IT'S... *KIND*... OF MAGIC

Magical Modernity
Book One

M.J. JACKMAN

It's...*Kind*...of Magic
(Magical Modernity: Book One)

ISBN: 978-0-9975549-1-5
Paperback version
© 2018 by M. J. Jackman

Published by LL-Publications 2018
www.ll-publications.com

Book layout and typesetting by jimandzetta.com
Cover art by Patrick Currier

Published in the USA
Printed in the UK and the USA

Also by M. J. Jackman

The Sid Tillsley Chronicles

The Great Right Hope

A Fistful of Rubbers

Acracknophobia

The Magical Modernity Series

It's...Kind...of Magic

(Coming Soon)
Steroids and Sorcery

Sign up now!

What Do Readers Say About M.J. Jackman's Books?

The Sid Tillsley Chronicles have often sat at **#1, #2. & #3** in Horror Comedy on Amazon!

Read real comments by critics and Amazon readers....

Book 1 - THE GREAT RIGHT HOPE

Long-time Amazon UK #1 Category Best-Seller!

"Not many books can make me laugh aloud. But I can't help giggling at regular intervals reading this series. Slapstick, childish and toilet humour. But delivered with a stroke of genius."

— *Caseypin*

"Haven't read a book that genuinely made me laugh as hard as Billy Connelly live in his prime till now. Kept reading and finished the others in the same week."

—*K. L.*

"I know there is an oversupply of homophobic, drunken vampire killer-novels but this is definitely the best in its class."

—*Kindle Customer*

"Kudos to M. J. Jackman for inventing an out-of-the-ordinary vampire tale and offering diversity within the realm of familiarity. I have already recommended *The Great Right Hope* to several of my friends, and now I want to recommend this book to all those who are stuck in the rut of the same old vamp groove and want to expand their boundaries."

—*Amy J. Ramsey*
Midwest Book Review

Book 2 - A FISTFUL OF RUBBERS

"More northern mayhem than it's possible to shake a stick at. Brilliant comic vampire novel that really deals with/nails homophobia in passing."

—*J. S. N.*

"Genius. This trilogy is a must read. I love Sid and the gang even though they're so wrong on so many levels. If you're looking for a funny read... look no further."

—*Caseypin*

"What I really liked about *A Fistful of Rubbers* is the interaction between Sid and the boys and the well-crafted dialogue. I really have not read anything quite like it. It is so refreshing to read a quirky and original vampire story that does not regurgitate the same old plotlines and characters that are so common in this genre."

—*Bitten by Books*

"Puerile rubbish. I usually stick with a book however terrible I find it but this was beyond the pail (sic). I even deleted it from my library just in case I downloaded it in error."

—*J. M.*

Book 3 - ACRACKNOPHOBIA

"A riot from the first page of book 1 through to the end of the trilogy. A mixture of the obvious and the subtle built into a believable world in which vampires and human beings co-exist creates a perfect environment for exploring the very real social conditions of our world. It's not often that something so much fun is so well thought through and then written so elegantly."

—*EMES*

"A thoroughly satisfying completion of the perfect trilogy, with twists and turns a plenty this book brings down the curtain on a cracking show."

—*D. S.*

"It's a mystery, a wonderment, how Jackman kept track of the twists and body count. Not even the most teeth-sharpened vampire aficionado will be able to guess how this one ends. I commend this book to all readers of both humour and vampire genres. Enjoy."

—*Geoff Nelder*
Cafe Doom

"Unfortunate drivel." — *R. S.*

The Great Right Hope
The Sid Tillsley Chronicles - Book One
M. J. JACKMAN

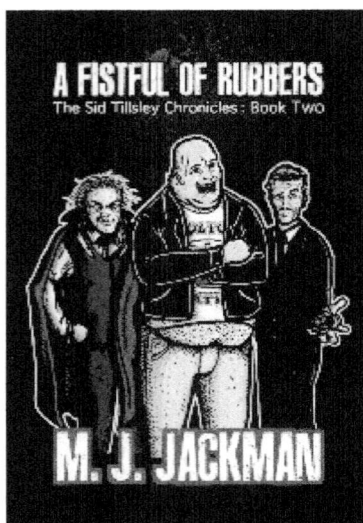

A FISTFUL OF RUBBERS
The Sid Tillsley Chronicles: Book Two
M. J. JACKMAN

ACRACKNOPHOBIA
The Sid Tillsley Chronicles: Book Three
M. J. JACKMAN

Get any/all of the *Sid Tillsley Chronicles* at Amazon!
UK: https://www.amazon.co.uk/Mark-Jackman/e/B0034PZJW2/
US: https://www.amazon.com/Mark-Jackman/e/B0034PZJW2/

Dedication...

This tome is dedicated to Maxwell David Ivanavicius, born today on 16th May 2014.* On this day I sorted out Chapter 27, which was a bit of a stinker until I made my moves on it. I also booked your Auntie Peel's Renault Clio (1.2 L engine, shark grey) in for a new tyre.** Achieve fulfilling things, little buddy. You couldn't have been born on a brighter day.****

* It took me a while to pull my finger out and finish this one. My god, four years!

** Clio's still going! I'm driving it these days. 108K miles!***

***This is in no way indicative of success in my career as a scientist or a writer. ☹ Shut up.

****Notable mention to his little brother Jenson who wasn't born when I wrote the original dedication. I'll get you a Teletubby or something.

Acknowledgements...

My fifth novel (need to sort the fourth)! Thanks to Graham Belfield, Lee Mallard, Dave Farmer, Patrick Jackson, Chris Day and Jason Knott for help with this one. Thanks to Zetta and Jim at LL-Publications for releasing another series of my books. Thanks to Pat for the awesome cover.

And thank you to anyone who bought The Sid Tillsley Chronicles, and especially those who left some extremely kind reviews on Amazon and Goodreads. You gave me the will to push on with this series and I really hope you enjoy it.

Prologue...

IN ANOTHER SET OF DIMENSIONS, an analogous world to our own grinds the wheel of monotonous life to a slightly different beat. In this parallel land, elves, dwarves, goblins, halflings, orcs, centaurs, and other weird and wonderful creatures live in mind-numbing tedium, desperate to make it though the working week and blow their wages on drugs, fags, and booze.

Some philosophers claim that given enough time, an infinite number of monkeys with an infinite number of typewriters would replicate *The Complete Works of William Shakespeare*. Even in the universes where monkeys had evolved to a point where basic administration and typewriter maintenance were a common skill set, throwing faecal matter and killing each other in blind animalistic rage remained surprisingly popular.

In every universe and on every world, wars wreaked havoc from antiquity to modernity. The scale of battle waxed with technological advancement and waned when everyone died because of the technological advancement. There was but one exception: on this Earth, from which this tale is told, there had been but a single war. The plural wasn't even in the dictionary, yet "LOL" and "muggle" were.[1] It was known simply as "the War." Admittedly, this does paint a rather peaceful and somewhat false image of this Earth's history. Life on Earth had been killing life on Earth for as long as there had been life on Earth. However, it was only about twenty thousand years ago that the species organised themselves into groups and fashioned tools sufficiently brutal so they could bludgeon each other to death in a more effective and rigorous manner. And once they started, everyone agreed that it would be a damned shame to stop.

In this warring but pragmatic world, it was difficult to refute evolution. With pinpoint accuracy, the divergence of sentient species had been resolved. Humans, elves, and dwarves descended from different lines of great ape; whereas goblins, orcs, and trolls descended from lizards. The centaurs' genetic background resulted from a rather promiscuous group of Amazon warriors and the sexual ineptitude of a local halfling tribe.

---

[1] For fuck's sake.

Even so, religion had thrived in the nineteenth century, with humans having a particular penchant for the weird, wonderful, and moronic. Yet even though evolution was accepted, with *The Origin of the Species* embraced by nearly all, divinity walking the earth was a historical and undisputed fact.

Uubla was a living god, and his kingdom a paradise. Uubla wielded magic, the manifestation of raw energy. Magic granted the ability to alter matter with the power of thought. In the world of magic, impossible did not exist; the only limit was the power of imagination.

Uubla created life. He materialised the fairies with one pure thought. The god and his fairy children celebrated peace and held the sanctity of life above all else. They educated, nourished, and cherished all the species descended from a big pond of muddy shit, and Uubla took it upon himself to end the War.

He'd appeared in front of a group of rampaging goblins and showed them the higher truths of the universe and the utopia that would flourish if people just stopped killing each other.

It wasn't his best idea.

News of the murder of Earth's true god by a seventeen-year-old goblin with Attention Deficit Disorder changed the planet's opinion of the divine. Slowly, the world pushed religion out of its mind and concentrated on evolution, glinting evil in its ever-changing eye. The phrase "survival of the fittest" was deconstructed and analysed. Data showed that "fittest" was directly proportional to "biggest arsehole"— and everyone knew who the biggest arseholes were.

Goblin society held no regard for the individual. Goblin commanders never hesitated in sending their armies to battle overwhelming, insurmountable odds, ending in certain inglorious death, sometimes just for the LOLs.[2] Historically, this was no different to any other species with total disregard for their proletariat subordinates, but the goblin commanders led from the front.

Back to the War, or rather the end of it.

It wasn't a human who first had the ingenious idea of not murdering everyone, and it certainly wasn't a goblin. It was an elf. Right here, in London, in the 1940s, Gundwir Echfelion changed the world by crossing Tower Bridge from the territory of the elf into the land of the human. He crossed the bridge and waved the white flag of peace. Subsequently, eight men from Tottenham, after watching the football and having headed into town for beers, kicked him to death.

In their defence, they hadn't known he was an elf vying for world

---

[2] It's in the dictionary.

peace. They hadn't even known he was an elf, which, it had to be said, wasn't a good defence. If the legends are true, Gundwir stumbled into them while walking past a fish and chip shop, spilling the greasy contents down a bright white football top, from which the stains were unlikely to be extracted. Violence and retribution had been swift and merciless.

The only good thing about living in a perpetual warzone is that there isn't much one can do to aggravate things. After twenty thousand years, it's difficult to "war harder." In fact, Gundwir's demise had the opposite effect. England's capital stood back and realised it had been a colossal tit. London stopped fighting. All of Britain stopped fighting. The world looked on and realised it had been equally tittish. The War ended. The miracle spawned a new age of love, or, more accurately, one of not quite as much murdering.

After Uubla's death and the subsequent Dark Age, magic had taken a back seat. Only a few studied the teachings of Uubla and passed them down through the generations. With the Renaissance, scholars and artists concentrated on the science and works of the ancients and nerds, rather than incantations and spells. The end of the War saw the beginning of the technological revolution. Now the general populous could look at cat pictures on the Internet, what need was there for magic in the world?

However, the technological revolution has not been a free ride. Improvements in healthcare and standards of living have led to a dramatic increase in the world's population, and Earth's resources are reaped without regard by a sole evil entity—The Corporation.

Pollution kills more people than the War did, and the undeniable climate changes points to a dire future. Greed, money, and power means there can be no other trajectory in the pursuit of progress, or rather, profit.

There is, however, an answer; one that the world isn't looking for. Magic could power the world in harmony with Mother Nature. The fairies left something behind, an item of power, hidden beneath the earth. In the right hands, the Lost Sword of the Fairy King could be used for the good of allkind. The Sword will only call to one pure of heart, one blessed with power and the will to save the world: the Chosen One.

Unfortunately, Dan Smith is, well...a bit shit.

Chapter 1...

"YOU'RE A LOSER, SMITH," were not words that usually initiated a successful yearly performance review, especially for someone called Smith.

Some would describe Dan Smith as pessimistic, but he'd protest at the reckless optimism. Conversely, some would describe Dan as a glass-half-full kind of guy, and regardless of Dan's remonstrations, they would be right. Dan's glass was, unquestionably, half full. Any more half-full and it would overflow, although some would protest at the reckless maths.

Dan's glass was half full of stagnant water. Stagnant water saturated with cholera medically diagnosed with "lack of get up and go." A half-full glass of stagnant water saturated with lacklustre cholera where a discarded condom floated, destined to sink, opened but unused, unsuccessfully deployed and pulled onto nervous, waning passion signalling a diminuendo of sexual mediocrity riddled with disappointment, ridicule, and the inevitability of her crawling back to Big Nev again.

Again.

However, Dan's gut feeling that his imminent performance review would be the worst of his twenty-five years of life, or rather, existence, had nothing to do with his can't-do attitude.

It had everything to do with Mr. Grak.

Dan drew in long, calming breaths, checking he had access to his inhaler on every fifth. He stood in Mr. Grak's office beside a tiny wooden stool, opposite the business side of the rich, mahogany, leather-topped desk that screamed opulence, decadence, and unnecessary company expense. Dan considered sitting down but came to his senses, his hand finding its pudgy, sweaty mirror image. Taking a seat without permission was an act of heresy in the Church of Grak.

The words, "You're a loser, Smith," hadn't been muttered under disdainful breath, they'd been bellowed. Mr. Grak accompanied his vocal contempt with a look reserved for murderers, rapists, and salaried street fundraisers.

It was the first thing Mr. Grak had said to Dan when they'd been introduced five years ago. A bold move considering it was Mr. Grak's first day—and he was working *for* Dan. Mr. Grak had quickly forced his way up the ranks of the company and Dan had only been his senior until mid-morning tea break—which Mr. Grak had forbidden Dan from attending.

With a final flash of straw-yellow teeth Mr. Grak said, "We'll get this done quick, Smith, because I can't bear to look at your stupid face any longer than I have to. Thirty minutes, max." Mr. Grak tapped at his watch, leaving his finger there. He wasn't emphasising the point, no. He brought attention to his watch because—

"It's a Rolex," he said. "In case you wondered."

Dan already knew. The last time he'd seen the watch, Mr. Grak had been exhibiting Dan's meagre payslip to the "lads" in marketing. Making Dan count the diamonds had been punishment for his interrupting the big reveal of the confidential, yet hilariously tragic information. To maximise the hilarity, Mr. Grak had printed the payslip out on paper watermarked with a naked picture of Dan, a picture Mr. Grak had taken after kicking in the door of the staff showers and bursting in with his iPhone.

Mr. Grak was the first in London to own an iPhone. Not many statements could better define a personality.

With a honed flick of the wrist, Mr. Grak angled the watch so the light pouring through the window danced within twenty-four twinkling diamonds, the light refusing to leave due to its love of crystalline perfection, a spectrum of colour courtesy of the stained glass effigy of himself battling the Nemean Lion. All this, embedded in eighteen karats of the most coveted of metals. Not just a talisman of beauty and design, practicality underpinned the essence of the timepiece, the watch, waterproof to depths of—

"Five hundred metres, Smith. I could dive half a kilometre under the ocean and still tell the time. That piece of shit hugging your wrist would die if I spat on it." He paused, grimacing at Dan's watch.

Dan slowly put his hand behind his back when Mr. Grak cleared his nostrils into his throat.

Suddenly, Mr. Grak jumped up, shoving back his bespoke office chair, a throne with casters. He bounded around the desk and shoved his wrist in Dan's face. Dan recoiled, fearing a punch or a wet willy or worse. Eventually, he opened his eyes to the familiar, insentient face.

"Twenty-four rocks, Smith. Rocks, yeah?"

Dan readjusted his large, faux gold-rimmed budget NHS glasses with inherent awkwardness. Mr. Grak looked to the heavens, mistaking Dan's tardiness for "retardiness."[3]

---

[3] The jury was still out on whether Mr. Grak was being offensive or he didn't know the correct word.

"Rocks are what we call diamonds, Smith. A peasant like you probably thinks rocks are probably, like, rocks or something." He made a noise from the back of his throat, a rumbling removal of phlegm which often escaped Mr. Grak's long pointy nose. From experience, Dan recognised it as a laugh.

The laughter desisted in a heartbeat. "Why the hell ain't you laughing?" Mr. Grak's eyes glowed red. Redder.

Upsetting Mr. Grak *was* an option, but it was a terribly stupid one. Dan summoned enough self-loathing to emit false laughter at his mockery.

Mr. Grak nodded, satisfied. He slid round the table and sunk back into the velvet violet lining of his office throne and incessantly drummed long yellow fingernails, more like talons, into the gilded mahogany armrests, little finger to index finger...little finger to index finger.

Mr. Grak's office said a lot about Mr. Grak. There wasn't a square inch of space without a picture, certificate, or award sporting his photo or name, mostly both, mostly twice. Mr. Grak clenched and unclenched his fists and said through gritted teeth, "You've just...got...one of those faces that people love to hate, Smith. Especially me."

Dan shrugged apologetically. He'd heard it before, even from door-to-door Jehovah's Witnesses.

"It's just so pudgy and soft and pathetic." Mr. Grak tore the air with ripping claws. "And those rosy cheeks are just asking to be stamped on," Mr. Grak added as an afterthought. His foot thudding into the parquet floor was difficult to ignore. "And your hair is proper shit."

Subconsciously, Dan reached for his hair. It wasn't his strongest feature, a plain, mousey-brown colour, curly and frizzy, and susceptible to static and the unrelenting bombardment with avian faecal matter.

But at least he had hair! Wisely, he kept this observation to himself.

Mr. Grak's eyelid twitched. He was agitated at the best of times, a ball of nervous energy. He'd say it was because he was always on the go, ready for any adventure, desperate to take on the next challenge, not because he was coked up to the eyeballs, 24/7.

Maybe Dan should've interjected with some of the targets he'd reached and then smashed. He'd raised more money to aid rain forest conservation than any other in the London office, or the company for that matter. But Mr. Grak didn't care.

Others had stood up to Mr. Grak. Des from accounts stood up to him once, in the staff cafeteria, telling Mr. Grak he was fed up with being bullied, so Mr. Grak shaved him. With an electric razor he'd shaved Des in front of fifteen members of staff, none of whom had seen a thing. Mr. Grak shaved him. Everywhere.

Schools spend a lot of time trying to stamp out bullying, but Mr. Grak had made a rather successful career of it. So much so, it was a surprise schools weren't adding bullying to the curriculum. It's often said that bullies are cowards, but Mr. Grak wasn't. He was a deranged sociopath who'd punch anything in the face.

"Well?" said Mr. Grak, talon tapping accelerated. "Are you going to stick up for yourself?"

In another life, would Dan stick up for himself?

In another life, in his *other* life, he wouldn't need to.

In his *other* life...

Dan's muscles relaxed. Energy coursed through his veins. He yielded his corporeal body to the higher powers of... No.

No. Not here. Not now.

No one could know about his *other* life. Not yet.

Mr. Grak's got down to business. "Sit down."

Dan pulled the stool and—

"On the floor," Mr. Grak, said, dragging out the last word, tiredly. "You don't think you deserve a chair, do you?"

Dan sat cross-legged on the polished wooden floor. Dan had never expected to be bullied at twenty-five, which, in hindsight was a little naïve considering he'd been bullied for the twenty-four years previous.

Mr. Grak banged both feet on his desk. "Do you know why I hate you, Smith?"

Dan understood why people who didn't know the *other* Dan, the *real* Dan, might hate him, but Mr. Grak never went into details. He just said he preferred—

"Winners. I like to surround myself with winners, Smith. Winners like me." He stuck a long thumb into his protruding ribcage. "And women with biiiiiiiiiiiiiiiiiiiiiiiiiiiiiiiggg hangers."

Dan believed Mr. Grak to be the most repugnant collection of cells ever assembled, or excreted. It wasn't just the words. It was the way he held out his hands, palms upright, bouncing up and down, and the way he stared hungrily at his hands, reliving some conquest from his sick and twisted past in his even sicker and twistier mind. He told Dan about all his exploits, every last one. As well as punching any living thing on the planet, Dan would bet his life that Mr. Grak would hump any living thing on the planet too. Most likely at the same time as punching it. And not just living things.

The look on Mr. Grak's face, staring off into the distance where the most sordid of activities defiled nature's laws, nauseated Dan. Mr. Grak didn't need to tell Dan he was physically aroused.

"I'm physically aroused, Smith," he growled.

Finally, his hands descended from where they molested the office air, and, thankfully, other things descended too. He turned his attention back on to Dan.

"Well, bleedin' say something, then!"

Twelve minutes into his performance review, or rather, performance execution, and Dan hadn't said a word, until now. "S...s...sorry."

Mr. Grak threw his hands up. "Why did you say 'sorry?' Why? I'm insulting you."

"W...w...would you like me to st...stand up for myself, sir?" Dan squeaked. His voice had never fully broken and puberty had only been suggested.

Mr. Grak's face froze. He took his feet off the desk and leant forward, pointing his talon between Dan's eyes. "You try it, Smith. You see how far you get. Did you hear what happened to Nigel in logistics?"

Nigel from logistics had stood up to Mr. Grak once. In the staff cafeteria he'd told Mr. Grak he was fed up of being bullied so Mr. Grak shaved him in front of fifteen members of staff. None of whom had seen a thing. He'd shaved him. Everywhere.

Who carries an electric razor around with them? Mr. Grak didn't even have hair.

Mr. Grak leant back and put his hands behind his head, preparing to return to his favourite subject. "I'm a winner, Smith. Look at the awards on the walls, the pictures of me with celebs, the accolades, the fame. Look at these guns, Smith. Look at these weapons of mass destruction." Mr. Grak stood up and tensed his arms. They weren't particularly large arms, surprisingly skinny considering the damage they'd caused over the years, but the Mr. Graks of the world were always sinewy. "Do you know what these mean?"

"That you have an effective workout p...plan, sir."

"And?"

"You understand the b...benefits of good nutrition?"

"And?" He hadn't moved since taking up the macho pose and now he shook with tension. A bead of sweat formed on his gleaming skull.

"You—"

"If you guess wrong this time, Smith, I'm going to shave you."

Dan sat quietly. He didn't want to say it. Not again. He'd already said it twice today. It was time to grow a backbone and be the man he was in his *other* life.

"Saaayyyyy it," Mr. Grak cooed.

Dan closed his eyes and whispered, "You're a winner, sir."

"And don't you ever forget it."

Dan kept his eyes closed, not wanting to see the self-satisfied grin that would eat another piece of his soul. He couldn't have much left.

"What do you have up in your office, or rather your toilet cubicle, Smith?"

"Well, there's a p...picture of my girlfriend."

"Why she is with you is beyond me," Mr. Grak blurted out. "Five minutes with me and she'd know what it means to be with a winner."

Dan stared at the floor. "Yes, sir. I'm sure you would b...b...b...bang her into next week, sir."

Mr. Grak made a fist, deadly serious. "That's right, Smith." The only reason Dan was still alive was because Mr. Grak didn't get sarcasm. "And you wanna know why?"

Dan didn't reply. There was no need.

Mr. Grak pointed at himself with both thumbs while glancing in one of the many mirrors scattered around the room, all aligned to his throne. "Because I, I am the man."

"Well, g...g...g...goblin, sir."

Dan's breath condensed before him. He said that aloud?

"What did you just say, Smith?" The last time a tone had carried so much dread, a man had been shaved against his will.

Yet, somehow, Dan managed to repeat, "G...g...goblin, sir. You're not a man, you're a g...goblin."

Chapter 2...

"IF I MAY BE SO BOLD, SIR?" said Rillit.

"You may," said Mr. Somersby.

"You look utterly magnificent." Rillit closed the sentence with a breathless sigh, rehearsed and refined. Rillit was Mr. Somersby's faithful servant and confidante extraordinaire. A casual glance of the butler would betray the truth. He appeared bald on top, but if the light was right, the keen of eye could discern total coverage of freshly shaved follicles. Curly grey hair sprouted from the back and sides, but closer inspection would reveal gold roots, not silver. His face was ageless, not a wrinkle, not a blemish, and great horn-rimmed glasses (non-prescription) were the diversion.

The English gentry insisted upon encyclopedic academic knowledge from their butlers—also a BA, MA, and PhD from the University of Life.[4] A butler should be worldly wise, a font of knowledge, a gentleman's personal gentleman, but bereft of any Wodehousian smart-arsed nonsense. The greater percentage of a lackey's life spent in servitude, the better. The same blood type was also a bonus, although this was not the case with *young* Rillit.

Rillit was the ultimate butler, trained to serve the elite of the pinnacle of the zenith of the English gentry. Yes, he was young, relatively it must be said, and Mr. Somersby was well aware, but no one was schooled in the old ways quite as finely, and Rillit carried all the pomp and all of the circumstance that the English upper classes demanded. No organism on the planet could get a tongue so far up another man's arsehole. Not even a bi-curious anteater. Rillit was the best, and that's why he worked for Mr. Somersby, a man who floated above the definition of class.

"Magnificence is mandatory," said the boss of bosses.

Mr. Somersby's tailor was taking the final measurements of his latest commission, a suit that, when finished, would have cost in excess of nine million pounds. Nine million pounds may seem a lot of money for a suit, especially when considering nine million pounds could

---

[4] The University of Life is the most incorrectly cited establishment on the planet. 96 % of the population who adamantly claim their alumni status were, in fact, educated by the Life Polytechnic, where a sexually transmitted disease didn't guarantee entry, but it certainly helped.

provide fresh water for three quarters of a million people in a third world country for the rest of their lives, but, as Mr. Somersby quoted from a Channel 4 documentary: "There are over 1.5 billion people living in poverty, but there is just one Mr. Somersby."

Context and shit suits were for peasants.

Nine million pounds was pocket change to this corporate deity, and Mr. Somersby had wondered how he'd managed so long without having dragon's bone suit buttons. The dragon had been hunted specifically for its bones, specifically to be made into buttons, specifically for Mr Somersby's suit. A seventeen-ton leviathan, one of Earth's noblest and magnificent creatures, had been hunted through the forests of Germany and slain for eleven buttons, three for the breasts, four for the sleeves, one for the trousers, and three spares. Sixteen hunters were killed in the pursuit of Windbane, the Black Dragon of Bavaria, the *last* Black Dragon of Bavaria. The expedition had been especially costly in human life as Mr. Somersby demanded Windbane be taken alive so he could administer the *coup de grace*, personally, with a blood-diamond-tipped golden chainsaw that ran on oil rendered from baby whale blubber.

Windbane, six thousand years old, Guardian of the Secrets of Old Saxony, had begged for its life and its legacy, but Mr. Somersby had not batted an eyelid at sticking his chainsaw in its ear, for dragon bone suit buttons were really, really cool this year.

The rest of the dragon had been burned, pulverised, and turned into glue,[5] for if there's one thing a gentleman cannot abide, it is to attend a party where another man is wearing a suit with buttons made from the same dragon as he.

He stood in the decadence of his London office, the headquarters of The Corporation, gazing out across the city, smoking the finest of cigars with a glass of Henri IV Dudognon Heritage cognac. A Maybach waited for him in the car park, ready to take him to his private jet at a moment's notice. Another Maybach waited in the car park on the other side of the building, also ready to take him to his private jet, just in case he felt like walking a different way. The jet was ready to take him to any of his luxury homes spread across seventy-four countries across the globe, each one housing a harem of mistresses ready to pleasure him utterly.

In short, Mr. Somersby was not short of a bob or two. However, even though Mr. Somersby was the richest person on the planet, having everything money could buy just wasn't enough.

---

[5] Mr. Somersby also wielded the world's most impressive glue stick.

"Have you decided what to do with your weekend, sir?" said Rillit, refilling his master's cognac glass.

"What do you suggest?" Mr. Somersby held out his arm so his tailor could measure it.

Like all good lackeys, Rillit, was not about to give his own opinion as he'd been trained not to have one. He was trained to enhance the opinions of his betters. "How about females, sir? Do you want me to organise some females for the most ludicrous and majestic fornication?"

"Why, yes of course, Rillit. Am I not *the* Mr. Somersby?" he said, a tightness to his voice.

Rillit bowed his head. "I can't apologise enough, sir. How many women were you thinking?"

"How many do you recommend?" For once, Mr. Somersby fixed his steely gaze on Rillit. This was pressure. This was a test, and one that, if Rillit failed, could only end in *seppuku.*

Rillit stood a little straighter. "Well, sir, for a virile, animalistic sex-ravager, like yourself, and only like yourself, for no one on the planet can sex ravage so cataclysmically, I'd say...at least...erm...ten?"

The slight inclination of Mr. Somersby's head was all Rillit needed. The powerful gaze of the boss wandered until it scanned the London horizon once more, his London horizon. "Make it twenty."

"Certainly, sir. Sorry, sir, I wasn't thinking of the whole weekend. I was only thinking of the first night, possibly the first hour."

Mr. Somersby raised a sculpted eyebrow. "Are you saying I'll be done in the first hour, Rillit?"

"Oh no, sir. Oh no." Rillit shook his head so hard he was in danger of losing his glasses. "I thought that maybe after an hour had passed, the first girl would've maybe recovered enough for you to give her the ol' heave-ho again, with you being so virile and so voracious. I was thinking that..." Rillit stopped digging, and diverted his efforts to arse-kissing instead. "I better make it forty, sir. With your sex drive, it is a better estimate of the number of females you will require for a single weekend." Rillit held up a fist and shook it to indicate voracious virility.

Mr. Somersby's tailor delayed the inside leg measurement.

"And, Rillit?"

"Yes, sir?"

"No trolls this time."

"Yes, sir." Rillit's forehead furrowed and he asked, "Are you talking figuratively or literally?"

"Both, Rillit. Most definitely both."

Rillit was always keen to inform Mr. Somersby that his heterosexuality was almost as celebrated as his wealth. Rillit assured Mr.

Somersby that his attraction to the opposite sex was so strong, it altered the brainwaves of organisms around him. In other words, his heterosexuality was contagious. Hypothetically, if he walked onto the set of a gay pornographic movie, his mere presence would induce the bearded great bear of a plumber to fix the leaking U-bend, rather than take the dressing-gown-clad, plucked, shaved, and more-than-willing homeowner whom had called the plumber because he wanted his "waterworks seeing to," roughly over the Belfast sink. The mere presence of Mr. Somersby would result in the production of DIY self-help video *Fixing your Pipes*, rather than the commissioned *Bursting His Pipes 2*.[6]

Most men of such straight-firing caliber would've been content with a weekend of forty women waiting on them hand and foot, ready to perform the most mind-blowing of acts at the drop of the hat, but not Mr. Somersby. This weekend would be forgotten by Mr. Somersby by Monday afternoon, because Mr. Somersby was deeper than that. Mr. Somersby wanted more.

"Rillit?"

"Yes, sir."

"Make it eighty women."

"Very good, sir."

That extra thing wasn't just an extra forty women. Most millionaires and billionaires were often subject to epiphany: the realisation of life meaning more than physical possession. Apparently, the tender touch of a loved one was something money couldn't buy, yet Mr. Somersby was about to enjoy the tender touch of eighty loved ones, and the tender touch of eighty loved ones in a place conventional loved ones tended to ignore after a time.

"Where would you like to go, sir, for your sex festival?" asked Rillit.

Mr. Somersby examined his tailor's shiny head, a result of male-pattern baldness, unlike Rillit's. "Tailor, where do you think I should go?"

Forbes William-Smythe had been Mr. Somersby's tailor for nineteen years, and this was the first time the fearsome tycoon had spoken to him, which was quite surprising considering Forbes had inadvertently brushed the tycoon's glans with his tape measure well over a hundred times during his career.

"Erm...well...."

"Speak up, man," said Rillit to the flustered tailor, who ran the

---

[6] The first in the series was a cinematic triumph.

tape measure through his hands and back again as if it was a rope he considered hanging himself with.

"Well, sir, if you have eighty women in a luxury mansion, does it really matter where you go?"

"Yes," came the deadpan reply. "Yes it does."

"Oh, erm...." The tailor paled. "What about...erm...Spain?"

Mr. Somersby closed his eyes. "Rillit, kill this man."

Such a comment in the offices of most executives would be accompanied with laughter and a little friendly elbowing of ribs. However, this wasn't most offices. This was the office of the most powerful man on the planet, who happened to be completely insane.

"Portugal?" ventured Forbes.

Rillit the butler opened Mr. Somersby's extensive weapon cabinet, which took up a worryingly (especially for Forbes) amount of wall space. "Would you like me to kill him now, or would you like me to dispose of him...by other means?" Rillit ran his finger across the maces, swords, daggers, morning stars, and cudgels, but to name a few.

"Can we talk about this?" said the tailor, backing away towards the door.

In the offices of this executive, friendly elbows in the ribs were not the flavour of the month, but arrows through the face most definitely were. There was a twang. There was a thump. There was delighted applause. The tailor fell, a dead weight, and bled profusely over a no-longer priceless Persian rug.

"A fine shot, Rillit," cried Mr. Somersby, his clapping a rare show of approval.

"Thank you, sir. It's in the blood."

Of all the butlers employed by Mr. Somersby, Rillit had lasted, by far, the longest, and was the only elf to take the position. Only Rillit's pointy ears would give any clue to his kind, and he hid these beneath the masses of thick curly hair that sprouted out the side of his skull, sculpted into a bingo-hall barnet. Rillit wasn't just an arselicker, he was a bastard of the highest order. The symbiotic relationship was nothing short of perfect.

"I really hate Spain," said the boss, nudging the dead body with his foot. "It's the shape of it, I think. I hate the idea of being on someone's boot."

"I think you'll find that's Sicily, sir. Spain is the place where they kill all the bulls."

"Oh," said Mr. Somersby, examining a manicured nail. "I quite like Spain, don't I, Rillit?"

"Yes sir. I think it was the bull killing which excited you the most. I'm still sacrificing a bull in your honour, every morning, sir."

"Is that a Spanish tradition, Rillit?"

"Ancient Greece, sir."

"Ah, it matters not," said Mr. Somersby. "But keep up the sacrifices, there's a good chap." He ran a finger over his desk, the bloodlust waning, and he sighed. "The tailor was right, it doesn't matter where I go." He walked up to the window and took in all of London, before sighing a heavier sigh than the last.

"What's wrong, sir?"

"Do you ever feel you want more? Do you ever think money isn't the answer to everything?"

"No, sir, and by having the divine fortune to live in your presence for the past few years, I have discovered that money *is* indeed the answer to everything."

"There is one thing that money cannot buy, Rillit."

"If I may ask, sir, what is it you're looking for? What more is there than the ultimate world you've created?"

Mr. Somersby undressed in front of his servant. Rillit didn't bat an eyelid. It wasn't until Mr. Somersby was completely naked that he spoke. "Look at me. Before you stands the most powerful man on the planet. My muscular strength is incomprehensible, my mind is neurological perfection. The roots of my hair have been strengthened with titanium. My black locks will never fall from my scalp and there isn't a bed in the land I will rise from without an impeccable 'do. My skin cells are interwoven with Teflon. I cannot wrinkle, Rillit. I will look like a man of thirty until the day I die, which in itself is not certain. My body has been genetically altered into this sculpted rock that stands before you. My penis is a miracle of modern science. The pleasing aesthetics of my scrotum is both a wonder of art and a technological achievement akin to the transistor."

"Then what it is it, sir? What is it you seek? What *can't* you do?"

Mr. Sommersby slumped against the full length window. "Oh Rillit, all I care for, all I want, is to do what no one else can."

"And what is that, sir?"

"Magic. I want to wield magic."

Chapter 3...

"WHAT THE HELL HAS ME BEING A GOBLIN GOT TO DO WITH ANYTHING?" screamed Mr. Grak, who was indeed a goblin, and at this moment (and most moments) a very angry goblin.

"Nothing, sir," said Dan, frozen in abject terror. "I was j...just saying you're a goblin, n...not a man."

"I'm more of a man than you are," snapped the goblin.

"Erm, yes, sir, Mr. Grak, s...sir, but technically you're not." Dan regretted his words.

Mr. Grak leaned over his vast mahogany desk and lifted a threatening digit. "I'd show that girlfriend of yours what a man I am." The glint in Mr. Grak's eyes, the windows to his soul, steamed up.

"Yes, b...but you don't have human g...genitalia, sir."

"You saying I ain't got balls, Smith?"

Dan fidgeted, hoping to retreat down a safer path. "Figuratively speaking, sir, I d...don't know anyone with more balls than you, numerically, volumetrically, or g...gravimetrically. In all aspects, you really are the biggest ball man I know."

"Figuratively?" Mr. Grak mouthed out the syllables. "What's that supposed to mean?"

"Well, you don't actually p...possess any t...t...testicles," Dan mumbled.

Mr. Grak jumped out of his throne. "I ought to rip your bleedin' head off." Spittle flew.

Dan ducked, closed his eyes, and tried his best to cover his hair with his arms in case Mr. Grak was holding the razor. "But, sir, goblins don't b...b...breed like humans. You are physiologically d...different."

Dan prepared for either pain or depilation.

But there was no characteristic hum of an electric razor.

There was nothing.

Dan gingerly opened his eyes and looked out between the gaps of his arms. The yellow grin and the waggling brow bones[7] were devilish.

"Are you saying you want to see my *growspeck*, Smith?"

"N...n...no, not...n...not again," said Dan, as quickly as his stutter would allow.

---

[7] For goblins didn't have eyebrows.

The grin widened. "Well at least us goblins aren't stuttering, pathetic little fairies, like you."

Dan came out from hiding behind his arms, and in a rare air of defiance said, "I am not a fairy!"

The grin evolved into ghastly goblin giggling. It always proceeded the dropping of the F-bomb. He had Dan right where he wanted him. Mr. Grak changed tack. "When you look at me you see a goblin, don't you, Smith?"

"Yes, I see a goblin." Stuttering was forgotten.

"And why's that?" asked Mr. Grak, leaning back in his throne, making himself comfy by grooving his buttocks into the cushion.

Dan preferred the homicidal maniac side of Mr. Grak to this. "Well, you've got green skin."

Mr. Grak shook his head. "And there's me thinking we stamped out racism, years ago."

"Green skin is a characteristic of goblins as a whole. There isn't a goblin without green skin."

"So?"

"You've got st...sticky up ears." Stuttering returned. The half-life of Dan's confidence was nature's fastest phenomenon.

"So have elves," said Mr. Grak.

"But they're not green. And they have a penis and testicles."

"So? My *growspeck* can do things a penis and any number of testicles could only dream of."

Dan avoided dissecting the statement and said, "And they're tall."

The thousand-yard stare was back. "You calling me short, Smith?"

"Not for a g...goblin, sir, no. You're tall. Very t...tall, in fact. And, your biceps are perhaps the biggest I've seen."

Mr. Grak tensed his guns on impulse. "I'm taller than you, Smith."

"I know, sir," said Dan, sadly caressing his Cuban heels. "I am rather short for a human."

Dan didn't know if his vertically challenged state was a result of genetics. He didn't know his parents. They'd abandoned him immediately, and many foster parents had told him they could understand why. Unfortunately, things were not about to get better for Dan Smith.

Mr. Grak wobbled his lip and blew bubbles between cracked lips and, as if talking to a baby, said, "You're a little, ickle, teency-tiny fairy."

Again, the F-bomb.

"Yes, I've been told that before," Dan said, listlessly. "Countless times."

Mr. Grak got up and danced from foot to foot, japing like a jester, a jester who would batter you if you didn't laugh at his substandard capering. "You're a fairy loser. A ickle, teency-tiny fairy loser piece of dog crap," sang the dancing goblin.

"You know I'm n...not a fairy," said Dan. "You know there aren't any f...f...fairies."

"You don't believe in fairies?" Mr. Grak spoke in an annoying high-pitched voice, one that a goblin's imagination might surmise sounded like a fairy sympathiser. He slapped a hand across his open mouth. "Oh, I'm sorry. Doesn't a fairy die when someone says that?"

"No, sir," said Dan, sharply.

"I don't believe in fairies! Oh!" He gasped. "I hope I haven't hurt another little precious fairy!"

"Fairies died out eight hundred years ago. And they d...didn't die out because of p...people saying they didn't b...believe in them; they d...died out because your ancestors massacred them."

Mr. Grak drove his fist into the table. "And don't you forget it! We wiped them sissy little bastards off the face of the planet, and do you know why, Smith?"

"Because the medieval goblin society was full of homicidal, psychopathic, b...blood-thirsty maniacs with no respect for life or d...decency?"

Mr. Grak shook his head slowly. "Because we're winners."

"Ah," said Dan, tiredly. So very tiredly.

Goblins.

There wasn't a living thing on the planet that didn't detest them, and that included goblins themselves. Dan, who could see the good in everyone, found it difficult to see any good, whatsoever, in the entire sentient race. People make mistakes, sure. And one has to forgive and forget, but can total genocide really be forgiven? Three times? It wasn't just the fairies. The gnomes went before them, as did the pixies. Historically, the goblins seemed to have a real problem with anything cute and cuddly. In their defence, they'd calmed down a little since wiping the planet of the fair folks' gay abandon.

"Why do you work here, Smith?" said Mr. Grak.

"I like to do g...good deeds, sir."

Mr. Grak pointed at the photos and awards on the wall. "Look there, Smith. Good deeds everywhere, and I got rewarded for them."

"We do a lot of good work here at G...Green P...Planet."

"We?" he barked. "*We*, you idiot? *We* do a lot of good work?"

"Yes, sir," said Dan.

"Look at the wall, again, Smith. Who is the one standing with the celebs?" Mr. Grak got up and rapped a talon on a photo of him with a Z-list celebrity who was likely dead or making exercise videos for the Boxing Day sales.[8]

"You, sir."

Mr. Grak grabbed his suit lapels. "Look at my clothes, Smith. This pinstripe suit is from Savile Row and cost three grand. What are you wearing?"

"Jeans and jumper from a ch...charity shop. The T-shirt I was g...given for some volunteer work, and the shoes I m...made myself."

"Your clothes are shit, and only a dick would make his own shoes. The company bought me this suit." He flashed the lining. "They invested three grand in making me look good because I make things happen. You'll never wear a three thousand pound suit, will you?"

"No sir. In s...such a situation, I would have bought a hundred pound suit and put the other two thousand nine hundred pounds back into the ch...charity we work for."

"Pathetic!" announced Mr. Grak, "Utterly pathetic. Let me give you some advice, Smith. Green Planet was founded in order to save the Earth from the hazards of Global Warming. Do you get that, Smith?"

"Yes, sir. You know I'd d...do anything to save the environment." The determined look on his chubby face meant business.

"But what you don't realise is that charity work has nothing to do with charity."

Dan's determined face collapsed. "P...pardon?"

"Take that stupid look off your face and I'll explain. You're a charity case, Smith, so be thankful I'm doing this charity for free."

"Thank y—"

"I'm only going to dock this time off your wages and not steal it out of your wallet as well."

"Err...thank...thank you, s..sir."

"Charity work is a business, see, and we are merely prawns. Well, you're a prawn; I'm more of a bishop, who is going to become a king."

"Do you mean a rook swapping with a king, sir," interjected Dan.

Ice formed on the office windows. "You a fag, Smith?"

Dan thought it best not to mention the prawns.

Mr. Grak went back to being the man. "Green Planet is a stepping stone to bigger and better things. As soon as a sweeter ride comes along...bam!" He slammed his fist into his palm causing Dan to jump. "I'm outta this shithole."

"Not me. Global warming is the biggest danger this w...world faces."

---

[8] The two activities weren't mutually exclusive.

Mr. Grak rolled his red eyes. "You really believe that, don't you? You're not even putting it on."

"We can make a difference."

Mr. Grak pointed at his awards again.

"No, I mean a real difference," said Dan, passionately, getting to his feet, his stuttering all but a memory. He gained confidence, becoming the person he was in his *other* life.

"How, Smith? Do you really think we're going to plug every oil well? Do you reckon the Yanks will agree to that? The Ruskies? And even if we did, we couldn't power the world by renewable energy overnight."

Dan placed his hands on the table and looked Mr. Grak in the eye. "No, but we can reverse the appalling damage we've inflicted on Mother Nature."

Mr. Grak's bored head rested on his bored hand. "How?"

Dan's crooked teeth did their best to form a winning smile. "Magic, sir. We can use magic."

Mr. Grak's laugh was infectious, like tuberculosis. It wasn't the effect Dan had hoped for. Mr. Grak sat back in his chair, his hands clasped over his belly, roaring. "Oh, Smith," he said, wiping a tear from his beady red eye. "I knew you were a loser, but I didn't realise you believed in magic! Not, like, actually believed!"

"Magic is real, sir. It's a universal ax...ax...axiom," said Dan, trying to ignore Mr. Grak's barrages of sporadic laughter.

Mr. Grak pulled out a monogrammed handkerchief (expensed) and blew his nose before throwing the cloth into the bin. "You don't believe magic can change the world, do you? Please tell me you don't believe that. Is this a wind-up? Is it?" He jumped off of his throne, clutching his sides as he guffawed, and put his head out of the office door. "Have you lot put him up to this?" he yelled at no one and everyone. "Have you organised a fairygram to come and tell me about magical pixie land?"

Every set of eyes stared straight ahead at the computer screen in front of them. Every mouth muttered a prayer to a relevant deity. Every hair follicle feared for its keratinised protein.

"You lot crack me up!" he said before heading back for more torture and torment.

"Magic is an underutilised f...force," said Dan before Mr. Grak could mock him further.

Laughter was over. Mr. Grak sat behind his desk and got back to business. "There's a reason magic isn't used, Smith. Do you know what that is?"

"We've forgotten the art," cried Dan, fervently pleading his case. "Magic has the p...power to end everything t...terrible in this world." He shook clenched fists, his passion carrying his words.

"By that argument, it also has the power to ruin everything good in this world."

Dan took a second to gather his thoughts. "Well...erm...."

It was a worryingly astute sentence from Mr. Grak, and the keen look in his eye caught Dan off guard. Strangely, Mr. Grak broke eye contact, readjusted his suit cuffs and said hurriedly, "But that ain't important, because magic is shit. Always will be."

Dan detested swearing, especially when it was aimed at his passion. "I don't think it's really fair to t...tar all magic with the same b...brush."

Mr. Grak picked a pencil off his desk and chewed at the end, making short work of it. "Why? It's all shit."

"It can be used for good."

Mr. Grak lifted a leg and broke wind loudly. "So can my fart, Smith. Methane can power turbines that make electricity. Electricity can turn on lights, switch on computers, boil kettles. I don't see you celebrating my arse in your spare time, even if you do spend most of your time kissing it."

Dan didn't defend himself, mainly because he was gagging. Goblin emissions were extremely toxic to humans, technically a carcinogen.

Mr. Grak laid the boot in a bit more. "It takes a half hour to utter a spell that will light up a room, and then it only lasts for a minute, tops. It takes me a second to turn on a light switch."

Dan pulled in enough oxygen to speak. "But electricity relies on fossil fuels, and they are d...destroying the environment."

"And Green Planet is here to save it."

"B...b...but if we just used magic, we'd be—"

"Out of business," said the goblin, matter-of-factly.

"We're not here to line our p...pockets!"

"I am. I'm making a mint." Mr. Grak scowled at Dan's indignant expression. "Take that fairy-look off your stupid, tiny fairy face! Look, if magic is so great, why does no one, and I mean no one, not a single person on the planet, use it?"

"The art has been lost. History speaks of cities completely dependent on magic. Thousands of p...people's lives were made comfortable without environmental harm. Mother Nature gifted us magic and we threw it back in Her face, and now we are d...destroying Her."

Mr. Grak leaned back in his chair and cleaned one of his long pointy ears with a talon, wiggling it. The squelching sounds were impressively loud and nauseating. "Do you know who used magic, Smith?" said an unimpressed goblin, staring at the large packet of luminous gunk he'd accumulated on a razor-sharp claw. "Fairies. Your lot."

"I'm not a fairy."

"Well you should be."

"The f...fairies were—"

Mr. Grak's raised, bony, wax-laden digit silenced Dan who worried as to its destination.

"The fairies used to ponce around in their blue bell woods, singing about the trees, the sun, and what sprinkles they'd put on their cupcakes. They were so far up their own arses they wouldn't give us goblins the time of day."

"They had c...constructed a society centuries ahead of its time where there was no c...crime, no disease and no p...poverty. Your ancestors were still eating their own faeces—"

"We decided to teach them a lesson," continued Mr. Grak, undeterred.

"I don't think g...g...genocide counts as a lesson, sir."

"And what good did their magic do them?" he said, patronisingly.

"Before or after the massacre?"

Mr. Grak grinned at that one. "Electricity has changed everything, Smith. Do you honestly expect magic to reverse the greenhouse effect when it's not even powerful enough to heat a small greenhouse, let alone cool it?"

The truth was, Dan didn't know how, but he was convinced there was a way. There was something stirring deep within him. He could change everything. Somehow, he could save the world.

Mr. Grak looked at his Rolex. "Right, time's up. No pay rise for you again this year. Now, get out of my sight."

"Yes, sir," said Dan, slightly upbeat. It was a better pay rise than last year.

Mr. Grak got up and walked him to the door. "See you at home, yeah?" he said, patting Dan on the back, who momentarily mistook it for a show of affection until he felt the soiled talon wipe down his T-shirt.

A bigger mystery to Dan, greater than those thwarting him from unlocking the secrets of magic, was why he'd agreed to flat share with Mr. Grak.

Chapter 4...

DAN HAD *ANOTHER* LIFE AWAY FROM THE WORLD OF GREEN PLANET, a life driven by the divine, a link to the arcane.

Dan drew nearer to his mastery of the ancient spells of Anglor, Earth's ancient, magical realm, lost centuries ago and now all but forgotten. He came ever-closer to fulfilling his dream of becoming a wizard, the last wizard. For in this modern age, no other wielded the might of magic, the spirit of nature, the all-power.

Or so he'd believed.

Dan sat in a circle beside visionaries, like-minded radicals with the foresight to see what the world could be. Only they fully comprehended the heinous crimes inflicted upon Mother Nature each and every day. There was no way to halt the unrelenting stampede of progress, and only by calling upon magic and witchcraft could the world avoid inexorable destruction.

Three hooded figures sat in a circle, their hands linked, a single candle on the floor in front of them, burning purple, all else shrouded by darkness, something greater than the absence of light.

"Danoclees Dunlorian, are you worthy?" uttered a deep voice, from beneath a dark hood. The robe did little to disguise the immense size of the individual, so vast the candle flame drew towards his mass.

"I am worthy," said Danoclees Dunlorian. This was the *other* Dan. This was Dan Smith's alter ego, an apprentice of magic, and a champion for good. Danoclees Dunlorian was Dan's ancient name. Generation after generation of failed wizards were unable to conjure, unable to bend reality with their mind. Dan would put an end to the abysmal tradition. Tonight, he'd succeed where all before him had failed.

Dan threw back his hood.

"I, Darkstar, see you, Danoclees," said the massive figure, pulling back his hood to reveal a portly man in his early twenties, carrying a considerable number of chins, all riddled with acne. His eyes were enormous, magnified by his glasses with lenses so thick they were likely bulletproof. The curliest hair erupted from his head and sprouted sporadically in every conceivable dimension, a display of infinite entropy, in ginger.

Darkstar said, "For us to bypass the laws of matter, for us to delve between the worlds of mathematics, to understand the substance of vacuum and the absence of time, we must unite and strive for the higher power: the will of the universe, magic."

"HARRRRRRROOOOLEN!" All three chanted the ancient word of power.

The last hooded figure spoke, "Danoclees Dunlorian, are you worthy?" The voice was female, a slight figure producing a powerful tone.

"I am worthy," said Dan.

"I, Hammerbeam, see you, Danoclees," said the female, pulling back her hood to reveal a third human, again, in her early twenties. She was even spottier than Darkstar and her glasses even thicker. She shared the same greasy skin and untameable ginger hair. She looked like Darkstar—if he was rendered.

"HARRRRRRROOOOLEN!" said all.

"Darkstar," said Hammerbeam, "it is your honour to call forth the spirits and their powers, to infuse the might of the world, to fill the very core of Danoclees Dunlorian with raw magic." She turned to Dan. "Danoclees. Are you willing? Are you worthy?"

"I am willing and I am worthy."

Darkstar clasped his hands together, only just managing to link them around his belly. He bowed his head, closed his eyes, and began the ancient ritual. "Hmmmmmmmmmm," he intoned, a deep note, long and unwavering.

Hammerbeam put her hand on Dan's shoulder. "He is breaking through. He will find the answers in the ether. He will connect you. It is your destiny, Danoclees."

"Hmmmmmmmmmmmmmmmmm—" Darkstar's eyes snapped open in horror, his body tensed, every muscle contracting, jiggling the blubber encasing it. "It's... It's... Oh no."

"What is it?" said Hammerbeam, her eyes wide with panic.

"Something is...." His face contorted, a mix of concentration and pain. "Something is coming through."

"Not again!" cried Hammerbeam.

Darkstar took quick sharp breaths. "Gotta stop...got to...stop it...coming through...."

"Oh no!" said Dan. "Darkstar, you can't let this happen. You must control—"

VRRRRRRRRMMMMMMMMMMRRRRRRRRRRRRRRRRIIIIIIIIIE EEEEEEPPPPPPPP...P...P...P.........P..............PRRRRRrrrrrrrrrrrrrrrrrrr mmmmmm....P...P...P...P.......................prm...

"You've bloody ruined it again, Craig!" said Dan, clutching his nose and wafting his hand in the air. He got up and turned on the light, destroying the mystical, smelly atmosphere.

The wannabe magicians stood disappointedly in Dan's bedroom. The bed was pushed against a wall to maximise space. Some would call the room geeky. Dan called it Geek Chic. The chic refused to comment.

There were a lot of posters of wizards, witches, and warlocks. Mostly, there were posters of dragons. Dan had always wanted to see a real-life dragon, and had dreamed of it since he was a boy.

"I'm sorry! I didn't mean to," said Craig. "I was holding it in for sooooo long and I got too excited."

"He does this every time," said Hammerbeam, otherwise known as Chantelle. "Every time!"

"I can't help it!" he said, pulling the tight-fitting robe out from a terrible, terrible place.

Chantelle slapped his belly. "You could try eating less."

"I need to eat!" he pleaded "I'm a skin troll."

"You're not a skin troll. You're Chantelle's brother," said Dan.

The purported skin troll, with difficulty, crossed his arms. "Well, I reckon I'm adopted."

"You're not adopted, Craig," said an exhausted Chantelle, taking off her robe and throwing it in the corner of the room. Underneath she wore jeans and a faded, retro Iron Elf T-shirt.

"If I'm not adopted then why am I ten times the size of you?" he said, grabbing his belly while considering her stick-thin frame.

"I don't know, I honestly don't," she said. "Because you eat at least twenty times as much!"

"Will you please stop bickering," begged Dan. "I honestly thought we were on to something." He blew out the purple candle with his sigh.

"On to something?" asked Chantelle. "Dan, we've been meeting here every week this year, and all we've heard is Craig's wind."

"It's not wind. It's a skin troll roar."

Both Dan and Chantelle rolled their eyes.

The door burst open, and although the literal breath of fresh air improved the situation, the accompanying bitter wave of disappointment soured it. "Oh dear lord, not again, Dan," said Michelle.

"Michelle!" Dan squeaked. "I didn't know you were coming over." His stomach turned as he followed her wandering, disapproving gaze across all of his magical paraphernalia and Lego.

"Well, I'm certainly not staying." Michelle's evil stare and bitter frown did little to detract from her astounding beauty. The skin troll's jaw dropped open, which began a sequential and rhythmic lowering of all his chins. The skin troll had not seen Michelle before. He wasn't used to being in the same room as a woman such as this, or any unrelated female for that matter.

Michelle's appearance was always a matter of heart-attacking shock. Strangers in the street would stop Michelle and Dan and, driven by impulse, aggressively ask her, "What the hell are you doing with him?"

Both how and why this union developed was inconceivable. Why would this prototypical ten out of ten, this earth-born Aphrodite, this ultimate rendition of the female form who walked in adoration and bathed in the worship of gynephiliacs the world over—become Dan Smith's girlfriend?

Why indeed?

Blue eyes, blonde hair, long of legs and full of breast, yet Michelle's beauty transcended stereotypical specification. A quintessential dream girl, too radiant to grace the mundane heteronormative dreams of the average *Dungeons and Dragons* enthusiast, and too radiant, even, for the dream world of a skin troll, a place as sinister and dangerous as a dark lord's nightmare.[9]

They were an unlikely couple. Others had struggled to understand the connection. Michelle was rich, powerful, commanded a genius intelligence, and modelled as a hobby. Dan was poor, ugly, and awfully shit. People said opposites attract. These people were idiots.

She'd popped in to see Dan after her nightly gym session, and the Lycra combined with her splendour was breathtaking, which was why the skin troll suffered a mild asthma attack.

Michelle's lip elevated to an even more disgusted angle. "Shut that fat blob's mouth," she said, casting a death wish on the wheezing mass. Not a kind comment, but not many comments that came out of Michelle's mouth were. It was, however, a valid comment for the skin troll drooled on to the carpet.

"Don't call him that!" said Chantelle.

"What are you going to do about it, you skinny nerdy bitch?"

Michelle was, as Dan put it, "direct."

Chantelle backed down, like all people did when Michelle was being direct.

Michelle's fondness of demonstrating the techniques she'd learned while earning several black belts in the martial arts backed up her directness. She massaged her temples. "Dan, I thought I'd told you to stop playing this bullshit?"

---

[9] And often with the addition of feet.

"I...I...know what you told me, Michelle, but this isn't *Dungeons & Dragons*."

"Yeah," said Chantelle, "we'd stopped playing that, like, an hour ago."

Dan closed his eyes.

"You're all pathetic." She crossed her arms. "Then what *are* you doing?"

Dan stared at the floor while the skin troll continued to drool on it. Only Chantelle piped up, "We were practising magic."

Once uttered, the words couldn't be recalled. The only thing that would've disgusted Michelle more would've been barging in on Dan having a threesome with two skin trolls.

"Not again," she said, working her temples with extra vigour. "For the love of god, Dan, I'll leave you if you don't get rid of these losers. I'm not sure if it's worse because you're the head loser."

And with that, she slammed the door.

"I'm not a loser...," he said to the closed door. "I'm a wizard," he mumbled.

"What a bitch!" said Chantelle, only when she was certain Michelle was out of ear shot.

"Don't call her that!" said Dan, instinctively.

"Well, she is a bitch, isn't she?"

Dan paused for a second, before regaining himself. "No!"

"Really?" Chantelle's fists found her bony hips. "So she's kind, warm, and loving, is she?"

"Well...well, no," Dan admitted. "Our relationship isn't one of them lovey-dovey ones, if that's what you're asking. Both of us aren't into writing poetry for each other, composing sonnets, leaving soppy messages, and that sort of nonsense."

"You do all of those things, all of the time," said Chantelle.

"I know, but she doesn't."

"So what kind of relationship have you got then?" asked the purported skin troll.

"Well...." Dan rubbed his chin. "W...well...," he said, becoming increasingly flustered, before turning defence into offence. "It's better than your relationship!"

"How dare you!" cried the outraged skin troll. He'd have pointed a finger but for the effort. "I've been dating Violet for three months now."

"Dating? Yeah, right, you've never even seen her," said Dan.

"I bloody well have!" Craig lifted a chin in the air, defiantly.

"Yeah, but only through a webcam," said Dan.

"Don't be such a git," said Craig. "Loads of people date online!"

"Yeah, and there's nothing wrong with that, but you've only ever seen her on the Internet. You've never met her in real life."

The skin troll scratched some eczema festering in between a couple of neck folds. "Well, yeah, it's not like I can actually see her, is it?"

"Of course you can see her!" said Dan, throwing his hands up. "That's the whole point of a healthy relationship!"

"Not that simple." Craig shook his head, then his chins. "She's a gorgon."

"What?" asked Dan. "A g...gorgon? You're j...joking! A gorgon?"

Chantelle shrugged her agreement.

"Craig, you can't date a gorgon."

The skin troll's mouth dropped open in shock, and he said, with right on his side, "Well, I couldn't if I was a racist like you."

Dan held a finger up and shook his head from side to side at the serious accusation. "No, I'm not b...being racist. I am not a racist!"

"That's what racists say!" countered Craig.

"No!" said Dan "I just don't think it's wise to date someone you can't look at without being instantly k...killed."

"We've made it work so far," said a stubborn skin troll.

"But, you haven't even seen her!"

"Surely that's a good thing?"

"No, b...but..." Dan paused, it was difficult to argue with logic.

"Well, we're still happier than you and your horrible girlfriend!" said Craig, with a satisfied sneer.

Dan was about to give the skin troll a piece of his mind when the lights went out and a cold wind whipped around the bedroom. Instinctively, Dan pulled his robe tight, and the wind desisted as fast as it arose. A golden glow appeared in the middle of the three would-be magicians, but it wasn't the candle, this was something else. The glow brought warmth and Dan drew towards it, wanting to bathe in it and become one with it. The glow crackled and golden lighting danced around the room before it struck Dan between the eyes. It ran through his veins and fired across the synapses of his nervous system, sizzling, titillating, tantalising. He sensed power, raw power. He'd never experienced such a thing, but he knew exactly what it was.

I see you, Danoclees Dunlorian .

"Who s...said that!" shouted Dan, desperately turning this way and that, hunting for the source of the words which reverberated from every surface. "Is one of you doing this?"

His two fellow wannabe magicians were statues. Chantelle frowned at the grinning Craig, his chins in mid-wobble. A string of spittle connected his fat, wet lips, frozen in time and space.

I see you, Danoclees Dunlorian. Only I know of what you're truly capable. Only I know of the good you will bring to the world. You can save the planet, Danoclees. You can, and you will.

"What's g...going on? Show yourself!" Dan turned back and forth, desperate to find the voice. He spied a reflection in the window. When his eyes focussed, it disappeared. He turned quickly. Before him stood a bespectacled old man with a long white beard, wearing a flowing, iridescent robe and a wide-brimmed hat. He held a mahogany staff, long and smooth, and on the end sat an orb which contained within it the source of the glow: golden lightning. Magic!

The old man winked over his golden spectacles, and then he was gone. Darkness returned.

The lights came on, and...

He was in his bed.

He was alone.

"What the—?" he said, looking around. He pulled back the covers. He was in his Spider-Man PJs.

I see you Danoclees Dunlorian, the voice whispered through the ether. *I see you.*

Chapter 5...

MICK THE KNIFE WASN'T YOUR RUN-OF-THE-MILL, EVERYDAY KIND OF ELF. With the creation of Mick, the mould hadn't been broken, but it had been tampered with. Elf genetics dictate grace and beauty, yet Mick was not graceful, nor was he beautiful. Some people might say Mick was beautiful in his own kind of way. These people were idiots.

It would be quite easy to judge Mick. He was, perhaps, London's most prolific felon, and he wasn't a petty crime sort of chap. Somehow, without the aid of a pretty face, rippling muscles, or five minutes of self-abasement on reality TV, and with possession of a caustic personality legally registered as a handicap, he'd managed to sire an awful lot of children.

To date, Mick had not proven a natural father.[10] He'd been absent for the birth of all his children, and from all of their lives too. He was consistent, one had to give him that. It was difficult to ascertain whether his absence had been a positive influence on his spawn, all of whom were utter bastards. It wasn't the kids' fault they'd unwittingly inherited the majority of Mick's aggressive and domineering bastard DNA.

So yes, it would be easy to judge Mick.

Most people did.

The 1400s marked the beginning of elven dominance. With the development of the English longbow, elves discovered their propensity for sniping, or as the dwarves called it, "playing posh ponces in trees." Technological progression engineered more efficient means of murdering thy neighbour. The elves took advantage of the extra range and power gifted by gunpower, killing anything setting foot within a half-mile of their forests that was shorter than six feet and didn't have pointy ears. The dwarves regretted some of their more derogatory comments.

However, Mick the Knife wasn't a bow man, nor was Mick the Knife a gun man.

Mick the Knife was a knife man.

And right now, Mick was also a whisky man, who found himself on a bender in Liberty's after yet another violent crime spree.

---

[10] Not for an elf, anyway. For a lion he'd make the tenth percentile of greatest dads, but that's only because he hadn't eaten any children. So far.

Depending on one's social status, one could describe Liberty's as a cosmopolitan kind of joint. Its patrons hailed from every continent with a diversity of clientele that would test a zoologist. To provide for all walks of life, Liberty's served drinks and foodstuffs catering to all the peoples of the globe.[11]

If Liberty's was situated in Chelsea, it would have been flavour of the month, frequented by It Girls, footballers, and successful stockbrokers. But Liberty's wasn't situated in Chelsea. It sat slap-bang in the middle of Lewisham, which meant it attracted a different kind of arsehole. Liberty's entertained the worst that every race, every creed, and every colour had to offer: psychopaths, murderers, degenerates, and worst still, Mick the Knife. On a positive note, no one had thrown up on the pool table, yet.

"Whisky," said Mick the Knife, sat at the bar, staring into his empty glass. As per usual, it was standing room only in Liberty's, the crowd jostling to get served, with drinks and punches thrown in common courtesy. Still, a six-foot circle, a safety zone, cordoned the Knife. Even here, his reputation floated above contestation.

"Hiyaaaa, our Mick." The Liberty's landlady was more than capable of dealing with the Knife's shenanigans if need be. Her legs were like tree trunks and her arms like ever-so-slightly smaller tree trunks. The monstrous arms dragged knuckles across the floor, which, over time, had gouged channels in the floorboards, delving a micron deeper each time she passed. When last orders were called, there were no arguments, not since the time a stone troll had kicked up a fuss and she'd chiselled a very rude word onto his nose.

Scouse landladies. Nothing scarier.

"Whisky coming up." She took his glass, turned around, and added a shot from the optic. "Three quid, luv." She waited until money hit the table and plonked the spirit on the bar.

He banged it back. "'Nother."

"Someone's flush. Who you robbed this time," she asked.

"Some rich halfling wanted to go on some *quest*," said Mick, shaking his head and struggling with the concept of the last word. "Twat deserved robbing, if you ask me."

She turned up a lip, smothered thick in bright red lippy. "Big, brave Mick the Knife, huh?"

Big and brave?

Mick certainly wasn't big. He was just under six foot, the only elf to drop below that magic number, and although it could be argued that

---

[11] Booze and crisps.

he was slender, as elven-kind were, he was more scrawny, skinny-fat at best. He did a poor job filling his clothes, his bones giving them the appearance of a poorly constructed tent. The garment, however, had come from a distant, evil land, constructed by the servants of a dark lord in some horrendous Asian sweat shop. His limbs, ribs, and other bony protrusions were destined to rip through the ultra-flammable tracksuit at any moment.

Brave? The bravery of the criminal classes was a hot topic in the world of white, middle-aged, right-wing English human males. For a reason as tragically pointless and unexplainable as whales beaching, these men felt the need to express their views by means of Internet comments on the websites of right-wing newspapers, and all held a common belief that Mick the Knife was not brave. Not in the slightest. In fact, he was so "unbrave" (Duncan Grant 56, Chigwell), that he "should be hung by the neck until he is almost dead, before having his scrotum removed, unfurled, set alight, and used to suffocate him." The wives of such moral gentlemen held complementary views. Jan Grant (51, Chigwell) said he was "no better than a filthy paedo who'd burn in hell. And my husband would love nothing more than five minutes in a locked room with him."[12]

Elves were clean shaven, primarily because they couldn't grow a decent beard, and the dwarves laughed at them and questioned their sexuality. In reply, the elves mocked the dwarves because the female of their species had beards, and the elves said the male dwarves secretly wanted to sleep with the other male dwarves because of this. When all was said and done, the two sides managed to agree on at least one thing: the thousand year battle on the matter and the resulting destruction of an estimated 153 million souls was bloody well worth it.

Mick sported the wispiest of wispy beards. Even Gerald, playing darts in the corner, and who was a wisp, launched arrows with smug satisfaction knowing someone out there possessed less body in their beard than he. Mick's wispy beard only broke ground where the acne hadn't left a vicious reminder that Mick was an even uglier teenager.

He pulled off his baseball cap. Almost-golden locks fell greasily to his shoulders. Mick was a strawberry blonde, a receding strawberry blonde. More accurately, Mick had a greasy ginger skullet. It meant he was angry.

Very, very angry.

Sometimes, Mick thought he'd been dealt a bad hand in life.

He tied his lank hair into a ponytail and put his cap back on. He

---

[12] It is unclear what the five minutes would entail.

hammered down another whisky and slammed his glass on the table, demanding a reload.

The door to the pub opened and an elf walked in. Three-piece suit. Fancy. The nearest patrons raised their noses and took in the air. Cologne was stolen, not worn. He was a beauty, too, but they all were. Well, nearly all of them were. Only a scientist in a lab packed with cutting-edge gene-identification technology could recognise this social intruder as the same species as the Knife, and then they'd conclude their fancy science machine was broken. This newbie couldn't be a tourist as he was in Lewisham. No one purposefully visited Lewisham for fun. A businessman for sure. The elf realised his mistake: it wasn't rocket science with the stares and the silence.[13]

The elf's eyes widened and he turned to leave, but...

"Oi, blondie!" said another elf, a bonier elf, a shorter elf, a gingerer, greasier elf.

Business Elf made the mistake of looking back. Mick, swaying on his seat, beckoned him in with a bony finger. The crowd parted, leaving a gap between predator and prey.

"Now then, Mick. None of that nonsense," said the landlady. "It ain't even kicking out time. I ain't having you scare off the customers."

Mick's eye firmly held on to Business Elf's suitcase, and he salivated. "What you got in there, blondie?"

The elf stood straight, jaw clenched. He hugged the suitcase to his chest. "That is none of your concern, sir."

"Oooooh, sir!" said a few of the patrons, mocking tones not carrying the fabled cockney cheekiness and charm, which no one on the planet had ever witnessed in real life.

Mick edged himself off the stool and stumbled, catching himself on the bar.

Darts no longer thudded. Pool balls no longer clattered. A more entertaining game was about to kick off.

The blonde elf turned to look at the door, but a crowd of onlookers had congregated in front of it, and their crossed arms and stern faces said they weren't keen on moving.

"I hope there's more than your lunch in there, posh boy," said Mick.

"There's nothing of use to you in here," said the elf, sweat appearing on perfect skin.

Mick flashed a decayed grin and reached inside his horrible

---

[13] Sound had already fled the pub as it didn't want to see any trouble and it wasn't a grass.

tracksuit top. The handle of the switchblade knife gleamed from the pool table lights. Maybe the drink was taking its toll, but Mick dropped the knife before he could release the deadly blade. "Shit."

Another blonde—a beardless dwarf, of all things—picked it up, rolled his eyes and handed it back to the drunk elf. Mick offered him a wink, and carried on towards his target.

There was a reason he was called Mick the Knife, and it was a reason which Richard Crummington (47, Bury St. Edmunds) had very strong online views about.

Chapter 6...

LONDON.

"When a man is tired of London, he is tired of life; for there is in London all that life can afford." Words as true today as when they were written.[14] London was a magnet for the rich, the famous, the power-hungry, the people who turned the world.

In London, there was all that life could afford.

Yet 99.999% of the population couldn't afford it.

For them, London could be really, really shit.

However, people made the city, and London housed ALL the people. The multi-cultural centre of the world was home to a member of literally every sentient species, all coming together to collectively grudge a £7 pint.[15]

Dan walked the London's streets, concentrating on dodging the people who made the city. For Dan they made it dreadful. It was Friday night. He'd worked late into the evening, failing to complete the extra tasks Mr. Grak had piled on him. At least, Sisyphus had a fighting chance. Mr. Grak said the extra work was punishment for a terrible performance review, but it was a weekly occurrence so the goblin could leave early. It's what winners did. Apparently.

Sober-navigating the streets when the pubs kicked out was a chore for all, but for Dan it was a dangerous operation. The drunk and Dan did not mix. The same way a drunken yob felt the need to consume a kebab, they also felt the need to punch him in the face.

His face was the only explanation. On his first day of school he was punched more times than he was spoken to. It wasn't like he was particularly clever and thusly beaten because of superior grades. Even the smart, nerdy, and unpopular kids beat him up. When he was thirteen, Dieter Goo, school nature quiz champion, Mathlete, and Warhammer Fantasy Battle exponent, had stuck a Level 9 Skeleton Archer so far up Dan's nose, surgeons had left it there. And there the skeleton remained, still at Level 9, destined to live its life in mediocrity and snot, just like the rest of us.[16]

---

[14] Samuel Johnson, London, 1777.

[15] Samuel Johnson wouldn't blink at a £7 pint. Dead flash was our Sam.

[16] He'd had dreams. He'd had hopes. Who didn't? But it was different for Cartilage. Cartilage had potential. Precocious, ambitious, and driven, from a

Dan's size cemented his status as prey. He'd developed an impressive ability to roll with the punches. He wouldn't be the next superhero, but he wasn't black and blue in the morning. He was still ugly, punched in the face or not.

Sometimes, Dan thought he'd been dealt a bad hand in life.

Nope, London wasn't a friendly place, and the only reason Dan stayed here was because Green Planet was the most influential environmental charity in the world. It was here he could make the biggest difference, and that he did. Even though no-one knew who he was, he still made an impact.

If only Mr. Grak felt the same. Unfortunately, London bred Mr. Graks. It was all about earning the next million, getting to the top, and being a winner. Being a goblin wasn't the reason he was a horrible, vindictive, evil little beggar. Well, it wasn't the only reason.

Dan hoped Mr. Grak would be out of the flat, drinking with yuppies, snorting cocaine, and throwing his considerable bank balance at strippers.

Tonight, Dan would be alone, which meant he could practise magic to his heart's content. Magic was the answer, but unfortunately, like most things, he was rubbish at it.

---

young skeleton, he excelled with the bow, competing against children twice his age at local competitions and defeating them. He had brains, too, not literally of course, but he was a straight-A student, and great things were predicted. He wanted to be an officer in the army. Everyone thought it was inevitable, his teachers, his parents. He'd earn his degree in a red-brick university and breeze into officer's school. Nothing could go wrong. Then he met Liz and she changed his world, his perceptions, and took his heart. They were smitten, destined to marry and have 2.4 skeletons, travelling the world with the army with him as an officer. Then the accident. It wasn't his fault.... It wasn't his fault, damn it! Seventeen, just passed his driving test. It was raining, throwing it down. He was late, rushing down country roads to pick Liz up from the train station. A bunny jumped into the road, cute as a button. He swerved. Instinct. He woke three weeks later. He was lucky. Pah! *Lucky?* His...face. The scars on his bones. Liz said she didn't care. She said it didn't matter, but he could see the sorrow in her eye sockets. She thought him a freak. Shallow. He turned to drink. The grades slipped. He got into fights. Hurt some people. Liz left him. She didn't care. He joined the army, no qualifications, no hopes, just hate. Drill Sergeant Boney McBone Le Bone saw through the angst and the rage and found a way into his heart, and unlocked his potential. He freed Cartilage from his emotional prison. He helped Cartilage let go of his irrational hate. He made peace with Liz. He reached Level 9 faster than any recruit in Skeleton Army history. He became the skeleton he was meant to be. Then he got stuck up a nose.

"Oh, I don't know, you might be better than you think."

"Eh?" Dan's mind had wandered again, but hadn't expected anyone to actually talk to him.

"I said, young man, that you might be better than you think."

"Eh?" said Dan, again, looking for the speaker, turning quickly, doing his best to avoid the drunken rabbles.

And in the blink of an eye, there he was, the old man from his room! His white beard stretched down to his waistband with his white hair blending into it, held in place by a large pointy hat. His eyes sparkled behind golden spectacles. Grey robes dragged on the wet ground, but the water didn't soak into the fabric. The rain fell, but it bounced off him and didn't wet him. A wide grin split Dan's face as he marvelled at the seven foot long staff the gentlemen held, glowing, protecting him from the rain.

"You! You were in m...my room. You're...you're a wizard!"

And so are you. The words rattled around Dan's head, but the wizard hadn't moved his lips.

"No, I'm a loser," said Dan, on instinct.

The wizard examined Dan with a serious stare, looking over his glasses, penetrating him with X-ray vision, looking at the Dan on the inside, the real Dan, the one that mattered. The wizard cracked a smile.

"No you are most certainly not, Danoclees Dunlorian."

"What d...do you mean?" said Dan, completely bemused.

"I, my young friend, am Gambledolf."

"G...Gambledolf?" said Dan, struggling to get his tongue around the name, but delighting in every syllable.

The wizard laughed. "Yes, Danoclees. Gambledolf. We should meet, you and I."

"Where? When?" barked Dan, desperate to know.

"You'll know." And, with a wink, Gambledolf disappeared in a puff of purple smoke.

"RELAMINARUS!" announced Danoclees Dunlorian and flourished his wand.

Nothing.

"PELAREEMANARUS!" he cried, with a flourish somewhat more vigorous.

Nothing.

After the encounter with Gambledolf, he was determined to harness magic, Dan stood in his bedroom, furiously pointing and twirling the wand he'd bought off eBay. The main focus of the wand's thrusting was the wall light. It remained untroubled. To make the light bulb glow, a voltage was required to force electrons through a thin wire resulting in resistance, resulting in work, resulting in heat and light. Every part of the process was reliant on natural phenomenon: the composition of the metal, the elements and their electronic structure, all were slaves to the laws and the whims of Mother Nature.

All Dan had to do was persuade the electrons to listen.

Persuasion was perpetual energy.

"GRAMANANRAREELUS!" he yelled.

Nothing.

"Bugger," he concluded.

He collapsed on his bed, exhausted. The tungsten bulb had defeated him. Persuasion, that was all. With his head on the pillow he flashed his wand, almost lazily, and muttered, "Expelliremarmus."

Illumination.

Incandescence.

Brilliance.

Radiance.

Glory and majesty!

He'd bent the will of nature to his demands. He was a wizard!

"I did it! I DID IT!" He jumped to his feet and into the air, giving it a damned fine punch.

"What are you so happy about, Smith?"

Things had been a lot better when Dan was on the ground. His beaming face fell with his landing. Mr. Grak wasn't out living the high life with fellow lowlifes. Mr. Grak stood in the doorway, finger on the light switch. Not only did it mean Dan was no closer to his dream, it also meant he was going to have to spend the night with his boss.

"I thought you were g...going out?" Dan asked the goblin, who wore his infamous, fluffy white dressing gown. He'd just got out of the shower.

"Can't be bothered. London's been so boring lately."

"B...boring?" said Dan, incredulously.

"Yep. Make me a cuppa."

Dan obediently followed Mr. Grak through to the open-plan living area and dutifully put the kettle on.

Mr. Grak turned on the TV and sat down on the couch. His dressing gown was infamous for a reason. It was a bit on the short side and Mr. Grak's *growspeck* was a bit on the large side.

A *growspeck* was not an attractive organ and terrifying to behold to non-goblin entities. This was not a belief Mr. Grak shared. To him, his *growspeck* was a celebrated organ of totalitarian sexual dominance, one that was likely to be immortalised in a statue, or at worst, preserved in formaldehyde for future generations to marvel at in a museum and for children to ask, "What's that, Miss Saunders?" And Miss Saunders would say, "Children, that is the greatest sexual organ ever known, and the one regret I have in life is not being alive when the owner was brandishing it."

And Miss Saunders would have biiiiiiiiiiiiigggg hangers.

"That woman of yours is waiting for you," said Mr. Grak, eyes on the television screen as he scanned the channels.

"Michelle?" Dan said, surprised, pouring the water for Mr. Grak's tea over the side of the mug. "I thought she was at her sister's?"

"Smith, when I tell you you're a loser, I'm doing it for your own good, you know?"

"Yes, Mr. Grak. Th...Thank you, Mr. Grak." Dan took the teabag out early so it wasn't as strong as Mr. Grak liked. It was as passive aggressive as he got.

Mr. Grak got up and put a DVD in the player. Dan prayed it wasn't another goblin porno. "Remember, Smith, I'm a winner. I've been banging sap's women since my *growspeck* oozed into place. You need to grow a pair."

Dan swallowed some vomit. Seeing Mr. Grak's *growspeck* had made him nauseous, but contemplating its use while looking into one of its many eyes took it to the next level. Goblin sex was a thing of nightmares. Goblin sex even made goblins sick.[17]

"She's in the shower if you were wondering." Mr. Grak frowned at the tea Dan was adding milk to. "I don't like mugs, Smith. I like a cup and a saucer. Mugs are for mugs, losers like you, and builders—who are idiots, and long-distance lorry drivers—who are murderers."

Dan transferred the contents of the mug to a cup.

"No!" said Mr. Grak with a raised finger, while pressing play on the remote control with another. Goblin porn. Hardcore goblin porn. German hardcore goblin porn. German hardcore goblin megaporn.[18]

Dan put the kettle on.

Dan often questioned why he was housemates with a goblin who hated him, belittled him, and had once eaten half his cat, Spartacus. Mr. Grak had left the other half so Dan could find it and learn his lesson. Dan's hamster had taken the brunt of the punishment when Dan asked what the lesson was.

"She's in the shower. Why don't you go in there with her?"

---

[17] Part of the courtship ritual.
[18] Not downloadable.

suggested the sordid goblin, his lips pursed at the action he was watching, the screen flashing green, pink, yellow, green-pink, yellow, green, vomit, pink.

Dan vomited into the bin.

"What did I tell you, Smith?" he said, mockingly. "If I was you, I'd be in there, and when she reached for a loofah... BAM! My *growspeck* would be waiting."

Dan wiped his mouth with some kitchen towel and tried to find a happier place in his head, one where there were no *growspecks* and where Spartacus was still alive and had never taken part in Mr. Grak's avant-garde interpretation of Schrödinger's thought experiment.

"Well, you're not me, are you, Mr. G...G...Grak?"

"Very true, Smith. Very true." Mr. Grak put his hands behind his head and relaxed, his legs spread to accommodate *changes*. "If I was you I like to think I'd have committed suicide as soon as I experienced conscious thought."

"We're waiting until we're m...m...married."

Raucous laughter carried through to the adjacent flats until it was finally silenced by Mr. Grak's convulsions. The occupants would never complain. Dominic from 5a had complained once. Dominic had made a big scene, telling Mr. Grak he was fed up of the noise coming from the flat when Mr. Grak was watching goblin pornography, so Mr. Grak had shaved him during a resident's meeting in front of fifteen of the neighbours. None of whom had seen a thing.

"What's so f...funny about waiting t...till we get married?" said Dan when Mr. Grak could breathe again.

Mr. Grak wiped tears from his eyes, and then his nipples, where a percentage of his tear ducts were located, and managed through the laughter, "You really are the most pathetic fairy alive."

"I am not a fairy!" Dan boiled, or, rather, gently defrosted. "Look, you can insult me, but d...d...do not insult Michelle."

"OK, OK, bring me my tea!" said Mr. Grak, coming to the end of his tormenting heckling.

Dan stomped over and gave the grinning goblin his hot beverage, but Dan made a point of not even saying thank you when Mr. Grak took it.

"And what's going on in here?" said a tired voice from the door to the kitchen.

Dan's heart melted, as it did every time he set eyes on Michelle. He'd cried the first time he'd seen her, which was partially because he'd just been punched in the nose by a yob, but mainly because of her radiance. She'd come to his rescue by breaking his attacker's ribs with a spinning back kick. And then she'd picked Dan up out of the gutter and asked him out! He'd never been asked out before, or asked anyone else out. He'd certainly struck gold first time. In some ways, he was the luckiest guy alive.

She was so beautiful, even with no makeup and her long blonde hair tied up in that weird towel thing that women did which sort of scared him. She commanded the presence of an Amazon princess, strong and beautiful. She was his princess, his Wonder Woman.

"Get us a beer!" said Mr. Grak to this princess.

"Get it yourself, you hideous piece of shit!" she snapped at him.

Dan wanted to be somewhere else. He clenched his buttocks at the awkwardness of it all. Every time Mr. Grak and Michelle were in the same room, the unstoppable force met the immovable object, and instead of solving the paradox, they both took a break to make Dan's life hell.

Michelle poured her scorn on her boyfriend, turning her back towards the goblin. "And where have you been anyway? I was expecting you back hours ago."

Mr. Grak was quick to point out the reason. "Useless git had the worst end-of-year appraisal in the company. I was forced to give him some extra work as a punishment, like a detention."

"Is this true, Dan?" Hands on hips meant trouble.

"I b...broke all my t...targets and was t...technically the b...best performer in the company. He always makes me stay behind on F...F...Fridays! Always! Even if there isn't any work on!"

Michelle turned to the goblin. "Is this true?"

"I'll remember this on Monday, Smith." Mr. Grak pointed a threateningly talon at Dan before getting back to the filth on the screen and turning up the volume.

"You can't p...pile any more work on me," he whined.

"Don't be such a chump, Dan," said Michelle, who turned to Mr. Grak and said, "You're overworking him."

Mr. Grak spread his hands. "He's the one who wants to save the world."

"And switch that rubbish off!" she snapped.

Dan turned to Michelle, but daren't look her in the eyes. "I've got to work on Sunday, too."

Through gritted teeth she said, "You're meant to be taking me out for the day, remember?"

"Yes," he said, guiltily.

She paced the room. "You're standing me up? And after what happened the other night?"

"I don't think it's technically possible for him to perform," said Mr. Grak, grinning, looking extremely pleased that he'd stayed in for the night.

"Shut up!" said Michelle. "Dan, what is more important than me, your girlfriend?"

"London Zoo is p...p...presenting its first p...polar bear c...cub."

"Stuttering: Level 9000!" jeered Mr. Grak. "It's nearly reached the highest echelons where his virginity lurks."

Michelle threw up her hands. "Why would I give a shit about a polar bear?"

"P...polar b...b...bears represent everything that g...global warming is destroying. The polar ice c...caps are melting. In the wild, the p...polar bear population has been reduced to fifty pairs. We're doing our best to increase the number through c...captivity, but most zoos have been struggling to get the females to c...c...con...conceive."

"The lads ain't doing the business, ey?" said Mr. Grak. "Are you sure you ain't a polar bear, rather than a fairy?"

"I am not a fairy!" said Dan, defiantly.

Michelle walked in between Mr. Grak and Dan. "And you're not taking me out because?"

"Because, Michelle," said Mr. Grak, "your boyfriend needs to run a story on the event, otherwise he is going to get his arse sacked."

"Why don't you stand up to him?" said Michelle.

The truth was, Dan wanted to be at the event at London Zoo more than anything. The plummeting population of the magnificent animals was a tragedy. The so-called civilised world didn't care it was ripping the environment to pieces. The staff at the zoo worked round the clock ensuring the little cubs had the best chance of survival in this bleak world, and their hard work was paying off. That little bear would be a symbol for Green Planet and their efforts to reverse the effects of global warming.

"Well? Why won't you stand up to him?" said Michelle, not happy to be repeating herself.

"Yeah," piped up Mr. Grak, "why don't you stand up to me?"

Dan's mouth gaped.

"Come on," said Michelle, tiredly, when no answer came. "Let's go in the bedroom away from that horrible turd." She took Dan by his pudgy, sweaty paw and led him to the bedroom.

"Give us a shout when he can't perform."

"Shut up, you horrible goblin bastard!" she cried.

Chapter 7...

MR. SOMERSBY PACED ACROSS HIS LONDON OFFICE, sipping a tumbler of whisky. Pacing was anomalous. Everything in his life ran like clockwork, there was never the need to pace.

Things had changed. He'd killed a lot of people over the past couple of days, and although that wasn't anything out of the ordinary, the murders had been through frustration rather than pleasure. His desire had not being fulfilled. The failure boiled his blood, figuratively, which had led to several would-be wizards' blood being boiled, literally. Mr. Somersby wasn't certifiably insane, for there was no one insane enough to certify him, but even he'd admit that he was feeling a little bit cranky of late.

Currently, Rillit was testing his patience, another rare occurrence. Rillit was his finest employee, and Mr. Somersby had developed an unusual relationship with the young elf, one where he'd feel slight remorse at murdering the pointy-eared servant.

In Rillit's defence, Mr. Somersby had placed a rather difficult task in his hands. Even though murder was off the menu at the moment, maiming was becoming a distinct possibility as a starter, followed by a main course of castration and a dessert of crucifixion.

"Rillit, please tell me you've you found a suitable expert on the subject of the arcane," said Mr. Somersby, closing his eyes and pinching the bridge of his nose with his thumb and forefinger.

"I believe so, sire," said Rillit, cold sweat forming on his fawning forehead. "I have found another potential employee for this afternoon. Would you like to see him now?"

"Yes, but only if he's an impeccable candidate, Rillit. I really hope you're not about to waste yet more of my time. There are better things I could be doing."

"Like sex ravaging, sire?"

"What else?" Mr. Somersby's head cocked to the side. "Did you just call me sire, Rillit?"

"Yes, sire."

Mr. Somersby nodded slowly. "I like that, Rillit."

"I'm glad, sire, and you'll be pleased to know that I've organised a session of sex-ravaging after your interview with one of Britain's finest wizards."

Mr. Somersby took a seat and crossed his legs. He took another sip of whisky. "Proceed."

Rillit paused, internal deliberation raging inside him, yet nothing showed on a face trained to be stone. "If…if I may say, sire," he said, tentatively, "tracking down competent wizards has proven frightfully difficult. I have scoured the lands and I think magic is all but forgotten in the world."

A groomed eyebrow rose. "What is it I say about excuses, Rillit?"

In a monotone voice, Rillit recited, "Excuses are for employees fifteen seconds from evisceration."

"You'll do well remembering that, employee."

If Rillit was able to stand straighter, he would have. "I present," he announced, looking at a card he had drawn out of his pocket. "Derek…." He turned the card over, looking for something more, something arcane. He found nothing. His pulse increased. He repeated, "I present Derek," with a slight break in his voice.

Rillit opened the door to the office and looked out, and then he looked from side to side, and then he looked down.

"Oh god," he muttered.

The potential wizard/employee/victim ducked under the butler's arm and entered the office/crime scene, walking confidently, walking tall—idiomatically, not literally.

Putting on an air of confidence to hide inability is only useful when dealing with the intellectually inferior. When dealing with intelligence, shrewdness, and violent mental illness, then the reason for one's air of confident ability best be ability.

If Rillit was pale before, it now appeared he possessed less blood than the last candidate wizard to have passed through Mr. Somersby's doors. It took all his will not to chew at nails, and if the windows weren't bulletproof, he would have thrown his worthless body into the blue yonder.

Through narrowed eyes, Mr. Somersby judged the book by its cover. "So," he said, "you're a wizard?"

"No, sir, I am not a wizard," said Derek. He wiggled his fingers. "I am a magician."

"A magician," said Mr. Somersby with terrifying calmness.

"That I am, sir. That I am," said Derek with a flourish of his cape and a twirl of a cane. To his credit he was smooth and very fluid.

"And you are called Derek?" asked Mr. Somersby, slowly.

"Yes, sir. Derek. Derek the Debonair."

"Ah!" Never had such a simple exclamation carried so much weight and foreboding. "And you are a—?"

"Magician!"

"Yes, I know that, but what are you?"

"A debonair magician, sir," said Derek, with a waggling of the bushiest of brows.

"Ah." This exclamation was a judgment.

Rillit did his best not to lose the contents of his stomach. If he was holding a blade, he would have done.

Whether the magician was debonair or not was questionable, but what was indisputable was that he was small, pudgy, balding, and had the most horrendous pair of feet outside of a farmyard. There was only one species which ticked all those boxes and that species was a halfling, and if there was one thing that Mr. Somersby hated, amongst many, many others, it was a lazy, good-for-nothing halfling. Mr. Somersby hated virtually all living things. The only things he didn't hate were endowed with teenage breasts, so maybe it was unfair to call him a racist, but he was.

Derek shuffled nervously on the spot, pulling at the collar of his white shirt. His cheap tuxedo did little to impress the boss, nor did the ill-fitting top hat. Derek was unaware of the danger he faced and that Mr. Somersby transfixing stare was akin to a great white shark's, not that a shark had seen a spinning bow tie before. But Derek was a natural showman, so he took a deep breath and did what he did best: he put on a show.

"Good evening, ladies and gentlemen. I am Derek the Debonair," he announced, his arms raised in greeting to an imaginary audience.

"Ladies?" asked Mr. Somersby, looking around him. "What are you talking about?"

"I...I...." The flustered magician mopped his face with a poker-dot handkerchief. "Erm...Good evening, gentlemen and...erm, gentleman, I am Debonair Derek, no—Derek the Debonair."

Mr. Somersby slowly turned his gaze over to Rillit, who was attempting to swallow his own tongue. Mr. Somersby turned back to Derek, who was juggling.

"What...what...are you doing?" asked a confused boss.

"I am juggling, sir."

"I c...can see that!" Mr. Somersby performed the first stammer of his life. "But, but it isn't even impressive juggling. You're just using three balls."

"Really?" said Derek, almost seductively.

"Yes, really!"

"Prepare for more than three balls! Prepare for amazeballs!" cried the halfling, momentarily losing concentration, allowing the multicoloured spheres to scatter far and wide. "Not again!" he cried, and ran around, panting, picking them up, his belly causing problems with reaching the floor. Finally, once all were recovered, with the exception to the one he lost under the sofa, he took another grubby ball from his pocket and went back to juggling, this time keeping a furious eye on the flying objects.

"What...what am I watching?" Mr. Somersby was close to upset, and this new feeling was confusing him greatly. It wasn't fun at all. This confusion was the only thing keeping Derek's liver inside his body.

"It was just one mistake!" said Derek out of the corner of his mouth. "Everybody gets one!"

Mr. Somersby pointed at Derek with a questioning, waggling finger, and tried to say to Rillit, "This...this...this..." He was so outraged he could barely speak.

Derek, concentrated on his A-game. When things were going bad, the best thing was to bombard with magic. "I want you to think of a number between one and ten," he said.

"Why?" asked Mr. Somersby, a very valid question indeed.

"For the sake of magic," said the debonair one, sweating with the effort of juggling.

"Six," said the tycoon.

"No! Not yet," said Derek. "And it can't be six."

"So pick any number between one and ten, but not six?"

"And not yet!" said Derek, walking closer, jaw locked with the extra concentration. "Just think of a number. OK, think of a number, but don't think of the number of balls I'm juggling. Think of a number. Not how many witches there were in Macbeth or how many blind mice there are, or how many balls I am juggling, just concentrate on a number. Have you seen *Free Willy*?"

Mr. Somersby started to turn red in the face. Rage corded his neck and threatened to throttle him. "I don't...I don't believe this is happening."

"Is it three?" yelled the magician, halting his display and catching the balls, well, one of them.

"No." said Mr. Somersby, staring at the ball that had bounced off his foot.

"Four or five or two?" ventured Derek.

"No," said Mr. Somersby, distantly.

Derek wagged a finger, "Are you sure it wasn't three?"

"Rillit?" Mr. Somersby turned to his faithful servant.

"Yes, sire," said the elf, hoping for a burial and not to be left in the car park to be picked apart by crows.

"I take it you asked for a demonstration of the applicant's magical abilities before this stage?"

"Yes, sire, yes, I did."

"And did you supervise the interview, personally?"

"Erm, no, sire. No, a mistake I can promise you will never happen again," said the unnerved lackey.

"Be a good chap and go have a word with whoever put young Debonair Derek on the list."

"Derek the Debonair!"

Rillit winced at Derek's interruption, which was accompanied by his spinning bow tie lighting up and making a whizzing sound.

"Yes, sire. Immediately, sire. Would you like me to escort Deb—" Rillit checked himself. "Derek the Debonair—"

Mr. Somersby silenced him with a raised finger. "No, I'd like to see if Derek could teach me some magic."

"A magician never reveals his secrets," said the halfling with a coy chuckle.

Not able to watch any more without spontaneously combusting, Rillit turned on his heel, left the office, and went to castrate someone with a rusty spanner.

"Now, Derek, where were we?" said Mr. Somersby.

"Giv' us a sec', I'm knackered!" Derek took off his top hat and gave his red, balding head a scratch. A large white rabbit took the opportunity to escape its sweaty prison.

"Not now, Perseus!" he cried and desperately chased the large white bunny around the office at a pace which did not worry the floppy-eared co-star. After a minute, Derek gave up the ghost, his hands on his knees. He wheezed and spluttered. Perseus took to nibbling on a priceless side table.

Derek had been taught to bombard with magic, so that's exactly what the halfling did. There was a finale to perform, and he wasn't one to disappoint. He stood up straight, looked the dumbstruck boss of bosses squarely in the eye, offered him a digit, and cried dramatically, "Pull my finger!"

Chapter 8...

DAN SHUT THE DOOR OF HIS BEDROOM TO THE HAUNTING SOUNDS OF GOBLIN PORNOGRAPHY. Michelle whipped the towel off her head unleashing the mass of long, straight, orgasm-inducing blonde hair. The smell of her shampoo washed over Dan, exciting and embarrassing him in equal measures. The towel wrapped around her middle hit the floor and Dan managed to close his eyes in time, keeping them tight shut, not wanting to take advantage of her.

Michelle dried her hair, rubbing it with a towel. "That horrible goblin bastard is right. You are a loser, Dan."

On instinct, Dan opened his eyes as he gathered his breath to defend himself. He caught a glimpse of her hard, yet curvaceous, bronzed and wonderful body before he slapped both hands over his eyes and turned his head away, to give her the privacy she deserved.

Michelle looked to the heavens. "Dan, I know we are waiting for holy wedlock before we actually do it, and I'm fortunate that you respect my wishes, but isn't there a single part of you, one in particular, that wants to take me over to the bed?"

There was indeed a part of Dan that lusted so, and his jeans were making it all rather uncomfortable. "Nnnnggghhhhhh," he managed.

"My father wants me to leave you," she said, when it became apparent he wouldn't turn his head. "It's OK, I'm wearing clothes now."

He turned back quickly to vent his concern, only to be tricked. She wasn't wearing any clothes at all. "Nnnnggghhhhhh," he managed, again, as he turned back around.

"My father can't stand you," she said, relishing the words.

"But he hasn't even m...met me!"

"And you don't need to meet him. The fact he hates your guts makes all this worthwhile." She threw on a pair of jeans and a cut-up T-shirt and made them look like she'd spent hours at a stylist.

Dan peeked through his fingers when he heard her sit down and withdrew his hands from his face. He wanted to ask if her dad's utter disapproval of their relationship was the only reason she was with him. He didn't though, scared of hearing the truth. "He really does hate me, d...doesn't he?"

"Yes, yes he does." Her blue eyes shone with delight. "You're a thorn in his side."

Sometimes, Dan couldn't believe he was dating *the* Mr. Somersby's daughter. Michelle couldn't help who her parents were, but the fact she worked for her father and The Corporation were daggers to his heart.

"I know he's your father and all, and I know he's very rich and powerful, but some of his c...crimes against the environment, Michelle," he said with a mild hint of venom. "Sometimes, I'd like to...I'd like to..." Dan nearly made a fist, but only managed a weak claw.

Luscious pink lips pouted seductively. "What would you do to him, Dan?" she asked, moving closer, trying to bring out his darker side.

"I'd shut down that C...C...Corporation of his for a start," he said, pursing his lips in quasi-anger.

"And then what?" asked Michelle, grabbing him by the hand.

Thinking it over, Dan realised that was it. He didn't want to actually hurt Michelle's dad, even if his company, The Corporation, was almost entirely responsible for melting the polar icecaps. Michelle's dad had wiped out a large chunk of the rain forests, and was well on his way to finishing the job. Ninety percent of his workforce were children from third world countries, and Michelle's dad was the reason for those third world countries. However, if push came to shove, and Dan had the opportunity, he wouldn't harm the man himself.

Michelle sat expectantly on the end of the bed, waiting for Dan to detail his planned dissection of her dad, and he felt compelled to say something, even though he had nothing to say.

"I'd...I'd give him a bloody good talking to."

Her face dropped. "You're a loser, Dan."

"I know," he said dejectedly.

"My father thinks you're some big shot in Green Planet. He doesn't know you are some jumped-up goblin's lackey."

Dan did more for Green Planet and the actual planet itself than anyone else in the company, but he didn't bother arguing the point. People thought he was a loser, and along the way they'd convinced him too. "Sorry to disap...p...ppoint you. I am who I am."

"It's a shame. Isn't there any chance for promotion, or for you to push yourself forward?"

"I want to save the p...planet, Michelle," he said, firmly. "I need to be on the ground, where it counts."

"Really?" She crossed her arms. "What have you managed so far?"

His eyes drifted towards the dressing table where a large, dusty tome was sitting, waiting for him. She clocked it, got up, walked over, and leafed through it, dust swirling under the table lamp. "What's this?"

"N...N...nothing, j...just something I've b...b...b...been reading," he said, the tightness in his voice and the extra stuttering gave him away.

"This isn't another spell book, is it?" She groaned. "Please tell me you're not spending your nights, when you're not boring me, trying to perform little spells and parlour tricks?" She slammed the book shut. "Please, no? You couldn't possibly be going against my wishes, could you? Not after our last chat when you were wasting time with them pathetic nerds."

"I...I...," he stuttered. "Magic can reverse g...g...global warming, Michelle."

"You're not just a loser. You're an idiot, to boot," she said, shaking her head in disgust and throwing the book in the bin.

"This world once ran on m...magic and there was no g...g...global warming and p...polar b...bears weren't being starved to death because the p...polar icecaps were intact."

"And there was no shopping, no HDTVs, cars, Caribbean cruises or anything else fun, for that matter."

"Magic is d...directly linked to Mother Nature. We can use magic to reverse global warming. Mother Nature will only t...take so much before she fights back and allkind will be brushed aside."

Michelle's lips tightened. "My father wiped out twenty per cent of the Amazonian rainforest in order to build the world biggest water park and multiplex cinema. If she was going to kick off, I am pretty certain she would have done it by now."

"Your father is a m...monster," said Dan with an attempt at a growl.

"Yes, he is a complete prick, which is why I'm with you, but he has the world's biggest Ferrari collection." She sat on the bed and took his hand. "Listen, this magic has got to stop. You're looking like more of a fool every day, and there's only so much that I'd do to annoy my father. I don't want to leave you for that homeless goblin who lives in the flat's recycling bin and will drink a pint of piss for a fiver. Look, get the picture of the polar bear, wipe its arse, and throw a snowball at it, but then I want this nonsense to stop. I want you to get to the top of Green Planet and show my father what for. Do you understand me?"

"Yes," said a downtrodden man.

"Right, I'm going home," she said with a start, getting to her feet.

"I'll walk you back," said Dan.

She burst out laughing. "If I was mugged, how would you help?"

She was right. There was nothing he could do about it.

Not yet.

But...

Magic would change everything.

Chapter 9...

DAN AWOKE IN FRONT OF A GREAT ROUND DOOR. He blinked, and then he rubbed his eyes, and then he blinked again. "Eh?"

Something wasn't quite right. He could have sworn he'd woken up to go for a wee. He looked down. He was still in his Spider-Man pyjamas and he couldn't decide if that was a good thing or not. He didn't need a wee any more, which was concerning.

The door before him was enormous, embedded in a great wall of yellow stone which stretched as far as Dan could see to his left, to his right, and up above. He stood on an empty cobbled street which ended here at the door. Behind him lines of Tudor-style houses meandered, leaning at impossible angles. Everything was so...perfect, perfect just for Dan.

"Where am I? How...how did I get here?" he asked himself. He had to be dreaming, but everything was so vivid. He gave his arm a pinch.

"Owww!" he said, unsure of what he'd accomplished.

This couldn't be a dream. His imagination didn't stretch far. Most of his dreams were of Mr. Grak shaving him or of him wetting himself. Sometimes, they weren't even dreams. He checked himself for dampness.

Then he checked himself for baldness.

Everywhere.

His pubes were, by far, his best feature.

Curiouser and curiouser.

There was a great creaking of metal on metal, and with a crack of golden lightning fizzling from the door's hinges to the night sky, the huge door swung open. Light streamed out, blazing like the midday sun. Stood at the threshold was Gambledolf, in magnificent form. He wore a blazing golden robe which possessed a life of its own, dancing around him, liquid gold in zero gravity.

"Come through, my dear boy," said the wizard with a broad grin, leaning on his staff. "We have much to discuss."

"Where am I, Gambledolf?" asked Dan, shielding his eyes from the golden glow.

"You are here, my dear boy."

"And where is here?"

"Somewhere you are not," said the wizard with knowing mischief.

"Eh?"

Gambledolf laughed and his beard shook. "Your attire may suggest you are dreaming, and in some way you are. You're safely tucked up in bed, back at your flat, snoring away." He shut his eyes and the orb on the end of his wand glowed bright. "Although, when I say 'safely tucked up in bed,' I may be giving you a false sense of security."

"What d...do you mean?"

"Your goblin housemate is currently stealing money from your wallet." Gambledolf sucked air in through his teeth. "And now he's urinating in your shoes."

"Ah."

"Ah indeed," said Gambledolf, still with his eyes shut. "And, now, unfortunately, he's taking a photograph of your private area and giggling."

"Yeah, he does that," said Dan, awkwardly.

"And now he's...oh." Gambeldolf opened his eyes and blushed a deep red.

"What is it, Gambledolf?" asked Dan.

"I...err...he's...Why *do* you live with him, Danoclees?"

Dan changed the subject. "So this is a d...dream?"

"Yes and no. Your body is in a dream-like state, but your consciousness is here. Forget the technicalities. Come in! Come in!"

The wizard beckoned Dan into the hallway, where Dan's breath was taken from him, and only partly because of an inflammatory respiratory disease.

"Wooowwwwww!" he managed, taking in the cavernous hall of wonders, lit with golden orbs that flew hither and thither wherever the eye was turned, as if the lights knew where one focused.

The room was a museum and a fun house all rolled into one. Contraptions on the walls, their purpose incomprehensible, turned turbines and powered pistons, belching out purple and gold steam. Ancient maps, parchments, and bizarre artefacts and curios sat on tables and plinths. Anthropomorphised robots bustled, cleaning the floors and dusting the tables, occasionally farting out small golden lightning bolts.

"They're p...powered by magic!" Dan cried.

Gambledolf laughed and clapped his hands. "Why of course, dear boy! You didn't think I'd be using coal and gas did you?"

"But...but!" said Dan. He was impossibly excited, until, that was, he caught another glimpse of his Spider-Man jammies, and said forlornly, "There is no way this isn't a dream."

Gambledolf raised a finger. "Your conscious being controls your thoughts and actions here."

"But that doesn't mean this wonder is real, does it, Gambledolf?"

Gambledolf sighed. "No, it doesn't."

Dan took in the spectacle and yearned for it. He could reach out and touch it, but this was too good to be true. He accepted the inevitable.

Gambledolf placed his hand under Dan's chin. "But it just so happens that all of this *is* real."

Dan let go of a little bit of wee.

"And I happen to live here." Gambledolf twirled on the spot and glided through the hall. "Come now, dear boy, we have much to discuss!"

Dan entered a child-like state of wonderment, following the wizard through his home where the vibrant energy of raw magic flashed from artefact to figurine to contraption to doodledad. Magic emanated off the hundreds, maybe even thousands, of wonderful and mystical objects and diddelytrapdads and jiggymcdallythings that filled the enchanting cottage, or castle, or whatever it was.

Dan wanted to say so much, but he was spellbound. "Your place is well ace!" he managed.

Gambledolf's deep laugh soothed Dan's soul. "Why, thank you, Danoclees, but, I must say, you haven't seen anything yet."

"Ace!" Dan jumped up and down with glee and his glasses fell off his nose. Luckily, the lenses were so thick there was no chance of them breaking.

They reached another great door, this one twice as large as the front one. The majestic wizard turned and, leaning against the door, faced Dan. "I have not taken anyone into this room for two hundred years. You will be the first, my boy."

"Why me?"

"Because magic is you and you are magic," he said, grandly.

"Ace!" Dan gave the air a damned fine punch.

Gambledolf bowed and, as he did so, the door opened and Dan was forced to cover his eyes as a wonderful, warm and inquisitive light encompassed him and somehow entered him, probed him, and weighed him.

"Behold, Danoclees Dunlorian, the Last Realm of Anglor."

Squinting, Dan, entered the room, and as soon as he crossed the threshold, unlimited power flowed through him, awaking something dormant and powerful. His eyes grew accustomed to the light and, if he was awestruck before, he found himself in a land beyond his wildest dreams.

"Ace!"

"I thought you'd like it," said Gambledolf with a wry grin.

This was everything the hall was but multiplied by a squillion. The room crackled with the golden radiance of pure magic. In this glorious library, golden bolts of magic jumped from book to book and across the room to pedestals and grand plinths on which stood jabberdacklewigs and stumpynickerdads and loudymcnuggetcracks. The ceiling stretched up as far as the eye could see, and around the circular room, the size of a cricket pitch, telescopes were set up for the purpose of seeing farther into the heavens. Animals, the likes of which Dan had never encountered and dressed in the most ostentatious of clothes, sat conversing, playing games or musical instruments. This was beyond fairy tale and the imagination of allkind.

"This is like, proper ace, Gambledolf!"

"Yes," said Gambledolf, his lined face freezing for a second. "You've already mentioned that a few times. Let's take a seat."

Two thrones waited for the wizard and the potential one. Beautifully ornate works of art depicting scenes from millennia ago, great battles and acts of heroism were carved into the frames. Dan tested out the ancient timber and upholstery and was amazed at the comfort. The timber actually moved with him so he could find the most comfortable position. It was like lounging in a La-Z Boy, not sitting on a millennia-old throne.

"Drink, my lad?"

"Eh?"

Dan wasn't paying attention; he was too busy looking around at the cool stuff and working his arse into the chair.

"Would you like a drink?" asked the wizard.

"Yes, please. Have you any Fairtrade orange juice?"

From a small table next to the sitting area, Gambledolf took an empty goblet and placed it in Dan's sweaty hands of excitement.

"You can have anything you want, anything in this world, or any other for that matter. Are you sure you want—what was it?—the juice of an orange?"

"A Fairtrade orange."

Gambledolf's bushy white eyebrows knitted together. "What constitutes a Fairtrade orange?"

Dan began to recite. "Fairtrade is all about better prices, good working conditions, sustainability, and fair terms for farmers and workers in the developing worlds. Fairtrade fights the injustices of conventional trade, which discriminate against the poorest, and therefore weakest, producers. Fairtrade gives the little guys control over their lives."

Gambledolf worked it through in his head and asked, "But it's essentially an orange?"

"Yes."

"And out of everything you could have in the world, you want orange juice."

"Fairtrade orange juice."

Gambledolf shrugged. "Fairtrade orange juice, yes."

In an instant, the goblet in Dan's hand turned cool. Inside was an orange coloured liquid. "Wooooowwwww," he said, with child-like amazement.

He drank the juice and grinned. It tasted just like the stuff he bought from the Co-Op. A small burp escaped his lips. He wasn't expecting the gold bolt of magic to fly out of his mouth with the escaping carbon dioxide. "Do it again!"

Gambledolf smiled. "I think you were the one who burped, Danoclees."

"I meant the drink." Dan swirled his goblet. "Can you make the drink appear again?"

"My dear boy. It wasn't me who did it."

"Who was it, then?" said Dan, looking over the back of his chair.

Again, Gambledolf's deep laugh echoed, and the golden energy of magic danced with his mirth. "Why, you, of course."

"M...me?"

"You."

Dan stared at the empty goblet and thought of orange (Fairtrade), once more. A small flash of gold caused him to blink, and in the millisecond it took to open his eyes, juice (Fairtrade) had filled the cup. The grin tested the muscles of his face.

"I can do magic. I can do magic!" he said.

"It's in your blood, and it always has been."

"So why couldn't I do it before?"

Gambledolf placed his hands together and his fingers to his lips. "This is a special place. Here you can tap into your true potential, but once you cross the boundary and step from Anglor into London, you will not be able to harness the power, not yet. That is, not without training. If you weren't able to harness magic, you would never have been able to enter this realm. You, my boy, are gifted and destined for incredible things."

Dan trembled with excitement. "Can I visit this place when I'm awake, and not just in my dreams?"

"Unfortunately, you can't. Things have...changed." Gambledolf's bright expression dimmed like the sun disappearing behind a cloud.

"I know they've changed," said Dan. "I know pretty much everything there is to know about magic's history—"

"No, you don't," said the wizard sharply. "In fact, there are none who do except the Order of Magi." Gambledolf settled into his chair and enthralled Dan by revealing the true history of the world.

"Once upon a time, we, the Order of the Magi, ruled this land for the good of allkind. The fairies were gone, slain, and their graves desecrated by the goblin hordes. We were all that was left of the world of magic. We tried as best we could to capture the essence of the fairy kings, but alas, we are but a shadow of what once was.

"Magic was all we had to maintain peace between the four powers: goblins, elves, dwarves, and men. They grew restless without the fairies to guide them. Each was desperate to dominate the land, and with power came the desire for more. The War descended into unparalleled savagery, catalysed by the forging of steel and discovery of gunpowder." Gambledolf removed his hat and ran the rim through his hands. The wizard's long, thick grey hair rearranged itself so it wasn't tickling his face.

"Magic has played no part in world affairs for over a millennium, Danoclees. The Order of Magi thought things could get no worse, but we never envisaged that the War would end."

"But surely that's a good thing?" asked Dan.

"Aye, you'd think so, laddie, we all did, but unfortunately, the races joined forces to create the world you know today, and that meant a new common enemy: Mother Nature. The technological revolution is destroying her, Dan. You know it, and in your heart you believe magic is the key. It is not coincidence that you feel this way, my boy. It is your calling."

"I knew," said Dan, staring into space. "I always knew...."

"Anglor is dying, Dan," Gambledolf's voice wavered. "Magic is our connection with the natural world, and we are slowly cutting off our bond. If it is severed, there will be nothing to protect us."

"From what?"

"Everything. Since the birth of this planet, it has been ravaged by ice ages, volcanoes, meteorites, plagues, famines. Mother Nature is yin and yang. She is destructive. Yet she is the bringer of life. We must respect her. We must love and fear her in equal measures.

"The fairies found a way to connect with Mother Earth, relenting to her power, and through this we gained her protection. Without it, it is only a matter of time before we are wiped out and Mother Nature will do it without a care. Allkind cannot dominate a planet. We are nothing compared to the elements, and we have forgotten that with our *science*." He spat the word. "She will punish us accordingly, mark my words."

"Can't you ask her not to?"

Gambledolf stared straight through Dan. "She doesn't live down the road. I can't give her a ring."

"Oh, oh right," said the potential wizard, concentrating on his fruity beverage (Fairtrade).

"The only way we can rekindle the link is by forging strong our bond with the Earth."

"How?" asked Dan from the edge of his seat.

"A quest, Dan. A quest."

"To go see Mother Nature?"

Gambledolf blinked a couple of times. "She doesn't live in Middlesbrough, Dan. Mother Nature isn't a woman. Mother Nature is figurative speech for the life essence of this planet, its soul if you will."

"Right, gotcha." Dan raised a thumb.

Gambledolf paused for a second and gathered himself. "To reconnect, magic must grow strong in the world once more."

"I've always said that, Mr. Gambledolf. I b...believe that magic can reverse global warming."

"Yes, Danoclees!" said the wizard. Now, he too, leant forward in his chair, "And that is why you're here."

"Really?"

"Your voice called out to me, Dan, from the ether. I was drawn to your passion. Magic is your ally. I can sense it. Even here, in Anglor, you shine like a beacon."

"So why have I always been crap at it?"

Gambledolf's serious face was replaced with one of mirth. "Because you are held tight by the bonds of society, my boy. I will set you free, if, that is, you are willing to embark on an adventure?"

Dan shrunk back into his chair, his fire waning. "I d...don't know if I'm cut out for adventures."

Gambledolf placed a hand on Dan's knee. "But you've already started upon it! You will show the world what it is to be a wizard. You have the power to stop global warming, Danoclees, and you will save the Earth with the power of Anglor, the essence of magic."

"Even though I'm a b...bit rubbish at it?"

"Not with this you're not, Danny boy!" Gambledolf pulled out of his cloak a mahogany wand. It was only small, less than a foot long, but it crackled and fizzed with golden energy. "Not with this."

Chapter 10...

"PLUMPORIOUS" WAS A VERY UNFORTUNATE NAME FOR A DWARF WHO STRUGGLED WITH HIS WEIGHT. In this age of equal rights, non-discrimination, and political correctness, the powers that decided who could be ridiculed without any chance of reprisal had decreed that the short of stature and the large of frame remained acceptable targets. One saving grace was that he'd never inherited a cruel nickname, as the kids at school could never come up with anything more hilarious and cruel as Plumporious.

Sometimes, Plumporious felt he'd been dealt a bad hand in life.

Racism within a species wasn't an issue in this world. It was hard for a white person to persecute a black person for the colour of their skin when a horde of goblins had burned down their town, executed the townsfolk, and waggled their *growspecks* on the corpses for no other reason than boredom.

As a gay dwarf, his sexuality was not ridiculed, it was an age of equality, after all. Even though he wasn't mocked for his sexual preferences, being a dwarf who deplored digging in dark, dank caves and grubby nails was a cause for one tough upbringing. Plumporious had been forced to move away from his northern homeland where his father, and his forefathers, for as long as records were kept, had mined deep into the hills in search of buried treasure—that was, until the mines had been destroyed by the terrible Dragon.

Plumporious had moved to the glorious south where people appreciated the finer things in life, and he was one of the finer things in life. He was a vision of pomp, of effulgent decadence, one the northern subspecies could not comprehend. He was a vein of gold in the darkness, the shining diamond in the pit of eternal night, but alas, his father had not seen the real treasure in his mines.

"Oi! Fatty! Kebab house is that way!" shouted an orc from the other side of the street.

Plumporious held his head high and strutted past with the air of the magnificent. Although London was home to the beautiful people, and was often a place where one could enjoy opulence and the grandiose while basking in the company of the blessed, London was also home to some despicable cretins. It just so happened that one of those cretins had decided to partake in ungentlemanly behaviour.

"Oi, fatty! I'm talking to you."

"Leave me alone!" cried Plumporious, hastening his pace.

The orc gave pursuit, drunkenly stumbling after the dwarf, kebab in one hand, can of strong lager in the other. He was abhorrent. His skin was like dark green leather, and Plumporious, who understood everything about genetic beauty challenges, could not excuse anyone not investing in a suitable lotion or cream. The orc's leathery skin was covered in scars, and the football top screamed hooligan. Naturally, the head was shaved, even though orcs were capable of growing majestic manes.

"Who ate all the pies! Who ate all the pies! You fat bastard, you fat bastard, who ate—"

"For goodness sake, must you be so crass!" Plumporious stamped his foot and turned to face the green-skinned thug who was laughing his ugly head off. His blue Millwall F.C. football top was covered in beer and food stains.

"Crass? Who says crass?" The orc grinned, delighting in annoying the small, chubby ball of majesty. "It rhymes with ass. Hur-hur-hur." The orc's canines sprouted out of his mouth and tapered into a razor-sharp hook, quite terrifying. Most decent orc folk, the ones who mixed in Plumporious's circles, filed their teeth down and whitened them to a state not unlike the clouds circling Mount Olympus.

"Most educated gentlemen, when presented by a thug with the manners of a dung beetle, would use the word *crass*."

Plumporious' scathing put down didn't have the desired effect. Rather than the orc slapping his hand over his mouth, tears streaming down his face, and running home to throw himself on his bed to cry into his pillow until he fell asleep, the orc grinned wolfishly.

"Maybe you should stop reading them word books, fatty, them dickcanaries, and get your arse on a treadmill."

Plumporious called upon all his restraint not to run home and throw himself on the bed and cry into his pillow until he fell asleep, but he did shed a little tear.

"Hang on, what's a dick canary?"

"You tell me. Here, do you want some of me kebab?" The orc held out the kebab towards Plumporious. It oozed out of the side of the pitta bread and onto the pavement with a gut-wrenching splat. "You going to eat that?" The orc pushed a bit of cabbage with his Doc Martin.

The sound of Plumporious's hand slapping across his mouth echoed off the surrounding buildings. "That's disgusting," he mumbled through his fingers. "I think I'm going to be sick."

"What sort of fatty are you?" said the orc.

"Firstly, my weight has nothing to do with you. Secondly, I have a slow metabolism. Thirdly, why are you following me?"

The orc continued to grin. "I was just saying hello. Just being friendly, like."

"Really?" asked a suspicious dwarf.

"What are you, anyway?" asked the orc, looking Plumporious up and down.

"What in blazes do you mean?" Plumporious lifted his chin proudly.

"You a short fat man or a tall, fat halfling?"

"How dare you!" cried the dwarf. He tapped his chest with his finger. "I am a dwarf of the North Hills, I'll have you know!"

The orc scratched his head. "You ain't got a beard."

Plumporious didn't have a beard, although shaving three times a day couldn't remove his perma-five o'clock shadow. He was a young dwarf, thirty years of age, and would be ruggedly good-looking if it wasn't for the lingering puppy fat. He wore his awesomely thick bleached blonde hair swept back, and it always proved a nightmare to straighten in the morning. His impeccable skin was a testament to a devotion to moisturisation. The little gold earring in one ear was cute. He wore it to soften his image. It was unnecessary.

"And, what the hell are you wearing?" said the orc, pointing at Plumporious's threads with the hand holding the kebab.

Plumporious backed away so there was no chance of the garlic sauce dripping on his loafers. "My pantaloons are by Gucci, my shirt is by Vivien Westwood, and my waistcoat is Armani." Plumporous looked the orc up and down. "The clothes I interior design my house in are more stylish than that horrid, ghastly top of yours."

"What did you say?" The wolfish grin was gone, leaving something far more terrifying: an orcish grin.

"I said...." Plumporious was suddenly aware of the part of the town he'd wandered into.

"Oi, Reg!"

Plumporious flinched at the volume of the orc's cry directed across the road to a figure which appeared to be a mountain. As the figure drew closer, Plumporious realised it was a mountain—well, part of a mountain. The mountain troll was wearing a blue T-shirt, much like the orc's, although the troll's shirt likely started life as a tent.

Reg's head slowly turned with the sound of rock grinding on rock. His beady eyes, pinpoints of blue light, focussed on the bullying orc. His mouth split like a sinkhole opening, revealing diamond teeth. Reg lifted a hand, and waved. "'ello, Gordon, mate," his deep voice boomed.

"Come over here, fella," said Gordon. "This little pork pie has got something to say about our team."

Reg's forehead furrowed, making a mini-version of the Grand Canyon. He crossed the road, his stony knuckles dragging across the tarmac. A finger caught in a drain, but it didn't slow the monster. He ripped the metal drain from the concrete which offered no resistance. In one motion, he launched it over the shops and houses, discus-like. Plumporious waited for a crash, but it never came.

"Uh...uh.... I can explain," stuttered Plumporious, a cold sweat appearing on his forehead, which he dabbed at with a Ralph Lauren hankie. He backed off, not looking where he was going. With placating hands upraised, he left the relative safety of the bright lights of the streets and backed into an alleyway. "I can explain everything."

"Not well enough, I don't think, fatty," said Reg, his cracking knuckles carrying the noise and ferocity of an avalanche.

Plumporious's back hit a wall and he let out a squeak. "Maybe, maybe we can come to some other sort of arrangement?" said the dwarf, pushing a stray hair back into the mass of blonde.

"Like what?" said Gordon, taking a bite out of his rancid kebab.

Plumporious waggled his eyebrows.

Reg looked at Gordon. Gordon looked at Reg.

Reg's grin was menacing and lewd. Gordon threw his kebab on the ground and it splattered all over Plumporious's Jimmy Choo shoes.

The orc and the troll closed in.

Chapter 11...

DAN JUMPED OUT OF BED WITH A START. Never before had he jumped out of bed. Never before had he possessed the adrenaline or the motivation to enable him to do so. His bed had always been something to crawl from, the gravity of the forthcoming day crushing him into his pillow.

There was no question whether his encounter with Gambledolf was a dream or not. It was too vivid, too real, and not to mention he'd never woken up with nine inches of wood in his hand before.

"EXPELLIANUS!" he cried with a waggle of his wand and the room illuminated! He was a wizard!

He danced around the room waving the wand Gambledolf had given him. "I'm a wizard!" he cried, dancing a jig and giving the air a damned fine punch. "I am a wizard! I AM A WIZARD!"

"No, you're a loser," came the voice of Mr. Grak from behind his bedroom door. Two seconds later the door opened without a knock or a "may I enter?"

Dan panicked and struggled to hide his wand from his goblin housemate. He turned his back and covered it up as best he could.

"Too late, Smith, I already saw your tiny fairy pecker. That thing's even smaller than a goblin baby's *growspeck*, which starts off inside the body I must add."

Dan pulled the duvet off the bed and wrapped it around him. "Look, just g...get out!" he said, tripping over his duvet and falling onto the mattress.

"You gonna make me?" Mr. Grak pushed out his chest and started towards the apprentice wizard.

Dan had a wand in his hand, a wand capable of actual magic. Spells danced on his tongue, longing to be released, spells he hadn't known until his encounter with Gambledolf. He could humiliate Mr. Grak. With this wand, he had the power. Unlimited power!

He could shave him.... He could *shave* him!

Everywhere!

...but, that wasn't Dan.

"Well, loser-boy, you gonna make me?" said the goblin.

"No," said Dan, wishing he could be more of a bastard like Mr. Grak and also wishing he wasn't wearing his Spidy jammies.

"Didn't think so." The goblin turned to leave. "Now put the kettle on and make me a cup of tea, or I'll post the pictures I took of you last night on Facebook."

Dan's head dropped, and once more he regretted accepting Mr. Grak's friend request.

"And I turned the air con on an hour before taking them." The door slammed.

Dan's head dropped further. When he mastered the ancient rituals and laws of Anglor, he was going to magic himself an extra couple of inches for sure.

For the next hour, the apprentice wizard kicked and chastised himself for what was either weakness or compassion, depending on the point of view. Was it because he didn't want to hurt the goblin, because Dan was a pacifist at heart? Was it because he was a good person and that two wrongs didn't make a right? Unfortunately, Dan was well aware of the reality: he was scared of Mr. Grak grabbing the wand off him and sticking it up Dan's arse before he could cast a spell.

There were more important things than the pettiness of revenge. There was the matter of saving the planet, and that started with saving the polar bears of London Zoo. He was about to publicly harness the forces of nature. However, the usual outfit he wore to harness the forces of nature, the robes he wore when messing around with Craig and Chantelle, felt a little silly. Gambledolf wore cloaks that seemed to be part of him, organic, a vision of times gone past and times yet to come. One day, that would be him, but for now, old jeans and a *Power Ranger* T-shirt would have to suffice; an outfit that didn't scream "hero," more "virgin."

To the zoo he went. It was rare for him to see much daylight as he spent so much time inside the HQ of Green Planet, including weekends and bank holidays. This was a glorious day, made all the better for the field assignment. Dan had a skip in his step and something quite wondrous happened: no one, not a single person, punched him in the face. Maybe it was the newfound confidence he'd gained from becoming a weaver of the magical arts, or maybe people could sense the power within him, but Dan walked straight down the pavement and only had to deviate his path out of common courtesy.

Into the zoo, the magical battleground, he ventured, paying the entry fee through Green Planet and then adding an equal donation to the zoo's upkeep from his own money. Dan even made eye contact with the girl behind the desk, a pretty elf, who didn't spit in his face or tell him she wished he was riddled with a rare, tropical wasting disease.

The polar bears weren't on show until 2 p.m., so Dan had a little time for sightseeing. He gambolled around the zoo. He saw the lions and the tigers and the penguins and the kangaroos and the monkeys and the snakes and the wolves and then the penguins again because they were his favourites, because of their funny waddles.

And then Dan visited the more unusual animals: the razor-billed death-sniffing griffon, Odin's horn-toed manticore, the five-fingered chimera of Fife, red-backed earless harpies, and then he saw the penguins again, because they were his favourites. Their waddling antics just cracked him up.

As a Green Planet employee, he was here to report on the day's events and relay them back to the Green Planet leadership team. However, he'd been gifted with the power of magic, and now he could do so much more. He could show the world the plight it faced. With ten minutes to go until the grand opening of the polar bear pit, it occurred to Dan that he'd never made a political statement, nor had he any idea how to go about making one. He'd watched others make them. Old Betty from the flat below had set herself on fire outside the Houses of Parliament in protest of the cutbacks to the old age pensioner's heating allowance. It failed to carry any impact, her being a fire nymph and all. The fire brigade hadn't even bothered putting her out, but it was a statement, nonetheless. She'd written in to *Loose Women* to try and get some air time, but they'd told her to "get to fuck."

Not knowing how to make a political statement about the ever-increasing threat of global warming, ten minutes before making the aforementioned political statement, would have worried most, and under normal circumstances, Dan would have passed out after losing control of all his bodily functions. Now, things were different. He had magic and righteousness on his side. He was fulfilling his destiny and he was going to save the world.

After seeing the penguins again.

Next to the penguins was the polar bear pit, the largest and finest in the world, a *tour de force* in fake icebergs, cold water, bear-proof barriers, and plastic cod. Here, mummy and daddy bear would raise a family, and once the little ones were old enough, they'd set out on their own adventure. Maybe they'd help sustain the failing population in the wild. Maybe they'd find themselves in other zoos with similar breeding programmes. What was certain was these two cute balls of fluff were a beacon of hope for all who feared man's careering path to self-destruction, and Green Planet wanted the rest of the world to know all about it. So prestigious was this day, the Mayor of London would unveil the zoo's greatest work of conservation in its illustrious history.

London's mayor, Lady Opalstone, was a strong leader, literally, being a troll and all. There's no such thing as a glass ceiling when you have a can-do attitude.[19] Lady Opalstone's position was well-earned. She was tough on crime, personally, and often accompanied the boys in blue on Saturday night patrols in the city. She was also there for the little guys too, but that didn't mean she was going to look favourably on the little guy about to interrupt her.

The mayor stood in the bear pit with mummy, daddy, and baby bears. Daddy-bear had tried to maul Lady Opalstone to death, but she had given the fur on his head a ruffle, rolled him over, and tickled his belly before sending him off with a little pat on the rump. An emasculated Daddy-bear sat next to the pool, staring into his reflection in the water, blaming his mother's neglect for his anger issues.

The mayor didn't need a microphone to address the crowd. Her voice boomed across the zoo. "I am so pleased I was invited here today, as I believe we have a responsibility as a nation and a global community to preserve this wonderful species, and all the species of the Earth."

Dan watched from the back of the large crowd assembled around the polar bear enclosure. He stood on a park bench so he could see over the heads, and, more importantly, so they could see him when the time was right. He'd never been good at public speaking, and interrupting someone who was extremely confident at public engagement and also one of the most famous people in London was pretty far out of his comfort zone. He put his hand down his trousers and grabbed his wand for confidence.

"Excuse me," he cried weakly, holding up his hand like a child might, asking the teacher if they could go wee wee.

Predictably, he was ignored so he tried shouting a little louder.

"Sit down, dickhead," said a middle-aged dwarf, stood just in front of him with his arms crossed. He had a couple of kids with him who were messing around, punching each other in the stomach. He was very tired, very disgruntled, and utterly joyless, like all middle-aged fathers of all species, on all worlds, and in all universes.

Dan flushed red and did as he was told.

I see you, Danoclees.

The voice in his head! Gambledolf! He was with him! Or rather, the spirit of Anglor was with him. It mattered not that he had the body of a weak and feeble human, for he had the heart of a wizard.

Dan got back up on the table, took his wand from his pants and touched it to his lips. "HEAR ME!" His voice enveloped everything.

---

[19] And, perhaps more importantly, the power to smash through the glass ceiling and pummel the chauvinistic scumbags into pools of their own excrement.

Magic was he, and he was magic. Even the animals were silenced, except the red-backed earless harpies.

"What a prick," said the middle-aged dwarf.

All faced him, dumbfounded, trying to work out why anyone was stupid enough to interrupt the mayor. Dan cleared his throat and cried, "Behold, the majestic polar bears!" The stutter was but a memory. "Friends, you do not fully understand their plight. The polar bears face extinction. Every day, the icecaps recede."

"She just said that, you muppet!" said the middle-aged dwarf, who had given up trying to control his kids and concentrated his fury onto the short-arsed interloper.

Dan did his best to ignore him. "Every day, the polar bear must forage farther for food. We're killing the planet."

"Who's that idiot?" asked the mayor to her aide, cracking her knuckles.

Dan continued, ignoring the bone-cracking noises, which echoed off the walls of the polar bear enclosure. "The industrial and technological revolutions have sent us too far down the path of self-destruction. We can no longer turn back. Allkind's lust for urbanisation is a force too strong, and allkind's reluctance to pursue green fuel will be its downfall. We cannot stop what our leaders call progress. However, we can heal the dreadful wounds inflicted by All, but not with without employing a different approach, one not considered for over a millennium."

"And how can we do that, young man," asked the mayor. "And bear in mind that if you don't come up with a good answer for wasting our time and making a farce of what should have been a wonderful event, then you're going to help the plight of these bears by feeding them with your worthless flesh."

Dan did not cower. Anglor was with him. "Fear not, good mayor. I have the answer to all our problems in the palm of my hand."

"And that is?" she asked.

He held the want aloft. "Magic," he cried.

The crowd booed and hissed. Rubbish, paper cups, plastic bottles, and half-eaten burgers with side-helpings of negativity arced towards him.

"What a bellend!" said the middle-aged dwarf.

The mayor's lip turned up in a snarl, but Dan steeled himself, unperturbed. He gained confidence with every passing moment. He waved his wand, which bought a barrage of laughter and then more rubbish.

"BEHOLD!" he cried.

He pointed the wand at the enclosure. Two security guards ran towards Dan with the intention of causing him as much harm as possible in as short a time as possible. But before they could get near him, a purple lightning bolt shot out from Dan's wand and struck the Daddy polar bear between the eyes. The bear's eyes slowly crossed, his mouth foamed and steam shot out of his ears.

"Stop it, you madman!" came a shout.

"You're killing him," cried another.

"What a complete spunktrumpet!" said the middle-aged dwarf.

The lightning ceased, leaving a purple glare temporarily burned into the crowd's retinas. The bear fell slowly, landing on his back, all four paws pointing to heaven, where the crowd assumed he now resided. Smoke trailed away from his fur. Deathly still he lay.

"Arrest that man!" cried the mayor. Her knuckles found her palm. "And have him taken to my offices for questioning."

The crowd winced.

"No!" cried Dan, with enough authority in his voice to stop the approaching guards in their tracks. "Hear the pain of Mother Nature for yourself. Behold!" he cried.

The bear wasn't dead at all. He rolled onto his front and struggled up to sit on his haunches. His eyes uncrossed. He shook his head. He scratched his tail.

And then he spoke.

Chapter 12...

MR. SOMERSBY SAT ON THE EDGE OF THE SOFA, HIS HEAD IN HIS HANDS. On a table in front of him sat a dangerously large tumbler of whisky. He blew out a heavy breath and levelled his head, focusing on the spirit. He took a long draw. A five o'clock shadow lurked guiltily on his manly jaw. Things were not as they should be in the world of the boss of all bosses.

From the doorway, Rillit coughed.

Bloodshot eyes fixed Rillit a threatening stare before they swept back to the glass of amber poison.

Rillit coughed again.

"What is it?" asked Mr. Somersby. "You're lucky you're not dead, elf," he mumbled into the now-empty whisky glass.

Rillit ignored the drunken raving, bowed, and formally announced, "I present...Draknarkus."

"I've seen enough pathetic excuses, Rillit. Leave me be."

"Sire," said the elf, unable to suppress a grin, "I've found her."

Mr. Somersby's eyes shot to the door.

She propped herself up against the doorframe. A sharp black suit hugged strong, athletic lines. A crisp white shirt, buttoned to the neck, was almost hidden by voluminous black curls. Flat black shoes, practical, nothing for show here. Only a few lines on her face gave her age away, forty? Fifty? Difficult to say. This one was different to the others. Oh, this one was something else entirely.

She straightened, and crossed the threshold. The room darkened with her entrance. It could've been coincidence, a cloud passing in front of the midday sun, but the cold shudder running down Mr. Somersby's spine told him otherwise. He sobered immediately.

More striking than beautiful, Mr. Somersby found her wry grin devilish. Satanic eyes, black, unnatural. He shivered.

This was Draknarkus.

And while Mr. Somersby was considered the most powerful person on the planet, he now had a worrying suspicion there were different kinds of power in the world.

"Are you a magician?" he asked, his standard opener after a recent bad experience.

"You could call me that," she said, examining black nails.

"Or would you say you were a wizard?"

She flicked an imaginary piece of lint from her sleeve. "You could call me that," she said. There was an Irish twang, only slight, as if she'd moved away from the Emerald Isle long ago.

"I really don't like magicians," said Mr. Somersby. He pulled out a handgun from his jacket pocket and pointed it at her, a slight, liquor-induced tremble in his hand. When it came to gunning sentient beings down in cold blood, Mr. Somersby was not one who'd discriminate, man, woman, puppy. Being a psychopath certainly gave one an edge.

Draknarkus smirked, ignoring the firearm. She walked to one of the great office windows, his gun tracing her movement. She gazed out across the rooftops of London. "Magnificent view, Somersby."

"That's Mr. Somersby," his voice was ice.

She smirked again. "I'm sure it is. Not bought yourself a knighthood, yet?"

"You dare mock me?" he said, taking a tighter grip on the gun. Mr. Somersby was not used to mockery or jokes. He was not included in The Corporation's Secret Santa for good reason.

She turned to look at him over her shoulder. A smouldering wink left him breathless. He was drawn to her. He wanted her and he wanted to please her. But how could this be? He thought women over twenty were past it.

She turned back to the view. "I hate London, laddie. I can't stand multi-culturism. Life was better before we all pretended to get along. You know where you stand with a good war. The lines between good and evil blur, and heroes and devils decide the fate of the world." Her finger traced a pattern on the glass. "How I miss battle."

Mr. Somersby loosened his collar. This woman beguiled him. He'd no idea if she could wield magic, but this woman, this...witch... Draknarkus was blessed with a hidden power that screamed from the darkness. "What are you?" he muttered under awed breath.

"I am...." She contemplated the question with an inclination of her head. "Complicated." Her attention was drawn upwards. "Why is there a halfling strung up by his ankles from the roof."

Derek the Debonair, red-faced from the blood that had pooled in his head, waved cheerily at Draknarkus as he swung with each gust of wind.

Mr. Somersby tapped his lips with his fingers. "I haven't decided what to do with him, yet."

"I hate halflings." She walked over to the drinks cabinet and picked up a decanter. "May I?"

Somersby shrugged and Draknarkus poured herself the smallest of measures. She sniffed it, closed her eyes, and drew in the vapours. "John Sheed Roberts Reserve."

"Impressive," he said, slowly. Still he held the gun firm.

"Your limited tongue and sense of smell cannot fully appreciate this liquor. The fact you keep this masterpiece in a decanter, where the angels rob you every day, proves that even if you did have the faculties to enjoy it, your stupidity would waste it."

His eyes narrowed. "Why would you insult a man holding a gun?"

"Because he wastes good whisky," she said. "And that should not go unpunished." She put down the glass, untouched.

"And you can appreciate it, I suppose?"

"That poison, that libation, that intoxicant is a history lesson. From the volatile chemicals, I can sense when it was made. The rocks the water filtered through speak to me. I can be part of that time. What does it tell you? Nothing. For you, it is an expense, an extravagance. Why do you keep it?"

"It's expensive. It tastes good. And that is the only bottle left in the world. That whisky represents me: unique and the subject of jealousy."

"Unique? You?" Her tongue played across her teeth with her amusement. "I can see a million of you from this window. You just happen to have a few extra quid in the bank."

"A few extra...?" he trailed off. A vein on his forehead pulsed. "Do you know who I am?"

She laughed heartily. "I do, I do, and it means nothing to me, Somersby. I could have all this if I desired, and I could take everything from you if I wanted to live such a one-dimensional existence."

He bared his teeth. "I'm gonna stop you right there, bitch. You better have the goods to back up that fancy mouth of yours, otherwise my elf Rillit is going to shoot you in the face with his bow and arrow."

The drawing of a bow string attracted Draknarkus's attention. Her head tilted to the side as she weighed the elf. "He isn't going to do that."

"And why not?" said Mr. Somersby.

"Because I'll kill you if he does." She snapped her gaze back on the boss. He recoiled, even though he was carrying a weapon.

Somersby's eye twitched. "What do you mean?"

"I won't kill him. In fact, I see huge potential in your elf lackey. If he tries to kill me, I'll kill you with the arrow fired at my heart. Make your choice. Call it a test, if you will." She gave a careless shrug and Mr. Somersby another cold shiver.

The boss hesitated. He never hesitated. "I've got a gun. He's also a trained assassin. What chance do you have?"

"I am a magician. I am a wizard. I am a witch. The powers of darkness long to feel my caress. Do you think I care for such primitive weapons? Do you think I'm concerned with the physical world, with your Newtonian laws which bind you to the mundane?"

Somersby lowered his weapon. "What do you think, Rillit?"

"I think she's more convincing than Derek the Debonair, sire."

"That will be all, thank you, Rillit."

"Sire." Rillit relieved the tension of his bow string, bowed to Mr. Somersby, and then to Draknarkus, and left the room.

"Why are you here?" he asked.

"Good question. Astute. I'm glad of that. I feared you to be an idiot. A rich and powerful idiot, but an idiot all the same."

He ignored her jibe and poured himself a whisky. Draknarkus took a seat behind his desk. Even though this human, this witch, had not demonstrated any magic, Somersby sensed she was so much more than he, and he didn't need to pull her finger to find out what she was capable.

Why, oh why, had he pulled that short stubby finger?

"You want to wield magic. Why?" she asked.

"The same reason I want to smell the rocks responsible for the taste of this whisky."

"Which is?"

"Because I cannot."

Draknarkus clapped her hands together. "Perfect."

"And why do you want to help me?"

There was the wry grin again. "I never said I did."

"Then what do you want?" he said, his patience coming to an end.

"The same as you."

"More?" he asked.

"More," she said.

"And how do you intend to get more?"

She smiled broadly. "With your help, dear boy."

"And what do I have that you do not? Or are all your boasts merely hot air?"

Her eyes narrowed for a millisecond, and she took to playing with a couple of stray strands of hair. "You have power in this world; power over the government, money, resources, all things I do not cherish or value. Unfortunately, I need access to these things if I am to acquire *more*."

"And 'more' is?"

She paused, and turned to watch the swinging halfling. "Mesmeric, isn't he?"

Somersby's banged the window with his hand. "Well?" he demanded.

"Unlimited magical power," she whispered when Mr. Somersby was fit to burst.

It was relief unlike any orgasm Mr. Somersby had experienced. He also spied a chink in her facade. "I thought you said you could have all this if you wanted it."

Her nostrils flared. "Yes, but I'm running out of time," she conceded. "I need these things and I need them fast. There is an artefact, a weapon, a sword that was not made for cutting, but to channel magic. The Lost Sword of the Fairy King."

"Sounds like bull shit," he said, but she had his full attention.

"With the Sword in my hands I could harness the powers of nature. I could rule my world, not your pitiful land of gold and stocks and shares, but a world of true power. I could infuse magic in you, Somersby. I'd gift you your heart's desire...and the Lost Sword of the Fairy King is your only hope."

"Why the sudden rush? Why do you need me?"

"I'm glad you're not an idiot." She got up and walked back to the glass of whisky she'd left on the drinks cabinet. "Events have passed. There is another who seeks the Sword, one who has evaded me for a long time."

"And he's too powerful for you, I suppose?" he said, smugly.

"No, that's not it, but there is one who could be. There is one who could be truly all-powerful." She knocked the whisky back, but didn't acknowledge its finery. "I fear my old adversary has found the Chosen One, and he has awoken a power inside him that has lain dormant for centuries."

Chapter 13...

"WHAT THE FUCK JUST HAPPENED TO MY GODDAMN HEAD!" shouted the polar bear, grabbing his skull with his paws. "SHEEEEIIIIIIIIIITTTT!"

Never had the outraged, animalistic screams of a mob demanding justice and blood been silenced so fast. The dumbstruck crowd turned from the dumbstruck Dan to where the polar bear was being anything but dumbstruck. All lips mouthed the same half-word: "Wha..?"

The bear shook his head and then tapped the side of it with a massive paw, as if shaking the water out of his ear. "WHAT THE FUCK IS COMING OUT OF MY GODDAMN MOUTH?" he cried.

"Wha...?" said the mayor.

Unsurprisingly, this was not what Dan had expected. Yes, he'd wanted to grant the bear the power of speech, and while he was ecstatic he'd bent nature's will with his own, he was confused why a polar bear would be so foul-mouthed.

Dan reasoned it was because of the state of the ice caps. He regained himself, cleared his throat, and announced, "Noble creature!" He held the wand aloft. "I am the wizard, Danoclees Dunlorian, and I have—"

"WHAT THE FUCK KIND OF STUPID-ASSED CRACKER NAME IS THAT?"

"Did...did that bear just call him a cracker?" asked the middle-aged dwarf. Even his brats had stopped misbehaving. They stared, mouths gaping, tongues lolling, dyed all the colours of the 'bow with every synthesised E-number from the lollies they licked.

The bear surveyed the crowd with a look of dismay on his maw. He shook his head. "SHEEEEEEIIIIT."

"Noble creature!" called Dan.

The bear focussed on Dan and screwed up his face, looking him up and down. "WHAT THE FUCK DO YOU LOOK LIKE?" The polar bear looked at the mayor. "WHO IS THIS VIRGIN FAIRY-ASSED, MOTHERF—"

"I am not a fairy!" interrupted Dan with impeccable timing. "I fear you misunderstand the situation. I have given you the power of man's speech."

The bear's eyes widened. "OH, *YOU'VE* GIVEN *ME* THE

POWER?" He yelled, tapping his heart with a claw. "YOU'VE GIVEN ME THE POWER, HAVE YOU? WANT ME TO GET ON MY KNEES AND THANK YOU? SHEEEEIIIT! DID YOU HEAR THAT, JASMINE? WANTS ME TO KISS HIS ASS BECAUSE HE'S ARRIVED ON HIS FUCKING ICE-WHITE HORSE TO SAVE ME." He placed paws on hips, which looked somewhat awkward due to his anatomy. "SHEEEEEEIITTTTT."

Mummy-bear looked somewhat embarrassed, trying not to make eye contact with the crowd. The embarrassing-in-public, overly aggressive father phenomenon transcended the classification of species. Fathers showing off and displaying their self-importance in public arenas was a universal phenomenon, and possibly its greatest misfortune.

"GIVEN ME THE POWER OF SPEECH? I'VE BEEN TALKING ALL THIS GOD DAMN TIME, IT'S JUST YOUR SORRY ASSES COULDN'T UNDERSTAND ME BEFORE—" The polar bear cut off with a double take of his massive shaggy head. "WHAT THE FUCK ARE YOU LOOKING AT!" he said to one of the zookeepers, who stood as slack-jawed as everyone else. "I'VE HAD ENOUGH OF YOU STARING AT ME ALL DAY LONG, EVEN WHEN I'M TAKING A SHIT, EVEN WHEN I WAS MAKING THESE LITTLE UNGRATEFUL BASTARDS," he said, to the cute balls of fluff, playing together on the ice, oblivious to proceedings. "I OUGHTA BITE YOUR GODDAMN HEAD OFF!"

"Noble creature!" cried Dan, attempting to get back on track. "Please, I need you to tell the people about your plight and that of your brethren."

"WHAT THE FUCK ARE YOU ON ABOUT?"

"Will...will you please stop swearing?"

"OH, YEAH THAT'S RIGHT! SHUT ME UP? SHEEEEEEEIIIIT. I'VE GOT ANOTHER IDEA—KISS MY ASS!" The bear turned and indicated to an area south of his tail.

Dan carried on regardless. "Will you please tell the people of the plight the polar bears face in the Arctic?"

The bear threw up his paws. "AND HOW THE FUCK WOULD I KNOW ABOUT THAT? MY SORRY ASS WAS BORN IN A PARK IN SHANGHAI. I AIN'T EVEN BEEN NEAR NO NORTH POLE. LOOK AT YOU JUDGING ME FOR THE WAY I LOOK, YOU RACIST PIECE OF SHIT, MOTHERFUC—"

"I am not a racist!" cried Dan, wagging a finger. "And why...why are you t...t...talking like that?" With his uncertainty, the stuttering returned.

"LIKE WHAT?" said the bear, head cocked to one side, begging his adversary to dig himself deeper. "LIKE WHAT?"

"Like... like...erm...." Dan shuffled on the spot, trying to find the right words. "Never mind," he said dismissively, and drew on his inner strength, his new-found power. "It matters not. I will give you the power to see your species' plight, to see through the eyes of the polar bears of the North, where every day is a battle, a quest to survive. Tell us what you see, oh mighty creature." Dan held up his wand once more. "Behold!"

The bear backed up on the ice. "HEY, WATCH IT WITH THAT SHIT, MAN. I'VE SEEN *COPS* ON THE TV, MAN. YOU FUCKERS SHOOT FIRST AND ASK QUESTIONS LATER, MAN. SOMETIMES YOU DON'T EVEN ASK ANY QUES—"

The bear was cut off by a purple beam flashing from the wand. It latched on to his forehead like a great magical tentacle.

"....AHGAHTABABABGABARGAGAJHNVAFRRGRG," said the polar bear just before purple foam poured from his mouth and his eyes rolled around his head. The crowd watched on, half in shock at the speaking bear, half in shock at all the purple.

The flashing lights vanished and the foam ceased pouring from his mouth and disappeared in the wind. The bear's eyes rolled around to the front and they found focus. He blinked a couple of times, and then a single tear fell from the corner of his eye.

"I SEE...." His voice breaking with emotion. "I SEE—"

"Yes?" pressured Dan.

"I SEE...." The bear was interrupted by a loud pop and then a gasp from the crowd. Several people fainted, and for good reason. All who were still conscious, stared wide-eyed at the bear, and then at the ice, and then at the bear again. The polar bear looked down at the ice where his paw was. His paw being on the ice wouldn't normally have been a note for concern, but it wasn't attached to the rest of him. The bear picked it up, dripping with blood, and examined it with a strange fascination. He held it up to the light where it exploded.

"MOTHERFUCKER!" he cried.

The first three rows of onlookers and the mayor were splattered with blood, gore, toenails, and soft white fur. The only thing louder than the screams of the children were the screams of the mutilated polar bear.

"MY LEG! MY GODDAMN LEG!"

The blood drained out of Dan's face. He held the wand at arm's length and dropped it, desperate to get away from it, shaking his hand like a spider had crawled on it. Magic wasn't supposed to harm! Magic was the earth's saviour! He didn't know how to fix the mess he'd caused the poor bear, the poor bear he'd sworn to protect!

The tail was next to explode, covering the ice with blood as well as splattering the penguins in the next pen, who thought this all utterly hilarious as a seal had told them what utter bastards polar bears were.

"MY TAIL! MY GODDAMN TAIL!"

Chapter 14...

CHIEF DETECTIVE MERES PULLED ON HIS CIGARETTE. He took it out of his mouth and stared at the embers. "You know what, Reed? I haven't had a fag in fifteen years."

Reed, sat adjacent to his superior, fidgeted in his chair. Reed said nothing. There was nothing he could offer. There was nothing anyone could offer.

With the cigarette in hand, Meres gestured at the glass in front of him. Beyond the glass, in the interrogation room, a centaur sat on his haunches, staring ahead, unblinking, unmoving. "That bastard is the reason I'm going to become addicted to these things again, and no doubt the reason I'm going to have a heart attack before retirement."

Again, Reed said nothing. This wasn't the chief. The chief was granite. The chief was a constant in this world. There were bad guys, there were the good guys, and there was the chief. The chief was London's white knight, the tireless enforcer of the law. He was the mayor's go-to guy, some said the prime minister's too. He was London's tireless safety net.

Was.

"Give me another," he said to Reed, gesturing with his hand. Reed would've coaxed anyone else out of it, but not Meres. If he wanted a cigarette, he was having a cigarette. Reed threw the packet on the table. His lighter followed.

Meres picked up the packet. Shaking, scarred hands knocked a cigarette out of the packet, and he placed it between tight lips. He was ugly, weathered. Scars tracked his face, all from his days as a rookie. He'd thrown himself at trouble and made mistakes, dangerous ones, but he'd always got his man, or whatever it was he hunted. After a while, there were no more mistakes.

Tatty clothes and shoes worn through, Meres had no time for fashion. He commanded a fearsome appearance, yet after thirty years on the force, this had him spooked. He didn't take his eyes off the centaur.

"Are you ready to question him again?" asked Reed, tentatively.

The cigarette grew brighter. "It's my job, Reed."

"He's the guy who hit the Natural History Museum, isn't he?"

Meres dipped his head, only the slightest of inclinations. "That's one way of putting it."

"Sir, I've got to ask. You've dealt with serial killers, rapists, terrorists, extremists. Is this guy really that bad?"

Meres leant back in his chair and rubbed his unshaven face. "Yes."

The word carried a doom that made Reed shiver.

"Reed?"

"Yes, Chief?"

"You're going you have to deal with this one."

The chief's words crushed Reed into the chair. The chief had just asked him to step into a situation he couldn't cope with. "Chief?" asked Reed, needing clarification.

Meres stubbed out the butt of the cigarette, taking out his frustration on the filter. "He's just...he's just...such a...a wanker!"

REED GRIPPED THE DOOR HANDLE. He wasn't trained for this. If Meres couldn't cope then no one could.

Under his breath he said, "If no one can deal with it, might as well be you." He opened the door to the centaur's interrogation room. The centaur didn't move, didn't flinch. They'd left him stewing for six hours, but he looked fresh, more determined. They'd not softened him at all.

Appear weak when you are strong, Reed told himself.

Reed pulled up a chair in front of the centaur. He was big, but they all were. Centaurs were a mighty race, quick to anger and devastating in combat. They were proud creatures and justified in their vanity. Haughty at best, arrogant at worst, and who could blame them when they had the chiselled torso of Heracles, the boyish good looks of Adonis, the grace of Apollo, and a twenty-five inch penis on the flop.

He was ugly for a centaur, with a big lantern jaw begging to be punched, and it looked like people had obliged over the years. His hair was thick, but greasy, dark brown with a few straggling greys. His black eyes sat too far apart and his protruding forehead made him look slow and stupid. He was anything but. He was devious and conniving and very dangerous. He wore a faded, ripped T-shirt that covered the natural musculature all centaurs carried. No centaur trousers for modesty, though. Reed wasn't surprised.

He kicked off the interview. "Why the Natural History Museum?"

Bang. The centaur focussed his stare on Reed who instantly turned away. Reed called upon all his resolve to face the monster. A slow grin formed on the centaur's face. A few yellow teeth were missing. "I wanted to see the dinosaurs."

"Really?" said the detective, folding his arms.

The centaur focused on the two-way mirror. "Why hasn't that bitch WPC been back with my chair?"

Reeds lips tightened. "You know why. There isn't a chair."

The centaur placed a giant hand on the table to balance, and lowered his top half under the table to examine Reed's seating arrangements. "You've got one."

"You've been through this with someone else. There isn't a centaur chair in the police station, or anywhere else for that matter. There's no such thing as a centaur chair."

The centaur sneered. "Nothing more racist than a pig, huh?"

Reed collected himself. "I'm not being racist. There is no such thing as a centaur chair. There isn't a quadruped on the planet that has need for a chair. It's physiology."

The centaur disengaged his stare and considered the cell he knew to be empty. "Got any wheelchairs?"

"Yes, of course, but what's that got to do with anything?"

The centaur folded his arms. "So it's OK to stick me on the floor, but those lazy bastards get the luxury of a chauffeur?"

Reed's eyebrows nearly reached his dark fringe. "I...what? What did you say?"

"You heard, pig."

"That's...that's a horrible thing to say." Meres had warned him not to get caught up in the centaur's games as there was no hope of winning. Reed regained himself and got back to the task at hand. "Why the Natural History Museum. Why hit that? Was it political?"

"I wanted to see the dinosaurs."

"Tell the goddamn truth!" Reed's fist banged on the table.

"Don't lose your temper with me, boy." The centaur started picking off the end of his nails, throwing the dirty keratin onto the interrogation table while Reed chewed the inside of his mouth to ribbons.

He's just trying to wind you up, he kept repeating to himself. *You're better than him.*

"The Natural History Museum was full of children for god's sake," said Reed.

"They should have been in school," argued the centaur.

"They were on a school trip!"

"Must be posh kids then."

"So it *was* political?"

The centaur threw his hands in the air. "Bloody hell, you're making it out like I bombed the place. I only went and saw the bleedin' dinosaurs."

"You might as well have bombed the place—and you did a hell of a lot more than see the dinosaurs." Reed regretted leaving his cigarettes with the chief.

"Well the place should have been more centaur-friendly, like this place, you racist pig!" The centaur spat the word "pig" and big, green globules of saliva splashed on the desk.

"Why would we make the place centaur friendly?" asked Reed.

"You disgust me!" said the centaur, spitting on the floor this time.

Reed fantasised about the centaur being turned into a thousand tins of dog food. "Do you know how many centaurs live in London?"

"No."

Reed leaned back in his chair. "You. Just you."

"So?"

"Do you know how many centaurs visit London each year?"

"No."

"None."

The centaur shrugged. "So my mates don't visit me. They're dicks, what's your point?"

"Why would London Council change the entire infrastructure of a city based on the need of *one* individual? Especially as no centaurs want to come here in the first place!"

The centaur folded his arms. "Maybe they would if it was centaur-friendly."

"No. They wouldn't. There are two hundred-and-nine centaurs living in the UK, and in a survey conducted by the government, not a single one of them said they had any intention of visiting London because they preferred the countryside."

"But I—"

Reed cut him off and pulled a sheet of paper out of his jacket. "Even you filled the survey in and said you didn't want to live in London because you, and I quote, 'think cockneys are pricks.' And you drew several pricks on the survey. And then you moved here the following week."

The centaur frowned. "That's meant to be anonymous and confidential."

"No it's not. You even wrote your name on the top, and your phone number." Reed slid the piece of paper across the desk. "A government employee tried phoning you but you kept farting down the phone."

With a chuckle, the centaur screwed up the survey and threw it back at Reed. "Look, just arrest me or let me go. I ain't done anything wrong, pig."

"Not done anything wrong? Not done anything wrong?" Reed screeched. "You defecated in the National History Museum."

"So do lots of people."

"But they use the toilets."

"But there isn't a centaur-friendly toilet. There's loads for your disabled buddies, and half them lazy bastards don't even work."

Reed grimaced. "I...I...can't believe you said that."

"Truth hurts," snapped the centaur.

Reed held his tongue and his pride in an attempt to get back on track. "Look, even if there wasn't a toilet, you could've had a word with a member of staff."

The centaur placed a hand on his chest and gasped. "That would have been embarrassing."

"And shitting in front of a hundred kids on the feet of the animatronic Tyrannosaurus Rex isn't?"

"It wouldn't have been if the little perverts had turned the other way, like I asked them. You should arrest them for being little deviants. As soon as someone tinkers with one of them they cry blue murder!"

Reed went outside in search of a cigarette.

Steve the Centaur was the world's biggest dickhead. He only lived in the nation's capital because it was the place where being a dickhead affected the most people. Not many people were arrested for being a dickhead. People were arrested because of a specific crime, which they committed *because* they were a dickhead, but on several occasions, Steve had been arrested for simply *being* a dickhead.

Reed came back in the room.

"You gonna charge me then, pig?"

"Yep," said Reed, sharply.

"What for, pig?"

Reed put his hands on the table, gripping it hard and leaned over until he was a foot away from the centaur. "I'll make something up," he whispered so the tape recorder wouldn't catch it.

Sometimes, Steve felt like he'd been dealt a bad hand in life.

Chapter 15...

"NO! I DON'T B...BELONG IN HERE! They'll eat me alive! I'm the g...good guy! I'm the g...good g...guy!" screamed Dan.

"Tell that to the polar bear's mum," shouted the prison guard before slamming the cell door shut.

"It was an accident!" The prison guard locking the metal door ended Dan's protests. "I was trying t...to save them. T...to save...." he muttered. He drove both his fists against the door which didn't make the racket he'd hoped for, just a dull, barely audible thud, inflicting bruises on his peach-like flesh. He rested his head against the cold, unforgiving steel. He shut his eyes, not ready to take in the surroundings. He didn't want to know who and what waited for him.

This was prison, and not just any prison: this was Brixton, the worst prison in the country. It suffered from appalling conditions, riding on the edge of lawful. The prison was rife with drugs, violence, and extreme prejudice towards anything little and vulnerable. The dregs of society were thrown here because they couldn't function in the real world. Murderers, rapists, and worse called this place home, and now, so did Dan, and all he wanted to do was save the world. He never wanted to blow up bits of a polar bear.

No one wants to blow up bits of a polar bear! Except seals.

How long would they keep him here? What would the inmates do to someone so weak and so soft? Here, he was bottom of the food chain. He was bottom of the food chain on the outside world, too, but the consequences here were somewhat more dramatic. On the outside he could run, but here he was locked up. This was his worst nightmare come true. The prison guards wouldn't help, that was certain. They'd told him as much. The British were fiercely protective of their animals, even if their animals had been flown in from Shanghai.

Whatever Dan's fate, he was about to find out.

"How wonderful, Michael, we have company!"

Dan cocked an ear. In a pressure cooker of psychopaths with nothing-to-lose and don't-care-if-they-die-in-pursuit-of-revenge attitudes, over-the-top camp was not a tone he'd expected to hear.

"Make yourself at home, young man, there's plenty of room," said the voice, cheerfully.

Dan removed his head from the steel gateway of his captivity. His body temperature hadn't warmed the metal. Dan turned around to a wide grin and teeth so white they shone like a beacon of hope in the darkness.

"Hello!" said the dwarf, waving merrily.

"Err...hi," said Dan, a little perturbed and half-expecting the small, extremely well-groomed dwarf to transform into a homicidal maniac at any moment and bludgeon him to death with whatever he held in his well-manicured hand. Hair straighteners, Dan realised.

"I'm Plumporious," said the dwarf, hand now holding straighteners on his heart. "And you are?"

"Erm...D...D...Dan." Dan had never seen a dwarf with straightened hair. In terms of grooming, this dwarf didn't have a beard at all, and Dan had never heard of a female dwarf trimming her beard. Plumporious had waxed his chest, visible because a couple of buttons on his shirt were undone. He was perhaps the most depilated individual Dan had come across outside of Mr. Grak's realm of influence. Dan gave a double take. Plumporious wasn't wearing a prison-issue shirt, but designer silk pyjamas.

"Hi, Dan, pleased to meet you." Plumporious offered a hand that Dan shook, surprised at the silky softness. Dwarves were renowned for their hands of granite. "So," he said cheerfully. "What brings you here?"

"I...I...w...w...what I m...m...."

Plumporious gave a camp and dismissive wave of his hand. "How rude of me! It's none of my business. Can I make you a cup of tea?"

"T...t...tea?"

"Or coffee if you like?"

"Erm...yes. Erm...tea, p...please."

Plumporious went to work, turning his back on Dan to attend the tea-making facilities. "I'm going to use the bone china. New guests are rare. Take a seat," he called over his shoulder. Porcelain clinked as it was packed away.

The cell was tiny, but that wasn't necessarily a bad thing as Plumporious was small, even for a dwarf, although he was still the same height as Dan. There were four bunk beds in the cell, only twelve feet square. Dan took a seat on one of the lower decks.

"Don't even think about it, pipsqueak" came the growl from the shadows before Dan's bum hit the mattress. Dan jumped up in shock.

"Don't worry about him, Dan. He's just a big ol' grump," said Plumporious, soothingly. "Do you want a cup of tea, you old brute?" he called under the bunk, which was eye-level for him.

A grudging grunt and nothing more.

"I'll take that as a 'yes,' then," said Plumporious, digging out a cheap mug from under his bed. He whispered to Dan, "I'm not using the good china on him."

Dan backed away from the lurking stranger, and Plumporious sensed his discontent. He placed a hand on Dan's shoulder and said, softly, "I'm going to assume you've never been in prison before, and this is your first night?"

The surreal meeting with this friendly dwarf had taken Dan's mind off the bitter reality of it all and he wilted when he remembered.

"Dan, it can be a little bit scary sometimes, but don't worry about a thing. I promise nothing bad will happen. Most of the other fellows are OK once you get to know them. Sugar?"

"One p...please." Dan considered the steel door again, and shuddered. For the moment he was safe, but what waited beyond the boundary of that great protecting door? He jumped when the kettle clicked off after reaching the boil. "I...I didn't think we were allowed a k...kettle."

"Welllll," said Plumporious, bullishly, "the guards let us have a few creature comforts. The grunting ruffian under the bed there has a bit of a reputation and they give him a few privileges to keep him happy."

Dan's eyes were instantly pulled to the shadows of the bunk where cigarette smoke gently blew into the small cell.

"Not that it works. He's always a right misery guts! Here." Plumporious offered Dan his tea. "This will take your mind off things."

"Thank you."

Even though the cell was small, it was remarkably homely. There were even a few pictures on the wall, prints of some of the classics, Caravaggio, Blake, Munch, and Turner, and there was a bunch of flowers in a vase in the corner. The duvet covers weren't prison issue either, nor were duvets.

Dan took a sip of the tea. It was very good. "Is...is there a t...toilet in here?" he asked, realising the tea would rip through him.

"Of course!" exclaimed the dwarf. "We're not animals, Dan. In fact, I had the guards put up a curtain around it for a little bit of privacy. Not that *he*," Plumporious indicated the smoking shadow, "ever uses it." He put his hand in front of his mouth and stage whispered, "He's quite disgusting if truth be told."

"Get bent," said the shadow.

"Disgusting!" said the dwarf, irrationally emotional, which caused the word to come out as almost a squeal. "You're a disgusting pig, Mick."

"Yeah, yeah, now give us my cuppa, ya 'orrible little woofter."

This time Plumporious did squeal, a high-pitched squeal not belonging in a high-security prison. "You're an animal! An animal I say."

Plumporious threw the mug of tea he'd made for Mick into the toilet. He dived into the shadows, opposite Mick, into his own bed, sobbing like a heart-broken teenager.

Awkward silences were not what Dan had expected. He'd expected pregnant silences, ones that proceeded to give birth to gratuitous violence, broken bones, and fates worse than death. With Plumporious sobbing, Dan built up the confidence to engage his other cell mate.

"So your name's M...M...Mick?"

"No, it's Mick."

"That's what I said!"

"It really wasn't," said the shadow.

"Stupid, horrible elf!" cried Plumporious.

"Pipe down, tubby," said the elf, with an amused tone.

Plumporious wailed and yelled, "That's the real reason they call you Mick the Knife, because you cut people's feelings into tatters, you wicked monster!"

"Mick the Knife!" Dan blurted, his hand slapping over his mouth as soon as the words that, when connected together in the right order, made the most dangerous proper noun in London, had left his lips. A wave of dizziness hit him and he grabbed on to the bunk.

"Yeah, what's it to you?" The elf leaned out of the shadows, fag in his mouth, eyes glowing in the darkness, a dog-eared dirty magazine in his hand titled *MELFs*.

Now Dan feared what was *inside* the cell. Mick the Knife was London's most infamous criminal. He used to have at least three or four episodes of *Crimestoppers* dedicated to him every year. You could even buy his biography in those high-street bookshops specialising in the autobiographies of Z-list celebrities who'd spent two weeks in a reality TV jungle eating kangaroo anuses so that people would like them again.

"Please don't k...k...kill me!" cried Dan, holding up his hands as if it were a stickup.

Mick the Knife shook his head, rolled back into the shadows and leafed through the magazine. Dan's heart pounded, in danger of exploding. He climbed onto the top bunk above Plumporious, as far away from the sociopath as he could.

Suddenly, Plumporious stopped crying. "What's that noise?" he asked, lifting his head from his arms and cocking his ear to the wind.

There was a noise, something in the background that carried over the prisoner's shouts and screams of turmoil and hardship. The noise gained rhythm, percussion growing louder, something approaching. The prison quietened as a result, all curious as to what could make such an alien noise in a place of rigid familiarity.

"It s...sounds like...like a horse?" said Dan.

"You're right, it does," said the dwarf, all tears forgotten. "Mick, what do you think?"

"Where's me cuppa?"

Plumporious shook his head. "I don't know why I put up with you!" He rolled out of his bunk and reboiled the kettle for a fresh brew. The faint rhythm grew louder and louder. "Sounds like the clippety-clop of hooves," said the dwarf.

They stopped outside. Plumporious handed Mick his tea and then placed his ear against the door. He quickly withdrew it when a key entered the lock.

"Mick, what have you been up to?" asked Plumporious, suspecting the worse of his cell mate.

"What? Apart from using your pillow to dry my bum with after a shower."

"You are despicable, Michael! Absolutely—" The door swung open and cut off Plumporious's rant. His jaw dropped. "You must be joking?"

"You must be joking?" said the enormous centaur. "You can't expect me to sleep in there!"

"Get in the cell and shut up, Steve," said one of the four guards surrounding him.

The future cellmate snorted, which carried a lot more weight when half your DNA was horse.

Plumporious closed his eyes and muttered under his breath. "Smile and be pleasant, Plumporious. Be a fine host. Remember what your mother taught you." He opened his eyes, self-pep talk completed. "Good evening!" he said, cheerily. "Are you planning on joining us?" The cheery voice wavered only a fraction while the dwarf eyed the centaur up and down and considered the logistics.

"No," said the centaur, crossing his arms.

"Get in the cell or you'll be in for another tazering," said a troll, rhythmically slapping a giant club into his hand.

"All right, screw, but don't think I'll forget this," said the centaur. Steve considered the space in front of him, cocking his head. "I'm going to have to back in here." He did a three-point turn on the gangway and reversed into the cell. The door slammed shut, millimetres from his nose.

There wasn't much space in the cell before there was a horse in it. For Steve to reverse, both Dan and Plumporious had to get into their bunks. They were cooped up like battery hens.

"Well, isn't this cosy?" said Plumporious, trying to make the best of the horrible situation.

"Cosy?" said Steve. "Bleeding cosy? The pigs told the screws to punish me, and I reckon they've done the same to you. This ain't right. Centaurs ain't even meant to be in this nick!"

"Oh well," said Plumporious, "guess we're all in it together, at least. Would you like a cup of tea?"

"A cup of tea?" asked Steve, looking over his shoulder. "You serious?"

Plumporious climbed up the side of the bunk and sat next to Dan. From there he could engage the centaur in conversation. "You a coffee kinda guy, then?"

The centaur screwed up his face as he considered the dwarf. "Why the hell are you on this wing? This is where they put the psychos. How come no-one's beaten you to death, yet?"

Plumporious's hand found his breast. "Well, I do try to be polite, courteous, and righteous. I guess even the most deranged of inmates can appreciate a little class."

Steve scoffed, "Yeah, right. So what did you do to get yourself in here?"

The dwarf found other things apart from Steve to look at. "I like to keep that private," he said, flustered.

"Yeah? Well, I could have a good guess, and it's probably the reason you haven't been carried out in a body bag. I guess your boyfriend is under here." Steve ducked his head to look in the shadows of the bunk, where the uninterested elf was puffing away.

"Mick the Knife!" said Steve, eyes widening.

Mick ignored him, and, instead, addressed Plumporious, "'Nother brew."

"You could at least say please," said Plumporious, before climbing over Dan and down the end of the bed near the sink. It was the only way to the floor because of Steve's bulk. He put the kettle on again.

"I never had you down as a babysitter, Mick," said Steve.

"Makes a cracking cup of tea," said Mick, between puffs of his cigarette.

"I bet he does. What is he? Currency?"

"Currency?" asked a confused Plumporious.

"Yeah, Mick rents you out for the evening."

"How abhorrent!"

Steve laughed his horseshoes off. "And who's my other cell mate?" Steve turned to Dan: huddled, hugging his knees, trying to find a happier place in his head. A grin split the centaur's large skull, which closed in on Dan for a better look. "Well, well, well, what do we have here, then?"

"That's Dan," said Plumporious. "Be nice to him, it's his first time in prison."

"I can see that," said the centaur, and then almost offhandedly added, "Well, at least they've caught him now."

Dan stirred. He wasn't blessed with street smarts, but he had an inkling this wasn't going to end well.

"What do you mean?" asked the dwarf.

"Well, it's always good when they finally bring a *nonce* to justice."

The word "nonce" reverberating around the prison, silenced it. Suddenly, a common enemy united them all. The relentless pursuit of paedophiles by the population staying at Her Majesty's pleasure was a point of British national pride. Montgomery McStewart (56, Basingstoke) would be utterly delighted. He'd left dozens of comments on tabloid newspaper websites based on the average British criminal's detestation of the "cowardly scum-maggots" who committed such crimes.

Dan's defence was poor at best. He said nothing, transfixed by the fearsome features of a centaur, and also by his echoing accusation. He wobbled his lip.

"This one your bitch as well, Mick?" asked Steve.

"Careful, son...," said the elf, stubbing out his cigarette. Steve, taking the sensible option, said nothing. Everyone in London knew of Mick the Knife and the things that he, or more importantly his knife, were capable. Steve himself was as tough as they came; not because he was a trained fighter or worked out, but because he weighed half a tonne and had iron shoes nailed to his feet. Still, Steve decided to focus his attention back on the little guy. He was a tosser like that.

"How come you ain't dead?" Steve roared with laughter as Dan's face paled and he fell in and out of consciousness.

"Leave him alone," said Plumporious, prodding the centaur in the side. "It's his first night."

"And probably his last." Steve made the sign of the cross. "Right!" He clapped his hands together. "Where's the bogs?"

"It's behind you, why?" asked the dwarf.

"Because I need to go."

"But...." The logistics of the sleeping arrangements could be solved, but Plumporious hadn't considered excretory matters. "But...but...no. You...you'll have to hold it."

"Not gonna happen," said Steve, looking through his legs at the white shower curtain that Plumporious had fitted. Steve kicked it to one side, ripping it off the hooks. "This is gonna need some precision bombing, this," he said, closing one eye.

"You...you can't!" begged the dwarf.

Steve backed up until his back legs straddled the white porcelain.

"Wish me luck!"

"No!" screamed the dwarf.

"Bombs away!" Steve's face took on a strained expression and the veins on his neck stood out.

"NNNNNNOOOOOOOOOOOOOOOOO!" screamed Plumporious, clutching his skull with both hands—resembling said artwork.

"Sorry about that," said the centaur, who wasn't sorry in the slightest. "I thought I was a better shot."

"You...you...HUERRRR...I...I can't believe you...HUERRRR." Plumporious couldn't speak without heaving. The smell wasn't particularly bad as most of Steve's diet consisted of hay, but it was still an unpleasant concept. Plumporious, not for the first time, broke down, and the only thing breaking the sound of desperate sobbing was the sound of dry-heaving.

Dan lay back into his bed and shut his eyes. "Yep," he said. "I'll be d...d...d...d...d...d...d...dead tomorrow."

Chapter 16...

INEVITABLY THE SIREN CALLED, the oscillating banshee of the morn. Hypnos had passed Dan by, and Morpheus was not called upon. There were no dreams of wizardry, no escapism while tormented in conscious nightmare. Death was upon him. Imminently, the door to his cell would swing open, which in itself wasn't an issue. However, the other inmate's doors opening would likely to lead to an altercation or two before breakie.

He didn't belong here. Yes, he'd maimed a polar bear, which was, technically, a crime. But he was sorry, so, so sorry. It was an accident. Surely they knew it was an accident. He didn't deserve to be locked up in a maximum-security prison, with no chance of bail, and without a trial. He'd questioned the legality of it all, but his cries had fallen on death ears, and then one of the interviewing officers had given him a wedgie and marched him, in discomfort, to the cells where things had not improved.

One of his cellmates was a violent psychopath. Another was a complete and utter arsehole, and the other was quite lovely. The guards must have put him in with Plumporious for a shoulder to cry on. They'd known he wasn't a criminal from the moment they'd been driven through the front gates, screaming like a toddler waiting for his first injection. He feared the accuracy of the analogy.

And now he was here, moments from death. It wasn't fair. Life wasn't fair and it never had been.

"Rise and shine, everybody!" The ever-cheery Plumporious knocked the cheer levels up a notch. "Shower time!" He stood at Steve's side, in front of the cell door, quite at home in his flowery kimono, holding a bag of lotions and potions.

"Can't be bothered with showering," said Steve, wiping the sleep from his eyes. He'd been forced to sleep standing up, which wasn't a big deal for a centaur, but he'd certainly made a fuss.

"Please, please, please tell me you're joking?" said a disgusted dwarf with a passion for hygiene.

"No, I ain't joking. I ain't going in there so you can watch the other blokes prance around with their wangers swinging."

"How dare you!" Plumporious converted disgust to outrage.

"Don't try to pretend this isn't your favourite part of the day," said Steve.

"Grooming is important," he said, convincing a stray hair on his forehead to join the rest of its fabulous friends. "You should take it a little more seriously, yourself. Your tail is absolutely covered in...in...faeces." Another dry heave escaped the sensitive dwarf.

With difficulty, Steve looked behind him and gave his tail a swish. An odour filled the cell, and it wasn't a pleasant one. "Yeah, you're right."

Another dry heave from Plumporious was followed by a high-pitch squeal. "You've flicked some on my pillow!"

There was the click of a relay. Electricity hummed, and then, in turn, each door unlocked, numerous steel bolts slammed back into place. Dan clutched his ears.

The centaur left the cell, swinging his arms when he had enough room. He stretched his arm across his chest, and swished his tail.

"It went in my mouth! His tail went in my mouth!" Dry heaving took over once more.

Dan stayed in his bed, under the covers. Communal showers were something he'd feared since his first Physical Education lesson in primary school. He'd never been comfortable with nakedness. The vulnerability of his puny, pale, and pudgy body magnified when there were no clothes to hide under. Dan had avoided local swimming baths his entire adult life. Showering in a high-security prison was definitely a kill or cure approach for tackling his phobia.

Mick the Knife swung his legs out of the bed. He pushed himself to the edge of the mattress, got up, and yawned. Mick had slept naked. The morning had been kind enough to present him with a rude awakening, but no sense of modesty.

Dan averted his eyes. This elf was feared across the entire city, and there were more horror stories told about Mick the Knife than of BBC Christmas parties in the 1970s. He, too, slung a towel on his shoulder. He swaggered on to the gangway with the naked confidence of a seventy-year-old man in a swimming pool changing room, sporting a scrotum with the surface area of a parachute.

He could have at least hung the towel off the end.

"That nearly took my eye out!" Plumporious shouted.

Mick popped both his heads around the door, back into the cell, and said to Dan, "Don't show any weakness or you'll be dead by breakfast."

The unexpected gesture warmed Dan's heart, and gave him the confidence to get out of bed. His feet touched the freezing floor tiles and he yelped, a sharp reminder of the cold heart of this prison and its occupants. He wore the clothes he came in with. His hands shook so much he doubted he could unbutton his shirt. He grabbed the towel he'd been given and left the cell, sticking close to the elf, for the great, terrifying unknown would be more terrifying once it was known.

SHOWER TIME wasn't proving as awful as Dan had feared. He'd taken up a strategic position next to Mick the Knife, which meant anyone who wanted to beat him into a pulp had to walk past Mick washing his bits. Steve had, as promised, not bothered to shower. Plumporious was in his element, singing along to his favourite Bananarama tunes. Dan was surprised the dwarf, and only the dwarf, had access to a waterproof radio, and Dan doubted the shower cap was prison-issue.

"Forg...g...give me for saying, but you d...don't seem the type to end up in a high-security p...prison," said Dan to Plumporious who showered next to him, applying one of his many conditioners. "In fact, you're one of the nicest people I've ever m...met."

The dwarf waved a camp wrist. "You're too kind, Dan. Thank you. I must say, I don't feel at home in here and I'm often putting on a brave face. The prison-issue clothes really are ghastly, and I usually love to dress up in uniform."

Mick the Knife shook his head.

"Would you like to try one of my shower lotions, Dan? This one," he said, pulling a bottle out of his waterproof travel case, "is a mix of elderflower, jasmine, and ginseng. It is quite invigorating and moisturises the skin far better than the soap they provide here, which I strongly believe violates human rights."

"I'm OK, thanks," said Dan, politely. "But how on earth d...did you manage to g...get hold of moisturising shower g...gel?"

"The guards can be quite pleasant once you get to know them," said the dwarf, scrubbing an armpit.

Mick laughed out loud.

"Why are you in here, P...P...Plumporious?" asked Dan, frankly.

"Hmmm, yes, rather embarrassing, I must say," said the dwarf, not making eye contact, washing his other pit.

Mick said, "Yeah, Plumpy—"

The dwarf wagged an angry finger. "Don't call me, Plumpy, Michael." The dwarf sighed, and addressed Dan while massaging yet another lotion into his scalp. "I'd chanced upon a couple of young gentleman while on an evening stroll, and at first I thought things were going to turn ghastly, but, funnily enough, we became romantically entwined, caught up in the moment, if you will. London can do that to a soul. Have you ever experienced that, young Dan?"

Dan's eyes narrowed. "I'm not sure what you m...mean."

"He was arrested for soliciting," said Mick.

Plumporious's eyes shut tight, as if the word had physically assaulted him. "Thank you. Thank you, Michael."

"He's always inside for it," said Mick.

"I have expensive tastes, you see, Dan. My outfits are not just a fashion statement, they express my people's culture and also the plight of the homosexual dwarf from the North."

"He's a drama queen," said Mick, grinning, thoroughly enjoying himself. "He's just bitter that his arch rival, Rudi von Shortspunk, has won Gay Dwarf of the North for the past five years running."

"Shut it, Michael! You know I hate that...that bitch!" said the dwarf, pointing a loofah at the laughing elf. He turned to Dan. "My parents...my parents find my lifestyle...." He tapped the loofah on his chin. "Let's say—difficult. They don't understand." He used the loofah to wipe away a tear. "I...I was outcast!"

"Yeah, I bet you were," said Mick, chuckling away.

"What's that supposed to mean!" snapped Plumporious.

Mick held up a hand, laughing, the other remained washing his bits, which were scrubbed clean a long time ago.

"You two know each other p...pretty well," said Dan.

Mick grinned, yellow and black teeth not softening the sentiment, and Dan didn't inquire as to why.

"And what are you in for, Mick?" he asked.

"Stabbin'."

"Ah," said Dan. He should've known.

Mick's presence had kept Dan safe in the showers. Now they headed back to the cells and Dan stayed closer to Mick the Knife than a toddler following its mummy. To Dan, the prison had transformed since his arrival. When he'd arrived, it'd been a medieval dungeon, dark and dismal, illuminated by fiery torches. Blood had run down the walls from torture chambers and excrement was flung from the cells, with the groans and shrieks of the damned and dying.

It wasn't that bad....

It was still bad, mind; a dilapidated Victorian prison, filthy and neglected. Dan had only seen one rat, and he hadn't screamed and run away. Prison was toughening him up, big time. He'd even had a poo without making a paper blanket to stop the sound of the splash.

The inmates had been every bit as fearsome as Dan had imagined. There was an even spread of the races, which had surprised Dan as he was expecting a lot more goblins, not that he was racist, not towards the other species, anyway. Apart from the occupants of his cell, lots and lots of muscles covered in lots and lots of tattoos were the fashion of the day. But none of the inmates had bothered him so far, and he had the presence of the Knife to thank for that.

The corridor opened out into the open-plan hub of the prison. Several levels, serviced by gangways, ran around the quadrangle, the common area. Over the railings, nets stretched across from gangway to gangway served as protection from landing to death. The common area had a pool table, table tennis, and a TV. It all appeared remarkably civil. It was deserted except for a small group, who could only be classified as small in the numerical sense. One of their number was especially not small. He sat on a table, which bent under his weight. It was obvious to Dan he was the leader as everyone looked to him as he lectured. Also, nothing said "leader" like six hundred pounds of muscle. Yet there were a few oddities about the fellow.

"Why is that ogre wearing a s...smoking jacket, and why is he holding—" Dan counted, "twenty-one volumes of the *Encyclopaedia Britannica?*"

"Because he dropped the other eleven," said Mick.

"Ah," said Dan, thinking of a suitable way to rephrase the question. "Why did he carry the complete *Encyclopaedia Britannica* under his arm?"

Mick placed his foot on the railing and tilted his head. "That there happens to be the daddy of the prison."

"The daddy? What's a daddy?" The colour drained from Dan's face for the thirtieth time of the day. "Dear lord, I d...do not want to be mummy!"

"It ain't like that," said Mick. "Well, not in this particular case, you'll be pleased to know. The daddy is the head honcho, the guy who runs the place."

"I thought the warden ran the p...prison?"

"He does, officially, but he won't kill you for not washing his socks for him."

"And that ogre would k...kill someone for that?" said Dan, incredulously.

"Oh yeah, it's a respect thing—and he hates laundry."

"I see." Dan backed away from the gangway. "Why is he wearing glasses and smoking a pipe?"

"He's a sensitive soul is our Obadiah," said Mick. "He's trying to combat negative stereotypes."

"I d...don't understand," said a perplexed newbie to the world of Banged-up Britain.

"Well, ogres are very good at smashing things with their fists and crushing things with their feet," explained Mick. "Obadiah Ulysses Jacobsen over there happens to be the best at it, and that's one of the reasons he's inside, and it's entirely the reason he's the daddy."

"I must say," said Dan, "he has an unusual l...look for an ogre."

"It is rather avant garde," said Plumporious.

"Obadiah has an issue with the world's stereotypical view of ogres being murdering, bone-crushing, spleen-ripping, liver-stamping psychopaths." Mick lit up a fag. "And the fact that Obadiah *is* a murdering, bone-crushing, spleen-ripping, liver-stamping psychopath should only be mentioned by people not particularly keen on their bones, spleens, and livers.

"Ogres are good with their fists but they ain't so good with their heads, unless we're talking headbutting, and then they're second only behind minotaurs and, formerly, the unicorns, until the goblins killed them all and hacked off their horns and pretended they were *growspecks*." Mick grimaced at the thought. "Old Obadiah is trying to convey a more intellectual image, hence the pipe, encyclopaedia, and smoking jacket. Those glasses aren't real, and his real name is Wayne."

"So where d...d...did he come up with...Obadiah...Ulys...wha?" said Dan struggling to get his tongue around it.

"Obadiah Ulysses Jacobsen. And you better not get his name wrong. Make sure you call him by *all* his names otherwise he'll be carrying twenty volumes of the *Encyclopaedia Britannica*. You see, the other eleven volumes were dropped on people's heads, repeatedly, until their brains came out of their ears and messed up the pages. What's in a name, huh?"

Dan's legs gave way and he caught on to the railings.

"Just stay away from him, although, as the new kid, chances are he'll come looking for you."

"Mick, I know you have a reputation as the most d...dangerous person in all of London, b...but thanks for helping me. You seem like a really n...nice guy."

Mick gazed upon Dan as one gazes upon dog poo stuck between one's toes after a walk on the filthy beach of a deprived seaside town.

Chapter 17...

MICK THE KNIFE WAS PROVING AN UNEXPECTED ALLY FOR DAN, who, remarkably, had been assaulted less in his walk around prison than he was on his morning walk to work. Making it through to lunch time without being killed was a pleasant surprise.

Three of the four cell mates sat in the canteen, trays of food in front of them. The clippety-clop of hooves announced the approach of the fourth member of the unlikely quartet, much to Dan's dismay. Steve put his tray of food on the table and awkwardly kneeled down on the floor.

"No centaur seats. I'm the only centaur in this entire prison. What's that about? Shouldn't even be in here! Bastards!"

Plumporious dabbed his lips with a napkin. "What on earth did you do to end up in here, Steve?"

"Been set up, again," said Steve, shaking his head. "All I did was take a dump in the National History Museum, and now I'm up for Regicide."

"That's so unfair!" said Dan.

"I know. If I do get out, I'm gonna stand on the bollocks of every one of The Queen's corgis in protest. No—all the corgis in London. Bastards."

"It's not their f...f...fault!" said Dan.

"Victimless crime," said the centaur, stabbing the meatballs on his plate as if they were attached to something fluffy and bred into a shape detested by nature.

The entire population of the prison sat in the vast canteen. Humans, elves, dwarves, trolls, goblins, and orcs, to name but a few, chowed down on slop. Logistics were not a simple matter. All the species had differing nutritional requirements, which were mostly ignored. All had different toilet habits, and the variability in size and shape caused many issues, which were mostly ignored. Most prisons separated the species to cater for the needs of the prisoners. Brixton didn't. Something as trivial as "genetic race" became irrelevant when the common denominator was "maniac."

"What have you been up to, Steve?" asked Plumporious, cutting up his Caesar salad. The dwarf's greatest mortal enemy was carbs. "I didn't see you in the shower this morning, but I must say you smell somewhat better."

"Yeah, screws hosed me down in the yard. Discrimination it is. Since then, I've been doing the rounds. Even though I'm the only centaur in the place, and that means I'm doomed to a life of discomfort and hatred for my physical size, my splendour, and boyish good looks, I've discovered there is one thing far worse that one could find oneself manifest."

"Such as?" asked Mick.

"I'd say the worst possible scenario is to be the only fairy nonce in the entire prison," said the centaur, indicating Dan.

Dan blinked. Then he turned to look behind him, hoping that Steve was talking about someone else, but found a brick wall. He had another go at blinking and it didn't help matters. He turned back to face Steve, considerably more terrified than the last time he'd seen him.

"Well there ain't any other fairy nonces in the prison, are there?" said Steve. He shook his head and pointed his plastic fork at Dan. "A despicable monster, *and* an idiot! You deserve what's coming to you, son."

Dan's eyes widened and the colour drained from his chest (it didn't bother travelling as far north as his head anymore). "What? Wh...wh...wh...what have you done?"

"What do you mean what have I done? What have *you* done?" said Steve, aggressively, stabbing his fork into an over-cooked carrot. "You're the one in here for noncing, you filthy bastard. Hanging's too good for your sort."

Dan leaned across the table and whispered desperately, "But...but...I'm not here b...b...b...because of...because of that..."

The centaur crossed his arms. "Then why are you in here for?"

"GB...B...B...BH."

"What the hell is GBBBBH?"

"Grievous b...b...b...bodily harm."

Steve managed to spit out "Bollocks" as well as a lot of his food in Dan's face, in between fits of laughter.

"I b...blew off a p...p...polar bear—"

"AND HE INTERFERES WITH ANIMALS!" yelled Steve over his shoulder. His intended audience sat together in a corner, staring with murderous intent at Dan. One of the group was three times the size of the others, and that was Obadiah Ulysse...Uly...Dan had forgotten his name.

He was dead.

Steve gave the gang a big thumbs up and pointed at Dan before turning back to the table.

"What?" he said, before shrugging his shoulders and getting back to his slop, not appreciating the stern look Plumporious admonished him with.

The dwarf patted Dan on the back who wailed into his food. "Why did you tell them Dan was a...was a...one of those despicable things?" Plumporious said.

Steve chewed it over as he chewed his dinner. After swallowing the mouthful, he said, "That's a good question."

"You must have a reason!" said Plumporious under a hushed breath.

Steve looked into the air for some inspiration, rubbing his chin thoughtfully. "You'd think so, wouldn't you?" He popped another carrot into his mouth without a care in the world.

"They're gonna k...k...kill me," wailed Dan. "They're gonna k...k...kill me."

The ogre and his cronies drove fists into palms, drew fingers across throats, and performed some other gestures which Dan couldn't quite decipher, but was pretty sure he wouldn't enjoy them. Dan had never seen a group of people so collectively angry, mainly because he'd never been to a football match or a bingo hall in northern England. There were fifteen of them in total, mostly goblins, a few orcs, a couple of humans, and an elf. All were rippling with tattooed muscle, and all had the strangest of stares. With the exception of Obidiah, all of them had completely blue eyeballs.

"Who...who are they?" said Dan.

Mick gave Dan the rundown. "The Blue-Eyed Boys. Nastiest gang in this prison, or any prison for that matter. Genuine crazy bastards. Obadiah founded the gang a few years ago. The initiation to join the gang is to, after killing at least half a dozen people, have your eyeballs tattooed blue. The pain is close to unbearable."

"How do you know?" asked Dan.

"Had it done," said the elf with a shrug.

His cellmates squinted, looking from one of Mick's brown eyes to the other.

"I never knew!" said Plumporious. "How come I can't see it, Mick?"

"I'm clever, me," he said, tapping his noggin. "I thought the tat was a bit shit, so after I'd gone through the stupid initiation, I had my old eyes tattooed onto my new eyes," said the elf matter-of-factly.

The others shared confused looks. "Can you repeat that, please?" said Plumporious.

"I had my eyes tattooed onto my eyes so it wouldn't look like I'd tattooed my eyes."

"But...but...why?" asked the dwarf.

"'Cos I'm 'ard."

"Oh, Michael," said Plumporious, shaking his head.

Mick jutted his head forwards in a way only the "well 'ard" could. "And they all get given a blue ring when they join too, to signify they're members."

"If you know them, they'll listen to you, right?" asked Dan, with hope in his heart.

"'Course. Done a few jobs with them on the outside. That's why I had my eyes done, you know, for a bet. Most of them are nutcases, but they leave me alone."

Dan's head rose from folded arms. "Can you t...talk to them? Will you ask them not to k...k...k...kill me," he said quickly, desperately.

"Well, I reckon I'd hold enough sway to convince them not to kill you—"

"Oh thank you, thank you, thank you!" said Dan, grabbing Mick's hand and kissing it.

Mick pulled his hand back and wiped it on his top. "If you hadn't been done for noncing."

"Filthy bastard!" cried Steve. "Hanging's too good for your sort!"

"But I haven't! I haven't! I haven't!" Dan sobbed. "You m...m...made it up, you awful m...m...monster!"

Steve couldn't stop giggling.

"Unfortunately for you," said Mick, "they don't know that."

Steve gave Dan a pat on the arm. "At least you were killed doing what you loved."

"I have d...done nothing wrong and now they're gonna k...kill me," sobbed Dan into his sleeves, "because you've made up some awful, awful stories about me."

"Don't worry, Dan," said the ever optimistic dwarf. "It will be all right. They're not going to kill you."

Mick said, "They're gonna kill—"

"I know," said Plumporious before Mick finished the sentence.

Dan wailed.

"Look on the bright side," said Steve, "I hear you got a visitor this afternoon, before the exercise yard."

"What are you on a...b...b...bout?" asked Dan, blubbering, every letter "B" accompanied by a spit bubble.

"Well, you'll have your chance to say goodbye to your loved ones before they stab you to death on the football pitch."

Dan had no more tears left to shed.

"Hopefully," continued the centaur, unrelenting, "they'll kill you at the start of the exercise session, rather than the end."

"Why's that?" asked Plumporious.

Steve said, "He doesn't look like he enjoys sport that much."

"I prefer it to d...d...dying!"

Steve threw his hands in the air. "No wonder no one likes you. I try and help you look on the bright side and you throw it back in my face."

"You're the reason for my imminent s...s...s...tabbing!"

"The worst thing about a prison stabbing-to-the-death," interjected Mick, "is that no one can get hold of proper knives, so they have to fashion their own stabbing-to-the death device."

"Whatever do you mean?" asked Steve, with mock interest, a fist holding up a quizzical chin.

Mick explained. "Well, the gang that Dan has made the mistake of upsetting—"

"I haven't d...done anything!"

"You tell that to that polar bear's mum," said a passing prison guard.

"—are also known as The Spork Gang," Mick finished.

"The Spork Gang, you say?" asked Steve, grinning at Dan.

"Yep. They stab their victims to death with a spork."

"Is that possible?" asked Plumporious.

"It takes a certain degree of skill, but mostly a lot of determination. It's definitely the worst way anything can die," said Mick, knowledgably.

"You're sporked." Steve nudged Dan. "Get it? Did you get my joke?"

"Leave me alone!"

"Don't be like that!" said an offended centaur. "I thought we were friends?"

"No, we are NOT friends!" said Dan in a rare show of defiance. "You're the reason for my imminent d...d...death."

"It's not just the death," said Steve. "They'll probably have their wicked way with you first."

"Every cloud...," offered Plumporious.

"SMITH!" came the booming cry of a guard, who was either a mountain troll or a small hill.

"Yes, sir," said Dan.

"Your visitor is here. Best make the most of it, son. I hear you're getting sporked to death afterwards."

"What!" exclaimed Dan at a frequency reserved for bats. "You know! And you're not g...going to do anything?"

"Not after what you said," said the troll, pointing a finger as thick as Dan's arm. "You're lucky I don't spork you myself."

"I haven't said anything!" he said desperately.

"Pull the other one." He pointed at the centaur. "Steve told me the rumours you were spreading about me mam."

Chapter 18...

UNDER THE GUARD OF A SHORT BUT INCREDIBLY STOUT OGRE AND A DWARF, a much dwarfier dwarf than Plumporious, who sported a thick, wiry beard and a face full of scars, Dan was marched to the visitor centre. His burly protectors were the only thing keeping him alive. With the Knife out of the picture, the prisoners had united under a banner of hatred towards Dan. The riot guards, effective and as brutal as ever, had brought order, and the prisoners had been sent back to their cells. Each cell erupted with Dan's passing, the inmates clawing through the bars, desperate to rip him to pieces. Still, his first day of high school was worse.

Magic. Magic bore the brunt of responsibility. Yes, Steve the Centaur had masterminded Dan's impending death, but he was only a catalyst, speeding up the process. It would have happened eventually...probably by tea time.

A twang of guilt inspired a sigh. It wasn't really magic's fault; it was his inability to perform magic, that or the wand Gambledolf had given him was a Friday-afternoon job. One thing was certain: magic was not going to save him from this predicament. He no longer possessed his wand, and even if he did, he wouldn't know what to do with it. He didn't want to harm anyone else. "Except that centaur," he muttered between gritted teeth.

He prepared to say goodbye to his beloved girlfriend, or at least he assumed he would. No one else would visit him. Craig the skin troll wouldn't show up. The only thing more debilitating than his agoraphobia was his laziness. Chantelle wouldn't contemplate a visit to a prison with her irrational germ phobia and her rational homicidal-maniac phobia.

Oh, Michelle, he thought. Regrets, he had a few, but one in particular. He wished he hadn't been such a nice guy about the whole sex thing. He was going to die a virgin. Then he remembered what Steve had said about The Blue-Eyed Boys and realised he wasn't going to die a virgin at all.

"Through there, nonce," said the ogre.

The dwarf pushed him, and Dan hit the floor sliding across the tiles. "Yeah, and for what you said about old Ted's mum. I'm gonna make sure The Blue-Eyed Boys have a bit longer to work over your rottin' corpse."

"I never said anything about his mum!" protested Dan.

"That's not what Steve told us, nonce," said the ogre. "His mum never played Backgammon with Burt Bacharach!"

"I never said anything of the k...kind!" Dan screwed his face up. "And how is that even offensive?"

"Shut it, nonce! *You* know!"

Dan pushed himself off the floor and dusted himself down. He opened the door to the visitor centre and the guards slammed it behind him with a shout of "Booth Six."

There were half a dozen booths where prisoners talked to loved ones across a Perspex barrier with telephones. Dan was well aware of the movies, where, without fail, inmate's lovers, wives, and girlfriends flashed the more private of areas, giving their sexually frustrated men something to help them through the lonely week.

However, there'd been no wanking goblins in *The Shawshank Redemption.*

Dan kept his eyes glued on the floor and walked past the booths, counting to six. He looked up. Michelle was not waiting for him.

A goblin waited for him.

Thankfully, this goblin wasn't handling his *growspeck.*

Unfortunately, Dan had seen this goblin handling his *growspeck* before.

Many times.

Once at a funeral.

Mr. Grak was quite an unexpected visitor. A surprise, yes, but not a pleasant one.

"Smith, heard you've been diddling."

Dan didn't need the telephone to hear the goblin. He fell into the seat and picked up the phone. "What d...do you want?"

"Justice to be done, you dirty bastard!" Mr. Grak yelled, banging his fist against the Perspex with every syllable.

"Who t...told you?" asked Dan, dejectedly.

"A centaur."

Dan closed his eyes in despair. "How on earth has he managed to speak to everyone, and even p...people outside the p...prison?" Dan sat back and slumped in his seat. "Why are you here, anyway?"

"I don't want to be, Smith." Mr. Grak straightened his tie. "The directors of Green Planet made me come down here to tell you you're fired. We've arranged for some reporters to wait outside so I can give a statement about how we're doing everything we can to ensure London

Zoo's first disabled polar bear has at least some quality of life. AND it isn't diddled."

"Is he OK?" said Dan, leaning forward, his chubby forehead pressed against the screen.

"He'll live, although with the filth that's been coming out of his mouth for the last forty-eight hours, I'm not sure that's a good thing, but don't you worry about that. The only thing that matters to you is: you're fired."

"Big d...deal. I'll be d...d...dead in two hours."

Mr. Grak examined some lint under a talon. "Do what you want, Smith, you don't even work for me anymore. I can't tell you what to do. Although I've gotta say, death is the best idea you've ever had."

"It's not suicide, I'm g...going to be murdered!" said Dan.

The goblin shrugged. "Well, if you're not murdered, suicide is a good move for you. It's not like you had much to live for before you got arrested."

"I'm going to be m...m...murdered!" Dan cried.

Mr. Grak rolled his eyes. "You always were such a drama queen, Smith!"

"Drama queen?" said Dan with a squeal. "The Blue-Eyed Boys are going to k...k...kill me."

Mr. Grak whistled. "I've heard of them, Smith. Why did you go and upset them for?" He shook his head, as if chastising a poor choice of pizza topping.

"That b...b...bloody centaur made up some lies about me," Dan's protests came in the form of high-pitched squeals.

"That hot girlfriend of yours will be devastated when I tell her you're in prison. She is not going to be impressed with the reason for your incarceration, either."

"She doesn't even like p...polar bears, or any animal for that matter."

"She'll forgive you for that, but there's no way she'll forgive you for your other heinous crimes."

"You know I'm not—"

"Yep, she'll be pretty upset," said Mr. Grak, cutting him off, looking away into the distance. "It doesn't look good on her. I can just see it now." A slow, sickly, and lecherous leer formed.

"It's a lie. P...please don't tell her!" Dan pleaded, banging on the dividing screen. He put the telephone between his jaw and shoulder and held his hands together in prayer, begging his former boss. "She'll be a mess."

"And I will comfort her."

"But—"

"With my *growspeck*."

"Ah."

Mr. Grak winked at Dan, a horrible, slow, sordid wink. It was his *growspeck* wink.

"Goodbye, Smith. You should be grateful I put up with you as long as I did. I carried you in your professional and your personal life. I was your rock. Look how you repaid me?" Mr. Grak did a "mic drop" with the receiver and got to his feet to leave.

This was the last time Dan would set disdainful eyes on his former boss and flatmate. This was his moment. There would be no repercussions for his actions because: A) a bullet-proof divide separated them, and B) Dan would be dead soon. He didn't care if Mr. Grak shaved his corpse. He had nothing to lose.

"Mr. Grak," shouted Dan, so the goblin would be able to hear him.

Mr. Grak halted. "What is it now, Smith!" he yelled, looking at his watch. "Haven't you got better things to be doing, like dying?"

Dan's confidence waned as soon as the goblin fixed him with his penetrating red stare. "Nothing...It's nothing..." His head dropped. He got up to leave and then stopped.

No.

He was Danoclees Dunlorian, and even if he was about to be sporked to death with a runcible spoon, he was going out with his head held high.

"Mr. Grak?"

Mr. Grak stopped and rolled up his sleeves. "That glass is bullet-proof, but it doesn't mean it's goblin-proof."

"You're...you're...y...y...."

"I'm what, you stuttering fairy idiot?"

"You're not...you're not." Dan Smith stepped to one side and let Danoclees Dunlorian step forwards. "Sometimes, you're not a very nice person." His words had wings. He turned on his heel and swaggered out of the room like Charles Bronson.

Chapter 19...

DAN SWAGGERED. He'd never swaggered before. But after his Hollywood-esque farewell to his former boss he walked tall, almost 5'0" in his Cubans. The swagger took a great deal of concentration. An onlooker would assume he'd soiled himself. Concentrating on looking cool was the sole reason Dan failed to notice the obstacle barring his path on the gangway ahead.

"Well, well, well, look what we have here then?" The rumbling nature of the ogre's voice shook Dan's bones, and any onlooker suspecting Dan swaggered because of a Hollywood-esque farewell to a former boss would be mistaken.

"H...h...hello," Dan squeaked.

"I've been meaning to have a word with you," said Obadiah, peering over his glasses. He leant against the wall, leafing through a mighty tome that looked like a pocket dictionary in his huge and fearsome hands.

"W...w...why?" said Dan, fearful of unfashionable cutlery.

"You're the new guy, and me and my Blue-eyed Boys have heard some...devices...about you?"

"D...D...Devices?" said Dan, bemused.

The ogre leant closer, his vile breath washing over Dan, who fought every instinct to recoil and waft his hand in front of his nose. That never went down well. "Yeah, devices."

Dan, clueless, offered. "Erm...good d...devices?"

"Not good devices." The ogre thumbed through the book he'd been reading and slapped a giant finger on the page. "Substandard devices," he said, a proud look on his face. Dan couldn't tell if the ogre had puffed his chest out as it was permanently enormous.

If these were the free streets of London, Dan would've legged it, but there was no point legging it in prison. He had to deal with this now, although the best course of action was unclear with the ogre talking utter gibberish.

Dan tried politeness. "With all d...d...due respect, sir, I'm not sure what it is I've d...done."

"I like polar bears," said the ogre. "Polar bears are fluffy and cuddly." Only a six-hundred-pound killing machine could consider an eight-hundred-pound killing machine both fluffy and cuddly. "And you blew his arm off!" he said with a snarl, before chastising himself. He held up a finger, mouthed "a moment," and turned to his font of knowledge. "What I meant to say was not 'And you blew his arm off,' but 'and you...,'" several seconds later, "...gusted his...," several seconds later, "...appendage...," several seconds later, "...sour."

Dan gestured at the book he was carrying. "Is that a thesaurus?"

"No," said the ogre, flicking through to T. "It's a vocabulary."

"Ah."

"All the...slowdowns in here can't...." There was a pause as he flicked through the book to find U. "...cognise my...highbrow ...declarations." The sentence took three minutes to complete. Obadiah beamed the beam of the learned.

Dan worked the sentence through. "All...the retards," Dan winced, "in here can't understand my intellectual words?"

The ogre mouthed the words slowly, counting on his fingers for some unbeknownst reason, and nodded excitedly. "That's what I'm saying. Yeah, that's exactly what I'm saying."

Dan let out a huge breath.

Obadiah weighed Dan, looking him up and down (which didn't take very long), tapping his lips. He concluded and said, sagely, "I was going to stand on you, but, 'cos you're smart, I'm gonna give you a chance. To become a member of the Blue-Eyed boys, you've got to tattoo your eyes and cut an elf's ears off and stick 'em up a dwarf's arse. But, I don't think you're a physical fella. I'm gonna have to make the initiation different, because of your big brain."

Unsure of the best course of action, Dan alternated from shaking vigorously to nodding vigorously.

"But," Obadiah raised a massive finger. "You can gain protection from us *if* you play a game." He consulted his mighty tome once more. "Limericks with the...male founder."

Dan tapped his chin. "Riddles with the Patriarch?" he ventured.

"Yep...I mean...erm...yes. Riddles with the Patriarch, yeah."

The game sounded ominous, but Dan had no choice. "OK, I've always enjoyed r...riddles." If he could work out what the ogre said, the riddle would be simple enough. Dan bet his life on this.

"Right," announced Obadiah. "I'm leaving to communicate you a limerick, and if you get it healthy, you on the air."

Dan worked it through, "I'm g...going to tell you a...riddle and if you get it...right, you...you..." he panicked. "On the air?" he squealed, puzzled, stumped.

Obadiah cracked his knuckles. "On the air, you slowdown!" He thumbed through the tome aggressively until he found the word he wanted. "On the air: conscious, being broadcast, aware, sentient," he read.

"Oh, live!" said a relieved inmate.

"That's what I pissin' said!" The ogre slapped a hand over his mouth. Cursing and swearing were foolish and wicked practises. The ogre pretended it never happened. "If you get the limerick healthy then I'll tell you an alternative one."

Dan rubbed his hands, warming up. His life was in danger but nerds loved a game of wits where dexterity, strength, speed, and stamina weren't required. "And how many d...do I need to get right?"

"All of 'em," said the ogre.

"And how many riddles are there?"

"All of 'em."

"Ah."

Now, Dan was very good at riddles, and he proceeded to get every one correct, especially the one the ogre asked four times in a row. Obadiah was delighted too. Finally, he'd met his intellectual match, having spent years in prison associating with criminals with IQs that did not allow them to stretch past the base level of riddles, mostly consisting of repeat rounds of "Cock or Ball."

"Now then, Dan." For they were on first name terms. "You have solitary more limerick to get healthy, and if you get it healthy then I won't hallmark on you, and if you do get it healthy, I have a flabbergast for you." The ogre patted down his pockets, "Now where did I position my homosexuals?"

"Facedown?" volunteered the plucky riddler.

"Eh?" The ogre raised his eyes from his search. "Me fags, me cigarettes."

"Ah." Dan screwed up his face. "Is that in the thesaurus?"

The ogre ignored him and continued patting. "What have I got in my pocket?"

"That c...can't be the riddle?" said Dan, desperately.

The ogre's face lit up with a big grin. "Why not? What have I got in my receptacle?"

"It's not a riddle! It's not a riddle!"

"Yes, it is." Light gleamed off titanic teeth.

"You've g...got to g...give me three g...guesses!"

"I haven't got to do anything, but I..." He flicked through the book. "Self-determination."

"You will?" said Dan, bracing himself in case he was hallmarked on.

"Yeah, it's what I said. Right, you've got three...suppositions."

"A hand?" blurted out Dan.

"No," said the ogre, whose hand was snug in his pocket. Dan thought it best not to argue.

"A spork?"

The ogre took a spork out of his pocket which was more dried blood than plastic. "No."

"Ah."

"Last guess." The ogre tied up his shoelace in preparation of some vigorous hallmarking.

Dan threw up his hands. "Fluff or nothing,"

"That's two guesses," said the ogre with a wag of his finger.

Luckily, Dan wasn't able to soil himself a second time.

"Both of which are healthy," said Obidiah, giving the air a damned fine punch. Unfortunately, there wasn't much room between the ogre and the gangway above and he punched a hole straight through the grated steel. He didn't even notice.

"Really?" said Dan, hopefully. He stared at the torn metal. "B...both healthy?"

"Both healthy, but not right. There's something else in my receptacle that I will give you if you guess right." The ogre reached into his back pocket and fingered Dan's prize.

"So I have another guess?"

"Of course. I said three, didn't I?"

Dan used all his grey matter. What could it be? What could it be?

"Time's running out," goaded the ogre, a little excited. He pulled his hands out of his pocket to rub his hands in glee, and a ring popped out and rolled on the gangway, spinning to a stop. It was brightest of blues.

A ring! Mick said that all members of the Blue-Eyed Boys received a blue ring as membership.

"A blue ring!" cried Dan.

The ogre jumped with joy and punched some more holes in the gangway, all unintentional for he deplored vandalism. "My treasurable! My treasurable! You did it Dan. You've won!"

"So you're not g...going to k...kill me?" said Dan.

"No, I'm not leaving to eradicate you!" The ogre looked on Dan with the love one holds for their firstborn. He spread out his humongous arms. "You've just been accepted as an honorary member of the Blue-Eyed Boys!"

"Have I got to t...t...tat...t...t...too my eyeballs?" A little bit of sick entered Dan's mouth.

"No, of course not. You have to stick the elf's ears up a dwarf's arse for that." He patted his back pocket. "Now where did I put that blue ring?"

Dan bent down and picked up the ring. "Here!" he said, holding it aloft.

"Not that," said the ogre, slapping Dan's hand and sending the ring flying over the gangway.

"Eh?" said Dan.

"I can't give you your blue ring with that, silly?" said the ogre.

"Eh?" said Dan.

The ogre pulled out a tattoo gun and a well of ink from his back pocket.

Dan held on to the railings as his legs buckled for the fifty-seventh time of the day. "I thought...I thought you weren't going to tattoo me."

"Not your eyeballs, Dan. But you're going to get a magic blue ring of protection."

Dan thought the riddles were over, but then a horrible realisation dawned.

"Now, bend over and let's get them pants down."

The tattoo gun hummed.

Chapter 20...

EVEN THOUGH RUNNING AWAY from someone in prison was a futile task, Dan had run. He had run as fast as his puny legs could carry him. His flight or roll-on-his-back-and-beg-for-mercy instinct had kicked in, and he'd pumped his knees before thoughts of unbuttoning his trousers had entered his mind. Some may say it was prudish, but he really didn't want his bumhole tattooed by a forty-five stone ogre.

And for his actions, he was going to die. Obadiah Ulysses Jacobsen had screamed blue murder, not in his own special literary kind of way, but in a sentence full of blasphemy and heresy so vile, it put in question the universal need for sentient life. Dan was screwed, and he was about to face his newest enemy in Physical Recreation.

"Right then, you 'orrible lot. We're gonna play a game."

Dan, his fellow cellmates, and about fifty other inmates stood outside on the prison recreational field which could sport a full football pitch if the need required. It was favourable for the prisoners to burn some energy in the wholesome fresh air, rather than expending it on trying to murder the guards.

Everyone, with the exception of Plumporious, wore prison issue sportswear: the tiniest of shorts and the tightest of vests. Even though the sun was shining, Dan froze, hugging himself and trying to rid his ghost-white arms of the goose bumps. It was a balmy 23°C, but Death's cold hand rested on his shoulder.

The guard responsible for Physical Recreation took them through the details of the forthcoming activities. Jonesy was a Welsh minotaur. Wales wasn't the native homeland of minotaurs, but a few minotaur families had emigrated to the Valleys in the fifties and sixties. For some unbeknown reason, the nine foot tall half-human-half-cow monsters had not met the same degree of bigoted resistance as did the Patels.

Jonesy was an amiable sort of chap really, and had managed to cut violence within the prison by sixty per cent since joining the guards a couple of years ago. Sometimes, to find calm, all people needed was a soothing voice from the Valleys and the threat of being gored in the heart with three foot of razor-sharp minotaur horn.

Dan hoped Jonesy's presence would improve his chances of survival by a percentage or two. It was possible. He was big enough to stop Obadiah simultaneously ripping Dan's intestines out through his nostrils and his anus, as promised by the ogre. The group had been split into two, and Dan had been parted from his only two friends: Plumporious and the Knife. As luck, or perhaps fate, or perhaps a planned murder would have it, he ended up in the same group as Obadiah, every member of the Blue-Eyed boys—and Steve the Centaur. That was the worst part of it all.

Jonesy walked in front of the line tossing a small golden globe up and down. "Now, I have a little surprise for you all," he said, singing his Welsh drawl. "Who here has heard of a game called Quibbitch?"

Dan's head snapped up from where it had been permanently glued to his chest. "The lost g...game of the fairies?" he cried.

A couple of inmates in the line started laughing, until elbows were shoved into their ribs. "It ain't funny," one of them said. "He's a nonce."

"I am not a nonce!" shouted Dan in the general direction of the insinuations.

"Quiet! All of you!" bellowed Jonesy, who was instantly obeyed. "Especially you, nonce!" The snarling minotaur pushed a finger into Dan's chest. Dan recoiled, struggling to breathe. A hair-line fracture in his sternum was likely. Thankfully, the minotaur went back to walking the line, throwing the golden ball up and down.

"What...what d...did I do?" asked Dan to himself, under his breath.

From behind, Steve the Centaur whispered into his ear, "You shouldn't have told everyone he has a human dick instead of a bull's."

"For the love of—"

"Who here knows the rules of Quibbitch?" bellowed the minotaur.

Dan put a hand up.

"Anyone here who is not a nonce know the rules for Quibbitch?" Dan raised his hand higher, but it was ignored.

"Ain't it fairy crap?" asked a goblin.

"That it is," said the minotaur.

"It isn't c...crap!" cried Dan, unable to contain himself. "It was the most exciting, intriguing, and refined team game that graced the earth." When excited, his stutter always disappeared.

"Yeah, but I bet it was shit compared to football, weren't it?" said the goblin.

"No!" shouted Dan, full to the brim with indignation.

"I bet it was," said the goblin in full flow. "Ain't a better sport to watch than footy." There was a lot of rough sounding "yeaaahhhs" when he'd finished, the working class equivalent of a "hear hear."

"Football is a terrible game," cried Dan.

This received a sharp, collective intake of breath from his fellow inmates and a stern look from the minotaur.

"You don't do yourself any favours," said the centaur, into his ear.

Dan continued unabashed. "Quibbitch was played on broomsticks and there'd be two teams of seven: one Goalie, three Runner-afters, two Bashers and a Looker."

"A Looker?" asked an elf.

"They'd be on the hunt for the Golden Twitch."

"Indeed, Smith." Jonesy tossed the golden ball at Dan, which hit him in the chest. He hit the floor, wheezing. "Give me strength," muttered Jonesy under his breath.

"If it was a fairy game," asked a dwarf inmate. "How come fairy boy can't play it? Shouldn't it be in his blood?"

"I—*wheeze*—am— *wheeze* —not— *wheeze* —a fairy."

Dan struggled to his feet with the Golden Twitch in his hand. "The— *wheeze* —Twitch!" he cried, holding it aloft.

Various names were uttered under breaths, and many were shouted, especially the nastier ones. The minotaur picked up a large leather bag and opened the zip. He picked out a broomstick.

Dan's eyes widened and his heart pumped joy around his body. He'd dreamt of playing Quibbitch all his life.

"Smith, as you know so much about the game, you can be a Looker."

Dan jumped in the air and gave it a damned fine punch!

Ten minutes later the teams were set, ready to play. Dan'd never been so excited in all his life. Even though it would be dangerous, even though there were a team of murderous psychopaths ready to kill him (and that was just his team), he was going to play Quibbitch!

"Right, you 'orrible lot, Quibbitch is all about catching the Golden Twitch. Smith, you're a Looker and you've got to find it. Basically, if you get it, you win, unless the other team has scored a ridiculous amount of goals—I think. Doesn't matter, really." He scratched a horn. "I'll be honest, I really don't care."

"Jonesy?" asked the goblin who'd made the comment about football.

"Yes?"

"This Quibbitch lark...." The goblin dropped his raised hand on top of his head and gave it a scratch. "It sounds a bit, you know...shit."

"That's because it is. However, you're in prison for a triple murder, Floyd, so shut up."

"It's a fair point, Jonesy," conceded Floyd.

"Right," said Jonesy, clapping his hands together, "Smith, you're up against Shotgun Tony."

Shotgun Tony, a rather large and imposing orc, roared to the heavens and yelled an oath to the Dark Lord of Ruberia that another blood sacrifice was incoming.

Dan swallowed hard, but steeled himself, his bravery augmented by his broomstick. He closed his eyes. "You are Danoclees Dunlorian," he said under terrified breath, "and you can p...p...perform magic."

"Right, you lot, obviously we won't be playing real Quibbitch...'

Eyes snapped open. "W...w...w...w...w...w...what?"

"Think on your feet, boyo! We can't give you all a flying broomstick. A) you'd just fly away and escape, and B) there isn't such a thing as a flying broomstick, ya daft noncey sod."

Dan's shoulders slumped. He should have known it was too good to be true, as well as logistically stupid. And then another feeling overcame him. His heart pounded and it certainly wasn't pumping joy. His gut feeling that things were about to turn nasty was not astute, it was obvious.

He considered the broomstick in his hands. If this wasn't Quibbitch, then what the hell was it? Luckily, or unluckily, depending on one's point of view, Dan was about to find out. Jonesy explained the exact nature of the bespoke game in exquisite detail, the history, the intricacies, and the strategies.

"So let me get this straight," said Steve the Centaur, grinning at Dan. "This game of Quibbitch we're playing is really a Battle Royale, and whoever gets the ball to the other side of the pitch wins?"

"Yep," said Jonesy. "It's like American Football, but with no pads, and no rules." Jonesy chuckled. "To be honest, I wouldn't worry about the ball."

"So what are the brooms for?" asked a dwarf.

Jonesy slapped a stick against his hand with a crack. "Violence!"

He blew the whistle.

As a Looker in the game of faux-Quibbitch, Dan was the equivalent of a scrum half in rugby. His job was to get the Golden Twitch into the hands of his side's biggest forward, none other than Obadiah Ulysses Jacobsen.

That was never going to happen for many, many reasons but primarily because: A) Dan didn't want to go near the ogre, and B) being a nerd of the highest order, he wasn't capable of successfully throwing or catching anything. He certainly wasn't capable of transporting the Twitch across the field of play, dodging violence, and handing it off. Especially as the field of play was more akin to a medieval battleground than a football pitch.

So no, Dan had no chance of excelling in his role as faux-Looker without a miracle...some kind of *magical* miracle, perhaps...

DAN'S ADMISSION TO PRISON HOSPITAL became a necessity seventeen seconds *before* kick-off.

His opposing number was one of Brixton Prison's most impressively dangerous physical specimens. Someone of Shotgun Tony's size, strength, speed, and resulting momentum would be worth millions of dollars if he'd been born the other side of the ocean and joined the NFL. He'd be worth even more if he wasn't so keen on shotgunning people.

What may come as a surprise is that Tony wasn't able to break through the defensive line and stamp Dan into the mud, and it had nothing to do with Steve the Centaur's dominating defence. Centaurs were banned from the NFL for their ability to both drive through defensive lines and to become an impenetrable barrier, just by standing still. For being half horse, a breed capable of charging down a riot wearing nothing more than shoes, gave an unfair disadvantage on the field of sports.

However, even though the centaur was part of the defensive line, Steve started the game as a substitute and wasn't meant to be on the pitch. Unfortunately, Steve had got a little excited at the competitive nature of the day and pre-empted the whistle to charge the field. Jonesy thought it was all good fun, "just a little horse play" he'd called it, which had received an appreciative titter from the inmates.

It was debatable whether Steve needed all his strength to sack the Looker, his own Looker, especially considering the size difference, and that the sacking was from the rear, and that it wasn't really a sacking, more of a horrific trampling. However, Steve considered himself a fair centaur, one who believed in equal rights, and that's why he took the moral high ground and tackled the ninety-eight-pound purported fairy with the gusto he'd reserve for a cave troll threatening his gran.

On the plus side, Dan wasn't dead; on the negative side, once he'd woken from his coma and came to terms with his injuries and the subsequent drop in his quality of life, he'd wish he was. At least the coma ensured a comfortable bed for the night in the prison hospital, and another night of survival.

Dan awoke a day later, but his internal organs and seven of his ribs wished he hadn't. It was a miracle he was alive. Again, Dan didn't see this as a positive.

"What happened, D...Doc? What's wrong," he uttered, when the hospital doctor walked in, doing her rounds. The doctor was a female elf: young, blonde, and attractive as per usual.

"You're shit at Quibbitch, for a start. Jonesy said he'd never seen anyone put in such a piss-poor performance." She was a doctor, just not a particularly compassionate one.

Dan wiggled his toes, just to see if he could. "I remember walking on the p...pitch and then...then there was a...sound, like drums announcing my d...death. No—a charge—like the cavalry c...charge in the Battle of the Torinard, b...back in the fourteenth century. I think I had an out-of-body exper—"

"Let me stop the silly bollocks there," she said with a raised finger. "An inmate trampled you into the ground and you've suffered severe internal bleeding. I wouldn't normally tell you at this juncture, considering the stress of the situation, but there's something about you I just don't like, so I am pleased to inform you your injuries have led to a life expectancy decrease by around twenty per cent, being optimistic."

He closed his eyes. "And not b...being optimistic?"

"Ten per cent."

"But that m...means I'll live longer? Right?"

"Yes."

"Ah."

She looked at her watch. "I've got other patients to see."

"I thought there was only one ward in the p...prison hospital?" said Dan, looking around at the empty beds.

"The nurse will give your injection, shortly," said the doctor, heading for the door.

UNDENIABLY, THERE IS SOMETHING COMFORTING ABOUT A LARGE, rotund matron. Maybe it stems from the physical stability of the larger lady being able to bear the load on wide shoulders and solid hips. Dan had never considered the origin of such feelings, but embraced the matron's warming aura when she entered with his injection, her impressive shoulders barely able to pass through the door.

Although, she wasn't really rotund; she was far more muscular than rotund. And she didn't have wide hips. The broad shoulders tapered into a relatively small waist before exploding out again in the shape of rippling quadriceps. And she didn't look particularly matronly because she wasn't wearing a matron's uniform, but a prison uniform. And she didn't have dark hair with wisps of grey pulled back tight in a stereotypical bun. No, she had a skinhead. And the injection needle she carried, full of pharmaceutical-grade healing power, wasn't an injection needle at all. It looked more like a tattoo gun.

Through Dan's pained and hallucinogenic state, fuelled by the doctor refusing to give him any painkillers, he could discern and then firmly conclude that things were not looking up.

Behind the hulking figure of Obadiah Ulysses Jacobsen were two much smaller individuals who were just as unlikely to administer medical aid. They capered and danced and jeered and mocked.

"Look what we have here then, lads!" said a short, yet thickset goblin. He grabbed Dan's medical chart, squinting at the words which contained far too many letters to be pieced together.

"A little noncey fairy, by the looks of it, Liam," said a goblin identical to the one currently drawing a *growspeck* on Dan's medical record.

Dan's head swung from one goblin to the other, wondering which one was going to hurt him first.

"A little noncey fairy who doesn't know what side his bread is buttered on, Kevin," said Liam, the first goblin. "One who turned down an act of friendship from the Blue-Eyed Boys!"

"I p...p...panicked!" cried Dan. "I d...didn't mean it. I'm sorry!"

"Remorseful doesn't cut it," barked Obadiah, consulting his tome of alternative words. "You should have proven we'd catch up with you sooner or later. A dazzling map getting yourself put in the...sanatorium, but that weren't...leaving to...halt me coming in here for...lawfulness."

The goblin brothers looked blankly at their boss, then at each other, shrugged, and then to Dan they both said, "Yeah!"

Dan didn't need to translate to know what the ogre was saying or thinking. His hulking shoulders heaved up and down with quickened breaths. Testosterone raced around his body, persuading the extremities to damage something small and squidgy.

"I've got a great idea," said Kevin. "Liam, why don't you piss in his drip."

Liam giggled, a horrible goblin giggle.

"That's horrible, hurh-hurh-hurh." Obidiah's sinister laugh added to the evil and the general unpleasantness.

"Don't wee in my d...d...drip!" cried Dan.

"Why not?" asked Liam.

"Because of what he said," said Dan, pointing at the ogre.

It was a fair point, but one the Blue-eyed Boys were not prepared to accept. Liam climbed up nimbly and cut the drip bag open with a particularly sharp spork. "I had asparagus for tea." He dipped his *growspeck* in the saline solution which turned it green.

"NOOOOOOO!" cried Dan.

In a flash of light, he appeared.

Gambledolf was terrifying to behold. He held his staff aloft, and his face contorted with rage. The kindly old man was gone and in its place was an ancient power as old as the Earth, with Mother Nature's strength to destroy and desolate.

"YOU...SHALL NOT...PISS!" cried the wizard. He waved his staff in the direction of the offending *growspeck*. There was no flash of golden lightning, but before Liam's very eyes, his *growspeck* extended, which put a brief glimmer of amazement on his face—before the appendage twisted itself into a tight knot.

"Shit!" he cried.

There was another mighty flash and smoke filled the room. Dan coughed and spluttered and prayed that his asthma wouldn't kill him before he could hug Gambledolf. When the smoke cleared, the wizard and the crippled hero were alone. The attackers had vanished!

"Gambledolf, you saved me!" cried Dan, tears streaming down his cheeks.

"That I did, young Danoclees," he said with a kindly smile and placed a hand on his young apprentice's head. Gone was the storm, and like Mother Nature, Gambledolf showed he had the power for violence, but also for compassion, warmth, and nurture.

"What did you do with them?" asked Dan.

"They're back in their cells now, Danoclees, safe and sound. I wish no true harm to any living creature even if they themselves wish harm on others. Two wrongs do not make a right." Gambledolf ruffled Dan's hair and from his robe took out a vial. "Here, drink this. It will help soothe your wounds."

Dan drunk deeply. "I don't feel any better," he said, weakly.

"You will do, my boy," he said, and Dan trusted him utterly.

"I'm done, Gambledolf," Dan croaked, listlessly. His head found his hands and he sobbed. "I'm done with it all. I can't take any more. I don't belong in prison."

Gambledolf eyes glistened. "I'm breaking you out of here, Danoclees."

Dan closed his eyes. "I thought I was going to die in here."

"Well, you're not," said the wizard, placing his hand on Dan's shoulder. "You are going to fulfil your destiny and save the world. They will pardon you once you reverse the melting of the icecaps, young wizard. You represent a new epoch." Gambledolf twirled his staff. "You will be a wizard, Danoclees. Mark my words. A wizard!"

Chapter 21...

DRAKNARKUS AND MR. SOMERSBY stood on the roof of The Corporation Building. Even on such a fine day the sweet wind blew hard this far above the London streets. Mr. Somersby absent-mindedly played with a rope looped through a pulley and around the foot of a crimson-faced but still-breathing halfling. The boss swung the rope so that Derek the Debonair, like a metronome, drifted over the balcony and back again. Draknarkus held on to Perseus, Derek's magical rabbit, stroking the snow-white fur between great ears. Perseus relaxed into the tickle.

"Your resources have proven most useful, Somersby," said Draknarkus. "Although the moon has only risen three times since we last met, there is much I have learned and there is much that has transpired."

"What did you expect?" he said, smugly. He gave the rope to Rillit, ever vigilant, who tied it to a hook on the wall. The halfling was safe, for now. He tried dancing a jig but it proved too difficult so he settled for a positive thumbs up.

"Exactly that, boss of bosses. I would not have sought you out if another path I could have walked."

Mr. Somersby leaned on the barrier at the edge of the building. He spat at the ants, the peasants, scurrying below. "Then tell me what I've invested my money in? The short amount of time has proven very expensive, and I am yet to wield the magic you spoke of."

Draknarkus leant against the barrier by his side. "It's not like you'll miss the money."

"That has and never will be the point."

She laughed into the rabbit's soft white fur. "Words only uttered by men who already own too much."

He took a cigar out of his suit jacket and Rillit was there in an instant, turning himself into a windshield and lighting the Cuban monster. "Well?" Mr. Somersby said to Draknarkus once his cigar smouldered.

Draknarkus turned, cradling the bunny in her arms, looking far across the city. "I have seen all in my mind's eye. Auspicious omens cross my path at every step. I know of what transpires, Somersby. Gambledolf has not been idle."

"Who is this...Gambledolf?"

"He's an old and powerful wizard. Gambledolf is my only match in the Order of the Magi," said Draknarkus, face tightening. "He's the only one who pays heed to the world we live in. The others bury themselves in books along with the past, and along with their future. His magic is the polar opposite of mine. Healing is something the old wizard excels at."

"And what about your magic?" asked Somersby.

"Mine is that of the shadows." A cloud passed in front of the sun. "The seduction of the night was irresistible."

"Is he more powerful than you?"

"Ha!" she shrieked. "No. Not even close. The powers of darkness know no bounds."

"So why do you fear him?"

She turned on him with a snap of her neck. "Be careful what you say, worm."

Mr. Somersby took a step away. Even Perseus stared at him. His eyes glowed red and his nose twitched with anger and loveable cuteness. The boss regained himself quickly. "Then what is the problem? Why even mention him?"

"The Lost Sword of the Fairy King was created for good, not evil, and it will not call out to me from its place of hiding. Nevertheless, once I have it in my power I shall wield it in a way its creator never thought possible."

"So you're saying you don't know where it is?"

She bared her teeth for a second, a flash of white against red lipstick. "That's exactly what I'm saying."

He folded his arms. "And this Gambledolf does?"

Cool serenity returned, her grip relaxing on the railing. "No. I don't believe he does, not personally, and the Sword will not call to him."

Somersby slapped both his hands on the rail in frustration. "Look, just cut to the chase. The mystery magic bullshit holds no sway with me, woman."

She bit her bottom lip, seductively, and looked the richest man on the planet up and down. "You have some attractive traits, Somersby, I will give you that." She put the bunny down on the floor and watched him hop away merrily. "If you were a bit younger I may have considered taking you into my bed."

"A...bit...younger...?" squeaked Mr. Somersby. Veins protruded from his neck. The old shoe being on the younger foot was a thoroughly unpleasant experience for him.

She smirked, and pretended to ignore his anger. "Only the Chosen

One can find the Sword. One person on this planet is blessed with infinite potential, and I believe Gambledolf has found him."

The boss reeled. Frustration grew as the black witch wrapped him ever further around her little finger. "What sort of bullshit is that? Chosen One? Infinite potential?"

She laughed. "And it is bullshit. All the goody-two-shoed fairy crap reeks of it. Can you believe they built an entire civilisation around it! However, even though it is bullshit, it cannot be ignored."

"So it's true? The fairies established a civilised world that ran on magic?"

"Yes, and there is one intended to inherit all the power that came with it. There is one born who is, alone, pure of heart. There is one who can wield the Lost Sword of the Fairy King and rise up, a power beyond power. The Sword will sing to him and him alone."

"Limitless power," Mr. Somersby murmured. "I need limitless power. Do you know where this chosen one can be found?" he said, evil lust in his heart.

"I didn't, no. But an acquaintance of yours knows exactly where he is."

"Cease with the riddles, woman!" said Mr. Somersby with a snarl. "What are you talking about?"

She motioned towards his office desk, and there, lounging in his chair with high heels resting on his desk, sat Michelle. Business suit, hair tied back in a bun, she looked quite at home in the most powerful seat on the planet. She took a slug of whisky from straight out of the bottle and winked.

Mr. Somersby grinned around his huge cigar. He always got what he wanted.

Always.

Chapter 22...

"AND HERE'S OUR LITTLE TROOPER!" said Plumporious entering through the ward door, a handful of posies in his hand. Mick the Knife was by his side, looking like he'd been dragged against his will, kicking his feet.

"These are for you, Dan," said the dwarf, looking for a vase. He grimaced at the lack of receptacle and placed them on Dan's lap. "I'll have the nurse send one in," he said, between tight lips.

It was the morning after Gambledolf's rescue. Dan hadn't expected visitors. He'd hoped Gambledolf was going to free him as soon as possible. He yearned for the safety of the wizard's protection. Still, Dan was touched by the visit. He'd grown fond of the unusual pairing of dwarf and elf.

"Thank you, Plumporious, b...but where on earth did you g...get flowers from?"

"I asked one of the guards to bring some in," said the dwarf. "I told him everyone needs flowers when they're poorly."

"And the guard you asked was c...convinced b...by this?" asked Dan, incredulously.

"After a special favour or two, he was," said Mick with his characteristic wry grin.

"Do be quiet, Michael! You are being intolerable lately," said a blushing dwarf.

"I didn't think I'd be allowed visitors," said Dan, allowing his lips to almost reach horizontal.

"The guards are quite decent, really," said the dwarf. "Some of them have got it in for you, but we chatted to a few of the nicer chaps." The dwarf spied an empty jug and clapped his hands. He filled it with some water from a glass by Dan's bedside (the doctor had placed it just out of reach), and arranged the posies. "Fabulous."

Dan heard a familiar sound, one that caused his entire body to convulse in an almighty shudder. The clippety-clop of hoof fall was usually a pleasant percussion. "Oh no," said the fallen hero.

"Where's the little shit!" came the cry from down the corridor. The rhythm grew louder.

"What is *he* doing here?" whispered Dan.

Plumporious sighed. "We couldn't shake him off. He says he feels guilty because you're injured."

"I should think so! He injured me!"

"Hello, mate!" shouted Steve, filling the doorway.

"Go away!"

"Don't be like that," said the centaur trotting in, immediately getting in Dan's personal space, knocking the drip stand over, tearing it from his arm, and then knocking his flowers over, much to Plumporious's disdain.

A tapping sound caused Dan to look in the corner. He did a double take. Gambledolf had appeared, gently rapping his staff on the tiles. Before he could say anything, the wizard placed a finger on his lips. Dan reasoned that only he could hear the tapping, administered at a magical frequency.

Dan gave him a longing look, hoping the wizard would magic the centaur's penis into a knot. The wizard wagged a finger, reading his mind. Dan couldn't wait to wield magic, but this time without maiming any of the world's most threatened species, that was, unless centaurs found themselves on the endangered list.

"Well, are you going to thank me then, nonce boy?" asked Steve.

"Thank you? Thank? You?" Dan shouted and grabbed at his head, the increased blood pressure making some injuries known. Since Gambledolf had given him the magic potion, he had started to feel better, but the centaur was bringing the pain back. "You almost k...k...killed me!"

The centaur's fists found his hips. "I bloody well saved you! The Blue-Eyed Boys were going to end you on the pitch and I stepped up to the plate and performed a heroic rescue. Next time I'll leave them to it." He folded his arms and lifted his chin indignantly.

Dan was in squeak mode. "P...Plumporious said you were feeling g...g...guilty!"

"Guilty?" It was the centaur's turn to squeak. "What for?"

"You trampled me into the d...d...dirt!"

The centaur threw his hands up, taking down the curtain rail surrounding Dan's bed. "I had to make it look realistic."

"How are you feeling, Dan?" asked Plumporious, squeezing himself between the centaur and Dan.

"I...I'm a little better now. I thought I was done for, though, I can tell you. I don't d...deserve all this. Where did it all go wrong? I only ever wanted to do g...good." His pudgy little face found his pudgy little hands.

"Yeah, right!" said Steve. "I've heard nothing but bad things about you since being in here."

"Why are you trying to get me k...killed!" cried Dan. "I've done nothing to you and you've t...tried to ruin my life from the minute you walked in that cell."

"Now hold on a minute there!" said the centaur, "Enough is enough."

"No!" said Dan, with unknown firmness. "I've had it up to here with you."

"It was just banter." Steve, hoping for support from Mick or Plumporious. It wasn't coming. "You know, bantz?"

"A b...b...bit of friendly b...banter does not involve attempted murder!"

Steve's head dropped and he stuck out his bottom lip. "But I bought you some grapes!" He lifted up a sorry looking package. Plumporious placed a perfumed hankie in front of his nose.

"That's a b...bag of horse manure," said Dan.

Steve retracted his bottom lip and laughed. "I'm just messing. Bantz! Everyone loves a bit of megabantz!"

"Not the victim!" said Dan. "And I'm always the victim. It's not b...b...banter, it's b...bullying."

"That's just selfish." Steve threw the "bag of grapes" on the bed, which spilled across the sheets. He crossed his arms again. "If ninety-nine people enjoy a joke, then the one who doesn't is ruining everyone's fun. Stop being that bellend! The need of the many, and all that."

Blood entered Dan's face and he reddened with anger. His face was surprised by the reversal of polarity.

It was time for the wizard to interject.

With a crack of smoke and much wheezing from Dan, Gambledolf appeared. "Gentlemen—Master Dwarf, Master Elf, Master Centaur—I am Gambledolf."

The three companions raised inquisitive eyebrows and gave each other a look, which asked the same question as their what's-going-on-'ere brows.

"What's going on 'ere?" said Mick, putting his eyebrow into words.

"Gentlemen," said Gambledolf, placing a hand on the shoulders of the elf and the dwarf, "we don't have much time. I have a proposition for you, and you've but a minute to decide your future. I warn you: your decision will have repercussions on the rest of your natural lives."

"What is it? Who are you? Where did you come from? What in heaven's name are you doing here?" asked Plumporious, looking around to see if any other men were going to appear out of nowhere. He'd seen the same trick pulled in the nightclub Pork, and the finale was spectacular.

"There is no time to explain, fine dwarf. What I can tell you in the short time that we have, is that I am inviting you on an adventure, an odyssey! If you are willing, if you are worthy, you will join me in a quest to the North to find the Lost Sword of the Fairy King."

"You're off your rocker, mate," said Mick.

"The Lost Sword of the Fairy King?" asked Steve, sneering.

"Yes, good centaur."

Steve pointed to Dan. "Surely, fairy boy there is already wielding the Lost Sword of the Fairy King, and from what the dwarf told me after the showers, it ain't a sword, not even a dagger. More of a strangely coloured bent needle."

"Hey! That's n..not on!" cried the wounded hero.

"Sorry, Dan," said the blushing dwarf.

The wizard reigned them back in. "Gentlemen, I can guarantee you this: if you follow me on this adventure, I will break you out of this prison. If you accompany young Danoclees to the North, I guarantee you will be pardoned by the authorities and you will become rich and famous beyond your wildest dreams. You have but a minute to decide."

"My dreams are...pretty wild," said the fabulous dwarf.

"I swear it," said the wizard. "What do you say?"

"You'll break us all out?" asked Mick

"What are your chances?" asked the centaur.

The wizard laughed. "No less than a hundred per cent, for I am an all-powerful Wizard of Anglor."

"If we're caught, it will incur huge sentences." said Dan. "We may never g...g...get out!"

"We're not getting out, anyway," said the other three, in unison.

"Have you all committed such terrible crimes?" asked Gambledolf, checking to see if he still had his wallet.

"Oh yeah," they all said in unison, without hesitation.

Uncertainty graced the old and wrinkled countenance of the wizard, "So, are you in?"

"I'm in," said one and all.

"Then it is settled. Nature has decreed its champions and you will quest forth to save the known world and bring a new era of love and light." He held his arms aloft. "Let the Fellowship begin!"

Chapter 23...

TO ANYONE WHO ISN'T A WIZARD, ESCAPING PRISON IS A PRETTY BIG DEAL. There wouldn't have been over eighty episodes of a U.S. drama written specifically about a prison break if wizards had been involved. It would have been one episode lasting a quarter of an hour, including adverts. Dan had hoped for some flashy spells, but none were needed. Gambledolf magically unlocked every door barring their path, and to Dan's disappointment, there'd been no whizzy-bangs or zooty flashdangos or ribbidy mcloomcstans. They'd pretty much walked out and no one tried to stop them. Gambledolf had told him that the best magic was subtle, hinting that mutilating innocent wildlife in front of hundreds of people and a live television audience was not subtle.

After leaving the prison, Gambledolf had woven powerful, magical disguises around each of them using the power of Anglor. To each other, they appeared as they always did, but anyone else would see a face they'd forget as soon as they'd passed by. The wizard had also kitted them out in some new clothes which had almost resulted in mutiny and a premature and disappointing climax to the mighty quest when Plumporious had been exposed to the colour scheme.

They stood in an abandoned warehouse. Gambledolf brought them here directly from the prison. Dan was uncertain why a wizard of Anglor would need a warehouse, especially one in such shoddy condition. The roof leaked and the dodgy repair job of the front door hinted at it having been kicked down a few times in the past. Dan thought Gambledolf would've used magic to clean the place up, but no. Instead, Dan had stood in a lot of vermin droppings, and one particularly large specimen appeared to be from a human. Everyone wondered what was in all the wooden crates, stocked from filthy floor to cobwebbed ceiling. There was more to this wizard than met the eye.

"The situation grows grave," said Gambledolf, giving them the final briefing. "The ice caps are melting faster every day. The polar bears are dying."

"'Cos of him!" said Steve, pointing at Dan who looked ashamedly at his shoes.

Gambledolf continued. "Master Centaur, Dan did not kill a polar bear, but, I guess, he did maim one. And I guess he hasn't done the cause any favours by turning the zoo's prize male polar bear into a foul-mouthed, crippled, and bitter beast who continues to call for justice."

"Bloody right," said Steve, his fist landing in his palm.

The wizard tugged at his beard. "And, again, the odds of success have been slashed, even though our plight is righteous and for the benefit of the world. I'm afraid to say it has been leaked to the media that Dan is a...a...it's quite horrible, I'm afraid. They said he is a...a...."

"Diddler!" shouted Steve, pointing an accusing finger. "Guilty."

"Yes, something to that effect," said Gambledolf. "The general public are up in arms. Dan's flat has been egged on a nightly basis and, unexplainably, middle-class housewives are driving a campaign to have Dan used in place of animals for the clinical trials of pharmaceuticals, while their husbands have campaigned to be locked in a room with him for five minutes, the reason of which, they are purposefully vague."

Dan stamped his feet in his version of a paroxysm of rage.

"You need hanging, you do, mate!" Steve said.

"You started the rumour!" Dan yelled, red-faced.

Steve folded his arms. "Well there's no smoke without fire."

Gambledolf got them back on track. "There is only one thing that can reverse global warming so that the planet can find a natural harmonious state."

"Renewable energy?" asked Plumporious.

"If only it was as simple as that, good dwarf. The global governments will only invest when it's too late. Their only foresight is the next general election."

"Magic is the key," said Dan, taking on a steely look, and a macho pose, feet spread wide, hands on hips. He'd have looked heroic if he hadn't reached for his inhaler.

"Aye. Magic, my boy," said Gambledolf, slapping Dan on the back, proudly.

"How?" said Plumporious. "I thought magic wasn't very good."

Gambledolf turned to Plumporious. "I'd like to disagree with you, friend dwarf, but you are right. Magic in its current state is not effective. My powers wane by the day." He raised a finger. "However, there is a way. There is a talisman, a concentrator of raw magic that can give us the power we need to shake the world, and the world has not been shaken in a positive way for millennia. My friends, you must recover the Lost Sword of the Fairy King."

"Is it his dad's?" asked Steve, looking at Dan.

"I am not a fairy!" said Dan, taking off his steamed-up glasses and wiping them on his jumper.

"Are you sure?" said Steve, "If you're not a fairy I'd be very surprised. You're small, plump, and a terrible, terrible fanny."

Dan stamped his feet again. "I am not a fairy!"

Steve gave him a knowing wink. "You embarrassed yourself in that prison, and us, your mates. I thought I was going to get beat up in the showers just for sharing a room with you."

"You didn't even have a shower."

"I was too scared to."

"It was all your fault!" Dan cried. He turned to the wizard. "Gambledolf, why has he got to come with us?"

The wizard raised placating hands. "The fairies were a peaceful race, Danoclees. You'll have to embrace their mindset if you are to find the Sword." He cast his gaze over each of the Fellowship in turn. "Each of you is a representative of your people. Your bond is your friendship."

"He tried to g...get me sporked!" cried Dan.

"Now then, Danoclees," said the wizard in a lecturing tone, "you must learn to forgive. Only an apprentice who is true of heart can find the Lost Sword of the Fairy King. Only with the world united can you find it, and that is what this Fellowship represents: a united world."

"But what about the goblins and the other races?" asked Plumporious. "It seems a little racist to leave them out."

Gambledolf leaned against a crate. "After the fairies' one true god, Uubla, was massacred, the fairies bore a bit of a grudge against the goblins. Racism? Yes, I guess in this day and age it could be construed as that, but can you really blame the fairies for not including the goblins in their plans? The goblin leaders committed some awful and lewd acts with their *growspecks* and the corpse of Uubla. Awful. No. Elf, dwarf, centaur, and man are the key. I do not believe it is coincidence that brought you together in that cell."

"But, Gambledolf, does it matter if we are all criminals?" asked Dan. "Am I not p...pure of heart?"

"Speak for yourself," said Steve. "I was innocent!" He stuck his thumb in his chest to emphasise the point.

"No," said the wizard, "your criminality is based on modern law. The Sword will sing to you, Danoclees."

"So diddling was allowed back then?" asked Steve, with a grimace on his face.

The wizard stroked his chin in thought. "I don't think it was, Master Centaur."

"Shut up!" shouted Dan at Steve.

"Where will we find the Lost Sword of the Fairy King, Gambledolf?" asked Plumporious.

The wizard tapped his pursed lips. "That is a question I have asked myself a thousand times."

"Well maybe you should have tried answering it," said Mick.

"Very good, Master Elf," said the wizard. "I have spent decades trying to decipher the riddles of the fair folk."

"So how come you haven't found the answer? You too old and thick to use the Internet?" asked Steve.

Dan gasped and Gambledolf's bushy eyebrows almost tipped his hat off his head. "My dear boy, I suggest you reign in that caustic sense of humour for the journey ahead."

"Why?" asked Steve, with a derisive shrug.

"Because chances are that someone will kill you."

Steve did not take the threatening scowl of Gambledolf lightly, and, to Dan's joy, he shut up.

"Where are you sending us, G...Gambledolf?" asked Dan.

The wizard paced the warehouse with his hands clasped behind his back, his eyes focused on his pointy shoes. After a few lengths he said, "I know the last fairy king died in Scotland."

"Well that narrows it down." said Mick the Knife. "You got any more than that?"

"Danoclees?" asked the wizard.

Dan closed his eyes and took a deep breath. "The fairies would've stayed close to Mother Nature. They'd have been drawn to the areas of natural beauty, the lochs, the coast, the Highlands."

"How does he know?" Mick asked the wizard, who was staring intently at his protégé.

"Magic," said Dan. "It's where magic will be strongest." Hope gleamed in the four eyes of the wizard's apprentice.

The wizard's face brightened. "Very good, Danoclees. Maybe you'd like to have this back." Gambledolf flicked his wrist and Dan's wand flew out of his sleeve. The old wizard caught it nimbly with thumb and forefinger. He twirled it in his fingers and offered it to the future wizard of Anglor.

"I'm scared that something bad will happen when I use it, Gambledolf," said Dan, staring at the wand offered to him.

"When the time is right, the magic of Anglor will flow through you, Danoclees. You must have faith, and you must find the Lost Sword of the Fairy King."

Dan humbly accepted it. The shenanigans at London Zoo weren't for the highlight reel. The screams of the polar bear echoed in his mind, along with the cries of several hundred people calling him a tosser. At least Michelle hadn't witnessed it, which reminded him. He grabbed Gambledolf by the sleeve. "I must see Michelle one last time."

The wizard raised a finger to his apprentice. "I warn you,

Danoclees. We cannot afford to be tardy or we will be caught. It is not just the police who chase us. There are others who seek the Sword. Every day I thank Anglor that I reached you, first."

"What d...d...do you mean?" asked Dan.

"Dan, I believe you to be the Chosen One. I believe you're the only one who can unlock the secrets of Fairy Lore. There are others that wish to use magic, but not for good like us, but for evil. Not the sort that plagues our cities, but true evil, the kind to enslave civilisation. Some want to rule the world, and everyone in it." The wizard's face was stone, but there was a fervent look in his eyes, one of fear. Dan couldn't comprehend how a master of the arcane could fear anything.

"D...d...do you know who?"

The wizard looked old and weary. "Aye, son, I do, and it is an adversary much stronger than I. It will be a race against time, I fear."

"Should I...should I be frightened, Gambledolf?" The wand trembled in his hand.

The wizard smiled. "You're a brave one, Dan." He put a comforting arm around Dan's shoulders and squeezed him tight. "Even though you don't know it, you're one of the bravest lads I've ever known."

The elf and the dwarf exchanged a look.

Steve tapped at his watch. "We gonna get on with it then? I'm bored out of my tits, already."

Gambledolf let Dan out his warm embrace, "Yes, Master Centaur, this is the beginning of your journey."

"So this is it," said Plumporious. "A quest! A quest to the North. We will have to adventure through the country, cross valleys, ascend hills, and all the time fighting our way against the forces of evil."

"Yep," said Gambledolf. "I've booked the flights. You leave from Gatwick tomorrow evening."

Chapter 24...

DAN ARRIVED AT MICHELLE'S FLAT AND RANG THE DOORBELL. It wasn't a big flat, but the lack of square footage had nothing to do with affordability. It occupied a most desired West End location. Dan concluded she was out, but rung the doorbell again, just in case. A minute later, Michelle opened the door. When her piercing gaze locked onto her boyfriend, she dropped her cup of green tea.

"Dan, what the hell are you doing here? Come in, quick!" she said, ushering him in.

She shut the door, locked it, and leant against it, bosom heaving. The tea saturated the carpet which, per square yard, cost more than Dan earned in a month. She wore her running outfit, the tiniest and tightest of Lycra shorts and top. There wasn't a bead of sweat on her soft skin, so she couldn't have hit the tarmac yet. "The police will be looking for you!" she said, looking out of the window to the car park full of Mercedes, BMWs, and Aston Martins. She turned back to him. "I can't believe you escaped—and I can't believe you maimed a polar bear! What on earth has gotten into you?"

He held his hands up, the quintessential bad boy. "I can explain everything, b...but I don't have much time."

"Were you followed?" she said, pacing from window to window, checking outside the flat.

"I don't think so. Listen, the p...polar bear incident was a complete accident. Look, you'll roll your eyes, I know, b...but I can wield magic."

"Yes, I know. It was on the news. Everyone knows. Everyone knows you used magic to blow that poor creature's leg off."

He wilted. "Look, something went wrong. It's all so new. I've g...got a wand, look." He drew it out and Michelle backed away. He quickly put it behind his back. "Don't worry, it won't go off. I'm not going to use it again until I know I can control it."

Michelle played with a lock of golden hair, twisting it around her finger. There was a glint in her eye. "How did you break out of prison? I can't believe you managed to stay alive."

He leant with his elbow on the wall, propping up his head. "Well, you know," he said, cock-sure. It had never been sure before.

"All my girlfriends thought you were going to get bummed and killed."

Dan screwed his face up. "Is that what they said?"

"It's what everyone said. Even the newsreader on the BBC said it, although she apologised straight afterwards."

"Well I got neither," he said, proudly. "I was b...busted out of the slammer by a wizard."

"A wizard?" she said, slowly. "You don't say!" She ran a finger down his chest." Can I meet this wizard?"

"Yes...ah!" he said, biting his bottom lip. "I shouldn't have told you that." The confidence waned. "Don't t...t...tell anyone, please."

"Of course I won't tell anyone," she said, with a pout that affected Dan in many places, one in particular. "But you can't run forever! What are you going to do?"

He took a deep breath and stood a little straighter. "You may find this hard to believe, Michelle, but I have a purpose, a destiny. I've always known it, always in my heart of hearts and in my dreams. This planet should, no—*needs*—to use magic to heal. And now, I'm off to do just that. I may die in this quest, Michelle, and I'm here to tell you that I love you. I'll always love you."

"Your stutter's gone." She took his face in her hands and kissed him hard on the lips. He kissed back. He pushed her back against the wall, kissing her for what could be the last time. He wasn't going to die a virgin. He was an adventurer now. Adventurers deserved to do a bit of shagging. He broke the kiss and took her by the hand. The look he gave, smouldering, sexy, enhanced by his magical aura would have sent her weak at the knees...or so he thought.

"So where are you going?" she said, as if he was popping to the shop for a pint of milk.

"It doesn't matter now," he said, breathlessly, trying to kiss her again.

"Yes, it does," she whispered back, mocking his breathless tone.

"No, it doesn't," he said, pretending her mockery was sexual desire.

"Yes, it does," she said, firmly.

"I can't tell you, Michelle."

"Yes, you will," she said, grabbing him by his hair, clenching her fist and pulling it back in front of his face.

"I...I can't," he said, staring at the retracted fist. He hoped his first sexual encounter wouldn't involve fisting but beggars could not be choosers. He tried to relax.

"Yes, you will, you little twat!" she said, spitting with her rage.

"Scotland," he blurted out a nanosecond later. "We're flying to Glasgow, but that's all I know. I promise!"

She pulled him up and against the wall. "Where are you—"

And then the doorbell rang.

"They'll leave in a second," she said. The very tip of her tongue licked the side of his face. It was back on!

The doorbell kept ringing, the caller not taking their finger from the button.

Michelle and Dan stared at the front door. At first, Dan didn't recognise the pointy-eared silhouette through the frosted glass, for he was caught up in what he hoped was a passionate moment, although it wasn't quite clear.

"Ignore it," said Dan, moving in for another kiss which was blocked by her palm in his face.

"I don't think they're going away," said Michelle.

"I don't care." He settled with kissing her palm. First base was first base.

She grimaced and wiped her palm on his hair.

"If you don't answer the door—" came the shout through the letterbox. Dan's eyes snapped open from attempted kisses. "Then I won't be able to give you your regular Friday afternoon seeing to."

Dan drew back, his face ashen. "No... not...this. P...p...please not this, and p...please not him. Not *him*. Anyone but him!" Dan fell to his knees.

"My *growspeck* is already in its second larval state of excitement," cooed the goblin.

Tears burst forth. "Why, Michelle? Why?" he cried, blowing a monumental snot bubble, which didn't burst, but was sucked back in when he took a breath for more sobbing.

There was a commotion at the door and Mr. Grak's *growspeck* oozed through the letterbox. "DELIVERY!" he yelled.

"You've got to be k...k...k...k...k...kidding me!" Dan pulled at his hair and rolled on the floor, kicking his feet like a toddler. "He always made me work late on a F...F...F...Friday and he always left early. And it was b...because of you, wasn't it?" he cried, pointing a finger of blame from his prostrate position.

Michelle took a few seconds looking upwards into the corners of her brain where the best lies were concocted. She came up with very little. It was difficult to explain the *growspeck* making a mess of the takeaway leaflet stuck in the letter box. Still, she gave it a go.

"How dare you!" she cried with mock outrage. "How dare you suggest such a thing!" She placed a hand on her wronged heart.

"*GROWSPECK. GROWSPECK. GROWSPECK!*" shouted the lewd

goblin, thrusting back and forth through the letterbox, leaving a sickly, acidic residue.

"OK, I admit it," she said, blasé. "But it's only sex, Dan. And it wasn't like you were providing me with any." She said it with the same level of remorse as she did when she used the last teabag.

"B...but, b...but, b...but, b...but him? Him! Why the hell with him!"

"The same reason I'm with you. The one thing my father hates more than green campaigners are green goblins. He's a racist and a bigot, what can I say?" She looked at her watch. "When's your flight, again?"

"I loved you," he cried. "I t...t...tr...trusted you. And with him? You know how he t...treats me?"

"Don't be such a fairy!" she said, with a dismissive wave of her hand.

Dan took out his wand.

"You want to see a fairy?" he said, with a flick of his wrist and mischief in his eye.

She backed away. The tears stopped pouring down Dan's chubby cheeks. "I'd never hurt you. N...never. You were my life, Michelle." He turned to the door. "Him, on the other hand."

"*GROWSPECK. GROWSPECK. GROWSPECK!*"

"What are you doing, Dan?" said Michelle. "I've never seen this side of you before!" She started forward, staring intently at the wand.

"And you'll never see any side of me again."

A purple bolt of lightning flashed from the end of the wand and attached itself to the end of Mr. Grak's world-class *growspeck*.

Chapter 25...

WHETHER IT WAS AN OVERSIGHT, whether the wizard was short on funds, or, as a master of the arcane, he was simply unfamiliar with air travel was unclear. What was clear, was that Gambledolf had not splashed the cash.

Budget airlines brought together the more *enthusiastic* of holiday goers. There was much vomit on the floor of Gatwick's departure lounge. Several people had tripped over several mounds of it. Many had added more when they'd noticed what they'd tripped in. Many simply added more. There was much noise, laughing and crying, mostly, with the odd warning shot fired by a petrified policeman. Some would have said the children frolicked, but the frolicking was a little too aggressive for that. The children were as dangerous and unpleasant as the stag parties, but at least the stag parties were predictable. The children ran rampant, throwing food, screaming, and driving their ride-on suitcases into the paths of the elderly.

Adventurers hoping to save the world should have travelled with a little more dignity. However Dan didn't care, for he was nursing a broken heart, and was keen to begin the journey and the next chapter of his life. Crying into a pillow for the past twelve hours had made him bleary of eye.

Mick the Knife was bleary of eye due to a hangover. He sat between Steve and Dan. Any child who ventured near was treated to his angry stabbing face, teeth bared, crazy eyes glaring. It didn't carry the usual gravitas, for he wasn't carrying his stabbing knife due to airport security procedures.

Steve the Centaur was bleary of eye because he was up all night causing general mischief in the neighbourhood. A paper bag of flaming dog poo on a doorstep is one thing, a black bag full of flaming horse manure is another. The old lady who tried to stamp it out was unlikely to survive the night.

And then there was Plumporious, positively magnificent, kitted out in his travelling attire of tweed jacket and button-down shirt. Like Narcissus, he was held captive by his reflection. He turned the travelling mirror this way and that, satisfied with every stunning angle.

"What a tight-arse," said Steve, looking at his budget airline ticket. "Is this the one where I've got to pay to have a crap?"

"I believe so," said Plumporious. "They become quiet ruthless if you don't buy one of their lottery tickets too."

"Yeah," said Steve. "I've heard about this airline. Getting on the transfer bus is a bit like the Royal Rumble, and they make sure it isn't big enough to fit everyone. You've got to fight for a place, and it speeds up the boarding process. Five or six people die each year from being caught in the doors and dragged along the road." He rubbed his hands. "I can't wait!"

"It's a good thing we all travelled light, otherwise we'd be having a nightmare checking in baggage," said Mick, looking at the long line where several of the elderly had died and been rolled to the side of the queue where they were picked apart by dogs. A single, apathetic member of staff checked them in, and not a single shit was given.

There was a polite, yet embarrassed cough. "One does not simply check in online," said Plumporious, gesturing to where his designer luggage awaited.

"Are you ready, my champions?" asked Gambledolf, returning from the toilets, reaching deep into his robes to zip himself up. "You don't seem very ready." The wizard glanced from face to face.

"Just hungover," said Mick the Knife, lounging back into a chair. "Leave it out. I ain't in the mood for any fairy mystical bollocks. I'm here, ain't I?"

Gambledolf waved his wand around Mick's head a couple of times who followed its arc and clutched his head. His hands dropped to his lap and he blinked. "Bloody 'ell!" he said. "You've got rid of my hangover!"

Dan awoke from his self-pity, his eyes shining bright through perpetual tears. The wizard winked at his apprentice and Dan said, "How come I couldn't see any golden lightning?"

"Not all magic requires razzle-dazzle."

In the background, Plumporious *Vogue*-ed.

"I simply gave a couple of Mick's tired organs a helping hand," said the wizard.

"Maybe you can help Dan's organ," said Steve. "It isn't tired, I guess, but the poor little fella has only ever had a helping hand."

"Shut up!" cried Dan, blushing in front of the wizard who had placed a hand over his mouth in shock.

Steve laughed and clutched his ribs.

"And what's up with you, Danoclees?" asked the wizard after his blushing subsided. "Why are you red of eye?"

"Never mind him," said Mick the Knife, "if you can cure hangovers you're sitting on a goldmine, mate!"

"Well, it doesn't work as easy as that. Magic isn't available to the masses, not anymore, not since the goblins ruined everything that is good in the world."

"They ruin everything!" shouted Dan, leading to an awkward silence within the group. Strangers within a five-metre radius shuffled a little farther away. Steve broke the silence with some sniggering.

Mick was first to speak. "Ah well, stuff everyone else. You can still cure my hangovers, can't you?"

"Yes, but only because I've spent time with you and now understand your chi meridians."

"Never mind that crap. It means I can get wasted every day of this stupid-arsed quest and won't have any side-effects."

"That would be corre—"

Before the wizard could finish, Mick sprinted to the crowded bar full of extremely drunk cockneys waiting to get even drunker in the bars of the continent than they did in the pubs of England.

"However, I won't be joining you for the time-being," said the wizard, when Mick was out of ear shot.

Plumporious' jaw dropped open. "What do you mean, you won't be joining us?" asked. "I chose my attire because it matched your robe. If I sit next to the Knife, I will clash horribly. This is dire news, indeed."

"How will we know what to do without you to g…g…guide us, Gambledolf?" asked Dan.

The wizard placed reassuring hands on both his apprentice's shoulders. "My boy, you've grown a lot in the last few days. Your confidence waxes, as does your ability to perform magic. Your stutter has all but gone! You are almost a wizard of Anglor."

Dan wasn't convinced. His magical attack on Mr. Grak's *growspeck* was his first act since his destruction of the polar bear exhibit. His magical attack hadn't the effect he'd desired. He'd wanted to blast the *groswpeck* into oblivion, instead he added a couple of inches in length and in girth. The fact that it caused the goblin some minor discomfort in pulling it back out of the letter box was Dan's only consolation.

"You will find your magical way, Dan," said Gambledolf, looking him square in the eye, enforcing positivity. "I've told you all along, you are the key to all this."

"But—"

"But nothing. It is time to save the world, Danoclees. Your disguises will not last forever. Stay away from populations. Time is of the essence. Good luck!"

And with a wink, he disappeared—

Through the exit, where he got on a bus.

Chapter 26...

"GOOD EVENING, LADIES AND GENTLEMEN. I am Morgan Alan Whiting Adey, your captain for this short jump from London to Glasgow. Flight time is usually eighty minutes, but we hope to reach our destination ahead of schedule as there is a slight tailwind aiding our journey. I'm pleased to say it is currently sunny in Glasgow, if a little cooler. We'll give you an update when we're in the air and have an accurate arrival time. In the meantime, Hazel and her team will take care of you and make your flight as comfortable as company policy will allow."

Silence followed the captain's announcement. No one had spoken since boarding. They sat, corpse-still, enveloped in darkness. Low-level lighting, skulking below swirling mist, had guided them to their seats.

The plane stank, and not just of the drunken hen and stag parties, but of fear, and not just that induced by the drunken hen and stag parties. There was a cold, lingering stench from the grave: rotting flesh, festering corpses, and a doomed afterlife. Although the smell emanating from the Glaswegian hen party returning home was arguably worse. In comparison, William Wallace hadn't come close to their decimation of the English peasantry.

No one said a word. No one sung a football song. Not a single baby cried nor did a single child complain or whimper. And certainly no one asked to buy anything from the airline shop, only because of the prices. There was a substantiated reason behind the carnal fear, one that had haunted man since time immemorial, and that was Hazel and her team, a new breed of air hostess that appeared with the arrival of budget airlines.

"HAHAHAHAHAHAHAHAHAHAHAHA!" The evil, cruel and wicked cackle haunted the cabin. At the front of the plane, just before the cockpit, an ethereal glow illuminated a face, if it could be called that. "I am Hazel, otherwise known as Hecate, and I will serve you on this flight along with my two sisters."

Two glowing faces appeared next to Hecate's. All three different, yet shared in the nature of the deformities: warts, growths, and hairs sprung from the most unlikely of places. Smiles that split faces revealed black tongues and yellow, sharp teeth. Sulphurous fumes blew heavily from deformed nostrils. The glow faded, the hideous faces disappeared, a moment's relief for the passengers until they realised the monsters stalked the aisles.

There are many ways to reduce the price of air travel in order to undercut competitors, and hiring three witches as cabin crew could be considered trailblazing, or an all-time low. The two were not mutually exclusive.

The lights rose. Witches abroad.

Rumbling gathered momentum. A hostess trolley appeared, being driven at pace down the aisles. A child made the mistake of dropping his toy and jumping off his petrified mother's lap to grab the cuddly rabbit. The trolley bore down on the infant, driven by insatiable bloodlust. The mother pulled the child out of the way in time, but poor Nibbles was decapitated by the wheels of death.

"I'll flush his guts down the toilet if he gets in my way again!" screamed the hag."

"I'm sorry!" cried the mother, covering her face with one hand and offering her child in a way of sacrifice.

The hag hissed and snarled and saliva dripped down her long, rotten fangs. She edged closer to the petrified toddler.

"I'll get a whisky, love," said Mick the Knife.

Inhumanly fast, the witch turned to destroy the perpetrator of the interruption. The fangs retracted. "Oh, hiya, Mick."

"Hey, Prickle," said the Knife once he clocked the hostess's face. "Didn't know you were doing this sort of lark? Change is as good as a rest, I guess."

"Aye, aye. I get to travel and meet new people. And it's like one big happy family here, what, with me sisters and all," she said, jovially.

Mick raised himself in the seat and stuck his head up, looking farther down the cabin, "Old Hellawyn is looking well. Her warts have cleared up a bit."

"Aye. They sell loads of cosmetics on these things," Prickle said, gesturing at the plane in general. "She's been trying all the latest potions and lotions, you know what she's like." She waved a hand. "She'll be finding herself a nice fella soon, I reckon." Prickle put a plastic cup of ice and a small bottle of spirit on his fold-down table. "That's sixteen pounds, please, dearie."

He sucked air through bad teeth. "Steep?"

"Aye, robbing bastards on here," she said, sympathetically.

"No bother," said Mick, casually. Mick hitched a thumb at Dan. "The fanny will pay."

Prickle moved like lightning. Her face an inch away from Dan's, she breathed Hell's taint into his face. "That's twenty-five pounds, you little shit." She opened her mouth and her black serpentine tongue lashed, giving Dan a vision of the bowels of Hades. He recoiled, covered his eyes and held out his wallet. She took it.

"See ya, Prickle," said Mick.

"Laters, flower," said the witch.

Dan's heart rate hadn't settled when another grotesque face appeared by the companions. "Eh-up, Mick."

"Hiya, Hellawyn." Mick waved.

The witch turned her attention to Dan, and her face transformed, taking on a vulpine character, a chimaeric hybrid formed in the depths of the Earth, away from God's light. She snarled. "You gonna buy one of our airline lottery tickets?"

"N...n...n...n...n...n...no, n...n...n...n...n...no th...th...th...th...thanks," he managed.

"No? No! NO! Don't you know it'll save the life of an abused kitten with diabetes, you little twat fairy shit!" she screamed at him.

"I...I... your c...c...c...colleague s...s...st...s...s...st...st....stole m...my wallet."

"Then give me your watch!" she screamed.

Dan held out his hand. His watch disappeared with the witch. He squealed and grabbed at his arm, blood soaking into his jumper. Deep nail marks had gouged out the flesh. He said to Plumporious, "Do you reckon Gambledolf realised how bad these flights were when he booked them?" he asked. "I overheard someone saying that the airline is legally entitled to sacrifice a passenger, once a day."

A small cockney man, decked in the finest of tracksuits and the most extravagant gold-plated necklaces, turned around in his seat and gave Dan a winning, gold-toothed grin. "Saves you four quid travelling with the witches, you know?"

"What?" asked Dan, mopping the cold sweat from his forehead with his sleeve. "They're op...optional?"

Cockney Man nodded enthusiastically, his gold-plated accessories jangling away. "There's a box you have to tick when you book your ticket. You can opt out of the sacrifice scheme, you know, with the ol' loyalty card, but four quid is four quid in my book, and the witches ain't so bad when you get to know them."

Dan's mouth opened and closed a couple of times before he said, "So you knowingly t...travel on here when there is a chance you'll be sacrificed to g...gods of the underworld?"

"One in a hundred chance, mate. You shouldn't be such a

pessimist!" The cockney reached over and gave Dan a friendly cockney punch on the arm.[20]

Dan tried to mouth words, unable to comprehend the man's stupidity. "How many times have you flown with this airline?" he managed.

The cockney shrugged in a very cockney fashion. "Dunno, twenty, maybe thirty times."

"And you're not worried you're going to die, all for the sake of saving four quid?"

"Done all right, so far, haven't I?" The cockney gave a very smug cockney grin.

"But you could die! You could die today!"

The cockney waved a dismissive hand. "Air travel is the safest mode of transport, you mug!"

"That's not what I me—"

"Besides," interrupted the cockney. "Chances are in my favour. Although I thought I was a gonner last year. Went away for a weekend with the missus, but we swapped seats when she had to go for a piss. That was a close one, I can tell ya!" laughed the cockney, pretending to wipe sweat off his forehead. "Phew!"

"So your wife...?"

The cockney removed his baseball cap and placed it to his heart. "Aye. It's the way she would have wanted to go. She was always into the psychics and that, loved the old tarot cards and that, not to mention a bargain."

Dan said, very slowly, "You lost your wife for the s...sake of four quid?"

"Do the maths, you mug." The cockney looked around him, hoping to find more equally tight cockneys who'd understand. "Say we took twenty flights, the both of us means a total of forty flights. Forty loads of eight quids, doubled up to sixteen quid for the two of us, that works out at £1240!"

"But you lost your w...wife!" said Dan.

The cockney lounged back in his seat with his hands behind his head. "Money in the bank, son. Money in the bank."

"Hang on," said Dan, playing with some mental arithmetic "You've worked the numbers out wrong, and then you've d...done the maths wrong with the wrong numbers. F...forty fours are £160. That's all you've saved."

The cockney relaxed even further into the chair as uncomfortable

---

[20] A lovely people. Simply lovely.

as any iron maiden. "Money in the bank, son. Money in the bank."

"It's absolutely disgusting," said a woman behind Dan. He turned in his chair to see an extremely skinny dwarf in a sharp suit, hair tied up in a bun, beard trimmed tight.

She caught his eye and vented her spleen. "How can they justify eight kilograms for hand luggage? It is an absolute farce! The in-flight magazine is bereft of content, and the quality of the pages is terrible! And talk about the legroom!" Her legs didn't reach the edge of the seat. "Don't you think it's disgusting?"

"Erm, I think there are more worrying things than the q...q...quality of paper they use for their m...magazine."

"Like what?" she snapped.

"Like the homicidal witches stalking the plane?"

"They're not so bad," she said, before feeling the quality of the sick bag and tutting.

Dan turned to Plumporious. "What is wrong with these people?"

"Oh, Dan, I didn't have you down as the judgmental type."

"We could d...die here!" he said through chattering teeth.

"Safest way to travel!" shouted the cockney.

"Speaking of risks," said the centaur, "they're about to read out the results of the lotto!"

At the front of the cabin, the three witches gathered around a brightly glowing cauldron, the light enhancing translucent skin.

"And the winner is...," Hecate said, while Prickle gave a drum roll on a bongo made of human skin, identifiable by the dolphin tattoo.

Many people on the flight said prayers, and some cried. Most hugged loved ones, and those on their own stared at pictures of significant others in wallets, lockets, and mobile phones that hadn't been stolen by the witches.

Only Steve sat, on his haunches, squeezed in the seats near the emergency exit, fingers crossed, whispering, "Please, please, please," over and over, staring at Dan.

Hecate rummaged deep into her cauldron before pulling out of the brew an owlet's wing. She shook the wing, flicking off the caustic liquid that burned the carpet where it splashed. She unfurled it and read, "Seat 27C!"

"Yes!" cried Steve.

Dan didn't need to look at his seat number. The other passengers cheered and hugged nearest and dearest and strangers who'd shared in the horror.

"Ah," said Dan.

The glow from the cauldron extinguished when a cold, bitter wind howled through the cabin. Dan was certain that whatever was going to happen next wasn't going to be enjoyable.

Three faces appeared at his seat. Dan backed away but it was futile. They closed in on their prey and in unison they said, "You're going to burn in hell, you sore-ridden shit-riddled perineum."

Chapter 27...

TRAVELLING IN ANYTHING BUT TOTAL COMFORT WAS INCOMPRE-
HENSIBLE FOR MR. SOMERSBY. He, Draknarkus, Michelle and,
inexplicably, Derek the Debonair and Perseus, were being transported in
unquestionable style in one of Mr. Somersby's Maybachs to his private
jet. From there, they'd be whisked away to Glasgow—where the glamour
was likely to end.

Michelle pointed at the halfling; she wasn't willing to look at him,
who was sat in the cream leather chair next to her, his hairy feet not
reaching the cashmere mats. "Does this...*thing* have to come with us?"

Derek looked up at her with sad, but forgiving eyes. "That's not
very nice, miss."

"And you're not very nice, you fat ball of stinking sweat!" Her
vocal blast knocked off his top hat.

"That's not very nice either," said Derek, gathering his hat. Derek's
clothes were torn and filthy, and his face red with windburn. He hadn't
enjoyed his stay at Corporation HQ, which was mostly spent swinging
from a rope by his hairy toes. Still, he was a true optimist and the view
had been superb. The persistent seagull trying to eat his pecker was a
low moment, but not every day can be a blockbuster in the world of light
entertainment.

Draknarkus, stroking Perseus under his chin, laughed heartily at
Derek's putdown. Even the bunny appeared to laugh, or maybe his nose
was itching. He'd become her firm companion since he'd first hopped
into the dark wizard's lap in Mr. Somersby's office.

Derek gave the fickle bunny a filthy look before beckoning him to
hop over with a calling digit. But Perseus the Bunny was going nowhere,
the traitorous cunt.

"How come you haven't killed him yet?" Michelle said to Mr.
Somersby.

He tapped at his manly jaw, thoughtfully. "I don't know. I've never
been so aggrieved by anyone in my life. He actually struck me dumb.
Watching this—" he gestured with his hand, "—this *thing* perform magic
tricks and sleights of hands, sent me into a paroxysm of rage, and I
haven't thought of a punishment suitable enough for him, yet."

"It wasn't that bad!" said Derek. "You never let me pull Perseus
out of my hat! That's a showstopper, that one!"

"That's because he'd escaped your festering hat and defecated all over a priceless Persian rug."

"Ta-daaaaa?" Derek ventured.

Mr. Somersby's eyelid spasmed and he reached into his coat for his gun.

"Wait!" said Draknarkus.

"For what?" said Mr. Somersby, his hand feeling very much at home around the cold handle of the pistol.

"He's going with us."

"What? Why?" asked Michelle and Mr. Somersby in high-pitch unison.

She snuggled into the bunny's fur. "Well, for one, I quite like Perseus here. Secondly...." Her eyes narrowed. "I can think of a situation where Derek will become very useful indeed."

Derek bowed in his seat, a button flew off of his waistcoat to reveal a hairy, fat belly. Michelle gagged and turned away from the halfling, crossing her legs and folding her arms. "Just pull over, and give me five seconds outside with him," she pleaded. "You'll never have to see him again. If you speed up, I can simply kick him out of the door. It will be as easy as that."

"No," said Draknarkus.

Mr. Somersby poured himself a whisky from a decanter in the arm rest. His lackey, Rillit, was not able to perform the task as he was driving the limo. "In what scenario could a halfling be useful?"

Draknarkus beamed at Derek, who, seeing the good in everyone, simpered back, a few teeth missing from all the sugary foods that had contributed to his mighty belly. "Just one," she said.

"Huzzah!" cried the halfling, and gave the air a damned fine punch.

"So be it," said the boss. He looked out of the window. "We are almost there."

"Good," said the black wizard. "We must hurry. Gambledolf is ahead of us. He will not stay long with the group, for he knows I'll sense his aura."

"This...Chosen One...," said Mr. Somersby, not enjoying speaking the words out loud, as if they validated his moniker. "Tell me about him."

Draknarkus signaled to Michelle who turned her attention to things outside the car.

"Well?" said the boss.

Michelle said, without looking at him, "It's best for your mental wellbeing if you know as little as possible."

154 | It's... *Kind...* of Magic

He sat forward in his seat and placed a tight, piercing grip on her knee, not that she showed any discomfort. "Why did you seek him out? How did you know where to find him?" he asked her.

"I was drawn to him. He *is* my boyfriend, after all."

The whisky tumbler in Mr. Somersby's hand shattered. "I...don't...like...you having boyfriends," he snarled.

Michelle couldn't hold back her amusement.

"Is it any surprise she's attracted to power?" said Draknarkus.

Mr. Somersby examined his fingers. The glass hadn't cut him. He was likely bulletproof with all the carbon nanotubes interwoven into the skin. "How did you know?" he asked Draknarkus.

"That she was intimate with the Chosen One?" Draknarkus waited for his grimace. "I could sense it. I could feel it when I first walked through Corporation headquarters. The aura of the Chosen One is faint still, but its origin is unquestionable. His aura will grow with his power. She was drawn to the power, as you are drawn to power. Peas in a pod, the both of you."

Michelle blew Mr. Somersby a kiss.

Draknarkus said, "In the world of the arcane, in my world, there is no such thing as coincidence."

They came to a slow stop, expertly performed by the chauffeur. The door opened and Rillit stood to attention. Mr. Somersby had added a few extra duties to Rillit's schedule since the incident with Derek, the chauffeuring being, by far, the most dignified. They alighted onto the runway where the jet waited, the door, which doubled as stairs, rested on the tarmac. Scantily clad hostesses were a-plenty, waiting on the runway and beckoning from inside the cabin. This was very different to the flight Gambledolf had booked from his dial-up Internet connection.

Mr. Somersby leant against the car, his foot on the wheel. He clicked his tongue while considering Michelle, Draknarkus, and the halfling. He came to a decision. "Rillit, you will accompany this...this...." He grinned the demented grin of the supervillain. "This Dark Alliance."

Rillit gave Mr. Somersby a double take. "But, sire," said the elf, uncertainty tugging his voice.

"What is it, Rillit?" said the boss, through gritted teeth, annoyed at his lackey's unlackey-like behaviour.

A lackey's place was beside his boss whose arse was to be kissed on an minute-by-minute basis. A secondment to field duty carried the risk of another lackey taking his place, and the unthinkable scenario of another lackey being *better* at arse-kissing than he. "Sire, who will organise all the...all the...." He cast a quick glance at Michelle and Draknarkus.

"All the what, Rillit?" said Mr. Somersby, who had indeed lost a great deal of respect for the elf since Derek arrived on the scene. "Spit it out, man!"

"Sex-ravaging, sire," blurted out Rillit.

The two women burst out laughing.

"Get out of my sight, Rillit," snapped the boss, spittle flying.

"Who will...erm...who will drive the Maybach, sire?" Rillit said, desperately, not wanting to leave his master's service.

Mr. Somersby clicked his fingers and a beautiful red-headed hostess standing beside the plane fell in at his side. "It's all covered, Rillit, including the sex-ravaging." The hostess giggled on cue. "Now go ahead, and look after young Derek here. I want to hear all about your adventures."

"Sire," affirmed Rillit, hanging his head as he pushed the halfling towards the plane.

"Draknarkus," cried Mr. Somersby, his hands aloft. "You will find me the Lost Sword of the Fairy King."

She turned back. The jet engines fired up, ready for takeoff. "But it isn't the Sword you want, is it, Somersby?"

"No, Draknarkus, bring me what I truly desire."

The black wizard smiled wryly. "We will follow the Chosen One. We will find him and take the Sword by force. Then I shall return with your gift, oh boss of bosses."

"Do not fail me, black wizard."

She laughed a high-pitched shriek, turned, and climbed the stairs. Michelle followed her up.

"And Michelle?" shouted Somersby over the din.

"Yes?" she said, looking back at him, tiredly.

"Don't I get a hug?" He held out his arms as wide as his smirk.

Chapter 28...

ALL'S WELL THAT ENDS WELL, OR SO IT IS SAID. Eventually, every member of the Fellowship landed in Glasgow alive, and all but one arrived in one piece. Ironically, Steve was Dan's knight in shining armour, although Dan had a sneaky suspicion it was Steve who put him in the predicament in the first place. Steve, along with some sweet-talking from the Knife, had convinced the witches to spare Dan from satanic human sacrifice, and, after a heated negotiation, they'd settled for chopping his little toes off, not even sending them to Hell, just flushing them down the toilet to fall thirty thousand feet and land somewhere in the north of England where no one would have noticed anything untoward for leprosy was rife. Steve had chastised Dan for not seeing the funny side. He could not wait to upload the video onto YouTube.

After the screaming had ended, and then the crying, and then some more screaming, Dan spent a fortune on toilet roll, which was charged for by the sheet, but at least he could walk off the plane, with assistance.

Reclaiming Plumporious' extensive luggage was time-consuming. It was fortunate it arrived in one piece as there'd have been hell to pay. The physical act of picking it all up was not a simple affair with Steve refusing to act as "a mule." Dan's limping added to the tardiness, as did Steve accidentally standing on Dan's feet and apologising, saying, "Sorry, I thought your other foot was the bad one."

Plus, an anonymous, horse-shaped tipoff to Customs and Excise that Dan had stolen Fabergé eggs and stuffed them so far up himself they were located beyond the lower bowel contributed to the delay. Only after Dan had been stretched to breaking point, figuratively and literally, did the adventurers finally make it through Glasgow Airport. Steve, always one to look for the positives in life, pointed out that it stopped Dan worrying about his toes.

It was here they discovered they'd no idea what they were meant to do or where they were meant to go.

"So what now?" asked Plumporious.

"Gambledolf said the fairy would know the way," said Steve.

Dan was in no position to defend himself. He wasn't even in a position to stand up or sit down, so he lay down on a bench in the foetal position and cried some more, being too tired to scream. The weather had turned and it was raining and blowing. His stumps, formerly known as toes, hurt. His heart hurt. His gastrointestinal tract hurt. And his bum was sore. These were bad times to be a sphinctally compromised adventurer.

"Well?" asked the Knife, tapping his foot. "We're waiting, Dan."

"I...I... haven't got a c...clue what we're meant to do," he said, his arm covering his face.

Plumporious sat on the bench next to Dan's head. "Have you got any idea at all? An inkling? A hunch? Anything?"

"Apart from the agony of my mutilated feet and d...defiled buttock region, I guess I am a bit p...peckish," he blubbed.

"How about we go get something to eat?" offered Steve. "There's a centaur-friendly nightclub somewhere in the city. We could have a few drinks, grab a bite, then go on to a club, maybe see some strippers."

"That sounds spot on," said the Knife. "Few beers and a few birds is just what the doctor ordered."

"Such a lager lout, Michael," said Plumporious, shaking his head.

"That's not what a doctor would order me," cried Dan. "I d...don't think Gambledolf wanted us to g...go on a lads' weekend on the alcohol," He removed his arm from his face and rubbed away the tears.

"Well, he shouldn't have put you in charge," said the centaur, aggressively. "If you have any better ideas then I'll be glad to hear them?"

Dan was stumped, and not just in the toe department. He was a bright enough lad, and not bad at thinking on his feet, but it was difficult now he didn't have proper feet. He'd no idea where to start looking or what to look for. Gambledolf had been so vague. His confidence in Dan was unsettling. Scotland was a big place, a big, scary place. Going to a nightclub in Glasgow was probably the most dangerous thing an adventurer could do. Due to his lack of toes, Dan couldn't even run anymore and Steve was already hailing down a cab.

"Let's get on it!" yelled the centaur. "You can get the first round in, fairy boy!"

"I can't. My wallet was stolen. I really think we should at least try to do something more...erm...aarrgghhh!" Dan tried to get to his feet but collapsed when his stumps were tortured by the eternal bastard that is gravity.

"Erm...aarrgghhh, what?" Steve stuck his finger in Dan's chest, who writhed on the ground. "You're lowering morale."

"I should p...probably go to the hospital—" Dan managed, taking deep breaths like an expectant mother in labour.

"It's not all about you, you know?" said the centaur.

"—and after that we should p...probably go to the local library and look in the arcane history sections. We may find something which will g...give us a lead."

"Let me get this straight," said Mick, scratching his ginger skullet. "Instead of a night on the tiles, you're offering us a trip to the hospital and then a trip to the library? The two shittest places on earth?"

Dan was very tired after his ordeal and loss of blood, and rallying the troops was tough on a good day. "Well, I know it d...doesn't sound like fun when you p...put it that way, but yes, fun will follow when we find ourselves on the road to adventure."

The other three companions exchanged glances. Steve stuck two fingers up in Dan's face, and left them there for an uncomfortable length of time. "Wanker."

Plumporious took Dan to one side. "They do have a point, Dan. Libraries are terribly boring, and Glasgow is meant to be a fantastic night out. Why don't we have a few drinks and then start our quest tomorrow? We haven't celebrated our freedom yet."

"We're not free, Plumporious. We are wanted p...people. Gambledolf said these magical disguises won't last much longer and we need to stay c...clear of towns and villages."

"He never said anything about cities, though, did he?" said Steve.

"No, but it was a g...given! If we're spotted, we'll be back in p...prison within a day. The witches could see through Mick's disguise, and Steve was telling everyone who I was at the airport. Security have my D...DNA now." Dan's head dropped. "So much of my DNA...." He grabbed the dwarf by his travelling coat. "I can't go back to p...prison, Plumporious. If we find the Sword, we have a chance of a p...pardon and a chance of freedom. Why waste it for a few drinks and a bit of drunken d...d...debauchery?"

Mick averted his gaze and Steve physically choked. Never had they witnessed such insanity. Plumporious explained to the sheltered hero, "Dan, you really should indulge in a little drunken debauchery now and then."

"Not when there's a planet to save." It would have been heroic if his legs weren't splayed and his trainers weren't covered in his own toe blood.

A cab pulled up. Mick and Plumporious jumped in, while Steve announced he'd keep up. One adventurer dragged his feet, but reluctantly got in.

"Right, then," said Steve. "Where are we gonna go first?"

"To a pub!" cried Mick the Knife.

"To Dick Van Dykes!" cried Plumporious.

"To A&E!" cried Dan.

Steve put his head through the cab window. "Well, the nightclub doesn't open until 1.a.m, so how about we start off at a pub, go laugh at the mincers in Dick Van Dykes, hit the club, and then go to bed while the fairy goes and gets his stitches? Everybody happy with that?"

"No," said Dan.

Plumporious added, "I'm happy with everything except the casual homophobia."

"That's good enough for me!" cried Steve. "Onwards!" he cried, and galloped up the road, slapping his buttocks as he went.

A FEW HOURS LATER, when three of the adventurers were worse for wear and one was being taunted for wanting a course of antibiotics rather than a giant Fish Bowl Jäegerbomb, the heroes managed to make it to Neiiiggghhhbours, the only centaur-friendly nightclub in Scotland, and the world for that matter. Many centaurs roamed the Scottish highlands, and were happy to venture into Glasgow for festivities.

A few dozen people waited in the queue, but it moved quickly, and luckily the bouncers had ignored Steve's accusations of Dan smuggling pills up his bum, which was now a physical impossibility.

Dan had been apprehensive of the nightclub, but then he'd been apprehensive of every pub they'd been into that night. The gay bar was the only place he'd felt comfortable as everyone had left him alone due to his sexually repellent aura. It really was incredible that Michelle had been his girlfriend, even if she wasn't a faithful one.

Neiiiggghhhbours was located down a back alley, as all such establishments tended to be. There wasn't a sign. There wasn't much except dilapidation. The bouncers did not look the kind who'd be keen on breaking up trouble, but the kind who'd significantly add to it. Eventually, they were all let in for a £10 fee, which confused Dan greatly as he couldn't reason why someone would pay to go into a nightclub.

"Are you sure it's a nightclub?" asked Dan as the bouncers pulled back the curtains to let them in.

"Yeah, why?" said Steve.

"Because it's disgusting," he shouted over the blaring music as they walked through the corridor to the main dancehall.

"All the best nightclubs are disgusting," said Steve. They all had to shout now.

"He's got a point," said Mick.

"The ones I go to aren't!" exclaimed Plumporious.

"Just because the bathroom floor gets mopped four times an hour doesn't mean it's not disgusting," said Steve.

The dwarf waved a dismissive hand and chuckled.

"Come on, lads," said the centaur, as they entered the main arena. He grabbed a beer off a table when the owner wasn't looking, finished it in a gulp, and threw the glass over his shoulder. He raised his arms aloft. "This is where the magic happens!"

Chapter 29...

"THIS IS WHERE THE MAGIC HAPPENS," was, perhaps, a slightly ambitious statement from the centaur. Neiiiggghhhbours attracted a certain clientele. Those going to Neiiiggghhhbours because it was centaur friendly were: A) centaurs, B) people who wanted to have sex with centaurs, C) people who wanted to fight centaurs, and D) the mentally deranged who tended to fall into all the categories above.

People came for the centaurs, not the décor. Neiiiggghhhbours was as run down on the inside as it was on the outside. Paint peeled off the plaster which in turn crumbled off the walls. Lighting systems did very little in the way of illuminating, and though the music was loud, it was not as the artist intended. By the smell of things, use of the lavatories was optional.

This was not the adventuring Dan hoped for. He'd hoped to meddle with magic and converse with nature, not avoid drunks who wanted to beat him up. Less hacking off of toes and deep cavity searches would have been nice too. One good thing about Glasgow was that the anticipated violence didn't feel so personal. In Glasgow, Dan always felt like he was going to take an imminent beating, but there was no malice in it, it was just a bit of harmless fun. In Neiiiggghhhbours alone, he'd watched several groups of people beat seven bells out of each other before hugging, snorting vodka, and then going at it again on the dance floor. Dan wondered why the Scottish didn't name the dance floor something else entirely.

Dan stayed close to Mick to avoid trouble. With the disguise of Gambledolf's spell, Mick's legendary name and image weren't able to deter potential attackers, but it didn't matter. Mick's inherent aggression was enough to deter violence and to deflect it to other, more innocent partygoers.

Plumporious enjoyed the attention from the punters. He mostly frequented gay bars and a bar of this ilk wasn't often treated to such magnificence. Steve was in his element, getting a lot of requests whispered in his ear from all races and genders, his caustic personality did not detract in the slightest, and he was aided by the ear-destroying music. His statement of "I will shag anything, anywhere, anytime, anyway, anyhow," had definitely boosted his popularity, a stark contrast to the last time he yelled it, at the start of funeral he wasn't invited to.

Steve struggled with the inconsistencies of people. Maybe he should have waited until the end of the funeral.

Dan stood, propped up by a pillar, away from the action. Steve sauntered over and shouted something in his ear. Dan couldn't hear anything apart from the blazing music. Steve came even closer and bit his ear.

Dan shooed him away and Steve trotted off laughing. Dan took himself off to a booth with his diet cola, the ordering of which had resulted in the barman pulling a knife on him, but luckily Mick had come to the rescue with a bigger knife. Dan sucked up the watered-down beverage, which was fizzing only because Steve had jostled him. Dan blew bubbles with his straw, finished it, and dumped it on the table. He hoped the rest of the guys would get just as bored soon, but looking at Steve and Plumporious on the dance floor, boogeying away, and Mick drinking at the bar, it was unlikely. How could everyone have a great time apart from him? He wondered, for the umpteenth time, if he was the problem.

Suddenly, the nerves in Dan's legs came to life and his leg kicked, like he'd received a tiny electric shock. He ignored it, dismissing it as nerve damage accompanying severed toes, but moments later it happened again, this time stronger. He rubbed at his thigh. That had hurt, although pain was nothing to him anymore. It was only after a third shock he realised the origin was his magic wand!

He took it out of his pocket. It crackled with magical energy. "What's happening?" he murmured.

Instincts possessed him. He no longer controlled his actions. He was but a slave to his sub-conscious that understood his true purpose in life and his ultimate destiny. He strode to the middle of the circular dance floor and people moved out of his way, not in disgust, but in awe.

The wand came alive in his hand and magic raged through his nerves and flowed through his blood. His senses heightened and time slowed. The world bathed in a different light: the golden glow of Anglor illuminated the truth, matter presented as a spectrum of energy, reality in its most malleable state. One had to look past the physical world. It was all so obvious.

But why here? Why now? Why was magic his to yield?

Danger.

The world spoke to him from the ether. Finally, the immensity of his quest became apparent. His second-sight gazed to the south. He wasn't the only one searching for the all-powerful Lost Sword of the Fairy King.

Darkness. It never strayed far from the light....

"It's a trap!" he cried, his voice booming with power. He held his arms aloft. "To safety, people of Glasgow!"

Ten minutes ago they would have spat at him, but not now, not after he'd revealed his true self. They obeyed. They understood. He spoke to their souls. They ran from the dance floor and the bar, out of the exits as far away as they could, desperate to obey the power that resided in the apprentice of Anglor.

Danoclees prepared himself for the challenge ahead. He must move and flow like water. He must become a light in the darkness and summon the goodness around him. He must persuade the world to bend to his will and battle the approaching evil.

"Ready yourselves!" he cried to his friends, who stood near the bar. Mick the Knife topped up his glass from the untended optic, Plumporious checked himself in a mirror, but Steve looked on, respect in his eyes. He understood Dan's prodigious power. Finally.

His friends could not help him in the battle ahead, but it mattered not. Doors tore from hinges. Wood shattered and splintered. Trolls charged through the entrance and the fire exits and more followed, scurrying in like ants on a colossal scale. They sprinted towards Dan, their massive feet splitting the wooden dance floor with every gargantuan footfall.

The few remaining partygoers who hadn't escaped screamed in fear, some fainted, some threw themselves to the floor, petrified for their lives. Dan grinned. Golden lightning danced off his body. His connection to Anglor filled him with absolute confidence.

There would be no prisoners taken this day.

His wand flashed as he moved in a kata-like dance, harnessing Anglor's might. The nearest troll flew back through a speaker with a crackle of blue sparks from the short-circuiting electronics and golden flashes from the arcane. The other trolls didn't pay attention, they were set on their target.

Gold spilled out of the wand like erupting lava. Trolls flew this way and that, crashing into walls and up into the rafters. Some he lifted up and bounced off the dance floor. Dan played with his foes. This was not a fight, but an exhibition, a demonstration to the world what magic was capable. Power was far more than the might of the arm, the pull of gravity. It was far more than anything science's haughty imagination could conjure. There were other forces in the universe: life was more powerful than all of them and Dan harnessed its essence.

Soon there was but one left, and now the slow-witted creature understood the futility of its mission. Dan aimed his wand and lifted the troll in the air.

"Who sent you?"

The troll said nothing, through fear not loyalty.

"I can manipulate the neurons in your brain, troll. I can lift the truth right out of you if need be. Who sent you?"

"It was—"

The roof caved in. A supporting stone pillar collapsed on the captive troll, crushing it like a grape, its insides spilling across the dance floor as writhing, stinking snakes. Dan stepped back from the mobile intestines.

The moon shone through the broken roof. It dawned on him: only one being was capable of such power and destruction—one that hadn't ventured into the cities of allkind for hundreds of years. Dan relished the challenge.

More of the roof collapsed and Dan only just got his wand up in time, sheltering him and his companions, still at the bar, from the debris. Wood, steel, and slate smashed into an invisible force field and diverted to safety.

Mick was too busy making the most of the free bar to notice.

Plumporious raised a double thumbs up. "You're doing awfully well, Dan," he cried.

Steve looked on, stony-faced, a curt nod a sign of his respect. Finally.

A roar drowned the night. Flames tore through the roof and Dan held up his wand once more, protecting him and those inside. It could be but one thing, and Danoclees Dunlorian had always dreamed of meeting a being born of magic.

"Dragon!" he cried, his voice filled with fear and excitement.

The old wyrme tore off the rest of the roof with powerful jaws and tossed it aside. It perched on the broken walls and glared in from above like a hulking carrion bird, hoping for spoils. It transfixed Dan in its hypnotic stare, the green orbs held him hostage. The dragon was a power beyond mere conjuration, this strength was as ancient and as vast as the hills.

The dragon licked its wicked teeth gleaming in the fire of the burning building. Nothing could withdraw Dan's gaze from emerald eyes of death.

"Danoclees Dunlorian!" The dragon's voice was deeper than the hole it crawled out of, rumbling the glasses and optics. "The man who thought himself a wizard."

Beads of sweat broke out on Dan's forehead and his glasses steamed up. He couldn't divert his gaze. He couldn't break the spell.

"You're not a wizard, Dan Smith, and you will never become one.

This world has forgotten magic, and once you're gone there'll be no more links to the sickening power of goodness. Only the last apprentice can find the Lost Sword of the Fairy King, the last relic of righteous magic. With you dies all hope, and this world—what it has become—deserves no hope."

"Who...com...m...mands...you?" Dan managed, although it was nearly impossible for him to talk, bending and testing the dragon's spell.

The dragon bobbed its head. "Strength. Bravo. One should never judge the power of an adversary by the fleshy bag of meat that surrounds it. Still, fleshy bags of meat cook so easily." The dragon roared and its fiery breath encompassed Dan. The flames wrapped around him, yet did not harm him or even singe a hair.[21]

"Doubt your tracksuit could have withstood that, Michael," said Plumporious, grinning.

Mick agreed and nailed a double rum.

"You underestimate me, wyrme," said Dan, and shut his eyes. A thunderclap reverberated to the heavens. He'd broken the spell of the dragon!

The dragon drew back. "What is that on your forehead?"

Dan sensed the symbol materialising on his skin when the fire had consumed him, an ancient rune of old white magic, one that could only be summoned by a being of destiny.

"The Scrotalus!" cried the dragon. "No, it cannot be! You cannot be he! You cannot be the One!"

"I *am* the Chosen One!" said Dan, with a voice that was not just his but of all nature. All of his skin glowed gold with the might of Anglor, and warm and wondrous light spilled from his mouth as he talked.

Dan pointed his wand at the dragon and golden lightning blazed from its tip. The dragon, born in the flames of the world, could not stand the brightness and intensity of goodness. The wyrme screamed and roared, a terrible sound, a memory of the world's first evil.

And then the dragon was away, beating its wings, fanning the fires, but desperate to escape from the world's new power.

"Are you chasing the dragon?" asked Steve, watching the hero approach. Dan lit up the three companions with his golden hue.

Plumporious looked Dan up and down. "Gold is usually so gaudy, but you've made it work." The dwarf examined the magic mark on Dan's forehead and gave it the nod of approval.

Mick poured himself another drink.

"You sure you're not chasing the dragon?" asked Steve, whose

---

[21] His pubes remained flawless.

mocking was over. He gave Dan a pat on the back and didn't even try to push him over.

"No," said Dan. "I'll leave that fight for another day," he said, placing the wand back in his pocket.

His magical spirit had awoken.

He was a wizard.

Chapter 30...

GAMBLEDOLF WAS NOT IMPRESSED WITH THE FOUR WALKING DEAD HEROES. After their big night out, they'd all passed out in a Travelling Lodge, and now the wizard was waiting downstairs for them, near the world's shittest breakfast station. He stood, tapping his foot, his arms crossed, glaring from elf to dwarf to centaur to man and back again.

"I didn't rescue you all from jail so you could frequent bars and nightclubs. I rescued you from jail so you could help save the planet."

He focussed his disappointment at Dan. "I'm most surprised at your behaviour, Danoclees."

Dan took a seat at a table. He grabbed his head with his hands, and used all his will to hold on to his stomach. "I don't know what happened, Gambledolf. I only had one d...drink. It wasn't even alcoholic but, b...but it channelled something inside me. Something ancient and arcane." He looked up with bloodshot eyes. "Gambledolf, I harnessed magic like never b...before. I...I fought a dragon."

"You did what?" said the wizard, his eyebrows bucking like rodeo caterpillars.[22] He grabbed Dan by the shoulders. "Tell me more, dear boy."

"We were in a nightclub and then something strange happened, something wonderfully m...magical." Dan retold the story and included every detail, especially the bits where he did cool stuff.

"I see," said the wizard, stroking his beard, pacing back and forth between the non-branded breakfast cereals and the tepid buffet. "A dragon has not entered a town for more than a century. Hmmm...why didn't it make the news?" Gambledolf considered the companions. "Dan, why are the others sniggering?"

Mick and Steve were close to losing control of their bodily functions. Their hands clasped their mouths, their faces bright red with the effort of subduing untameable mirth. Plumporioius looked on scornfully, although his acting fell as short as his stature.

"I...I don't know, G...G...Gambledolf," said Dan, placing his hands on his hips.

"Out with it, Master Centaur," said Gambledolf.

"I don't know nothing!" said Steve between giggles. Gambledolf's

---

[22] Yeah, they're a thing in this universe.

staff across Steve's buttocks convinced him to talk, but only after another giggle fit. "OK, OK, OK! Dan wasn't exactly *fighting* a dragon."

"Then what was he doing?" The wizard's face was thunder.

"He wasn't fighting one, but...." Steve drew it out. "He was *chasing* one."

"So he *did* chase the dragon!" said the wizard, nearly losing his spectacles in animated excitement. "This is amazing, Danoclees!" cried a joyous wizard.

"I didn't chase it!" cried Dan.

"You bloody well did!" said Mick.

"Pretty impressive, I've got to give it him," said Steve. "Especially considering I'd spiked his drink with acid, first," said Steve.

"Acid?" shrieked Dan.

"Yep, LSD. Big ol' dose too. You halflings are surprisingly resilient little fellas."

"I'm not a halfling!" cried Dan, clutching his head when the blood pressure added more pain.

"OK, fairy, then."

"I am not—"

"You were hallucinating," Steve managed between hysterics. "When you thought you were fighting a fire-breathing dragon and marauding trolls, you were actually—and this is the best part—convulsing on the floor and choking on your own sick!"

The elf and the centaur's laughter reached new heights. The volume offended the other, equally hungover, occupants of the Travelling Lodge, but they couldn't help smirk at the story. Plumporious tittered into a silk handkerchief.

"W...what...w...what are you on ab...ab...about?" said Dan.

Steve rubbed a tear off his cheek and said, "Yeah, the dwarf saved you by rolling you onto your side, and I drew a cock and bollocks on your head in permanent marker."

Gambledolf squinted over his spectacles at Dan's forehead and examined it more closely. "I was going to ask why you'd drawn an ancient fertility symbol on your head, young Danoclees. A mighty impressive set of gonads, I must say."

"The Scrotalus!" cried Dan, rubbing his forehead, sending his companions into more hysterics.

"Be thankful, Dan," added the dwarf. "I stopped him dragging you to a tattoo parlour."

"I reckon the smack must have added some awesome adventures!" said the centaur.

"You injected me with heroin!" Dan shrieked.

Steve waved his hand. "Don't worry. Don't worry. It was just a joke!"

"A joke! A j...j...j...joke!"

"Yeah!"

"How c...could anyone p...possibly find that funny? How?" Dan's eyes widened when a horrible thought hit him. "I hope you used a c...clean needle!"

"Well, yeah, course I did."

Dan breathed a huge sigh of relief.

"Based on a visual inspection," added Steve.

Dan hyperventilated.

"Well...," said Steve, "the floor looked clean."

"You found the n...n...n...n...needle on the floor!"

"Yeah, but it was part of the joke!" he explained to Dan, slowly.

GAMBLEDOLF HAD USED MAGIC TO CURE ALL THE HANGOVERS, an act he vowed never to perform on the adventurers again. He'd also removed the HIV virus from Dan's bloodstream (which Steve objected to, saying that Dan should be taught a lesson for his misuse of drugs) and removed the infections from Dan's amputations. Dan had hoped for more flashes of magic, not Band-Aids and Steri-Strips. The wizard had said there was nothing he could do about the *loosening*. Steve had offered a balloon, but it was not appreciated. Soon after, the heroes left the city of Glasgow with the utmost of haste.

There was adventuring to be done.

Gambledolf had hired a car, with a trailer for Steve, and transported them a few hours north of the city. They'd picked up supplies on the way from a Tesco Express, and now sat on a grass verge, taking a water break. They picnicked on one of Scotland's boundaries, the edge of the wilderness, the beginning of the Scottish Highlands.

The Highlands. Rolling glens and carpeting heathers. Snow on caps and rampaging rivers. Eagles soaring and stags braying. Capercaillie calling and salmon leaping. Pine stretching and harriers gliding. Otter fishing and marten hunting. And fucking midges.

"Well, Dan, where lies the hidden Sword?" asked the wizard.

"Gambledolf, why on earth do you expect me to have any idea? D...do you have any c...clue, yourself?"

The wizard rummaged in his Tesco bag for his chicken fajita wrap, part of a meal deal. "I may do, young apprentice, why do you ask?"

"You're very k...keen for me to use my instincts. Are you testing me?"

"Always," he said with a wink.

"Why?" said Dan, frustrated. He would have stamped his foot if he had all his toes.

"I need to know for certain you are worthy. Only if you are worthy, will the Sword reveal itself."

Dan's head dropped. "I...I don't know, Gambledolf. I just don't know."

"It is a difficult road you have chosen, Danoclees. Luckily, your friends are here to help." The wizard picked something green from between his teeth.

"Even me?" asked Steve.

Gambledolf didn't take his eyes off Dan. "*Most* of your friends."

"Where s...shall we start, Gambledolf? It could be anywhere!"

"As I said, your friends are here to help you. We will start with the dwarves," he said, looking at Plumporious.

"Moi?" said Plumporious, placing a hand upon his chest.

"Yes, good friend, you, or more exactly, your family that lives here over the border."

Plumporious paled. "Oh, oh no. I don't really want to be visiting them anytime soon." He took out his hanky and mopped his forehead.

"You must, I'm afraid, brave dwarf. I believe that within the stronghold of the Highland dwarves lies the key to locating the Lost Sword of the Fairy King. You must seek their council."

The handkerchief was put away and Plumporious got to his feet and paced. "But they really don't appreciate visitors."

"Nonsense!" said the wizard. "The hospitality of the Highland dwarves is legendary."

"But, Gambledolf, they're not hospitable to all—types." He shook his head. "Some of their views haven't progressed past 1967."

"Even so, that is where you must go." The wizard threw the plastic wrapper into a bush. Dan didn't mention it, but it didn't feel very one with nature. "And this is where I must leave you."

Dan closed his eyes in dismay. Bad things happened when Gambledolf wasn't around. "Where do you keep going, Gambledolf?"

"To hide our trail, dear boy. I was lucky finding you on the streets of London. Many wish to lay their evil hands on you, desperate to discover your mysteries. They will not act in kindness like I have. They will tear the secrets from your chest, secrets that could unlock the fabric of the universe, secrets hidden within the souls of all apprentice magi." Dan's blank stare made Gambledolf more blunt. "They'd dissect you alive, young Danoclees."

"Could you tear me in two, Gambledolf?"

Gambledolf's eyes sparkled. "Aye, lad. Aye."

The elf and the dwarf exchanged looks.

The old wizard stared at Dan's heart and a wanton expression flashed across his face, but he suppressed it, turning away and biting a knuckle. "But that is not my way. I champion good. The world spirit will call when it needs you." With a dramatic sweep of the arm, the wizard pointed to the North. "In the dwarven lands your soul will sing to the ancient powers."

"Are you sure, Gambledolf," said a squirming dwarf. "Are you one hundred per cent certain we need to visit?"

The wizard clapped him on the back, a clap full of heart and spirit. "You know better than anyone, Master Dwarf. I believe there is something deep under the hills, buried within your kin's homeland, in the halls of the Mountain King. You must journey to Dunhelm."

Plumporious closed his eyes and hung his head in defeat. "Oh, bugger, no."

Chapter 31...

GAMBLEDOLF HAD STOPPED HALF A MILE FROM THE MINE ENTRANCE, IN THE HAMLET OF ACHRIABHACH, IN GLEN NEVIS. Gambledolf had said it was impossible to get them any closer to the mine, for the way was too perilous and another path they must take. He'd said that maybe if he'd had a 4 x 4 he could have made it. Mick had remarked that the people carrier could easily make it up the drive to the mines, but Gambledolf had said he wasn't driving on gravel, not with the terrible excess fees on the insurance. He'd waved them off and sped away to the sounds of Hawkwind's *Warriors on the Edge of Time*. Even Dan would have admitted it wasn't particularly wizardly.

The home of the dwarves lay under the Grampian Mountains, the tallest peaks in Britain. Although they rarely strayed above ground, their back garden offered some of the most beautiful and dramatic scenery the country had to offer. Green hills rolled into granite-topped mountains. Streams escalated into rivers, and dippers flew hither and thither. High above, golden eagles circled, huge birds, but not big enough to offer a convenient *deus ex machina*.

The walk to the mines proved rather treacherous as in parts there were no footpaths and it was a bit muddy. No one had packed appropriate footwear, either. Oh, the life of the adventurer! Luckily, they didn't need to carry Plumporious's extensive luggage, and he'd slummed it by only bringing several changes of outfit. No evening wear.

Plumporious led the way. Every hundred steps or so, he'd stop and turn back to his companions and say, "Do we have to go?" And every time he'd receive the same answer from Dan, albeit with different degrees of stuttering, "Yes! We must p...press on and d...discover the secrets of the d...deep."

And Mick would say, "To be honest, I couldn't give a toss if we go or not." And Steve would make a wanker gesture in Dan's face.

Plumporious continued his trudge, ever onwards, ever upwards, destined to face his past. But he mostly trudged because the mud had completely ruined his suede loafers.

Nearly hundreds of yards they travelled, so far, they could only see the car park if they craned their necks. And they still had hundreds of yards to go, up and up, into the heady heights of Scotland's giants where fell winds and unknown enemies lay in wait.

Mick stopped and looked into the distance. He shielded his eyes to cut out the light and sighed.

"What is it?" asked Plumporious, fearing the worst.

"On the north wind, it comes," said the far-sighted elf.

"'Scuse me," snickered Steve. "Couldn't keep it in."

"A fart j...j...joke?" said Dan, condescendingly, crossing his arms. "Really?"

The centaur shook his head and then pointed at Dan's shoes, which he was showering in urine.

"That's d...d...disgusting!" cried Dan, running for cover, and trying to kick the urine off his shoes so it didn't soak through to his socks. "My socks!" he cried.

"What draws near?" said Plumporious, rubbing his hands and regretting not bringing his gloves. He joined the elf and craned his neck, but he was not as far-sighted as his elven friend.

"A light drizzle."

"As if the journey could not be more arduous?" said the dwarf. "If we don't hurry, I will have to parley with the elders with frizzy hair."

Luckily, our bold adventurers were almost upon their destination, and fortune smiled, for their path turned to tarmac for the last fifty yards or so, even though Dan had to stop, for he had a stone in his shoe.

At last, the heroes reached the gates of Dunhelm. Set in the hillside, beautiful heather made a natural frame for the great oak doors which were no longer the majestic, impenetrable barriers of legend. Broken and hanging off rusted hinges, violence wasn't the perpetrator here, but neglect. With a manicured nail, Plumporious picked off flaking paint from rotting wood. Subsequently, he squealed and wiped his dirty nail on Mick's back.

"How come there ain't any guards or security?" asked Mick.

Plumporious placed a foot on a rock, an elbow on his knee, and a chin on his fist in a time-honoured stance of yore. "Once upon a time, fanfares would have sounded from the surrounding hills as we approached. No dwarf would return home without one. It would've petered out once they saw it was me, but the point is—this was once a thriving community. The hospitality of Dunhelm was famed throughout the lands for beyond these broken doors are magnificent halls, a place of endless feasting. Last time I was here, the table decorations were to die for!"

"What happened here, Plumporious?" asked Dan.

He closed his eyes. "The Dragon came."

"Dragon?" asked Steve, looking to the skies. A centaur had few natural predators, but a dragon preyed on anything and everything.

174 | It's... *Kind...* of Magic

"Yes, and not just a dragon. *The* Dragon. She destroyed this entire community with a sweep of her talons, and it only took her a moment."

"Is she still here," asked Dan, who was half terrified, but half thrilled about seeing a dragon in the flesh. He'd dreamed of dragons since he was a boy. Once, he'd even chased one. Although that didn't go so well.

"No. She didn't even enter the mine. Her power was so great, she destroyed it all from outside the stronghold."

Mick, too, had his eye on the clouds, but he wasn't perturbed by the prospect of gigantic lizards. He'd stab one if it got tasty. "I didn't think there were any dragons left in these parts."

"No," said Plumporious, "not now, but here, Thatcher's legacy will last forever."

"Ah," said Dan, disappointed and relieved in equal measures. "So it's *safe*."

Plumporious gave a humourless laugh, a stark contrast to his camp giggle. "Oh no. The Dragon left terror in her wake. The ripples of her evil haunt this place. Let us enter." He looked back across the hills. "Say goodbye to the light, my friends."

Deep into the mines of Dunhelm they delved and darkness enveloped as soon as they passed the threshold under the mountain. Only the dwarf's eyes were accustomed to the dark, and each followed in turn, grabbing on tight to the shoulder of the adventurer in front, Dan, then Mick, and then Steve. The unknown closed in and the adventurers huddled closer. When someone uttered a word, echoes hinted at the scale lying beyond, but the black penned them in and claustrophobia crippled. A pin prick of light, never growing, was their destination, and Plumporious led them forever forwards and forever downwards into the bowels of the earth, the forgotten places. These mines once teemed with life. All that remained were the ghosts of glory past and the bitter taint of loss.

"You sure anyone lives here?" asked Mick. The roughest, toughest elf in the world was not fazed by the predicament. His eyes couldn't adjust to the dark and he turned this way and that whenever rats scuttled or water dripped, but it was not fear that drove him, and he was still up for some stabbin'.

"Yes, my uncle will remain. He will not move from this place, no matter what. We are a stubborn race." Plumporious kicked a stone in front of him in frustration that echoed off in the distance. "Still, he will not be happy to see family."

"Are you sure you want to do this, Plumporious?" said Dan.

"What choice do we have, my friend?"

"INTRUDERS! SHOW YOURSELVES!" The cry came from up ahead, but only Plumporious's dwarven eyes saw what confronted them.

Ahead was a bridge spanning a chasm. On the other side stood a lone guard, holding a great axe, and dressed ready for war with thick iron armour covering all but his head. His long, full beard hung down over his breastplate, and his head was completely bald. A tattoo of a spider's web covered his left eye.

The group reached the chasm and Plumporious put his hands out to stop the others walking over the edge. "Greetings, young Grundard!" Plumporious said. He waved his polka dot handkerchief across the bridge as a hello.

"What are *you* doing here?" said the Scottish dwarf, lighting a torch. The adventurers shielded their dark-accustomed eyes from the blinding light.

"Erm...just visiting. Just visiting," said Plumporious, casually, putting his hanky back in his pocket.

"And who are these lot?" Grundard said, pointing the axe at the rest of the adventurers.

"Who, these?" said Plumporious, somewhat innocently. "I've just brought some friends with me."

Grundard considered each in turn. "They're...they're not like *you*, are they?"

Plumporious's head dropped. Steve laughed out loud until it dawned on him that the dwarf guard was incriminating him too.

Dan stood shoulder to shoulder with Plumporious and said in his ear. "You don't have to take this. You aren't the one with the problem; these c...cavemen are the ones with the p...p...problem."

"Thank you, Dan, that means more than you could possibly know. However, my good friend, we must take this road if we are to find the Sword, and if that road is to be an uncomfortable one for myself, then I will take the weight upon my shoulders."

"Well?" shouted Grundard. "Are they like you?"

"No, I ain't like the woofter," shouted Steve across the bridge.

"Do shut up, Steve!" chastised Plumporious, before shouting. "No, I am the only one, like...*me*." he said, choking back emotion.

Grundard called back, "I'm going to have to speak to the boss, Plumporious. I'm sorry, but you know what he's like, and can you really blame him, after last time?" Grundard pulled a lever and the small bridge retracted before he went off to seek counsel.

"What happened last time?" asked Steve, grinning.

The dwarf took a deep breath. "You don't want to know."

"Was it bumming?"

"Shut up, Steve," said Dan.

A few moments later, the rattling of armour meant Grundard was on his way. "Plumporious?" he called as he reached the chasm.

"Yes, Cousin?"

"The boss said you can come in, but if there's any funny business, anything untoward, or even the hint of it, then he has ordered the guards to shoot you."

"That's rid...d...diculous!" said Dan. "How d...dare they t...treat you like this, like a c...criminal in your own home?"

Plumporious patted Dan on the back. "We must accept The King's terms. Don't worry, I couldn't possibly put myself in that position again."

"Pulled a hamstring?" asked Steve.

"Do be quiet!" said the dwarf over his shoulder, before addressing his cousin. "Thank you, Grundard. We will not dally long."

Grundard pulled the lever and the bridge extended, reaching the adventurers with a subtle click, a sign of dazzling engineering. The Fellowship crossed. "You know the way," said Grundard, backing himself firmly against the wall as Plumporious passed.

"You ought to b...be ashamed of yourself!" said Dan as he walked by.

Grundard gave him a confused look, waited until Mick, the last of the group walked by, and followed.

"Please, Dan," said Plumporious, "we'll be out of here in no time, just keep it all bottled inside you. It's what I do."

"This is outrageous! This isn't the fifties! People should be educated now. These p...people need to learn."

"Dan, just leave it OK?" asked the dwarf, giving Dan a steely look, quite different from his usual camp abandon.

"What's going on over there?" asked Grundard.

"They were touching bums!" cried Steve.

"We were not touching b...b...bums, you idiot!" said Dan to the centaur. "Not that it would m...matter if we were." It was Dan's turn to hand out stern looks, this time to Grundard.

The battle-hardened dwarf shook his head and ushered the group forwards. Eventually the tunnel opened out, growing ever larger, until they entered the Cavern of the Dwarves.

"Welcome to my ancient ancestral home," said Plumporious.

One could only see a hundred yards in any direction from the torchlight, an insignificant distance in the capacious cavern. Still, the craftsmanship, engineering, and artistry was breathtaking. The cavern stretched up beyond sight, but the millions of tonnes of rock were held up by interweaving arches, carved from the slenderest plinths, ornate and seemingly fragile.

"If only we could have visited before the Dragon, at the zenith of dwarven power. My father told me stories of when he was a lad, before he moved to the north of England, of how everyone feasted in this cavern and it was lit with ten thousand lanterns every night, and there'd be singing and dancing and everything was fabulous."

"Yes, but not truly fabulous," Dan said, pointedly. "Not one hundred percent fabulous?"

"Pack in the politically correct bollocks," said Steve.

"You are a brute and a thug, Stephen!" cried the dwarf.

"PLUMPORIOUS, IS THAT REALLY YOU!" the cry echoed around the now-drab and desolate hall.

"It is I, Uncle," cried Plumporious towards the golden throne.

They approached the throne where The Dwarf King lounged, one leg over the arm, munching on a chicken drumstick, the hot juices trickling through his beard that reached the floor. The Dwarf King was old, his face wrinkled, but strength lingered within his frame. His crown hung off the other arm of the throne. His long grey hair that mingled with his beard had receded, and a large scar ran from his chin, up past his nose, and over the top of his head.

"What brings you here," growled The Dwarf King, as gravelly as the rocks his people hew.

Plumporious's bright eyes scanned the hall. He folded his arms and did little to hide his sneer of disdain. "I must say the place has deteriorated since I've been away."

"That's no business of yours!" said The Dwarf King, picking another drumstick off the plate and devouring it with more vigour. The juices ran down his beard and he chomped away merrily with his mouth open. The juices found their way onto The Dwarf King's robes. Plumporious placed a hand over his mouth and gagged. The Dwarf King said, "I see you haven't changed."

Plumporious grabbed his lapel. "Tell me you're joking."

"That's not what I meant!" The Dwarf King took a bite of drumstick. "Are you still...you know, like you are?"

It was too much for Dan, whose confidence was ever waxing. "I am sorry, but I c...can't stand by and listen to this, king or no k...king, armed guards or no armed guards." He stepped forwards, the sound of cocking guns came from the darkness behind the throne, but he carried on regardless.

"Plumporious is a good dwarf. He is k...kind, helpful, and always in high spirits. How you can judge him based on his sexuality? How you can oust him and send him away from his home, his family and loved ones, is, quite frankly, d...despicable. Shame on you! Shame on all of you!" He swung a judging finger at The Dwarf King and all who lurked in the darkness.

The Dwarf King cast Dan an odd look with a screwed-up face, making the scar zigzag across it. He said to Plumporious, "Is...is he like you?"

"Of course I am like him!" said Dan. "We are all the same. All of us are flesh and blood."

The Dwarf King ignored Dan's fine words and pointed a freshly stripped chicken bone at the short bespectacled man who The Dwarf King, for some reason, had taken a very strong and instant dislike. "Does this friend of yours know what you're like?"

"He...he—" Plumporious's stutters were silenced by some stutters from an interjecting apprentice wizard.

"Yes, h...h...his friend knows exactly what he's like."

The Dwarf King spoke slowly, as if to an idiot, "You *really* know just how *extreme* my nephew is?" He threw the bone over his shoulder and took another drumstick.

"Yes, I do!" cried Dan. "And I would never judge him, mistreat him, or anything like that, just because he is g...gay."

The Dwarf King choked on a piece of thigh meat. After some violent coughing, the breath-constricting protein had been removed and wiped on his sleeve. The Dwarf King put his hand to his ear and said, "Sorry, what did you say?"

"I said you discriminate against P...Plumporious because he is gay." A hushed whisper spread through the darkness like invisible wildfire.

"I'm not sure what you've been told, young man, but no one has ever discriminated against Plumporious because of his sexuality. This is a modern and progressive society, I thank you very much."

Dan turned to Plumporious who was staring intently at his Jimmy Choos. Mick the Knife grinned inanely.

"What's going on?" asked Dan.

The hushed whispering ceased when everyone had caught up to speed. That left an awkward silence near the throne, one Dan could not quite explain. There should have been an awkward silence, but one based on The Dwarf King seeing the error of his ways and repenting for years of misdeeds, not an awkward silence caused by general confusion.

Dan said, "So if you're not discriminating against him because he's gay? Why are you d...discriminating against him?"

"I don't think you can really call it discrimination," said The Dwarf King.

"Well it sounds like d...discrimination to me, no matter what the reason." Dan did his best to stay elevated and safe on the moral high ground. "You weren't even g...going to let him in your house."

"And for damned good reason," said The Dwarf King with conviction.

"And why is that?" demanded Dan.

"Do you not know?" said The Dwarf King, slowly.

"Know what?" said Dan, throwing up his hands.

The Dwarf King leant forward in his throne. "That Plumporious is a psychopathic, bloodthirsty killer, the likes of which have not been spawned by a dwarf in over a thousand years."

Chapter 32...

THE DARK ALLIANCE STALKED GAMBLEDOLF'S CHAMPIONS. After landing at a private runway, they'd been whisked away from the airport in top-of-the-line Range Rovers, deep into the Scottish Highlands in search of the wizard of Anglor and his apprentice. Draknarkus had directed them, and her magical sense had taken them to Ben Nevis, the tallest peak in the Grampian Mountains and all of Great Britain.

They'd been forced to park up, continue on foot, and climb the hills in pursuit of the Chosen One. Draknarkus sensed his unmistakable aura. She stood atop a hillock, eyes closed, thick black hair billowing in the wind. She held her hand outstretched in front of her, sensing the ancient ley lines. She could only track the Chosen One from the ground, but helicopters were a mere phone call away. One of the Dark Alliance was hoping the phone call would come sooner, rather than later.

Derek the Debonair was frightfully tired. In his defence, he wasn't dressed for the task at hand and still wore the tuxedo he'd dazzled in back at Corporation HQ. The tuxedo had lost some razzamatazz. It was covered in an awful lot of seagull shit and turning muddier by the second. The flat-soled brogues weren't helping his cause, and he spent more time falling than walking. Hill walking wasn't his bag, nor was it any halfling's bag. Some folk believed halflings could do anything a human could do. These people were idiots.

Whereas it was fine to judge a troll or a minotaur on their volume and hardness, judging a halfling under the same criteria was considered a modern day *faux pas*. In this world of equal rights, stamping out stereotypical racism was technically impossible when genetics dictated a species in a language easily deciphered.[23] Irrefutably, 99.999% of elves were tall, agile, and graceful; 99.999% of dwarves were short, broad, and hairy; 99.999% of trolls were craggy, strong, and stupid; 99.999% of treemen were tree-like men; 99.999% goblins were arseholes; and 100% of humans were self-absorbed dicks.

---

[23] By science nerds.

Nothing would grant Derek the physicality to dominate the Scottish Highlands. Even with prior notice, no training regime would enable him to keep up, not even if he followed Claire Richards from Steps *5-Step Fat Attack with Claire Richards from Steps*. No, his slow metabolism, short legs, stupid feet, and his genetic addiction to smoking pipeweed and fags were insurmountable factors and could not be ignored. Although they had been ignored, which is why Michelle threw him into a bog.

"Why are we bringing this useless sack of shit with us?" she asked. Dressed in tight-fitting black clothes and a scarf flowing in the direction of her hair, she could have appeared in a catalogue for outdoor wear, if her foot was on a stone and not a halfling's head, holding it under the filthy water with her boot.

It was uncertain whether Derek's cessation of bubbles was a protest over his captivity or he was dead.

"Leave him be," said Draknarkus, without much care, looking on in amusement.

Michelle relinquished the pressure of her hiking boot and dragged him out of the water. He gasped for life. "That...wasn't... very...nice...," he managed.

"I can shoot him in the face if you want, madam," offered Rillit, testing his bow. A creature of habit, he wore the morning suit of a butler, but with many vests and long johns layered beneath.

Draknarkus raised her hand. Perseus, Derek's white rabbit, popped his head out from her coat. She put an ear to Perseus's nose, and laughed. "Even the bunny offered to rip his throat out."

"I don't know why you're all so mean," said the forever-optimistic magician, getting to his feet and doing a little dance to try and cheer everyone up. The near-drowning was forgotten. A mere jape, nothing more.

"The world is mean, halfling," said Draknarkus, bitterly. "God does not play nicely. Earthquakes, famines, tsunamis, murder, rape, torture, everything is natural. The world simply *is*, and what it *is* happens to be an evil piece of shit, one that love cannot conten—" She froze. Slowly, she licked her finger and held it to the wind, scanning the horizon until.... "There he is."

"Where who is?" said Michelle looking around.

"Gambledolf. I sense the old bastard." Draknarkus walked faster up the hill, much to Derek's dismay. She picked up the pace and she reached the summit at a sprint. Most of the others followed close behind.

"Where?" asked Rillit, craning his neck when he reached the top.

"Beyond the hill," she said, gazing into the distance "The Chosen One isn't with him. The Ch—"

"Don't call him that," interrupted Michelle. "Even being this near him makes my skin crawl."

"So why—*wheeze*—were you—*wheeze*—with him?" asked Derek, who had made it up the mountain with a herculean effort. "You—*wheeze*—should only stay with—*wheeze*—someone because of—*wheeze*—love!" He clasped both hands together and held them to his heart.

"I think I am going to skin you alive," said Michelle.

"That's not very—*wheeze*—nice!" said the smiling, fluorescent red halfling, "but—*wheeze*—I forgive—*wheeze*—you." He lit up a pipeweed.

"Just leave me here with him," said Michelle to Draknarkus. "Please."

Draknarkus ignored her. She sniffed the wind. "Gambledolf would've known I'd sense him. He's covering their tracks. Ha! Good luck, old man."

"Are we going to apprehend him? I've never punched a wizard," said Michelle, slamming a fist into a palm while staring at Derek the Debonair.

"No, we must follow closely and stay in the shadows. I know the old one's tricks."

"Is the Sword under these hills?" asked Rillit, surveying the ground beneath him, kicking a rock at the halfling who took it full in the knackers and fell to his knees.

"Shot!" cried Derek, between soothing rubs.

Draknarkus said, "No, elf, I don't believe it is. I believe that Gambledolf has charged Michelle's squeeze...." Michelle shuddered. "...with another errand."

"Stop being so cryptic!" demanded Michelle. "What's going on?"

"I've always appreciated your directness." Draknarkus pointed across a valley, at the base of a mountain capped with a dusting of snow. Her finger did not waver. "The Fellowship are with The Dwarf King, and Gambledolf hopes that something hides in the depths, something to help find the Sword."

"What now?" said the elf butler. "Shall we follow Gambledolf?"

"No," she said, pacing. "We must avoid him."

"Then what are we doing on this stupid hill?" asked Michelle.

"Good question," said the dark wizard, pondering. She turned in a circle, taking in every horizon, her dark eyes flitting this way and that. She concluded, almost smugly, "I think it's time we tested the Fellowship."

"Test them? How?" asked Rillit. "We must find the Sword. My master will not be pleased if we are not forever vigilant on our mission."

"Patience, arsekisser. We must play a sly game. We cannot find the Sword without the Chosen One." Draknarkus tapped her lips in thought and looked out to the west. "Yes, maybe we should see how the dwarves and their guests cope with a visit from the old enemy...."

Chapter 33...

BOTH STEVE AND DAN STOOD WITH ARMS CROSSED AND HEADS TILTED TO THE SIDE, CONTEMPLATING THE ACCUSATION. Plumporious being a "psychopathic, bloodthirsty killer, the likes of which have not been spawned by a dwarf in over a thousand years," on the surface, appeared somewhat far-fetched.

Steve said to Dan behind cupped hand, "Are you sure he didn't say he was the most emphatic man-thirsty mincer, the likes of which have not been spawned in a thousand years?" As usual, the whisper was heard by all, subtlety not being Steve's strong point.

Plumporious blushed. "The two titles aren't mutually exclusive."

Steve placed the back of his hand on Plumporious's burning cheek. "Psychopaths don't blush."

The psychopath turned a deeper shade of red, looking more at home at a side of a garden pond holding a fishing rod, rather than in a fifty-man brawl hooking someone's eye out with a claw hammer.

"Although I don't agree with your homophobic comments, Steve," said Dan, "I'm w...with you on the disbelief."

"Hmmmm...," said a deliberating centaur, his chin on his fist, his other hand supporting the elbow. He said to The Dwarf King, "You're definitely talking bollocks."

"Yeah," backed up Dan, "you could have at least come up with something a bit b...better than that, I mean, I c...can understand why you're embarrassed by your homophobia, but...but c...come on, he's not a psychopath!" Dan looked to Mick who merely shrugged. The king frowned, and then, sinking into his throne, let out a long and laboured exhalation. "I wish you were right, but unfortunately you are the one mistaken. How long have you known my nephew?"

"Well, I only met him a week or so ago," said Dan.

"And where did you meet him?" asked The Dwarf King.

"In...erm...." Dan coughed, embarrassed, and said under his breath, "In p...prison."

The Dwarf King did not look convinced. "You? In prison?"

"It was a big misunderstanding." Dan waved his hands in front of him, denying all accusations of—

"Diddling," said Steve.

The Dwarf King formed fists, and beyond the lights, in the

darkness, there was a murmur and talk of "hanging being too good" and the demands of "five minutes alone in a room with the bastard." Several dwarves left the hall to make comments online.

"No...No!" Dan turned on the giggling centaur. "Will you stop that, please?"

"No," said Steve, deadpan.

"He's making it up!" said Dan to The Dwarf King. "I was put in p...p...prison, because of a mistake!"

"And what a mistake!" cried Steve. "Only fifteen years old. Fifteen!"

"Will you shut up!" Dan snapped.

"With the makeup she looked older, I'll give you that, but—"

"THE POINT IS!" cried Dan. "Plumporious was not inside b...because of a violent temper, he was inside for the same reason you have ousted him: d...discrimination!"

"And that's why he was sent to the highest security prison in Europe, was it?" asked Mick, grinning.

"Yes," said Dan with finality, before contemplating the Knife's comment. "Although...actually that's a g...good point."

Plumporious now matched the colour of his outstanding ruby travelling cords. "I...I think I have some explaining to do, Dan," said the embarrassed dwarf. "I may not have been completely honest with you."

"You can tell me, Plumporious," said the non-judgmental adventurer.

"I was not inside because I *killed* anyone, let's get that straight, right from the start."

"Killed?" said Dan, struggling to get his tongue around the word.

"Admittedly, all those involved in the—'*fracas*,'" he added the quotation marks with his fingers, "probably wish they were dead, but I did *not* kill them."

"Although one of them is unlikely to survive," added Mick.

"Thank you, Michael!" added Plumporious. "I am quite capable of telling the story myself." He gave the elf one of his more fearsome looks, which only received another wry grin in return.

"As I was saying, I was the victim in this particular set of circumstances. I was insulted, verbally, and there was also the threat of physical violence in the air, too. An orc and a troll decided to pick on me when I was walking home, and I was forced to take action."

Mick finished the story: "He battered both of them unconscious and left them in dumpsters. He made it all the way home, and because his rage could not be satiated, he took an angle grinder back to the scene of the crime. He took all the troll's fingers off and was forced to go to

B&Q to buy some more grinding discs before coming back for his feet."

"And the orc?" said Dan, a cold sweat forming on his body.

"Oh, he's in a *really* bad way."

Dan stared at the dwarf, who casually pushed a lock of hair over his ear after examining the split end. "Are you...are you sure?" asked Dan of Mick.

"That's tame by his standards," said The Dwarf King.

"So you didn't banish him because he was g...gay?"

"God no. A lot of gay dwarves move to the city; most youngsters do, really. It's a simple life here in the mines, dirty work too, with no time for fashion or anything like that. Plumporious, there, would never have stayed, even if he wasn't kicked out. Although, the diva thing didn't help matters. Combining that with the ferocity of a sabre-toothed mantadragon, the pain threshold of the nerveless spiderharpy..." The Dwarf King shook his head and rubbed his face tiredly. "My brother said it took half of the Royal Special Guard armed with water cannons and tear gas to calm him down after he saw last year's Autumn range."

"Plumporious?" asked Dan of the cross-armed dwarf.

"It was a travesty, Dan," he said, with a stamp of a Jimmy Choo.

Dan wasn't giving up on his friend. He said to The Dwarf King, "Even so, you could have tried helping. You should channel his anger and his c...creativity into something c...constructive."

"We tried. We tried everything. But he's a psycho!"

Plumporious held up a hand. "Guilty, as charged."

"He had a loving upbringing, he's well-educated, he's had every opportunity given to him," said The Dwarf King.

"He's batshit mental," added Grundard.

"What about counselling?" offered Dan.

"No one will work with him. Not since he hung a psychiatrist by the eyelids because he wore socks and boat shoes."

Plumporious slammed his hand down on to his fist. "That was justified!"

Again, The Dwarf King shook his head, tiredly. "The only reason he wasn't put in prison for the rest of his life was that he never killed another dwarf."

"What has he killed?" asked Dan, staring unbelievingly at the small-statured dwarf who was polishing a cufflink.

"I think he has added all forms of sentient life to his list. He really is the harbinger of death," said The Dwarf King.

"He's batshit mental," said Grundard again.

"But I've never seen him lose his temper," said Dan.

"It's only a matter of—"

The clanging sound of armour hitting stone interrupted The Dwarf King, as a young dwarf ran into the hall. He bowed and took a knee, regaining his breath. His beard was short and he wasn't thickset, but wiry, if any dwarf could be called such a thing. He scanned the room, surprised by the visitors, spied Plumporious, and screamed.

"What is it Pernik?" said The Dwarf King, hurriedly.

"I'm sorry!" cried Pernik, ripping off his coat and throwing it on to the floor. "I didn't know you were here, Plumporious! I should never have worn black and navy, I'm sorry!"

"Forget that!" shouted The Dwarf King. "What do you have to report?"

Tears were in the young dwarf's eyes, but not because of a fatal fashion *faux pas*. "Goblins, sire! The goblins are coming!"

Chapter 34...

PANIC CONSUMED THE THRONE ROOM.

Goblins.

The old enemy.

Only the four adventurers, The Dwarf King, and Grundard had remained calm. The Dwarf King's subjects had scrambled in blind panic, wailing, tearing at their beards, embracing each other and crying. Eventually, The Dwarf King had calmed his subjects, and Pernik had led The Dwarf King and a dozen chosen warriors, along with the four mighty companions, towards the surface. They took up positions in a lookout chamber where Pernik believed the goblins would emerge. In days of yore, this was a strategic position, for it intersected two valleys, routes of attack from over-ground foes. Now it overlooked a car park. While they waited and the tension became palpable, Pernik briefed them on the forthcoming onslaught.

"There are many," said Pernik, his face pale with fright. "I've never seen so many."

"Calm yourself, boy," said The Dwarf King.

"We're doomed. This time we're doomed!" Pernik cried.

"And I said calm yourself!" The Dwarf King slapped him, trying to snap the young dwarf out of his despair, but the king was still strong and the slap took Pernik to the floor, where he remained, sobbing into his beard.

"No strength left under the mountains," muttered The Dwarf King under his breath.

"Fanny," said Grundard.

And then they heard it.

Booom. Booom. Booom.

"DRUMS! Did you hear that?" cried another dwarf.

And now the rest of the dwarves, with the exception of Plumporious, Grundard, and The Dwarf King, were wailing, beating their breasts, and tearing at their beards.

The Dwarf King muttered into Grundard's ear, "No strength left at all, my friend."

"Aye, fannies," said Grundard.

The ancient enemy was here. Since time immemorial the goblin had been the dwarf's bitterest foe. Both shied away from the sun, and both sought the comfort of the deep. The battles had been long, bloody, terrible, and difficult to see.

Booom. Booom. Booom.

Relentless drums reverberated, shaking the chamber walls and the nerves of the dwarves who'd endured torment for so long.

Booom. Booom. Booom.

Plumporious scratched his head. "Erm, why are you all so scared?" he asked. "The battle prowess of the Highland dwarves is legendary."

"We are a weakened community," said The Dwarf King. "Our strength waned, even before the Great Dragon. Only Grundard and I have experienced war. Now, the only dwarven bastion of power lies in the north of England, where your father is lord. The goblins know this. They know there is nothing we can do."

"But what about the p...police?" said Dan.

The Dwarf King laughed without mirth. "This is an isolated community."

Booom. Booom. Booom.

"Come," he said, forlornly, unlocking a great door that opened to the hillside. "We must defend ourselves as best we can."

"But you have us now," said Dan to The Dwarf King.

Steve burst out laughing. "Us?"

"Well," said Dan, "we have you, Steve, a mighty centaur."

Steve crossed his arms. "I ain't getting involved. Not my fight." He wasn't being cowardly, just an arsehole.

"Well we've got Mick and Plumporious," said Dan, taking out his wand. "And my magic!"

The elf, dwarf, and centaur all laughed at that, taking away Dan's newly found fire. He put the wand back in his pocket.

"No," said The Dwarf King, firmly. "We cannot risk a revenge attack from the goblins. We will not have the strength to defend ourselves once you are gone, and they will reap vengeance."

"What are you going to do then?" asked Dan.

The Dwarf King opened the door to the hills. "I wish I knew," he said, heavily.

The sunshine blinded all who had spent long in the deep. The ancient goblins never attacked during the day. Time changes everything. This new generation of goblins only roamed when the sun was high and blazing.

The dwarves and the companions took positions outside in the car park for people visiting the mine. It used to be brimming with top-end motors, and the dwarven lords made a fortune with pay-and-display parking. Those days were gone, and today it was more trouble than good, attracting persistent, local, late-night perverts. They'd tried writing to the council, but to no avail.

Booom. Booom. Booom.

Smoke billowed over the hillside, marking their approach, thick plumes of it reaching into the sky, choking the air. They travelled at pace, dangerously so. But it mattered not. Their lives were cheap and adrenaline was all life offered.

The goblins were here.

The vehicles that carried them were as deadly as they were horrifying. Six sat crammed in a Vauxhall Nova, 1.4 SRi, windows open, elbows propped on frames. The Nova had been lowered and a body kit applied. Seven had managed to fit into a Renault 5 GT Turbo. The exhaust roared, ready to fall off at a moment's notice. A battered Escort XR3i loomed menacing with several goblins hanging off the spoiler. And there were many others, terrible, terrible others, a nightmare from the blackest night of any honest MOT tester, not that any of these vehicles had MOTs, or the possibility of one...or insurance...or legal tyres.

Drums: no instrument inspired fear like it. Drum and Bass music was the enemy of the old, and the dwarves clutched their ears and ailing hearts. Car boots full of subwoofers sent out merciless bass, penetrating dwarven cores, shaking ventricles to the point of arrest and eardrums to the point of bursting.

A teenage goblin leaning out of the passenger window of a Vauxhall Corsa threw an egg that hit The Dwarf King on the chin, covering his beard in yolk. The goblins cheered triumphantly.

"Ace chuck, Jordan!" cried a yob.

"Little bastards!" yelled The Dwarf King, shaking his fist at the horrible, jeering teenage goblins wrapped in hideous track suits, baseball caps, and pus-filled acne.

"Surely there's something you can do?" argued Dan, as the goblins continued their assault, do-nutting the cars, sending waves of burned rubber into dwarven lungs.

"There's only a few of us left," said The Dwarf King, rubbing his yolky beard with his coat sleeve and coughing up some tyre smoke. "Only Grundard and myself can fight with our fists."

"But I heard guns being cocked when we were in the hall."

The Dwarf King shook his head sadly. "All show, I'm afraid. If we do anything now they'll just bring back reinforcements. They live on a vast council estate a couple of miles down the road."

Plumporious's petrified eyes were locked on The Dwarf King's beard. The egg dripping onto The Dwarf King's clothes horrified him, and he backed away from the goblins, laughing and jeering and opening fresh egg cartons.

"They're just bullies!" said Grundard. "They're always messing around with the old folks. It started as kids' stuff—egging their doors, ding dong dash—but it turned nastier. Soon it was stealing, pushing them over, throwing buckets of cold water over them. One poor old fella got pneumonia and died."

"And the police do nothing?" said Dan, furious.

"No, 'course not. They don't even go down the street these little bastards live on," said Grundard.

"Why don't we go inside," said Plumporious, grabbing Mick's arm and dragging him towards the entrance of the mine. Plumporious' saucer-wide eyes were unable to escape the hypnotic fix of egg-splattered fabric.

Dan's fire waned when the goblins parked up and got out of their cars. He wasn't keen to stand and fight now there was the possibility of an actual fight. "Maybe you're right, maybe we should go b...b...back inside."

"You're such a bunch of wimps," said Mick.

"Well are you going to do something, Michael?" asked Plumporious, hopefully.

"Ain't my fight," said Mick, as unconcerned as the centaur, who still laughed about the buckets of cold water being thrown over the elderly.

"Then come on in!" cried Plumporious, somewhat desperately. "I fear they're going to throw another egg and my travelling jacket is, naturally, dry-clean only. Come quick."

The goblins neared, continuing their brutal assault with grammatically questionable abuse. They were all male, and all were identical with different hue of tracksuit the only distinguishing feature. Their hair was greased down across foreheads, with baseball caps worn at identical angles as mathematically impressive as it was fashionably calamitous. Each pair of tracky bottoms were worn low, with the ever-present threat of revealed *growspecks* adding to the horror. If there's one thing worse than a goblin, it was a teenage goblin.

And then it happened.

And in slow motion.

For cliché dictates it to be so.

Running into the forefront of the battleground, a spotty goblin threw an egg in a direction he really shouldn't have.

Plumporious watched it all the way, but it was too late. It was too late for everyone. The avian ovarian missile struck him on the tweed travelling jacket, his favourite tweed travelling jacket, and he recoiled as if shot. He fell, knees striking the ground at the same time as the shell. He clasped the wound.

"I'm hit," he managed to the heavens, under laboured breath.

"It's all right," said Dan. "It's just a bit of yolk. It will rub out."

"It's all over! Game over, man! Game over! Go without me," he said, sobbing his heart out. "Leave me to die!" His normally rosy cheeks were deathly pale.

"Don't be silly," said Dan. "Come on!" he tried to pull the dwarf to his knees.

"Leave me!" Plumporious roared.

Dan jumped back. There was no camp chuckle, no quivering lip, no Plumporious. The dwarf fell forwards, his head cracking on the car park tarmac. He shook and writhed on the ground, his hands making fists, the cracking of bone spoke of a hidden power.

"What's happened?" asked Dan to Grundard and The Dwarf King. They completely ignored the goblins, only ten yards away, several of whom had weapons in their hands: blades, chains, and baseball bats. Grundard and the king stared intently at their quivering relative.

The Dwarf King said, "We must leave here."

"We can't leave him," said Dan.

"Run!" said TheDwarf King. "RUN!"

Mick was first to leg it. He'd seen someone spill a pint on Plumporious's suede shoes before, and even though Mick, in his stabbin' career, had been covered in more blood than most surgeons, there were some things he didn't want to see again. Everyone followed, Dan last— morbid curiosity and the lack of toes getting the better of him.

Another egg crashed into the prone dwarf. And another. And another. He writhed with every strike, with every crack of shell and spilling of albumen. When the goblins were just a few paces away, he stopped moving, dead still, and the goblins prepared to have their wicked fun.

The dwarf's eyes snapped open. He jumped to his feet. The first goblin entering the short range of plump fists was punched so hard in the face that six of his teeth came out with a brace attached. The goblin's head snapped right then left, and then back to centre. He would have mouthed "how?" but he didn't have a mouth left. Instead, he fell, unconscious. The teeth—still airborne—hit another goblin in the temple with such force that he was knocked out too.

This was not a snap of anger. This was the beginning of a long and extended onslaught of Achillean rage; one not quenched by power and glory, but only by drowning the enemy in their own blood.

A goblin stared from his two unconscious friends to the dwarf and back again. The knife in his hand wasn't the formidable weapon it was when he'd taken it from his mum's cutlery drawer. He considered the best course of action, but Plumporious's flying left hook took out eight of his teeth before any successful conclusions could be reached.

Plumporious's eyes burned red and he raised his fists to the heavens, yelling a brutal war cry: "ELPEEHS PU EKAW, LAER ERA SLIARTMEHC!"

The dwarves and the companions stood by the entrance to the mine. The Dwarf King said to Dan, "That's the secret war cry of our forefathers. It is passed down from king to king as part of our history. He'd never have heard it before, yet somehow he is a berserker of the old age, albeit, a camp, well-dressed berserker."

A group of five goblins got out of the XR3i and attempted to apprehend the dwarf. A raging ball of chub, Plumporious's fists carried weight beyond their mass. Punches and kicks bounced off him. Whether they damaged him wasn't discernible, but they didn't slow him. Within moments four of the five goblins were unconscious. The last wished he was, as his head was being repeatedly crushed between car door and chassis.

"You're dead, mister! You're all dead" shouted a particularly short and skinny goblin, running back to his car.

Plumporious chased after him, but the rage in his fists did not add speed to his legs. The goblin got into a passenger seat and the driver yelled out of the window, "We're gonna get backup! You're all dead, all of ya!" before racing away—after some obligatory wheel-spinning.

The Dwarf King's head fell into his hands. "We're done for. We're all done for."

But Plumporious wasn't finished.

He jumped into a car, the owner of which would be unable to drive for some time, as feet and hands and eyes were required for the operation of a motor vehicle. Plumporious slammed his foot down, and in a shower of gravel, set off in hot pursuit.

"Should we go after him?" asked Dan, stood on tipstumps looking over the horizon at the disappearing dwarf.

"I don't know," said The Dwarf King, pulling his beard.

Mick laughed. "Leave him well alone when he's in this sort of mood."

"But he's driving off to take on an army of goblins. Shouldn't we help?" said Dan.

"Nah," said Mick. "There's nothing you can do for them now."

Chapter 35...

THERE WAS A TIMID KNOCK ON THE DOOR. It was an embarrassed knock, a remorseful knock. Grundard had waited in the surface chamber for the AWOL mass murderer/fashion icon. Grundard opened the door, ancient iron hinges creaking. There, stood with metaphorical cap in hand and looking extremely sheepish, was Plumporious. He was filthy. His face was covered in soot and he appeared to have been rolling in blood and entrails.

Grundard tutted like a parent might if a child turned up later than his curfew time because he was too engrossed in a game of Headers and Volleys. "You better come in."

Everyone sat waiting in the throne room. The Dwarf King tapped his foot impatiently while Dan chewed on his nails worrying about the mental state of his friend.

"Well?" demanded The Dwarf King, looking at his watch. "What time do you call this?"

Plumporious held up apologetic blood-stained hands. "I'm sorry. I realise things may have got a little...out of hand."

"Out of hand!" shrieked The Dwarf King. "Wait till I tell your father you've been up to your old tricks again!"

"Please don't tell Daddy! I beg you!" cried the dwarf, falling to his knees, clutching his chubby murdering mitts together in hope and prayer.

"How many?" asked The Dwarf King.

Plumporious scratched his head. "Not...not too many."

"How many!"

"Four," he blurted out.

"Four what?" asked Dan.

"Dead," said Mick.

"D...d...d...d...dead!" cried Dan.

"I didn't mean to," sobbed Plumporious. "Well, in hindsight, I didn't mean to, I just sometimes lose my temper, and then, and then the bad things happen."

"What happened?" asked Dan, incredulously. The Dwarf King slowly shook his head and frowned.

"Well I can't remember—erm—much of it. I vaguely remember catching up with the other car and ramming it off the road and into a ditch. One of the dying goblins gave me the address of the supposed backup, and then I went round to tell those ghastly creatures that we were not going to stand for any more nonsense or bullying." Plumporious gathered momentum, his head held high. He had been attacked first, after all.

"And how did you tell them," asked The Dwarf King.

"Verbally," said Plumporious with much righteous chin raising.

"And?"

His head fell. "With firebombing."

"Oh, Plumporious!"

"What's that on your back?" asked Mick, walking up to the dwarf and examining him.

"Not sure. Why?" said the dwarf, straining his neck to see.

With a sickening squelch, the elf pulled out a blood-soaked tomahawk. Plumporious let out a high-pitched scream. "That's enormous! Is there much damage?"

Grundard walked quickly to Mick's side and slapped a hand over his mouth. "Oh, that's nasty. I'm going to have to sew that up."

Dan took a look and immediately passed out, much to Steve's delight who took a pen from behind his ear and called forth The Scrotalus.

"Hurry!" shouted Plumporious, taking off his waistcoat. "Before it's too late," he said, passing the garment to Grundard for repair.

LATER, after Plumporious's jacket was repaired to a suitable standard, and Grundard had sewn a hundred and six stitches into Plumporious's tomahawk wound, and Dan had scrubbed his head free of the Scrotalus, they all sat in the hall, enjoying The Dwarf King's chef's competent cooking.

Dan said to the camp dwarf. "You have to do something about that t...temper of yours, P...Plumporious."

The dwarf lay his cutlery down. "I saw counsellors when I was in prison, but it never does any good. For some reason I attract the wrong sort. Bullies see the flamboyance, the soft exterior of an ultra-camp homosexual and then have the audacity to complain when I break their limbs and crush their faces. If you're not prepared to take it, then don't even think about giving it!"

Mick chuckled.

"Michael!" chastised the dwarf.

"How come you never get angry with him?" asked Dan, gesturing towards the elf. "He's always rude to you."

"Oh, we go way back, and besides, I never really flip unless someone messes with my clothes. Strange, I know. When I was out shopping once, someone popped a button off my coat when they bumped into me and I made them eat all the buttons from all the clothes in British Home Stores. I did three months for that," he said, and then shuddered. "Can't believe I spent so long in British Home Stores."

Steve said, "So the reason you were given all the favours in prison, was because—"

"The guards are scared shitless of him," said Mick.

"It's not like I want to be a homicidal murderer, but I was born this way," said the dwarf, appealing to a judgmental audience.

"He'll never change," said The Dwarf King, allowing a small smile at last. "So why were you knocking on our door, Plumporious? You never did say why you were visiting."

"Well, to be honest, Uncle, I'm not too sure either. We're helping young Dan here on a quest to find some magical heirloom or other."

"Sounds like a load of bollocks to me," said The Dwarf King.

"I'd like to argue," said Dan, "but in t...truth, I have no idea why I'm here."

"Ah well, it doesn't matter," said The Dwarf King. "Most quests are shit if the truth be told. You only hear of the good ones, but a few duff ones slip through the net it seems. Any road, it's good to have a bit of company. We can put you up for a few nights while you work out where you're going. I'm sure the police will be along once they realise my nephew has been involved in another massacre, but there are many places one can hide in the mines."

"Thank you, sire," said Dan. "That would be most welcome."

"You got any booze?" asked Steve.

"Ha!" laughed Grundard. "We're dwarves! Of course we have booze! Dwarven beer is famed across the lands."

"Well let's go get some then!" shouted Steve. The centaur tilted his head towards The Dwarf King. "Because that old fart is boring the shit out of me."

After The Dwarf King's subjects had stopped shouting, and the guards had stood down, and the centaur had finished sticking two fingers up at everyone, including to The Dwarf King's gran, the four companions, all holding flaming torches, followed Grundard deeper into the mines to the famous dwarven brewery. They walked through myriad halls and corridors and Grundard recounted the history of the mines, which was mostly about rocks. They carried on ever deeper, heading for a depth where the temperature was perfect for fermenting ale.

After an hour of trudgery, Dan stopped suddenly. Something

inside him pulled him left, as if he'd swallowed a giant piece of iron and walked past a magnet. He rubbed his tingling tummy and looked left. There was nothing there except for a craggy rock face. He shook his head and walked on. This time the force was stronger, so strong that it pulled him backwards.

"Hang on, g...guys!" he said to the party. They all ceased their march and gathered around him.

"You're such an attention seeker!" said the centaur.

"What's this?" Dan asked of Grundard, placing his hand on the rock.

"Rock."

"And what's behind it?"

"Rock."

"Yes, but beyond that?"

"Rock."

"I know, b...but what—"

Grundard cut him off, "Whatever you're going to ask, the answer is rock."

Dan shook his head. "But—"

"Rock."

"Come on," said Steve, beckoning the group to follow him down the corridor. "Let's get wasted!"

"No!" said Dan, firmly. "There's something here. Something... magical."

Grundard shared looks with Dan's companions, who fidgeted with the arsty-fartsy awkwardness of it all. Plumporious mouthed the word "sorry" while Steve performed a wanker gesture with one hand and pointed to Dan with the other. Mick simply shrugged.

Dan ran his hand over the craggy rock face and then rubbed his fingers together. They tingled and sparked golden. He ran his forefinger across the rock.

"It's a k...k...k...kind of magic," he whispered. A thin line, bright gold, appeared where his finger traced. He didn't know why, but it felt right to draw a doorway.

"What is it?" asked Plumporious.

"Rock," said Grundard.

"It's a door," said Dan.

"Made of rock," said Grundard.

"There's something behind here," said Dan, running his hands over the wall.

"Rock," said Grundard.

Dan bit his lip in frustration and pushed the door, which was indeed made of rock, and, hingeless, it fell backwards, gathering speed with its descent. It was only millimetres thick, yet it hit the ground with an almighty crash, sending out shockwaves of dust. Beyond, a secret corridor beckoned. Dan puffed out his teeny chest. "See, there's more than j...just rock."

"No there isn't" said Grundard.

"Are you coming with me?" said Dan.

Plumporiuous nodded, and both Mick and Steve said, "If we have to."

Grundard had already left.

Dan pressed ahead, leading the Fellowship down the corridor and a golden glow intensified. Soon their torches were made redundant so they left them in wall sconces.

"I've never sensed so much magic, not since my dreams of walking through Anglor with G...Gambledolf."

"It's very pretty," said the dwarf, admiring the golden glow on his Moschino jacket. Mick shrugged and lit up a fag.

"This better not be nonce magic," warned Steve. The corridor twisted and turned and eventually straightened, the golden glow calling them onwards. They reached the source of the light, a golden shrine, a plinth made from the essence of magic itself, magic as matter, magic one could touch. Dan rubbed his hands across the surface of the plinth, on which sat a tiny circular amulet an inch wide. The amulet radiated gold light, but it was completely black, a physical impossibility. It was connected to the thinnest of chains, a hair's-breadth thick, as black as the amulet itself.

Something inside Dan told him to take it. He reached out, but didn't grab it. This was an ancient artefact. The power within it was startling, yet Dan didn't know if he could handle it. Before he touched it the aura engulfed him and all his questions were answered. This was from an age of sword and sorcery. This was an amulet of the fairies.

He grabbed it, and the golden light vanished. The only light was that of Mick's cigarette, the embers burning in the darkness.

"You've broken it, you twat," said the centaur.

Chapter 36...

"I SEE YOU, DANOCLEES DUNLORIAN." Gambledolf waited for them, not far from the entrance to the ancient mines of the Highland dwarves, in the pay-and-display car park. There was only one other car present, and the windows had steamed up. After glimpsing inside, Gambledolf had taken up position by leaning against the hired people carrier, red-faced and flustered.

The four companions approached the Wizard of Anglor, all shielding their eyes from the sun.

"How long have you been waiting here?" asked Mick.

"Just long enough, good elf. Just long enough." He tugged at his collar. "It took me a considerable time hiding your tracks in Glasgow. Secrecy is still our greatest ally. We are not in an open race to the finish, not just yet."

"Gambledolf!" cried Dan, embracing the wizard, who hugged him tight and ruffled his hair.

Gambledolf held Dan by the shoulders. "I sense you've picked up a little treasure on your journey."

"How did you know?" asked Dan, feeling the amulet under his clothes, warm against his skin, brimming with magical energy.

"Last night I sensed a surge in the good elements that make up Earth's magical background."

"You knew it was the amulet?"

"No, my dear boy!" He laughed, heartily. "Not until our warm embrace!"

The dwarf and the elf exchanged looks.

"I knew there was something hidden in the hills, and I'd always hoped it would be the amulet, but...." Gambledolf didn't take his eyes from Dan's chest. "Did it call to you?"

"Yes, it d...did," he said, happiness on his cherub face.

"You're even more powerful than I imagined." Gambledolf took off his hat and looked up at the deep blue sky. "It's going to be all right," he said to the winds. "Your saviour has arrived."

The centaur made a wanker gesture behind the wizard's back.

"I don't understand, Gambledolf," said Dan. "You keep saying I have p...potential, you keep saying that I'm powerful, but I can't do anything! I haven't d...done anything! The amulet stopped glowing when I laid my hands on it."

"He's right," said the centaur. "He's a useless tool."

"Quiet your tongue, Master Centaur." Gambledolf pointed his staff at Steve's mouth that didn't often know when to shut up, but got this one right. "Danoclees, your magical spirit hasn't awoken. Your magical soul is a slumbering giant, but it is stirring, and when it rises, a new epoch will blossom. You are the Chosen One, my boy."

Dan's companions shared unconvinced looks. Steve whispered loudly to Plumporious behind a concealed hand, "But he's proper shit!"

"Danoclees, what you have found—no, what *called* out to you and has found you—is an amulet of the ancient fairfolk."

"What's it called, Gambledolf?"

"It is called...." The wizard took a second's pause, and coughed. "The Amulet...of..." he coughed again, "...the Fairies. Yes, the Amulet of the Fairies, if I remember correctly."

The three companions, who weren't overly enthused with the world of magic, all shook their heads.

"Why is it so special?" asked Dan.

"That amulet was forged at the same time as the Sword. It is a key, a map to finding the Lost Sword of the Fairy King."

"How?" asked Dan.

"For it to call to you tells me two things. Firstly, that it would only reveal itself to someone good. The Lost Sword of the Fairy King, in the wrong hands, could bring destruction to the world. All power can be corrupted, and the fairfolk hid the Sword under the world and left this amulet, a beacon of good, for the future generations to find. Secondly, if the beacons are calling, the state of the world must be dire, indeed. For the ghosts of the ancient realm to release the Sword means Mother Earth is struggling and darkness looms. It is as I feared."

"Gambledolf, if the amulet hadn't p...presented itself, would we have found the Sword?"

"No. No, we wouldn't, Danoclees. I'd hoped it would call to you. Did I gamble? Maybe a little, but I'd call it an educated hunch. This plan I concocted centuries ago, and all I needed was a well of potential and a heart as pure as the winter snow." Gambledolf ruffled Dan's hair once more.

The elf and the dwarf exchanged looks.

"Do you want to use the amulet, Gambledolf?" asked Dan, fishing it out of his top. The sun bathed them all in its warmth, but not a photon bounced off the amulet's surface. "You could harness the magic. I can't even cast the most basic spell."

"NO!" Gambeldolf put his hands across his eyes. "I could not wield it. It would consume me, and I fear my heart is not pure enough."

The elf and the dwarf exchanged looks.

"So what are you saying?" asked Steve. "You saying the fairy's the Chosen One because he's never been near a woman?"

"I am not a fairy!" said Dan defiantly.

"His purity is his virtue," said Gambledolf.

"So he's all powerful because he has a hymen!" said Steve.

"I do not have a hymen!" cried Dan, clenching his fists.

"Because he has a *fairy* hymen?" corrected Steve.

"Friend centaur, I would choose your words wisely in future. If the inner wizard wakes up in young Danoclees, then he could turn you into his own pet hymen."

"That's kind of d...disgusting, Gambledolf," said Dan.

"I know," said the wizard, regretfully. "I didn't really think it through before I said it."

"So what now, then?" asked Dan, changing the subject.

"I am not going to lie to you, young Danoclees, I did not know exactly where to send you. I hoped, oh, did I hope that magic would find you, and I was right. I've never been so glad to be right. However, this part of the quest is not yet complete. The amulet you wear around your neck has a twin—"

"And what's that amulet called, Gambledolf?" asked Mick, smirking. Plumporious and Steve tittered into fists.

"And once you find that," said the wizard, loudly, ignoring the question. "The Lost Sword of the Fairy King will sing to you, and then we can and will save the world."

Dan played with the amulet beneath his T-shirt. "Where will I find its twin?"

Gambledolf paced. "The dwarves held onto the first, even if they didn't know it, and they held it in their most ancient settlement, which was my hunch. Another hunch says the second amulet lies beyond the Wood of Darbenham, the fortress of the elves of the dark, the old warring faction, yet another ancient enemy of the dwarf."

"Where is it, G...Gambledolf? Is it far?" asked Dan.

"It is many miles march from here, young Dan, and across difficult terrain."

Dan steeled himself. "And how will we f...find it?"

"One of your number knows where it lies," said Gambledolf to Mick, whose head was bowed, pulling on a cigarette.

"Are you coming with us, G...Gambledolf?" asked Dan, hopefully.

"Nay, son. Nay. I must stay here. Removing the amulet has

released a shockwave of magical force, something I have never experienced before. There have been a series of magical aftershocks. I must disguise your movements and put any would-be attackers off your trail. I fear there are many." He looked into the distance with far-seeing eyes.

"Are you in danger, Gambledolf?"

"Of course, my dear boy," he said, warmly, before wagging a warning finger. "Be under no illusion, you all are, but hopefully my diversions will keep you safe. I've hidden my secret house in the centre of London for all these years, have I not? And no filthy chav bastard has broken into it yet."

"Ah," said Dan, a little surprised at the unwizardly and socially derogatory language.

"Now come, friends, you must be on your way." The wizard unlocked the people carrier with a key fob.

"I must say, Gambledolf," said Dan. "I am not looking forward to the long road ahead."

"It won't be so bad, my boy," said the wizard, getting into the car and staring the engine. He wound down the window. "The Number 7 bus will drop you off right at the doorstep."

Chapter 37...

"THIS, I WAS NOT EXPECTING," said Draknarkus, flowing through the rundown street, taking in the sights, sounds, and smells, the latter of which was dominated by the smoke billowing up from houses and cars. Neon streetlights couldn't compete with the uncontrollable fires.

"What happened here?" said Derek, his lip wobbling. He surveyed the destruction with bloodshot eyes. "It's a warzone!"

Even Michelle was taken aback. "I hate to say it, but you're right."

Rillit consulted his GPS. "This is Lashley, a goblin town devastated in the '80s after the closing of the mines. It's a hotspot for drug abuse, mainly heroin, and, as you'd probably expect, education is non-existent. Crime is rife." He looked over the screen. "I don't think this could be classed as a crime." He put the device back in his pocket. He turned up half a lip. "Although the architecture certainly is."

Lashley was a council estate built in the fifties. Row after row of characterless terraces were, ironically, filled with some of Scotland's biggest "characters." Washing machines adorned gardens, and several of the burned-out cars looked like they'd been there a while.

Some goblins, mostly female, were out on the streets, crying and consoling one another, hugging their children. Some of the males were venturing into smouldering buildings, trying to rescue meagre belongings. Draknarkus stopped by a garden where an entirely family stood, watching flames take their possessions, their past, and their only shelter from the future.

"What happened?" demanded the black wizard, no concern in her voice.

The mother spoke, her deep Scottish accent, difficult to decipher. "The evil one came," she cried.

"Talk sense, woman, or you will truly meet evil," she threatened.

The goblin whispered to the ground, "The Black Rainbow came." She picked up a child at her feet and hugged him close.

"The what?" Michelle turned her nose up and moved closer to hear.

"Aye, the Black Rainbow," said another goblin, older with glasses and a dated, flowery apron, probably the grandmother of the family. "A dwarf unlike any other. On the outside he is as gay as the fairies and camper than a Carry On Christmas Special, but on the inside his heart is as black as the coal mined by his forefathers."

"One dwarf did this?" said Draknarkus, unbelieving, turning around and admiring the destruction.

"Aye, but not just any dwarf, it was the Black Rainbow."

"Interesting." Draknarkus turned to the company. "It appears Gambledolf is more calculating and far sneakier than I gave him credit. He is protecting the Chosen One with a group of bodyguards."

"I don't care about that," said Michelle, watching a male goblin fight his way back into a burning building. "I can kick anyone's head in."

"Calm the temper and think with your head, not your fists. One dwarf did this, on his own. One." Draknarkus turned back to the crying goblins. "Was he armed?"

"Not at first. The lads of the town tried to take him down, but he was too strong. The Black Rainbow is unstoppable. We'll have to arm ourselves with guns after this, the last thing this cursed town needs." The old goblin crossed herself. "He didn't stop breaking our poor boys. And, when there was no more fight left in the town, he brought the fire."

"How long did the attack last?" asked Michelle.

The grandmother said, "It is impossible to cool the Black Rainbow's flames. You've just gotta wait till his rage burns out."

Draknarkus took Michelle to one side. "I thought riling up the goblins would cause more of a problem for the Fellowship, but their attack was completely ineffective."

"What did you hope to achieve by this?" Michelle noticed that Derek, who was putting on a brave face, was entertaining some of the goblin children, making them laugh with his awful version of magic tricks.

"A test, no more," said the dark wizard with a dismissive, uncaring wave of the hand. "It didn't slow the Chosen One down. He was inexorably pulled to the amulet. It could be nothing else. I can feel the magical reverberations from when he dislodged it from its ancient hiding place. I can't believe it was here all along. The amulet's sister will be next on Gambledolf's agenda."

"Where will it be hidden?" asked Michelle, still watching the halfling who had a group of goblin children cheering and clapping.

"This one lived with the dwarves, so I imagine the other is with the elves. Which tribe, however, I cannot say."

Some of the adult goblins gathered round Derek, watching his pathetic attempts at hijinks, but it was enough to take their minds off their current problems. "We should leave the good-for-nothing halfling here," Michelle said.

Draknarkus's mind was on something else. She looked out into the distance and came to a decision. She called to Rillit. "I require the resources of Somersby, elf!"

"Yes, Draknarkus," said Rillit with a stiff bow.

"We're going to need a helicopter."

He stiffened, close to cracking. "I must say, madam, that expenses have been rather steep for such a short trip."

"Your boss can afford it, I'm sure," said Draknarkus with a sneer. "Once the second amulet is located, then it will be a race against time. We will need air travel if we are to apprehend the Fellowship once they lay hands on the Sword. We—"

Draknarkus was cut off by Michelle grabbing her arm. "I don't believe it," said Michelle.

"You don't believe what?" said the dark wizard, irritably, ridding herself of the unwanted hand.

Michelle pointed up the road.

Most people had the social awareness to walk in a respectful and dignified manner when passing though a state of emergency. Strutting was off the menu for most, except one.

He made a beeline for the biggest fires, so they'd make an impressive background for him to walk in front of. It added to the strut, augmented it. Some would call it inconsiderate, but he saw it as a gift, a gift of aspiration to a bunch of losers.

He was showing them what it was to be winner. He readjusted his *growspeck*.

And he'd probably bang a widow or two.

Chapter 38...

THE ADVENTURERS GROANED AND YAWNED AND STRETCHED THEIR BACKS AS THEY ALIGHTED FROM THE NUMBER 7. It had been a fell journey, even for a bus ride, of which, all are fell...so fell. This was worse than any bus ride home from town, unless it was a bus ride home from Manchester after 11 p.m. because there was nothing more dangerous than that. Nothing. Not even close.

Rumours of succubae stalking the bus routes of the UK had long been whispered around camp fires when horror stories were regaled, raising goose bumps and bringing to attention the hairs on backs of necks.

Dan had become remarkably animated when Plumporious had told him of the succubae, the female soul stealers who weakened their victims with unrelenting sexual activity. It made Dan nervous and extremely sweaty, but there was at least a spark of lust inside his pure and wholesome body. He saw it as a chance to get over Michelle and become a man.[24]

But it was not to be.

It transpired that succubae were indeed stalking the bus routes of the UK, but, much to Dan's disappointment, it also transpired that in this modern age, the succubae had been forced to change soul-stealing tactics.

Forty years ago, any heterosexual male of any species could be coerced into anything, no matter how stupid, dangerous, pointless, inane, or home-improvement related with just the hint of the possibility of a sniff of an opportunity of a whiff of tit.

However, over the past forty years, Sony, Sega, Microsoft, Commodore, Sinclair, Atari, Apple, APF, Unisonic, Zanussi, Coleco, Philips, Radio Shack, Granada, Binatone, GHP, Fairchild, RCA, Midway, Mattel, Bandai, Epoch, Casio, Sharp, SNK, Pioneer, Mad Catz, PlayJam, and Nintendo had assembled their finest and most voracious virgins, scientists if you will, to battle the call of the succubae.

Online video gaming was a masterstroke in contraception, with the male of average libido almost impossible to persuade into an early

---

[24] Who had partaken in sexual intercourse with a female.

night when he was only three experience points from levelling-up his Warrior Elf Lord's greaves from eight to nine, adding +1 to armour and enabling a customisable ye olde paint job. Wives and girlfriends had struggled, but soon stopped struggling, realising they were getting the better end of the deal. Succubae, however, faced extinction, so another path they forged.

Succubae had attempted to infiltrate the world of online gaming to entice their prey, but things had not proceeded as hoped. Before they'd even started playing the games, the hordes of young males had sensed, through misogynistic clairvoyance, that females intruded on their personal game space and time. Within seconds of logging on, the succubae had been shouted at and abused terribly, not in terms of language and offence, just by dire senses of humour. The succubae turned off their consoles, preferring a slow and lingering death, rather than listening to twats online.

Ironically, it was a victory for the legions of skin trolls out there, who would spontaneously combust in conversation with a woman outside the realms of Ethernet cables and WiFi. Their hearts were safe from the succubae, but, alas, not from inactivity.

The succubae, a parasite operating under the most unpleasant conditions, were amazed that the male half of the species was evolving into an even bigger collective bellend. So they thought outside the (X)box. Rather than stealing souls with sex, they drained the souls of young men by talking to them on buses. Their plan was as devious as it was devilish. They disguised themselves as a specific sub-species of the elderly. On the outside they were kind-looking white-haired biddies, bespectacled, tartan-wearing, humbug-giving, granny-reminding fogies. Young males would take a window seat and the succubae would pounce, taking the aisle seat, launching their attack with the opening of a humbug wrapper.

Nothing crushed a man's soul more than hearing an elderly lady rip into the blacks and the gays and the foreigns with reckless abandon and an unquenchable fire drawn from Phlegethon. This far-right sub-breed of the elderly would tear the soul from out of a young man's body with tales of cancer, friends dying through neglect of lazy Romanian nurses and cancer caught by sharing a toilet seat with gay black transgendered suicide bombers. And when the young man tried to escape, the succubae would feign arthritic discomfort and not get up in time. He'd miss his stop and his salvation.

This is what Dan endured on the Number 7. Even though he would never admit it, Steve was the only reason he'd escaped his predatory succubus. Succubae preyed on the weak-willed and Dan would have been stuck, listening (yet not having the heart to disagree) to the succubae's Nazi mantra, breathlessly chanted into his ear along with how her husband's golf course had gone to the dogs ever since they let a non-member use the club's phone to call an ambulance for a Traveller who'd been hit by a car on the road outside.

Steve, in his mind a hero, had head-butted the succubus who had relinquished a majority slice of Dan's soul and the centaur had set the wizard's apprentice free. There had been outrage on the bus, the other passengers not knowing the creature was a soul-stealing succubus, and, not to his credit, nor did Steve.

"THANK CHRIST FOR THAT!" cried the alighting adventurers, stretching cramped limbs and relieving stiff backs. The adventurers watched the Number 7 roll up the road, kicking out smoke.

"Well, this is as far as the road take us," said Mick. In the distance, about a mile across green fields where longhorns grazed and lowed, a forest spanned the horizon. Even from a mile away, it was obvious it wasn't your typical congregation of trees. Murders of crows and unkindnesses of ravens flew up to its boundary, but none ventured over the forest canopy. A mist oozed out from between the densely packed trees.

"What now?" asked Plumporious, pulling his summer jacket around him, regretting not bringing more of his autumnal collection. He'd left more of his luggage at his uncle's mine and was down to two cases.

"We have two options," said the elf. "We either: A) sack this shit off, or B) walk through the forest."

"I vote for the first option," said Steve, wiping some thin, elderly blood from his forehead.

"We can't sack it off!" cried Dan. "If we find the amulet we'll all b...but have found the Lost Sword of the Fairy King."

"Yay," said the centaur, sarcastically.

"It was a great surprise to discover you're Scottish, Michael. Why didn't you tell me?" asked Plumporious.

"Yeah, well I haven't been *home* for quite a while," said the elf, struggling to get his tongue around the word. "And these elves haven't got much of a Scottish accent anyway. They're cut off from the other communities because of their way of life."

"I guess the Scottish thing explains the ginger skullet," said Steve.

The elf stopped in his tracks and said over his shoulder. "What did you say?" his tone rung death.

Steve was an arsehole, possibly the greatest, widest, deepest, hairiest, smelliest, and pile-ridden of arseholes, but he wasn't an idiot.

His mouth gaped for a moment before he retracted his statement, "Auburn. Auburn skullet."

"Auburn, yeah," said the elf, pulling on a cigarette, and twiddling an unmistakable auburn lock. Mick got back to the path. "There're gonna be a lot of horrible surprises in the Dark Forest. There's gonna be a lot of bad things wanting to say hello."

"Such as?" said Dan, subconsciously moving towards the Knife for protection.

"Spiders as big as Steve here for a start," said Mick, spanning his hands as wide as he could. "But we don't have to worry about them because the worst thing in the forest will find us first: the dark elves."

"The dark elves," said Dan, slowly, his conscience having trouble with the second word.

"Yeah," said Mick.

"The *dark elves*," he said again, warily.

"Yes," snapped Mick, his patience waning.

Dan's conscience made its decision, and, as usual, it was on the side of outrage. "D...d...disgusting!" He announced, crossing his arms.

"What do you mean?" asked Mick, screwing up his face, looking to Plumporious who gave an unknowing shrug.

"I thought racism was stamped out years ago. The colour of someone's skin makes absolutely no difference to the person on the inside," he said, righteously.

"That's not entirely true," said Plumporious.

"Yes, it is" said Dan firmly.

"What about the Chameleon people?" said the dwarf. "The colour of their skin makes a massive difference to the person inside. If they're red, they're best avoided, and if they're purple they'll hump your leg."

"That's different!" said Dan. "But c...calling someone a *dark* elf, indeed! Indeed!"

"I'm not in the best of moods, son, and I'm certainly not in the mood for any fairy bollocks." said Mick, rubbing the back of his neck, tiredly. "What are you on about?"

Dan threw up his hands. "You might as well just go ahead and call them P...P...P...P..." The stutter was always a problem but he had another issue to contend with. "P...P...P...P..."

Plumporious crossed his arms. "Dan, where are you going with this?"

"P...P...P...P...P...Pa—"

"DAN!" yelled Plumporious. "Let me stop you there."

"You d...d...don't know what I was going to say!"

Plumporious crossed his arms. "I can't believe—I can't…. I am lost for words, young man!"

"No" said Dan, shaking his head and wagging his finger. "No, I'm not b…being racist!"

Plumporious took up a wagging finger too, perpendicular to Dan's, in the form of admonishment. "Yes, you are! Uttering such filthy words, I am surprised and, I must say, very disappointed in you, young man."

"No," said Dan, making cutting actions with his hands. "I was saying what *other* p…p…people might call them, what *racist* people might call them."

Plumporious's fists found his hips. "It was you who said it. I thought you knew better. I dread to think of all the terrible things you're saying behind my back."

"I've said nothing behind your back!" pleaded Dan.

"He called you a Bumbadier!" cried Steve.

"NO I DIDN'T!" Dan turned on the centaur. "Will you p…please stop making up lies?"

"No," said Steve.

Dan tried to plead reason with the dwarf. "What I'm saying is that you shouldn't name a race after the colour of their skin."

"They're not," said Mick. "They're named after the place they live, The Dark Forest, where daylight barely breaches the forest canopy."

"Ah," said Dan, taking off his glasses and cleaning them while trying to blend into the background, which usually wasn't a problem.

"Is that OK, Mr. Ku Klux Klan?" asked Plumporious.

"Don't call me that!" wailed Danoclees, politically correct in all aspects of modern life, except when it came to goblins. "And is what OK?"

"The Dark Forest? Or do you want to call it a Pa—" Plumporious closed his eyes and shivered. "I can't even say the despicable word!"

"No, p…p…p…p…"

"Don't say it again!" cried the dwarf.

"I wasn't g…going to. And I never said it in the first p…place!"

"You tried to!"

"You've g…got it all wrong," said Dan, squirming uncontrollably.

Plumporious turned away from the apprentice wizard. "Oh no, I'd say it is you who got it wrong, Danoclees Dunlorian, I would certainly say it is you."

Steve spat on Dan's jeans. "Shame on you."

Mick let out a massive moan and looked to the heavens. "If you bastards are gonna continue bickering, then I say go through the forest. If they kill us, then at least I won't have to listen to you anymore."

"Sorry, Michael," said the dwarf. He walked to the side of the elf and gave his friend a hug round the waist, who didn't reciprocate, but didn't pull away. "I can tell this is hard for you."

Mick lit up another fag. "Yeah, so let's get it over with."

The adventures adventured.

They approached the forests of the Dark Elf, where nature was worshipped rather than ravaged. The branches reached towards the wary travellers, beckoning them in towards its deadly heart, where being lost forever was but a moment away. The forest reached high into the sky, trying to suck the light directly out of the sun, for in the heart of the Dark Forest, Mick's native home, there was no light, and there was no hope. Yes, nature was worshipped, but nature was often cruel and malignant.

"I've heard t...terrible things about the elves of the ancient forests," said Dan. "They used to cast spells of the d...darkest magic. They were witches and warlocks who worshipped the suffering darkness brought."

"Well, they're certainly a bunch of tossers, that's for sure," offered Mick, throwing the fag end on the ground.

"I can't believe you litter, even in your native homeland," said Dan.

"At least I'm consistent," said the elf.

Plumporious slowed down as the forest approached, filling his field of vision. "We shouldn't go in. We should find another way of procuring the amulet." He pulled his coat around him.

"Yep," said Steve. "I don't like the looks of this. It's all right for you lot, but I bet none of you have ever caught your chap on a bramble bush."

The other adventurers winced, but none felt compassion for the unlikeable centaur.

At the edge of the forest, all stopped, except Mick who trudged forwards, eyes on the ground. Light could not penetrate through the gaps in the trees and not a sound escaped the bastion of bark. Mick disappeared between two gnarled trees.

"Come on, you fannies!" called the elf from the darkness. "It's the quickest way to get to the end of this shitty quest."

All the adventurers agreed, and all pressed on, for the quest was indeed shitty.

Chapter 39...

THE FOREST CLOSED. Ancient evergreens stood strong, thick, and dense, with no paths or tracks between them, not even those of animals. Daylight did not fall willingly through the canopy. The midday was like dusk, eventually turning to complete darkness with the waning of the sun.

"Do you know where you're g...going, Mick?" asked Dan, tripping over a root.

"Not a clue," said the elf, fighting back brambles and branches.

"So...well, why are we still walking?" asked Dan. "We could get lost for days in a p...p...place like this."

"That's if you're lucky," said Mick, pushing on. "Loads of people die in here, every year. They go looking for the enigma that is the lost dark elves. They get lost, and then wander in circles until their water runs out and they simply lay down and die, finally understanding why the dark elves were lost in the first place. I've heard of people dying fifty yards from the edge of the forest, next to a main road. The forest is so dense you can't hear the cars going past, even though they bomb past because there're no speed cameras."

"So where on earth are you going, then?" shouted Plumporious, trying to remove an epaulet from a bramble.

"If the amulet is going to be anywhere it's going to be in the Hall of Darbenham," Mick said. "The other amulet was in the dwarf shithole so it stands to reason."

"And you don't know where the Hall of Darbenham is, I presume?" added the dwarf.

"Not a clue," he said, pushing on.

"So what happens when we get lost and we're all on the road to starvation?" Plumporious's belly rumbled and he grabbed at it like a bullet wound. "Oh my god, I'm dying."

Mick said, "Don't worry, you could do with losing a few pounds, tubs, and it doesn't matter, for when we're lost there'll be the biggest bunch of wankers you ever did meet waiting to torment us."

"You mean in hell?" cried the dwarf, pointing at a toadstool, or rather beyond the toadstool into the depths of underworld.

"No," he said, grinning at the dwarf's theatrics, but then the reality hit home and the grin was cut short. "Well, it will be my own personal circle of hell, I guess."

"What do you m...mean?" said Dan.

"You'll find out," said the elf, grimly.

They continued to walk through the forest, or, rather, they continued to struggle through the forest, which had a life of its own, tangling with the adventurers at every opportunity. Not half a dozen steps could be taken in a straight line before a great tree or bush would bar the path. A thick compost, a result of the falling leaves and no indigenous animals to trample it down, made walking difficult.

"How long have we b...been walking for?" asked Dan, mopping his face.

Plumporious looked at his watch. "Three hours."

"Three hours! But I c...can still see the edge of the forest," said Dan, squinting at the dim glow on the edge of his vision.

"We had to double back," said Mick. "There were some impassable brambles."

"You're telling me!" said an uncomfortable centaur.

"Then why are we bothering with this stupid charade!" cried the dwarf, stamping his feet in the leaves and kicking at branches.

"You'll find out." Mick stopped and cocked an ear. "You'll find out—" He waited....

"Are you lost again, outcast?" came a musical voice from high in the trees.

"—about now," said Mick, with a sigh.

"The prodigal son returns," said a mocking voice from behind them.

Steve, Dan, and Plumporious looked everywhere for the voices that came from the trees themselves.

"He's in a worse state than when he ran away," came another gleeful voice, giggling.

"And he has a dwarf as a friend!" the mocking voice was dissected with contempt.

"That can't be a dwarf! He has no beard. Surely it is nothing more than an overweight halfling?"

Plumporious's sharp intake of breath pulled leaves off the trees.

"It's definitely a dwarf. Can't you smell him, brother!"

"How revolting! A stinky little dwarf in our beloved forest with his strange little clothes."

"Show yourselves!" cried Plumporious. "Stinky? Strange little clothes? You have no class!" He grabbed at the T-shirt under his jacket and roared, "This is Vera Wang!"

The dark elves giggled and laughed.

Mick stood with his arms crossed, tapping the foot of his bright white trainers. "All right, you've had your fun."

"Oh no, there is much fun to be had, outcast!"

"Why do they call you outcast?" asked Dan.

"He hasn't told them!" came a cry.

"They do not know!" came another.

Mick tiredly held up his hands, "Look, just take me to see the old man, all right?"

Dan blinked. He hadn't been able to see the elves, but now he could; like they were wearing cloaking devices and had switched them off or walked out of a giant Magic Eye poster. He blinked again. He'd never seen them materialise, not even a hint of movement. They were one with the forest. Dan couldn't help but marvel at their beauty. They were exceptionally tall and slender and graceful, yet seemed powerful and dangerous. Their hair was as black as the night, unlike the blonde elves of the city. Their eyes were black, too, and their skin as pale as moonlight. These elves were unlike the elves he knew, and a million years of evolution ahead of Mick the Knife and his ginger skullet. Their clothes were like nothing else, as if they'd been part of the forest and had grown into garments. This was a step back in time and was what Dan always dreamed of.

"Do you have any weapons?" asked the elf at the front of the group. A gold broche in the shape of an oak leaf clasped his cloak together and signified his authority.

Mick's knife appeared in the blink of an eye. The elves gasped as one.

"Have you still not yet learned the art of the bow, Michael?" asked the leader of the sentries.

"I ain't no wimp who can't face another elf, one on one."

"Well said, Michael!" Plumporious slapped him on the back.

"I like to look a man in the eye when I take him down," said Mick.

"Absolutely!" cried the dwarf.

"I ain't one to put a prick in a man's arse."

Plumporious mouthed the words "Call me," and made the universal phone gesture to an extremely handsome elf, who turned red, although he didn't say no.

"So, no, I ain't learned the bow, but I can show you how I can use this." Mick flourished the knife. "And yeah, you can take that as a threat."

The elves laughed. More made themselves visible, dropping to the forest floor or hanging from the trees, affirming Mick's dire destiny if he

215 | M.J. Jackman | 215

made a move with his infamous knife. The forest creaked with the drawing of bow strings.

"Mick, t...t...take it easy," said Dan, raising his hands.

Mick snarled, his lips drawn back to show crumbling yellow teeth. His eyes snapped from figure to figure. "I can take these bastards."

"No, no you can't," said Plumporious. "Not even with my help."

"Did you hear the dwarf?" said a voice from the trees.

"He thinks he's a warrior!" cried another.

"We have missed the War," said another.

"Look at his outfit! Is this what the dwarves wear for battle these days? How garish!" said yet another. Although one extremely handsome elf (no longer blushing) gave the top a nod of approval.

"They mentioned my Vera Wang top again...." A distant look came across Plumporious's face as it reddened with his rage.

"What do you want?" asked Mick, looking at the lead elf and taking the attention away from a dwarf ready to destroy every sentient being in the forest and then burn the entire thing to the ground and urinate on the ashes.

"I am Rickrond the Just, and you are trespassing in The King's woodland," said the leader, standing up straight, seriousness returning.

"The King?" said Plumporious. "The only royalty in these lands is the King Under the Hill and The Queen of England whom sits on the throne of Buckingham Palace."

The bowstrings tightened some more.

"Not all of us bowed down to servitude, dwarf. Here in the Dark Forest, we did not give up all our rights like the pathetic lords under the hill who relinquished everything for worthless titles."

"Proper twats, these, ain't they?" said Steve.

"Shut your mouth or I'll pin your tongue to the roof of it," said an elf holding his bow at full strain a foot from Steve's head. His hands were stone still, even under the incredible tension.

Steve obeyed, but shot a sly two-finger salute against his cheek.

"You will all be judged by The Dark King of the Forest. Do not expect leniency, outcast," said Rickrond to Mick.

Their hands were tied and they were blindfolded, not that it was necessary, for finding their way was impossible. They were led, stumbling and falling over low branches and roots, the elves mocking them as they went. Progress was slow.

"I thought the elves were a k...kind and fair race," whispered Dan to Mick.

"Yep, you'd be right if you were talking about the wood elves, high elves, and sea elves. Unfortunately, the dark elves are the goblins of the elf world."

Dan asked, "So why did you t...take us through the forest if you knew they were waiting for us?"

"I need to get to the end of this quest so you can do whatever you've gotta do and I can get pardoned. And, I need to see The Dark King."

"Why?" asked Dan.

Mick blew out a heavy sigh. "Let's just say me and him have history."

Chapter 40...

THE FOUR HOODED FIGURES WERE LED INTO THE SECRET GLADES, and eventually into Darbenham, the hall of the dark elves. Through the ancient doors and into the throne room they were marched, pushed, and prodded. Here they'd have their audience with The Dark King. The throne room did not match the caustic personalities of the guards that harried the four heroes. The entire throne room appeared to have been carved straight out of the forest and there was still verdant life within, with chairs, pillars and tables sprouting buds and leaves. The detail was exquisite, with animals and birds carved into various beams and walls, so lifelike, only the colour gave them away. Torches hung on the walls, reaching out into the room as to not damage the wood. This was where the wildlife of the forest congregated and bees buzzed and birds sang, for the animals were too stupid to know when the people around them were jerks.

The four's final destination was at the centre of the hall in front of The Dark King, whose throne grew from the ground. The Dark King was older than the other members of the court. He shared their thick black hair, yet a few grey hairs streaked it. He was heavily built and appeared a powerful warrior. What was most unusual was his dark skin. All the other elves of the court, of which there were about a hundred, male and female, had almost translucent skin, but not greasy as in the case of the Knife. All were beautiful and graceful, yet armed with a cold stare. They stood around the circular hall, leaving the adventures very alone in the clearing. All murmured at the sight of the unusual guests.

"Behold The Dark King," cried the herald, stood beside the throne, holding an immense horn that was almost as tall as she was.

An elf removed Dan's hood. He looked at The Dark King, and then to the other members of the court, and then back to The Dark King. He was sure racism was afoot. Sure of it, he was.

"Who trespasses on our sacred grounds?" said The Dark King. His voice did not carry the musical qualities of the other elves. His voice matched his title.

"Sire, look who returns," said Rickrond. He pulled the hood off Mick the Knife and the crowd gasped when ginger locks fell greasily to narrow shoulders.

"Michael!" cried The Dark King, rising from his seat. "Untie him immediately."

Heated murmurs spread through the congregation.

"You all right, Dad?" said Mick.

"He's your father?" asked Dan, looking from father to son, and back again.

"Hang on," said the dwarf. "This means you're a prince!" Plumporious high-pitched screech did a fine job of revealing the full extent of his jealousy.

Like Dan, the centaur looked from father to son and back again. "He's got to be adopted."

Deathly silence fell on the hall. All turned to the centaur. The Dark King's lip trembled. Steve scratched his mane. Mick chewed at a finger nail and looked thoroughly bored of it all.

"What did you say?" asked The Dark King, his voice, no more than a whisper and colder than an iceberg, carried a warning in titanic proportion.

Some could say that Steve had courage in his convictions. These people were idiots.

"I said, 'He. Must. Be. Adopted.'"

"And why do you think he's adopted?" asked The Dark King, trembling with rage.

The centaur looked The Dark King up and down. "Well you're a very dark king indeed, and—"

"Stephen!" cried Dan, "you can't say he's a d...d...dark king!"

Steve screwed his face up. "But he is The Dark King."

"But not a *d...dark* D...Dark King. The c...capitalisation is important!" said Dan under hushed breath, not that it didn't carry to the rest of the congregation.

"Are you saying I am not the darkest lord of the lands?" said The Dark King to Dan.

Dan was unsure of the best course of action. "It's irrelevant how dark you are!"

"But I am the darkest of all the kings, am I not?" The Dark King grew angrier at the insolence and rose to his feet.

"I d...don't know how to answer that," said Dan, honestly.

"Are you not prepared to announce my darkness?" cried The Dark King, eyes widening, spittle flying.

Dan sucked in air between his teeth. "I...I..."

"Cowardly, Dan. Cowardly," said the judgmental dwarf.

"I never said it!" cried Dan.

Thankfully, Steve interrupted. "And anyway," said Steve. "Mick's got a ginger skullet."

"Seize him!" cried The Dark King, jumping to his feet.

The guards surrounded the centaur. Steve rolled his eyes but put his hands forward so they could be cuffed. However, this was not London, and this was not the Met. This was a group of insular elves who lived in a forest in the Scottish Highlands and worshipped the darkness. Without a word, the guards beat Steve with chunky sticks and clubs until he hit the floor. And, when he hit the floor, and the elves were able to line up the shots, he was beaten harder and better.

Steve's three companions watched the horrific ordeal with great interest. This would have carried an attempted murder charge if this was in civilised society. Even for Dan, the pacifist, it was extremely satisfying to watch. The beating seemed unlikely to desist. Steve didn't cry out in pain, or for help, not because he was brave, but because he was unconscious.

"Are you going to intervene?" The Dark King asked his son, with interest.

"Nope," said Mick, caught up in the moment, throwing pretend punches in time with the guards.

While there was no corporal punishment in this modern, peaceful world, and while a civilised society could not be classed as civilised if it needed to call upon barbaric acts, scholars could argue there would be less arseholes kicking around if a few more bloody good public hidings were handed out when the need presented itself.

"Throw him in the cells!" cried The Dark King. The elves dragged the limp body of the centaur out of the room, leaving a considerate trail of blood.

"That was b...brilliant," said Dan. Both he and Plumporious, while fearful for their safety, were feeling more upbeat than they had done for days.

"What brings you here, my son," asked The Dark King. His face was stern but there was concern deep in those dark eyes.

Mick spoke to the floor, kicking his feet. iHisH

"We need to find some shitty amulet thing, Dad, and then we'll be out of your hair."

The Dark King frowned. "Is that the only reason that brings you here?" He raised his arms. "Do you not come to claim your right to the throne?"

Plumporious made a *squee* sound.

"Nah," said the elf, lighting up a fag.

"Do you not want to take up your birthright?" his voice boomed over the congregation. "Do you not want to take your true place as ruler of the dark elves?"

"Nah."

The Dark King whispered under his breath. "So you've come all this way and it isn't to see your mother and I?" He was angry, sad, and disappointed, all at the same time, in a way only a parent could be.

"Awww, Dad, don't be like that." Mick stared at the floor, and kicked his feet a little harder, in a way only disappointing children could.

"And you're still bloody smoking, I see," whispered The Dark King before knocking the fag out of his son's mouth. He remembered where he was and raised his voice. "You are heir to the throne. Look around you. These are your people, Michael."

Mick rubbed his chin and examined the congregation of dark elves that could one day call him The Dark King. He wasn't one of them. They were tall, graceful, beautiful, and intelligent, and he was short, ungainly, pig-ugly, and shit at quiz machines. "They're not my people."

This brought a mixed reaction. Whereas everyone knew, and were glad that Mick didn't consider them his people, they were still outraged that he'd say such a thing.

An elf taller than the others stepped forward from the congregation and into the centre of the hall. He appeared slender, but his forearms were uncovered and they looked like braids of steel. His hair was longer than the others, too, and it shone blue, even in the dull light of the throne room. The intensity of his eyes made anyone who caught his gaze look away. His stride spoke unwavering confidence and he was dangerously beautiful. "If he will not take the throne, then he must fight to leave it. It is the law," he said.

"I know, Jonquil," said the king, his jaw locked.

"My father, who is too ill to stand here today, has the next claim to the throne. I am his champion," Jonquil announced, and beat his chest once with his fist.

As one, the crowd drew breath through pursed lips. To them, Mick was an unknown entity. They'd no idea of the infamous reputation he'd built on the outside world, but they all knew of Jonquil, and his prowess in combat was legendary.

The Dark King looked from Jonquil, the mighty warrior, to his son. He said, heavily, "You know the law of the land, Michael. Only combat can free you from your duty."

Mick lit up again. "Yeah, I know."

"This is your last chance," said The Dark King.

"He's had too many chances already!" cried Jonquil. A few "hear hears" were mumbled from the congregation.

Mick stayed silent, concentrating on smoking.

"Then you leave me no choice," said The Dark King. He picked his staff up and held it aloft with an impending doom. "You must fight to the death for your freedom, Prince Michael—" there was a squeal from one of the audience "—and Jonquil you must fight to the death for the throne you so desperately desire."

Mick rubbed a fag out on the ancient floor. "But I can't be arsed, Dad. Can't I just leave?"

Dan whispered to Plumporious. "He's Mick the Knife. Why is he worried about a fight to the d...death? All his fights are fights to the d...death, other people's death!"

"Hmmm," said the dwarf, in a camp, but ponderous stance. "Yes, there is that."

"Michael," said The Dark King. "If you don't fight, then you will watch all your friends die and you will be executed."

"Now, just hold on a second!" cried the dwarf, raising a hand in appeal.

"So that's the way it's gonna be then," growled Mick. The strawberry blonde elf cracked his knuckles, did the cool thing the hardmen do in films where they crack their necks with a twist of their head—and then he fainted.

Chapter 41...

THE FOUR ADVENTURERS WERE COOPED UP IN A TINY WOODEN CELL, EVEN SMALLER THAN THE ONE THEY SHARED IN BRIXTON PRISON. There were no beds, and most of the floor was taken up with Steve's heavy-breathing, semi-conscious, haemorrhaging body. Mick, Dan, and Plumporious sat against a wall, their arms wrapped around their knees. The dwarf and the apprentice wizard were doing their best to talk sense into Mick the Knife.

"Listen, Mick," said Dan. "I'm all against violence and for love not war, you know that, b...but if you don't fight him, then we're all going to d...d...d...die." Even though his stutter was improving, he always struggled talking about his imminent death.

"I'm already dying," moaned the centaur. The pained voice pleased Dan immensely. Steve coughed and spat out a load of blood over Dan's shoes and socks. Dan's karma found neutrality.

"I ain't having them lot tell me what to do anymore," said the stubborn elf, more like a child than one of London's most feared felons.

"But you're Mick the Knife," said Dan. "You love st...stabbing things and k...killing stuff, and I don't think that Jonquil is very nice."

"He's a right wanker, he is," said the elf.

"Then why can't you do some of your s...st...stabbing on him?" pleaded Dan, ignoring the blood and phlegm soaking into his socks. "We c...can't let the quest end here. It's not our lives that are important, it is our quest! You've g...got to fight him!"

Mick took a deep breath—and then the breath fled his body along with any remaining confidence. His head found his hands. "I can't fight him!"

"Why? Is he an old friend or something?" asked Dan.

"No, he's a complete tosspot" said Mick with passive-aggressive venom.

"Then why c...can't you fight?"

Mick looked into Dan's eyes, and his bottom lip wobbled. "Because I can't fight."

Dan shook his head, convinced he was hallucinating. "Erm, sorry?"

"I can't fight!" said Mick. Torrents of tears rained down his pitted face, and he buried his head in his knees.

Plumporious shuffled nearer to the elf and put his arm around him. Mick abandoned his knees to sob into the dwarf's armpit.

Dan blinked rapidly. "Have I missed something here?"

The centaur was speechless. He lay, his mouth wide open and bleeding, staring at the elf. It was uncertain if he was confused or unconscious.

"I'm just a big *pansy*!" cried Mick, spitting out great bubbles of sadness with the pronunciation of pansy.

Dan put his hand on Mick's knee. "But you're Mick the Knife, the scariest g...gangster in London. I've seen d...dozens of TV programmes about you!"

"Yeah, it's amazing what a reputation will do for you," he said, sniffing. He pulled out a polka dot hankie and blew his nose. Now, he didn't look as menacing as on his photofit after a purported stabbing.

"B...but, b...but how?" asked Dan.

Plumporious gave a slightly embarrassed cough. "I think I may have something to do with that, Dan. You see, Mick and I have been friends for a while, and we've had, what you could say, is a mutually beneficial relationship. Mick, as a pacifist in London, was treated extremely badly, a prey animal, if you will."

"I know the f...feeling," said the Dan.

"I, as a gay dwarf—a gay dwarf with a few anger management issues, I might add, finding my way in the world—I also found it difficult to mix in desired social circles. So, Mick would take the blame for some of my more noticeable crimes. We became somewhat of a double act," he said, rather showbiz.

"So you're the most terrifying c...c...criminal in the UK, Plumporious?"

His hands clasped together in prayer. "I beg you not to tell anyone, Dan. I'd hate to have to cut out your beating heart and feed it to you."

Dan stared into the cold eyes of death, and looked away quickly. "So, Mick did all your t...time in jail for you?"

"Yes. Obviously, when Mick wasn't around I was arrested. It was why we had so many luxuries in our cells. I was most shocked when Steve here—" he gestured at the dying centaur, "—was placed in our cell. Any longer and I think I'd have been forced to complain, and I do dislike the awkwardness of complaining."

"So, Mick, why d...did you leave here?" asked Dan.

Plumporious talked, for Mick was busy sobbing.

"Poor Michael. Loved by his father, The Dark King, but a laughing stock to his people. You never told me you were a prince though, Michael. I thought he was rich, but not...not royalty."

Mick blew a snot bubble.

Plumporious sighed but continued. "Racism, sexism, anything – ism can never be stamped out or eradicated, not until there is only one person left on the planet, and I can guarantee they'll hate themselves. No one treats everyone the same, and everyone judges people by the way they look."

"No they—"

Dan's interruption was interrupted. "Would you cross the street if a goblin was coming the other way wearing a PVC gimp outfit and brandishing a fifteen-inch dildo?"

"Erm...fair point," answered Dan, honestly.

"Mick was the only ginger elf in the forest. If he wasn't The Dark King's son, what sort of life would he have led? Mick realised this and, for him, the position of power was not earned, it was given, a birth right."

"Where's the justice in that?" asked the elf, looking up from the dwarf's tear-stained armpit.

"It's just the way it is," said Dan. "Most people have their shitty lives m...m...mapped out from their first breath."

"So Mick went to the city, to London, determined to make it for himself and prove to his clan he was worthy to lead them. He went penniless and with only the tunic on his back."

"And what happened?"

Plumporious gave Mick's shoulder a squeeze. "Someone took the tunic off his back."

"I didn't have a formal education," said Mick. "I couldn't get a job. I ended up on benefits. I was officially a prince and I was claiming jobseeker's. There was nothing I could do. The longer it went on, the worse it got. If I'd stayed here, I'd have had everything. It's all right being a useless twat as long as you're a rich useless twat."

"So why d...did you want to come back?" asked Dan.

Mick shrugged. "All my stuff is here."

"There must b...be more to it than that?" asked Dan.

"Got to get that amulet somehow," he sobbed.

Dan patted Mick on the knee. "Poor guy," he said. "I know how you feel. You're j...j...just the same as me."

Mick's whole body tensed for a moment, but he said nothing.

"Are you g...going to fight, Mick?" Dan asked.

"When I said I can't, I really can't." Mick stared at his fists. "I'm really shit at it, you know, like you are at magic."

Dan bit the inside of his mouth. "So what are you going to d...do, then?"

The elf looked away into the distance and came to a conclusion. "I'm going to be stabbed until enough blood runs out of my body and I am given the luxury of dying."

Chapter 42...

THE DARK KING SAT ON THE EDGE OF HIS THRONE, incessantly tapping his royal staff on the floor, an outlet for nervous energy. The prisoners were brought out before him, Mick trudged along, head bowed. Only Steve was slower out of the blocks because of his terrible wounds.

Jonquil stood in the centre of the circle, swinging his sword with expert timing, the slashing of the air singing to the time of Mick's trudging. He stared down an already-vanquished foe. There wasn't a spectator in court who thought The Dark King would sit on his throne for longer than a fag break.

The Dark King stood. "Michael, will you fight for the right to leave Darbenham? If you win, you can leave, if you lose you will die and your friends will be put to the sword."

"Thank, God!" said Steve, clutching his spleen.

"Will you fight, Michael, or do you have a champion?" asked The Dark King.

Jonquil's swinging sword stopped dead in mid-air at the mention of champion. His steely gaze focussed on Mick and he mouthed the words "fight me."

Mick looked back at Plumporious, who reached up on tip toes and gave a hopeful wave. Mick turned to his father and asked, "May a dwarf fight for my honour?"

An angry murmur poured forth from the spectators.

The Dark King silenced the murmuring with his sharp tongue. "Our laws forbid it, as you well know. If you weren't my son, the dwarf would have died when he set foot in our sacred forest. They remain our ancient enemy."

Plumporious winked. "We can kiss and make up if you like."

The Dark King's eye twitched in anger. "What is your answer, Michael?"

Mick approached the throne. "I understand you have no choice on the matter, Father," he whispered, so that only his dad would hear. The Dark King closed his eyes tight shut at hearing his son's words, and a single tear that he'd held in for so long, escaped down a hard face. Mick sealed his fate. "Mum wouldn't want me fighting." He turned to the court. "I accept the challenge."

The court erupted in cheers. "Stab the ginger tosser in the liver!"

came a cry—and it wasn't from Steve. He was in too bad a state to cry anything but brine.

The Dark King seethed but said nothing, his face granite once more.

"See why I left," said the Knife to his dad.

The Dark King sat heavily on the throne. Now he was monarch, family ties were irrelevant. Mortal combat ruled this world, and it was time for blood spilling.

Three rounds would be fought. The first two rounds were to warm up the crowd. Only the final round would bring death. The first round was a boxing match, and the Queensbury Rules were not paid heed to in these parts. Jonquil beat Mick to a pulp inside a minute. Mick didn't land a blow, didn't even swing a punch. Some of the crowd had expected Jonquil to put on an exhibition, but that wasn't the case. The referee, a slight, elderly elf wearing a black-and-white striped shirt, had only stepped in once Mick was unconscious on the floor, his opponent astride him, raining down punches. They'd given him an hour for the cobwebs to clear. He needed more time—seven years in a gladiatorial camp would have been perfect.

Wrestling was next. The round would end when a combatant tapped out. In thirty seconds, Mick was banging on the floor like a hopeful teenager at an off-camera reality TV audition. Jonquil was strong, fast, and lean. Mick was—lean. After reluctantly releasing Mick from the arm bar, Jonquil spat on his opponent with the words: "You disgrace your species. Whatever species you happen to be."

Mick crawled over to his friends, their faces painted in encouragement, all except Steve who laughed his horseshoes off in between grabbing his ribs in agony. "This is hilarious! I've never seen such a one-sided fight in all my life!" He coughed up some blood.

"Thanks," said Mick coughing up some blood of his own.

"You didn't do so bad in the last round, Mick," said Plumporious, cheerfully. "I think he grazed his knee when he slammed you into the ground."

"Yeah, great," said the dejected elf.

"A graze can be quite painful, I can tell you," said the homicidal psychopath.

"And now we have the final round," shouted the referee above the din of the crowd, who mostly laughed and mocked. Only The Dark King sat quiet, his regal chin resting on his fist, not able to look at his son. The final round forced fatality. The other two rounds were to raise the blood, to make it interesting and inflict injuries that might affect the outcome of the match, but this was where the real entertainment began.

"Sire," cried the referee for all to hear. "What weapon would you have our combatants prove their worth?"

"The knife!" he said, desperation creeping into his voice.

Dan slapped Mick on the back. "The knife! The knife! He wants you to win. He wants you t...to win. You're Mick the Knife! You're the m...most famed knifeman in all—"

Mick gave Dan the most tired of looks.

"You've never s...s...stabbed anyone in your life, have you?"

"Of course I haven't."

"But Mick," Dan said, "if you don't stab Jonquil, then he'll kill you."

"I know," said the elf, taking the knife that the adjudicator handed him. He felt the weight, bouncing it in his hand. "Mick the Knife," he said. He gave a mirthless laugh, shaking his head. "I've lived by my reputation as the Knife for so many years, and now I'm going to die from it. There should be a saying about it or something."

"This is a battle to the death," announced the referee, grandly. "There will be no mercy shown to the loser, and none to the winner if he does not finish what he started. This hard land cannot abide weakness." He cast a sly look at Mick. "The future of the Dark Forest will be decided by the spilling of blood and the taking of life. Let's get ready for stttttaaaaabbbbbbiiiinnnnnn'!" he yelled to the rooftops, but his finale fell a bit flat.

The two gladiators circled each other for no more than a second before Jonquil jumped in and slashed at Mick's knife hand, drawing blood. Mick's weapon clattered into the floor. The deadly Jonquil laughed, and stood back, allowing Mick to pick up his knife. Jonquil slapped Mick's head with the flat of his blade as he bent over. Mick didn't retaliate, just rubbed his head and sucked air through his teeth.

"You could never be a king," said Jonquil.

"I don't bleedin' want to be," said Mick. "That's why I've been forced into this bollocks, you bellend!"

"Do not anger me!" said Jonquil, haughtily.

"Why? We're in a battle to the death. You can't exactly kill me twice, can you, you penis?"

Jonquil ignored it. "Soon you'll be forgotten. Your rotting corpse will not be given a burial. I'll rip out your eyes and spit on your brain."

"Why?" asked Mick, genuinely confused.

After not being able to come up with a retort to Mick's very good question, Jonquil attacked with added vigour. He cut across Mick's cheek and Mick grabbed at yet another wound. Mick didn't attack, just tried to stay away.

Dan looked on in frustration and despair. "Please, fight back, Mick!"

"I can't watch this!" said Plumporious, snarling. He rolled up his sleeves and stepped forwards. Suddenly every bow was drawn, but, not aimed at him, aimed at Mick.

The referee warned, "Step into the circle, dwarf, and you seal your friend's fate."

Plumporious gnashed his teeth but didn't take another step. "If he dies, I am going to burn this forest down and everyone in it."

Mick breathed and bled heavily. Jonquil hadn't broken sweat.

"I'm bored of this," announced Jonquil, pompously looking down his nose at his foe. He stepped forward, flashing his knife, but his foot came down on a piece of horse manure Steve had unwittingly left behind during his beating, and Jonquil slipped, landed on one knee, and dropped his weapon. He was there for the taking!

"FINISH HIM!" cried The Dark King, Dan, and Plumporious.

Mick only had to drive the knife downwards.

But he didn't.

Mick hesitated.

"I can't do it. I ain't a cold-blooded killer."

Jonquil on the other hand...

The lithe elf quickly regained himself, span around, and swept Mick's legs from under him with one of his own. Mick dropped his knife and Jonquil caught it. Mick landed on his back and Jonquil jumped on top of him, one hand around Mick's throat, the other holding the knife above his head, ready to drive it down and claim the throne. Mick, only moments away from death, looked up at the carved ceiling of the ancient hall, breathed one last sigh, and waited for his fate...

A small commotion broke out at the back of the hall, starting with a murmuring, and then shouting, and then much louder shouting, and then screaming, lots and lots of screaming. The elves jostled and bustled, desperate to get away from something less popular than a shit in a swimming pool. Whatever was coming through the crowd was short, for it couldn't be seen, but its path could be, as the elves who couldn't get out of the way were thrown out of the way. Eventually, it broke through the line of elves, and it couldn't have been less elf-like, although it did have pointy ears.

Mr. Grak still managed an arrogant saunter through the court, even while holding one elf by the neck and another by the hair, both of whom were desperately, and unsuccessfully, trying to break free. The guards followed him, bows drawn, trying to fix him in their sights, but he moved constantly, swaying like a cobra looking for an opening, ensuring his hostages were always in front of the arrowheads.

"What is the meaning of this?" cried The Dark King.

"Mr. G...G...Grak?" said Dan. "What are you d...d...d...doing here?" The return of the goblin sent the stutter into overdrive.

"Shut it, fairycakes. I've come to bring you in."

"B...b...bring me in? Wh...wh...why?"

The goblin, uncaring of the overwhelming odds he faced, or that he was in the presence of royalty, said, "Do you realise the damage you've caused Green Planet since you blew that polar bear's paws off and escaped prison? And then it came to light you'd been diddling all these years!"

"He's a nonce," said Steve, pointing from the floor.

"...just five minutes in a room with him," said several middle-aged members of the congregation, while several left to leave online comments.

Mr. Grak hushed them all with stares, and then went after Dan again. "After you escaped, all the attention turned on us. I'm here to bring you to justice," said Mr. Grak, twisting and turning with the elves' arrows.

"Who are you!" demanded the referee, who was swiftly kicked in the groin. He collapsed on the floor and was relieved the agony of crushed testicles by a kick to the jaw.

"Shut up!" said Mr. Grak, rather needlessly to the comatose ref.

"Who are you?" demanded The Dark King.

"I'm Mr. Grak," said the goblin with an unmistakable air of authority. "You can call me, Mr. Grak."

"How dare you address me in that way!" cried the monarch.

"Shut up, or you'll get a kick in the bollocks as well! What's going on here, anyway?" he said, keeping an eye on Jonquil who'd jumped off Mick and now paced like a tiger sizing up newly discovered prey.

"That's Mick's dad," said Plumporious, nodding at the king. "And Mick and this abhorrent Jonquil are having a fight to the death to see who will be the next heir."

"That's Mick the Knife ain't it?" said Mr. Grak, looking at the supine strawberry blonde.

"Aye," said the bleeding elf, lighting up a fag while enjoying the rest.

"And you're a prince?" said an unconvinced goblin executive.

"Soon to be a dead one."

"How come?" asked the goblin.

"Because I am going to kill him," said Jonquil, grandly, his chin held high, looking down the snootiest of snouts.

"And who are you, then, sunshine?" said Mr. Grak in a voice only Dan recognised.

"I am Jonquil, and after I have killed this pathetic excuse for an elf, my father will become king of this realm, and I will be the prince. And my first decree will be thus..." Hands clasped behind his back, he strolled around the hall. "That any filthy goblin who wanders into our beautiful forest is captured on sight and brought to me so I can kill them personally."

Mr. Grak's eyes glazed over in a way only Dan recognised. "I don't think you know who you're dealing with, boy."

"I am dealing with a dead goblin," said Jonquil, coldly.

"Is that so?" Mr. Grak said to the elf, in a tone only Dan recognised. Mr. Grak turned to the congregation and let go of his captives, uncaring of the bows trained on him. He raised his arms aloft and announced, "I am going to take Mick's place, here."

"But you can't," said The Dark King. "Proceedings are already in motion."

Mr. Grak landed another boot into comatose referee. "The ref doesn't mind."

"But, I am The Dark King."

"Who doesn't care if his own son dies?" Mr. Grak's arched brow bone was a judging one. Dan concluded it the only moral bone in his body.

Jonquil stepped forward, red of face and hot of blood. "Let me fight him, sire." Cool serenity had departed. "Let me cut his head off and place it on a spike in front of—"

Mr. Grak bounded across the hall at remarkable speed, a flash of green to an onlooker. Jonquil, a veteran of hand-to-hand combat wasn't fast enough, wasn't good enough. Mr Grak's forehead crashed into Jonquil's face with a sickening crunch. To the elf's credit, he did not fall. He grabbed his nose, a bloody waterfall, and slashed wildly at the goblin who ducked out of the way while sporting the wickedest grin that only Dan recognised.

Dan had only seen the grin twice before, both times in the staff canteen. This was the most feared of Mr. Grak's myriad bowel-loosening facial expressions. This was his shaving face.

Mr. Grak toyed with the elf, moving into range. Jonquil flashed his weapon but Mr. Grak was too fast, dodging and weaving. Jonquil tired quickly with the loss of blood and the pain. Mr. Grak took his opportunity. He nipped past Jonquil's flailing blade, grabbed him by his beautiful hair, and ran him skull-first into a torch sconce. The elf bounced off the wood and hit the ground, defeated.

But it wasn't over.

And it wasn't even shave o'clock.

Every elf turned away from the ensuing beating. They were bloodthirsty by nature, and had watched, with glee, the one-sided knife fight between Jonquil and Mick, but watching their champion ridiculed, crying on the floor and begging for it to end, was too much for proud hearts. Every body part bled, including his knee, which Plumporious pointed at and gave Mick a double thumbs up. Which was nice.

Jonquil crawled, tears wetting the wooden floor. Mr. Grak gave mostly double biceps poses to the horrified onlookers, and added a few "Hulkamania" poses for nostalgia. All that was left was for him to finish the job. He reached into his coat pocket and took out the weapon for the final act of degradation. The buzzing was an alien noise in the halls of Darbenham.

Mr. Grak shaved Jonquil. He shaved him. Everywhere. All looked on, appalled, as the goblin finished his work. To the goblin's credit, he was very efficient and left no cuts. Jonquil trembled from his prone position and clutched at fallen locks with shaking hands.

Mr. Grak stepped over him and marched towards The Dark King. He put the infamous weapon in his pocket and said, "Right! Who's next?"

"It's a fight...to the death," said The Dark King, weakly, watching Jonquil cry into his pubes.

Mr. Grak snarled in disgust. "If that's what you want, then you're next on the list for one of these, pal!" He shook a green fist. "Because I ain't killing anyone because some prick with a shit crown, who thinks he's better than everyone else, tells me to."

"Guards!" cried The Dark King.

As one, the guards grimaced and rubbed the backs of their necks. They shuffled a few millimetres towards the irate goblin.

"Don't even think about it!" snapped Mr. Grak, whipping out the razor and pointing it at them. They stared at it, eyes wide, as if it was a gun. None of them had seen a man have his pubes shaved against his will before. All mimicked statues and hoped for the best.

"Right, you lot," Mr. Grak said to Dan, Steve, and Mick, who was having his wounds tended to by Plumporious. "I'll catch up with you on the way out, but first, these tosspots need to be taught a lesson."

The Fellowship left the secret glade to a righteous hum.

Chapter 43...

No one had tried to stop the Fellowship leaving the halls of the Dark King. Mr. Grak had seen to that. Even though the elves were armed with bows and were considered experts by world-class Olympic archers, there was something about a bully with Mr. Grak's credentials that could force doubt into the mind. It was basic mathematics: miss once = shaved once.

Dan was still rather confused why Mr. Grak turned up in the first place.

They left the grounds of the elven halls and the surrounding glades and soon treaded with difficulty through the thick of the forest. Mick had known how to get out of the hall and the glade, but he'd no idea know how to get out of the forest. He'd just wanted to be away from the place. A great whoosh, searing the air, had them all craning necks to the sky. A bright red flare, barely visible through the dense branches, arced across the night.

"What's that about?" asked Dan, scratching his head.

"I have no idea," said Mick, placing a hand on Dan's back and shoving him along. "Come on, let's get out of here."

"Where?" asked Dan.

"Anywhere," said Mick, setting off.

Claustrophobia was quick to find them again, choking them and laying heavy on their hearts.

"Pissing twigs!" cried Steve.

"I'm sorry things ended up the way they d...did," said Dan to Mick.

"Eh?" said Mick, his mind elsewhere.

"You know, with your father, and that."

"Oh, right, yeah," he said, waving a hand, as if he'd already forgotten the damaging experience which would have corroded a fragile mind to mush. He didn't seem overly concerned with his cuts and bruises. He lit a fag and took a draw. "I'd hoped to reconcile our differences. I must say, I didn't think he'd put me in a battle to the death with a narcissistic assassin."

"A bald narcissistic assassin," added Plumporious with a wink.

"Shame that," said the centaur. "I was quite enjoying the fight until that goblin showed up."

"Are you OK, M...Mick, really?" Dan placed a hand on his friend's back.

"Gerroff!" Mick shrugged off the comforting small mitt of Dan.

Plumporious coughed. "Michael," he said.

Mick closed his eyes and counted to ten. "Yeah. Thanks for looking out for me," he said, sarcastically. "It was really hard, and stuff. You know...with the stuff."

"Michael!" chastised Plumporious.

Dan narrowed his eyes. "What's going on—" And then Dan's train of thought derailed. He sensed....

He sensed....

He stopped dead, but Steve walked into the back of him, sending him flying into a muddy puddle.

"Sorry, didn't see you there," said the centaur, kicking the muddy puddle over the fallen hero.

Dan didn't complain, or say a word, much to the centaur's annoyance. With difficulty, Dan pushed himself out of the boggy puddle with a mighty squelch. He got to his feet. No one helped him because two of his companions didn't care and the other now treated him like a leper, whispering "unclean" under his breath.

Dan closed his eyes and placed his fingers on his temples. "I can...I can...sense something."

"Is it sound?" asked Steve.

"No, it's...well, yes I do sense sound, b...but...." His eyes snapped open and he pointed through the trees. "There!"

"What are you talking about, Dan?" asked the dwarf.

"It's like the d...dwarf mines," he said, excitedly, jumping on the spot. He disappeared through the trees.

"Watch out for wolves," called Mick through the trees.

Dan reappeared through the trees a lot faster than he'd disappeared. "C...c...come with me!" he urged.

"What is it, Dan?" said the dwarf, irritably, "and stop jumping about with all that filthy mud on you! I'd hate to have to make you eat your bodyweight in fox poo!"

"The other amulet is through here, I know it!" cried Dan, giving the air a damn fine punch.

"There's nothing through there," said Mick. "Just a load more trees like there is in every direction."

"Just like Grundard said there was only rock in the mines?" Dan said. Mick acquiesed and they followed through the woods until Dan reached a tree, a tree just like any other. "This is it. This is a magic tree!" Dan cried.

"Stupid fairy," muttered Steve, rubbing his bits.

Dan ran his fingers up and down the bark of the ancient pine. "Magic runs strong through the roots." He reached out with both hands and wrapped them as far as he could around the vast trunk. "What do you have for me, old friend?"

Much to Steve's surprise, who was making a wanker gesture with his hand, a golden glow emanated from the leaves and they rustled, whispering magic secrets in a tongue no longer spoken and sounding like bird song and kitten purrs to non-magical ears.

Only Dan understood the whispers, and the golden glow sparkled off his wide grin.

A golden line ran up the tree from the roots, bisecting the trunk until it reached the top, and then, ever so slowly, with the creaking of bark and the splintering of timber, the tree split in half, falling, landing with a mighty crash, destroying the sinister silence of the foreboding forest. Gold light illuminated the darkness.

Lying in the centre was a shrine, a sister to the one in the dwarf mines. Sat on top was the source of the light, the second amulet, a mirror image to the first, a black amulet radiating golden light. Dan grabbed it this time, with no hesitation, and the power coursed through his body, the light extinguishing in an instant. He placed the amulet around his neck. The twins, like attracting magnets, snapped together, becoming one, and a magical shockwave threw Dan to the ground. The other companions kept their feet for they were made of sterner stuff, although Mick's tracksuit did sustain a small rip from the force. The trees shook back and forth, but not a leaf was lost for the blast of magic was sent by Nature.

Ancient, powerful knowledge awoke inside Dan.

He knew.

He knew!

It called to him like a beacon.

"I know where the Lost Sword of the Fairy King is hidden," he cried and grabbed the amulet around his neck. "This is the key! I know where it is."

Dan slowly got to his feet, his cherubic cheeks glowing. Pure delight lit his normally downtrodden face. For once in his life, Dan...was a winner.

"I'm going to save the polar bears! I'm going to save the world!"

Chapter 44...

THE DARK ALLIANCE WAITED ON THE OUTSKIRTS OF THE DARK FOREST in a pub car park, which wasn't particularly dark. Scenic but isolated, a travelling inn of old with a history longer than the publicans could comprehend. The Dark Forest to one side, and the gateway to the Highlands on the other, this was a place of power. A few locals had ventured outside to see what the commotion was. A couple of Range Rovers, engines running, waited, and the helicopter was ready for takeoff. The locals could be forgiven for being curious, but Michelle told them to "Piss off back inside, you nosy old bastards." They'd assumed a big, famous Scottish celebrity had flown in, like Susan Boyle, or...or...or Mel Gibson as The Braveheart or something.

The Dark Alliance was in the driving seat and Gambledolf and the forces of good had no idea what waited for them. The Dark Alliance's inside "man" had infiltrated Gambledolf's ranks and checkmate was but a move away. It was only a matter of time before—

"There it is, look!" cried Rillit, pointing to the heavens. The red flare shot out of the forest canopy and illuminated the moonless sky as well as dark hearts.

Draknarkus, who'd paced the car park, chuckled with a rare show of approval. "I must say your goblin boyfriend is a rather remarkable individual, Michelle."

"He isn't my boyfriend," she said firmly. "It's just sport sex."

Derek waggled his eyebrows at his sexually promiscuous captor.

Michelle sneered. "He has a *growspeck* the size of your leg, shortarse."

The halfling flushed a deep red. "It's the technique that matters," he muttered under his breath.

"Even so," said Draknarkus. "I never thought he'd infiltrate Darbenham and rescue those blundering idiots from certain death. I thought we were going to need Somersby's private army."

"He will *not* be happy when he learns of the expenses you've amassed, black wizard," said Rillit, scanning his finger down a tablet, tutting and shaking his head. "And I wouldn't be surprised if his private army comes into play when he sees your credit card bill."

"Once he possesses the Sword, he won't care," she said, with a dismissive flick of her hand. She contemplated the Dark Forest.

"Gambledolf placed too much hope in the Chosen One's bodyguards. The goblins of Lashley were one thing, but the elves of Darbenham are something else entirely. He always was an optimist, or, rather, a foolish, romantic."

"Why did he let them traipse through the forest unaided?" asked Rillit.

Draknarkus laughed. "Probably because the elves would have put an arrow in his saggy arse the moment they saw him. The old wizard has made dangerous enemies over the years."

"So what now?" asked Michelle.

"All of Gambledolf's efforts to hide the Chosen One and the amulets have been in vain," said the black wizard. "It will soon be a race to the Sword, and we have the might of Somersby's bank account to get us anywhere, fast. That tight arse Gambledolf won't know what hit him."

"They have to find the second amulet first, though?" asked Rillit.

"Yes, they do, and it is bound to lie somewhere in—" Draknarkus eyes widened and she grabbed at her head. She reached out to the car park wall to steady herself, and then doubled over. She blinked rapidly, her wide eyes unseeing. She fell to the ground, hard, landing with a mighty bump for such a slight frame.

Derek gasped. "Are you OK?" he said, genuinely concerned and rushing over to her side.

"They've...they've found it. They've found the amulet! The shockwave was like nothing I've felt before. They must be nearby. My god, the power." She licked her lips. "I can taste the residual magic." She pushed the concerned halfling away and he fell over the short car park wall. Draknarkus got to her feet nimbly. Perseus hopped over to her and she picked him up and tickled his ears.

"Judas!" said Derek from behind the wall.

Draknarkus stared at the forest. "I can pin point the amulet and the man who holds it. Our quest is nearly at its end. The final confrontation between good and evil approaches."

"What is your plan?" asked Rillit, taking out a mobile phone. "I must inform my master."

"Leave him out of it, for the time being," said Draknarkus, gripping Rillit with a powerful stare. The lackey held on to the phone, battling his duty and the hypnotic gaze of the evil witch. "He will only get in the way," she said lightly.

The phone went back into the pocket, but he looked to Michelle for guidance. She ignored his unspoken plea.

Draknarkus ran her finger over the sleek bonnet of the 4 x 4. "We should take the cars. They're inconspicuous compared to the chopper, and if I know Gambledolf, they will not be travelling fast, or in style. Hmmm...." She looked over at the helicopter. "But I *do* like travelling in style. The Sword is as good as ours, my people."

"Yay!" said Derek, and danced for their entertainment and for their morale.

"Can I take him into the pub toilets and kill him?" asked Michelle. "Honestly, it is no problem at all."

Derek cut his jig short.

Chapter 45...

GAMBLEDOLF WAITED FOR THEM ON THE OUTSKIRTS OF THE FOREST, leaning on his staff and smoking his pipe. He'd parked up a people carrier, even more disgusting than the last, in a lay-by near one of the country's most deadly establishments and its biggest killer: a greasy spoon. There was a public toilet here, too, which had never been used for its intended purpose.

"Gambledolf!" cried Dan, and ran up to the wizard who patted him on the head, ruffled his hair, and pulled him into a warm embrace.

The elf and the dwarf exchanged looks.

"How did you know we were here," asked Mick of the wizard.

Gambledolf inclined his head. "I always know where you are, good elf."

"Then why did you leave us trudging through that shit forest if you knew where we were?" Mick said, a touch on the aggrieved side.

Gambledolf wagged a finger. "Then it wouldn't be an adventure, would it?"

"You're saying that like adventures are a good thing?" said the wounded centaur.

"Don't you think they test the spirit as well as the flesh?" asked the wizard.

"After tearing my sack on a bramble, I got the shit kicked out of me by a load of poncey elves—and these bastards did nothing." Steve pointed an accusing finger at his companions, none of whom cared.

The wizard tipped his hat. "All part of adventuring, good centaur."

"Gambledolf, look what I have!" cried Dan, holding up the fused amulet.

Gambledolf grinned from ear to ear. "Danoclees, this lifts my heart. Anglor wants you to wield the power! Mother Nature calls to her champion!"

"So how come I still haven't got the confidence to use magic, Gambledolf?" he said, sadly, holding up his limp wand.

The companions tittered.

"The Lost Sword of the Fairy King will unleash the wizard in you, young Danoclees. Do not fear, power beyond your wildest dreams is near, and not just any power—good power, righteous power."

Neither Mick nor Steve looked convinced. Both turned lips up at the small, bespectacled saviour whose wand, in all fairness, did look a little more turgid of late.

Plumporious, ever optimistic, said, "It does look like it has an extra half inch on it."

"You are almost there, my young adventurers," announced Gambledolf. "You have both halves of the amulet, which Danoclees has united, and this will lead us to the Lost Sword of the Fairy King. You march to your destiny."

"Is this going to be over soon, I'm getting really bored," said the centaur. "And I think I've got a couple of broken ribs."

Gambledolf waved his wand at the centaur. "Yes, you have, majestic beast, and you are also suffering from internal bleeding, although not enough to kill you."

"Are you going to heal me?" asked Steve, hopefully.

"No," said Gambledolf, deadpan.

"Old fogey twat," muttered the centaur under his breath.

"Are you going to come with us for the final leg of the journey, Gambledolf?" asked Dan.

"Yes, my boy. I will accompany you to your destiny."

"That's brilliant news, Gambledolf!" Dan gushed.

"Alas, now it is a race. While the Sword will remain undetected to others, the magic blast unleashed from the fusing of the amulets will alert anyone with even a passing talent in the arcane. They will bear down on us with great speed."

"You not gonna hide our escape route this time?" asked Mick.

"If there were but two of me. Danoclees knows where we must travel, and I will decipher the paths we must follow. I will guide you and protect you from awaiting adversaries. It is a dangerous road we take."

"As long as you stick to the bargain, then it's all right by me," said Steve, who realised he'd said something untoward when Gambledolf stared at him like a hypodermic needle in a playground.

"Bargain? What b...bargain?" asked Dan.

Steve picked at his fingernails and whistled a non-descript tune. Gambledolf turned to Dan. "Unfortunately, not all your companions are as interested in the well being of the world as you, my young protégé."

"What do you mean?" said an innocent, if naive apprentice.

"I had to pay him to come along," said a grudging wizard.

Steve poked Dan in the chest. "Didn't think I'd be doing all this for nothing, did you, fairy boy?"

"I guess not," said Dan, looking dejected.

"Don't worry, young Danoclees, your other companions are here because of their free will."

Dan turned to his favourite two companions and beamed.

"I need a piss," said Mick, turning sharply and heading for the toilets.

"Anyone want anything from the café?" said Plumporious, turning and leaving before anyone could order anything.

"We must alight!" Gambledolf held up his staff, an action implying yet further action. "I fear the black wizard trails us, and there is nothing stalking this planet more dangerous than she."

"Will we have to c...c...confront her, Gambledolf?" asked Dan, fear touching his heart.

"If we are fast, we may avoid her." He stroked his beard and considered the people carrier. "But this vehicle is slow as shit at the top end, so they'll probably catch us up on the dual carriageway."

Chapter 46...

THUS BEGAN THE LAST LEG OF THE JOURNEY. Even though time was apparently of the essence, Gambledolf refused to take the people carrier (with a trailer for Steve) over fifty-six m.p.h., the optimum speed for fuel conservation. A helicopter had passed overhead several times, but Gambledolf had dismissed it with a wave of his hand saying it was nothing more than coincidence. The Fellowship were beginning to doubt the abilities of the white wizard, although Dan knew that underneath the bluster and the blunder, Gambledolf was a true warrior of Anglor.

Their destination was the west coast of Scotland, Oban, to be precise. Dan was the human compass. He felt important. He *was* important. He was going to be a wizard and save the world.

Gambledolf parked in a National Trust car park and cursed the heavens when he saw what they charged per hour. He made everyone get back in the carrier and they looked for cheaper, alternative parking, but there was none, only signs saying that if they parked on the roads they'd be towed. Gambledolf swore a dark oath that made Dan blush, and headed back to the National Trust car park. They waited for twenty minutes, asking people leaving the car park if they'd finished with their parking tickets, and when they'd all but given up hope, Gambledolf struck gold—and saved himself a few quid as an elf family had enough money left on their ticket to take them past 5 p.m. when the car park was free.

The wizard was on a high.

After leaving the car park, they followed a roughly hewn coastal path for a couple of miles, but it was all guess work. Dan could point to the Sword, but walking in a straight line in this wilderness on this winding trail was difficult.

The Fellowship had expected trouble, but, according to Gambledolf, there hadn't been a sniff of the dark witch. The rest of the Fellowship, however, were certain the low-flying helicopter had something to do with them, no matter what the wizard said.

But there was no evil lurking on the ground, not conventional evil anyway. The worst they'd dealt with was Gambledolf standing in dog poo. He was convinced the perpetrator was a West Highland terrier they'd seen a mile back. The Fellowship worked hard to convince the wizard not to go back and give the owner, an elderly gentleman, "a right fucking kicking," as the wizard called it.

The west coast of Scotland was a treasure enjoyed by too few. Sunbeams warmed even the coldest heart, and the whistling breeze coming in off the sea chilled even the fieriest of tempers. Waves lapped at the rocks below the cliff faces and seabirds called to one another in play, sounds to calm even the most aggressive of spirits. This was where the world would be saved, a magnificent testament to nature's wonder when left alone to flourish.

"We're getting closer! We're getting closer!" cried Dan.

"Can you perform any magic, yet?" asked Plumporious, hopefully.

Dan lifted his wand, which was definitely pointing above the horizontal. "I'm not sure. I think...."

"Hold, Danolcees," said Gambledolf. "You'll give our position away if you use magic."

Dan looked up at the circling helicopter. He opened his mouth to speak but Gambledolf hushed him. "Once you hold the Sword, cast spells to your heart's content. No force of darkness could oppose you." The old wizard smiled and so did his excited apprentice.

They drew closer. One didn't need to be a wizard nor a wizard's apprentice to know magic was afoot. Nature thrived. The Garden of Eden hadn't come close to this splendour, especially after some goblin teenagers got drunk on extra strong lager and made a terrible mess of it, burning massive *growspecks* into the lawn with petrol, and leaving things in the birdbaths unlikely to aid our avian friends in their quest for cleanliness. Yes, the goblins were caught, and charged, but no amount of community service would restore the garden to its unearthly goodness. Rehabilitation? "Nonsense! They hadn't learned a damned thing," asserted Brian Reginald (68, Guildford). He demanded the reinstatement of National Service, and although his requests had been ignored, he'd received three likes on "the Facebook."

This place was different. Not cultivated like the Garden, but wild. Birds wheeled above and landed on the outstretched arms of the Fellowship. Even Steve smiled when a robin landed on his shoulder and sung him a tune. He only grimaced due to his terrible wounds. Dan was only shit on thrice, and one of those times was a genuine accident. The flowers bloomed and the trees swayed. Concentrated walls of colour and delicious scents frolicked in the wind, ever changing. This was paradise.

"This is well ace!" said Dan.

"I must say, it is rather fabulous," said the dwarf. Butterflies completely covered his clothes and he danced, the staggering iridescence of their wings producing a colour that would send that utter bitch Rudi von Shortspunk into second place at last. "I'm a princess!" he cried.

Even Mick the Knife had some fun, frisking with the bunnies, although one bunny stood a little way off, all white, red eyes flashing awfully suspiciously. Awfully suspiciously with evil.[25]

Dan raised a hand and halted. "This is...." He paused and squinted at the vertical grassy cliff, reaching high above him and his fellow Fellowshippers. "It...?" he said, questioning his impulse and the amulet.

"Are you sure?" asked Gambledolf, running his fingers through the grass.

Dan's hand shook when he reached out to the cliff. He, too, ran his hands through the grass, and as he did so it pulled away from his touch, and kept pulling away, as did the soil, defying gravity and sliding up the hillside to reveal a gateway.

Gambledolf clasped his hands together and cried aloud, "I'd never have believed it if I hadn't seen it with my own eyes."

All the artistry and architectural finesse of the Vatican compacted into a doorway, six foot square. The stone door was the last barrier to the Lost Sword of the Fairy King. The millennia-old stone work had not weathered in the slightest. To observe all the intricacies of the work were beyond the wavelength of visible light. The door depicted the fairy king holding up his sword with all the species of the world (except goblins) stood before him, arms around each other, united. The stone mason had constructed something so realistic, one had to reach out and touch it to believe it was real.

"This is incredible," said Dan. "Is this magic, Gambledolf?"

"You'd think so, but no, although there is probably a spell protecting it from the elements. The fairies could work both stone and wood beyond anything we see today. They bent nature's materials to their will, or more likely they convinced them to dance." He closed his eyes and whispered. "If only they still walked the earth with us."

"Yep, I've got to give it to them," said Steve, "this is pretty good shit." The heart-breaking cracking of stone caused Dan to cry out as Steve ripped off a priceless figure of a fairy from the architrave.

"What are you d...d...doing?" said Dan.

"Having a closer look," said Steve "It don't matter, it's not like they're going to press charges. They're all dead, remember? This is a victimless crime."

Dan looked to Gambledolf for support but the old wizard merely smiled, and the reason for his mirth became clear. Where Steve had broken off the statue, the rock regenerated to make an identical copy

---

[25] Yes, he did do a bit of humping, but that was just to fit in.

one of the figure Steve desecrated. "Now, that is magic," said Gamble-dolf.

Steve, lock-jawed, said, "Wonder how it copes with piss?"

"There will be none of that, Master Centaur," said a frowning wizard. "Now, Dan, it is likely that no one has seen this door in millennia, and certainly no one has passed beyond it, for there is but one key."

Dan patted his pockets down. "I haven't got it."

"I think you have, my boy," said Gambledolf pointing to the amulet on Dan's chest.

"This is a key as well?" said Dan, holding the amulet up. It absorbed all of the sun's energy shining on it, but remained cool. A nightingale landed on top of it and entertained the Fellowship with a beautiful song. Dan danced to the music, and the nightingale didn't even try to peck out his eyes.

Gambledolf laughed merrily to the little bird's tune. "Yes, it's a key. As well as other things, I should imagine."

"How do I use it?" asked Dan, turning the joined amulet over in his hands, the bird flying onto the wizard's hat.

"You tell me," said the wizard with a wink, rubbing the hair of the young apprentice.

"So weird," muttered Mick.

"Tell me about it," said the dwarf.

Since the halves had been joined, there was no evidence it ever lived as two pieces. The door in front of Dan had no obvious keyholes. He had no idea how to…. Wait. There were two indentations where the sun and the moon shone down on the fairytale scene. However, no sun and no moon were present, only an indent. Both celestial powers should be there with the fairies celebrating being illuminated by both.

Dan took the amulet and pulled it apart. It split into two, easier than unfastening Velcro, but without the annoying ripping sound. He considered the pieces and they moved in his mind and transformed in his hands, becoming circular; one turned silver, the other gold. He placed the sun and moon in the sky and a golden slit appeared down the middle of the door.

"He's done it!" cried the wizard, shaking his head in awe.

"I honestly never saw that coming," said Steve.

The doors swung open. The stone was a micron thick, completely defying material science, let alone craftsmanship. Gambledolf stood in front of the entrance and addressed the adventurers.

"Gentlemen, you are privileged. You are each the first of your kind to walk in the world of magic, in the world of the fairy. Each of you, myself included, will be remembered forever for these footsteps." The wizard stepped aside and bowed. "After you, Danoclees."

With no trepidation, he all but ran through, and, like when he'd entered Anglor in his dream, he became saturated with magic: golden lightning sparked from his fingers and golden bolts shot out of his ears and nostrils. The others did their best to squeeze through, Steve having particular problems, being mostly horse. They had to drag him and push him at the same time. He grazed his cock quite terribly, and Gambledolf refused to look at it, let alone treat it.

The Fellowship descended several steps and assembled in a great hall, a far cry from the tiny entrance, and full of stone carvings as magnificent as those on the door. The circular hall stretched up to test the sight, and not a square inch of wall was free of sculpture. It must have taken centuries. Each of the Fellowship stood in admiration, and even Steve didn't have a detrimental comment, although his subconscious forced out a little fart in protest.

Opposite the entrance stood another door, enormous, reaching ever upwards, and, ominously, it was blood red.

"Come," said Gambledolf. He tried to close the door from whence they came, but it wouldn't budge. "Master Centaur, if you will," he said, gesturing to the door with his hand.

Steve sighed, but trotted back to the entrance. He grabbed the door and grunted and groaned with the effort of pulling the door shut. Muscles bulged under hair and grime, but it was all to no avail. "Bugger that," he said, wiping his face.

"With one less barrier, time, I fear, is against us," said the wizard.

He hurried back across the hall and approached the blood red door, the group in tow. As they drew nearer, each of them wrapped their coats and cloaks tighter, a chill taking their bones. The group slowed with each footstep. They reached the door and all shuddered with a dread, as if someone had told them the day they would die—and today was that day—and they'd be killed by sporks. Terrible thoughts pushed themselves into the minds of each of the adventurers, filling them with self-doubt and destroying their self-worth, except for Dan. The voices in Dan's head had nothing on the doom and gloom his own consciousness could muster. To him, it was a pep talk.

The door, however, was undeniably and intrinsically evil.

"What is this thing, G…G…Gambledolf?" asked Dan, shying away, not wanting to look at what should be the barrier to salvation.

The old wizard leant on his staff and suddenly looked very old, as if his bent back held the weight of the world atop it.

"Gambledolf?" asked Dan, grabbing at the wizard's sleeve.

"It...it cannot be?" he said, pale of face.

"Just spit it out, you doddery old twat," said Steve.

"This door...this is dark magic." The wizard put out a hand to touch the surface and quickly withdrew it. "This is the blackest form of magic," he managed, weakly.

"Whatever do you mean?" asked Plumporious.

"What he means," came a female voice from behind them, "is that this is out of his goody-two-shoes comfort zone."

The heroes turned and there stood the Dark Alliance. At the front stood Draknarkus holding the fluffy white rabbit, Perseus. Hands on hips and chin held high, she cut a ravishing figure, even with the black cloak wrapped around her. She swept her wild black hair out of her face and the triumphant grin turned Dan's legs to jelly.

Next to her stood Rillit the butler. He didn't carry the usual pomp, for he'd been in the field, and didn't have to impress Mr. Somersby. Stubble was clearly visible on the top of his head. Grey hair no longer hid blonde roots and it had started to straighten. Several stains disgraced his suit. He looked from the Fellowship to Draknarkus and clenched a fist in victory. "You came good, witch," he said.

But she paid him no heed. Her eyes fixed on Dan.

Just behind the witch and the butler was a filthy, bruised and battered halfling, red of face, and bald of head. He lay prostate on the floor, but looked on the Fellowship with a friendly twinkle in his eye. He didn't try to get up because there was a foot on his back, and connected to that foot was—

"Michelle!" cried Dan.

She took her foot off Derek and moved forwards to stand next to Draknarkus. "Piss off, Dan!" she said.

"How the devil did you find us!" cried Gambledolf. His fellow adventurers gave him a look which said, "you what, mate?"

Draknarkus walked lightly down the steps, leaving the Dark Alliance waiting at the top.

Gambledolf's shoulders slumped and his head fell forwards letting his hat fall to the ground.

Draknarkus cackled, and said to Dan. "No, he isn't the man for the job anymore." She winked at the apprentice wizard and he recoiled, not able to hold the gaze of evil. "No," she said. "This is more *my* kind of magic."

Chapter 47...

DRAKNARKUS STARED INTENTLY AT DAN AND HE COVERED HIS FACE WITH HIS HANDS. With her to the front and the satanic door behind him, he had never been immersed in such hateful evil, not even when he'd been surrounded by a group of teenagers who inexplicably hung outside McDonalds restaurants late at night.

"I see you, Danoclees Dunlorian," she said, her voice deep, husky and enticing.

"Keep away!" he cried. Her words invaded, sullied, and tainted him. He looked to Gambledolf for strength, but the old wizard's face was grey. He leaned on his staff, and to Dan, he was an old man, not a wizard of Anglor. "Gambledolf?" Dan ventured, but the white wizard said nothing. Dan was alone. Again.

Draknarkus stalked the hall, high heels clicking on flagstones. She examined each of the Fellowship in turn. None of them could hold her gaze, not even Steve. She finally got back to Dan. "The old bastard did a fine job of hiding you, didn't he?"

With all his might, Dan held her eye, but darkness was all he found, evil embedded in beauty. To inherit the powers of Anglor, he must prove his worth. He was so close, and righteousness was his ally.

"How long has your bloodline lay hidden?" She paced slowly around him, looking him up and down, weighing him.

"Leave him be, witch!" said Gambledolf with a surge of fire.

"I had no idea of the power he'd wield, grey one," she said, eyes only on the apprentice.

"Grey one?" asked Dan, looking over to his teacher.

"Ha!" shrieked Draknarkus. She said to Gambledolf, "You didn't tell him you were a white wizard did you?"

The elf and the dwarf exchanged knowing looks.

Dan turned to Gambledolf, who finally stood up straight from his resting place on his staff. "I am the servant of Anglor!"

"Don't you think it strange how the good guys always draw the short straw?" she said, examining a nail. "And to think, you were so close. You thought evil chased you, but, no, it waited," she said, nodding towards the red door. "The darkness always waits. It waits for everyone."

"What's happening?" said Dan, desperately. "What is that door? What should I do, Gambledolf?"

"You must do what you think is right, Danoclees." All kindly tones had gone. His voice shook with uncertainty and fear. He was out of his depth, drowning like his apprentice.

Draknarkus laughed heartily and clapped her hands. "Oh, very good, old one. Another test? Another test because you don't know the answer? And what if he understands the door's call? What if he can interpret the wants of Hades?"

"Quiet, witch," snapped Gambledolf.

She smirked, but said, with all seriousness. "Would you turn him over to me?"

"Never!" he said, banging his staff on the stone floor.

"What if he *belongs* to me?" She drew out the words, seductively. "What if he *belongs* to the darkness?"

"Hold your tongue!" He made a gesture with his staff and Draknarkus flashed a hand in the air. Nothing visible to the naked eye, the arcane plane was the medium for their spells.

"Still got it, I see," she said with a seductive wink.

He turned his back on her, placed his arm around Dan, and walked him to the door. "What do you make of it, Danoclees?" he said, under hushed breath.

Runes covered the door. Runes of a language lost had been violently and desperately scratched into the stone. Dan looked closer. The runes were graffiti, scrawled over intricate paintings, all composed in red...in blood? He examined the paintings: ghouls and demons devoured the world and all the races who'd walked it. Suffering. Torture. Murder. Sadistic revelry. This was a celebration of death and violent chaos painted in blood. He turned away, biting his fist.

The runes were there to contain the evil and hold it back from the waking world. But nothing could hold back the evil at the core of the universe. Life was but an extinguishing moment, pointless and irrelevant. The darkness always returned. The runes could only divert the tide of entropy, a moment of respite on a meaningless timeline. Now, the door sung to Dan its price, planting the message in his head, and he couldn't keep it out.

"A sacrifice must be made," said Dan aloud.

The old wizard said nothing, but closed his eyes. The black wizard clapped her hands together in delight.

"What does it mean, G...G...Gambledolf?" he said.

"It means exactly what it says, Danoclees Dunlorian," said Draknarkus. She stood in front of him and gestured to the door like a game show hostess would do to the star prize.

"A sacrifice?" Dan turned from the dark wizard to the light wizard and back again. "What kind of sacrifice?"

"I think you know," said Draknarkus, beaming.

"A sacrifice of l...life, of...," he faltered. The enormity of it all weakened his knees. He put his hand on the door to steady himself and the evil coursed from the door and into his hand, his life's warmth absorbed by the cold stone. He pulled his hand away. "The horror!" he cried.

"Fanny," muttered Steve.

"Seductive, is it not?" said the knowing black wizard. "There is so much I could show you, Chosen One."

"Leave him alone!" cried Gambledolf.

"A sacrifice of life...," said Dan, once more.

"And not any life," said Draknarkus. "You must sacrifice a sentient creature to pass the gate."

"But I thought the fairies were good?" said Dan, his bottom lip wobbling.

"So did I, Dan," said Gambledolf, tears poured down the old wizard's cheeks, just like his apprentice's.

"Well you guessed wrong, didn't you?" said Draknarkus. "Evil resides in everything. If you want to save the world by wielding the Lost Sword of the Fairy King, then one of your company must pay the ultimate sacrifice."

"Noooo!" screamed Dan, looking to his companions.

"Or," said Draknarkus. "I can offer you this worthless halfling." She stood back, and swept her hand towards the chubby star prize.

"That's not very nice!" said Derek, wagging a lecturing finger.

"Why else do you think I brought you along?" she said.

"For the company?" Derek danced a jig. "For the razzamatazz?"

"Shut up, for god's sake!" cried Michelle, and pushed the halfling behind her. Her strength and his physical ineptitude caused him to fall. She whispered to him. "Just be quiet and stay out of the way."

Derek thought he saw something different in her eyes. A glint was still there, but not of malice. Regardless, he heeded her words.

"One of us must sacrifice ourselves?" said Dan, the weight of the task fell heavily on him.

"Or the stinking halfling," said Draknarkus, rejoining the Dark Alliance at the entrance to the chamber.

"I don't stink!"

"Shut up," whispered Michelle and kicked him in the leg.

"Gambledolf?" asked Dan, hoping for wisdom, hoping for his

burden to be lifted, to be shared. The wizard remained silent, head bowed.

"What are we going to do?" said Plumporious.

"Yeah," said Mick. "I don't want to die, and I doubt anyone else does, apart from maybe the nerd," he said, indicating Dan with a bob of the head.

"I don't want to d...d...d...die," said Dan, appalled.

"Really?" said Steve. "Are you sure? Have you really put in the quality time to think it through?"

"What should we do, Gambledolf?" pleaded Dan.

Gambledolf gave his scalp a good scratch. "Well, Draknarkus has offered us the halfling." He raised both hands, palms up and tilting them like a set of scales.

"I must say," shouted Derek, "although I'd love to help, I haven't volunteered for such a thing, and I really don't want to die."

"We can't kill an innocent being!" cried Dan. Halflings were the only species that hadn't bullied Dan. Halflings couldn't bully anything apart from other halflings, and they were too lazy to do that. Dan saw a fellow victim of life. Derek's tuxedo hung in ribbons. Bruised and battered soft flesh poked between the rips in his clothes. And he appeared to be covered in rabbit bites. "No. No we can't," said Dan. "We just c...can't!"

Gambledolf put his hat back on his head, instantly regaining former grandeur. He tapped his bushy chin in thought. "If not the halfling, then I believe Steve would make an ideal candidate for a sacrifice." He said it with the casualness of a barman suggesting salt and vinegar crisps when he was out of cheese and onion.

"What do you mean, 'Steve would make an ideal candidate?'" said Steve. "I thought you were the good guy. I didn't think you'd be advocating a murder, especially my murder."

Gambledolf shrugged. "What choice do we have?"

"We could take a vote on it?" offered Mick.

"I'm not sure I like where this is going?" said the centaur, scratching his chin and working out his chances.

"All in favour of sacrificing Steve, raise your hand," said the elf.

"Now just hang on a minute!" said Steve.

Mick, Plumporious, and Gambledolf raised their hands without hesitation. Mick actually raised both of his for he was a man of strong and numerous convictions. Dan looked on, aghast.

"Stop!" cried Michelle.

Draknarkus snarled and her nose met Michelle's. "What do you think you're doing?" Her eyes burned, but Michelle stood firm.

"You can't sacrifice me. I'm Steve! Everyone loves Steve the Lovable Centaur! You can't be serious," he said, concentrating on Dan, who was, unfortunately for Steve, his only chance of survival. "You wouldn't even kill a wasp, yet you're willing to sacrifice your buddy Steve, lovable ol' Steve?" The centaur patted down Dan's lapels and grabbed his cheek and gave it a loving squeeze.

Dan never thought he'd sacrifice anyone, but he considered the last few days…. "Well, you did tell everyone in prison that I was a—what was it?"

"A diddler!" said the centaur in hysterics, before remembering his current situation and biting his lip. "But that was just a bit of banter!"

"And you did put chewing gum in my p…pubes every night of the quest. Every. Night!" Finally, Dan understood the lure of the dark side.

"Bantz!" cried Steve.

"And you took the time to remove all the b…bristles from my toothbrush and replace them with your own p…p…pubes."

"That one was megabantz!"

"Why are all your practical jokes p…pube-related?"

"They're not *all* pube-related?" said Steve.

"Name one?" said Dan.

"The time I injected you with heroin from that dirty needle and gave you HIV." Steve gave him a soft, banter-laden punch on the arm.

"We choose—" announced Dan.

"Think about your actions!" cried Michelle. "If you take a life—"

Draknarkus slapped her across the face with the back of her hand. "Insolent dog!" she said, seething. "What is wrong with you?"

Michelle wasn't deterred. "You can't do this, Dan!" she cried, dabbing blood from her lip. "You're not a murderer!"

Dan's mind was made up.

"We choose Steve the Centaur!" His words echoed around the hall and gathered momentum, building and building until the Fellowship and the Alliance were forced to grab their ears.

The booming ceased.

Silence.

"Shit," said Steve before he dropped onto four horsey knees and collapsed sideways, stone dead.

Draknarkus cried with laughter, Rillit smirked at the amusing display, and Derek breathed a huge sigh of relief.

"You've killed him…," said Michelle in disbelief.

"What do you care?" asked Draknarkus, eyes narrowed.

Dan considered the centaur lying on the ground, his tongue

sticking out, his eyes glazed, his thick pubis hair reminding Dan of unwanted foreign bodies in his mouth.

He looked up and shrugged his shoulders. "I thought I'd feel more guilt." He scratched his head. "I really did."

"So, what now?" said Plumporious, sneering his nose at the fallen centaur. "Corpses are just icky," he whispered to Mick, who rolled his eyes.

"We must drag his stinking corpse to the door and see if the offering is accepted," said Gambledolf.

"And if it isn't?" asked Dan.

"Worst things happen at sea, I guess," the wizard offered. "We can always try the halfling."

Derek gnawed at filthy nails.

It took co-operation of both good and evil to drag Steve's soon-to-be-rotting corpse to the Door of Blood. Dan placed a hoof on the great door, and on silent hinges, it opened before them.

Chapter 48...

ON TOP OF A SMALL STONE ALTAR, BEREFT OF DECORATION, sat the Sword, pointing upwards, balancing on its hilt, spinning slowly on its axis. The Sword was simple, yet undeniably beautiful. Its sleek lines, as sharp as when they were forged, split photons desperate to reflect from the wondrous metal. No jewels decorated the hilt; its beauty was purpose, not the materialistic twinkle of mineral. This sword was not a killing device, not in the typical sense of medieval weaponry. It was fairy-sized for a start, which meant it was better suited to carving a turkey than for cutting a marauding goblin's leg off.

The circular chamber, housing the greatest of treasures, was a suitable tribute. Carved into the rock were representatives of every species, a male and a female. Goblins were a notable omission. The statues stood twenty feet high, and each was dressed ready for battle holding stone swords similar to the one rotating in the centre of the room. The room curved upwards to a hole in the ceiling from which sunlight illuminated the Sword, which reflected the light and lit the room.

The Fellowship and the Alliance filed down the several steps into the chamber and parted, standing in separate halves of the circular pantheon. All stared on, transfixed by priceless treasure. After a momentous journey and a quest of wonder and intrigue, the adventurers had reached their final destination.

"There it is, Danoclees," said Gambledolf, unable to take his eyes off the treasure. All thoughts of the impending danger were gone. His life's work was before him. "There, before you, the Lost Sword of the Fairy King."

Gambledolf's hand found Dan's arm. "Take your rightful place as a wizard of Anglor." He nudged him towards the Sword. "Then we can save the polar bears together."

Dan approached, dry mouthed, footsteps unsure, everything he'd ever wanted within grasp.

"Stop right there!" said the black wizard, each word barked with authority.

Dan only turned because of Gambledolf's rushed intake of breath. Draknarkus held a gun in both hands. She looked down the barrel and obviously knew what she was doing for the gun didn't waver. "You aren't saving anything yet."

But Dan was merely paces away from the prize. He could almost reach out and touch...

"DON'T!" yelled Dranarkus, "...even think about it."

"Can't you use magic, Gambledolf?" asked Plumporious.

"We are evenly matched, my magi sister and I, and in such a position it comes down to a battle of physical strength. She is the one with the gun."

"And I am not afraid to use it. Not on anyone," said Dranarkus. "Don't even think about touching that sword, you little worm."

"I knew I should have come tooled up," said a regretful wizard.

Dan's eyes fixed on the Sword, even though a gun was pointing at him.

"If there's going to be an all-powerful master of the arcane walking this planet then it's going to be me," said Draknarkus.

She switched her aim to Gambledolf and moved forwards so that she stood before Dan, next to the Sword. "I can't believe the Chosen One made it all possible."

With power and speed that would have impressed Steve the Centaur, if he wasn't decomposing in the other room, she drove her foot into Dan's stomach, crumpling him to the floor. He wheezed and struggled for breath.

"She *is* evil," said Plumporious.

"And don't I know it," said Draknarkus.

"Good kick, mind," said Mick.

"Rillit!" she called. The elf drew his gaze from the Sword and took his place beside Draknarkus.

"Yes, ma'am?"

"Take your master's prize," she commanded.

"Certainly!" he said with a bow. Rillit approached the altar and without hesitation took hold of the Sword. He screamed an unearthly cry and bolts of golden magical energy flashed around him and smoke rose from his hand where it gripped the hilt. His curled hair straightened, revealing his pointy-eared shame, and golden electricity sparked across his glasses. A loud bang was followed by his airborne body, flying across the chamber, arms windmilling. He hit the wall and landed in an unmoving heap on the floor. His clothes and hair smoked.

"I thought that might happen," said Draknarkus tapping her chin with the barrel of the pistol. She walked over and prodded the body of the elf with her toe. He still drew breath, but not in a reliable fashion.

"Halfling!" she cried.

Derek took a step forward with his hands on his hips. "Can *I* help?" he asked heroically.

"Being of the darkness," Draknarkus began, "I was privy to the entrance price to this great chamber, and I brought you along as sacrifice. You may still be of use. I believe nothing evil can take the Sword, and I can't imagine you've ever had an evil thought in that pathetic brain of yours."

"It doesn't hurt to be nice," said the halfling. He walked over to the Sword and grabbed it without hesitation. It didn't burn him like it did the elf, but he couldn't budge it, even though nothing visible held it in place. It continued to spin and he orbited the altar.

"Pull it, you useless fat shit!" shouted Draknarkus.

"You do not understand," said Gambledolf, shaking his head. "No one may free the Lost Sword of the Fairy King, except the last heir to the fairy throne."

Everyone turned to face Dan, who'd rolled onto his knees since being kicked in the gut. He rubbed his belly and got to his feet, still wheezing. "What do—*wheeze*—you m...mean, last *heir*?" he said.

"Last *heir* to the fairy throne?" mouthed Plumporious to Mick.

Mick mouthed back, "If he's an *heir*, that means he's a...." He gave a knowing wink.

"Isn't it obvious, my boy?" said Gambledolf to his apprentice. "You are the true heir. Only you can free the Sword from its resting place."

"Heir?" Dan said slowly. "As in...heir? As in...*heir*?" he repeated again. "I thought you said I was from a line of wizards, not a...not an *heir* t...t...to a...a...?"

"You are the one true heir," said Gambledolf. "What don't you understand?"

"But that m...means...," Dan trailed off, not wanting to state the obvious.

Gambledolf stated the obvious, and didn't pull the punch. "It means you are the last of the fairies!"

Dan closed his eyes tight. Devastating as the news was, in the cold light of day it wasn't entirely surprising. Only two things gave him comfort: 1) Steve the Centaur was not alive to hear the revelation, and 2) Mr. Grak wasn't around to—

"I BLOODY KNEW IT!"

Mr. Grak stood at the doorway to the pantheon. The grin on his face told Dan he'd heard everything. "I always said you were a little poncey fairy! I bloody knew it!" Mr. Grak capered, jumping up and down and pointing.

Father Time is the biggest bastard of them all.

"This is the shittest adventure, ever!" screamed the last heir to the fairy throne.

Chapter 49...

DAN SAT ON THE FLOOR, his back to the altar, hugging his knees with his head lying on top. Technically, it was known as a sulk. Between sobs he said, "I've spent my whole life being c...called a f...fairy. I thought everyone was b...bullying me, but they were only stating a f...fact." Dan looked up. "How can it be bullying if it's a fact?"

"It can be bullying," said Plumporious, trying to make him feel better. "People have called me fat, and they've said it in a derogatory way, as if there was something wrong with me."

Mr. Grak, in convulsions of laughter, rolling on the floor, pointed at the dwarf while trying to pull enough air in to his lungs to fire some insults, but he couldn't, and doubted he'd ever be able to talk again.

"And d...d...did you d...do anything about it?" asked Dan of the dwarf, ignoring Mr. Grak as best he could.

"I guess I did feel a little better after I'd broken their bones and bathed in their blood. Bullies are terrible people," said the dwarf, looking over at the green-skinned interloper.

Dan continued to sob. "I just sat there and t...took it, all those years. All those years trying to p...p...pretend I was something I wasn't. But I am a fairy! I am a f...fairy!"

Scientifically speaking, goblin cackling now carried the ubiquity of cosmic microwave background radiation.

"And that is why you control the power of Anglor, Danoclees Dunlorian," said Gambledolf, warmly, choosing to ignore his apprentice's negativity.

"Why didn't you t...t...tell me?" asked Dan. "I mean, I would've still c...come on this q...quest if you'd just said you n...needed me because I'm the last heir to the p...poncey fairy throne."

"It's not *that* poncey," Gambledolf countered.

Draknarkus groaned, thoroughly bored. "Just pick up the goddamn sword, you moaning little bastard!"

"No! Why sh...should I?" said Dan, from his primary sulking position.

"Because if you don't, I'll kill you," she said, waving the gun, just in case he'd forgotten.

"And then you won't have your precious sword," he said with fire.

"Good point." She tapped her lips with the barrel of the gun again. "So, I'll shoot you in the bollocks instead."

"Ah," he said, squeezing his thighs together.

Then, in the tone one would save for a baby, she said, "Now pick up the Sword, you sugar-coated little munchkin fairy!"

"It's not like he needs them anyway," said a goblin who'd finally rediscovered the power of respiration. Michelle tittered as well.

"Shut up, you!" cried Dan to a former colleague. "You've d...d...done nothing but make my life hell, and now you're here m...m...making it even w...worse. If it wasn't enough to ruin my j...job, have g...goblin sex with my g...girlfriend, and racially ab...abuse me, you're now laughing at my d...d...destiny!"

"Dan, calm down," said Plumporious.

"No, I'm not c...c...calming d...down," he said, getting to his feet. "I am g...going to take this sword, and I am going to magically shove it up a g...goblin's arse."

Without ceremony, he grasped the handle and the room illuminated with the warm golden glow of the arcane. He pulled at the Sword, but it didn't move. The sound of harps filled the pantheon.

"I see you, Danoclees Dunlorian," said a wondrous voice drifting down from the heavens. "Are you worthy?"

"Probably not," snapped the disgruntled fairy, "but I d...don't think that really matters, d...does it?"

The heavenly voice gave a heavenly sigh. "Are you worthy?" it asked again.

"Yes, I'm bloody worthy," he snapped.

The voice asked, "Are you pure of soul?"

Dan massaged his temples. "What does that mean?"

"Are you a virgin?" said Gambledolf whispered in his ear, not considering the acoustics of the room.

"Did it even need to ask?" said the goblin, coughing and spluttering. "Can't his magical ancestors sense his magically intact fairy hymen!"

"I d...do not have a fairy hymen!" shouted Dan.

"Hymen" took on a haunting echo.

"Are you pure of soul?" the voice asked again.

"Are you s...s...saying that only a virgin f...f...airy heir could pick up this b...bastard sword?" said the now-extremely disgruntled virgin fairy heir. "Un-p...p...p...p...pissing-b...b...believable."

"Well?" asked the heavenly voice, impatiently.

"Yes, I'm a virgin!" he said, exasperated. "But I don't have a hymen."

Mr. Grak was close to losing a lung. Everyone else giggled behind polite hands too, even Derek chuckled, who, himself, did a remarkable amount of shagging considering his physical appearance and financial status.

The harps reached a crescendo and the heavenly voice announced. "Then I relinquish the Sword and pronounce you Queen of the Fairies."

Dan pulled the Sword free, which continued to glow golden. He waved it around a bit, but his heart wasn't in it. "Hang on. D...d...did you say *Queen* of the Fairies?"

The voice was silent. Mr. Grak clawed at the stone flagstones, writhing in the agony of uncontrollable laughter, convinced that his body could not survive much longer.

"I guess," said Gambledolf, gingerly, "it was a recorded message and they expected a queen. Don't worry, you're not really a queen."

"I know I'm not a b...bloody qu...queen!" cried Dan. "And it wasn't a recorded message, it knew my bloody name!"

"Maybe it sensed your hymen?" suggested the helpful wizard.

"I do not have a HYMEN!"

HYMEN!

HYMEN!

Hymen!

Hymen!

Mr. Grak passed out.

Hymen!

Hymen!

Hymen!

Hymen!

Hymen!

Hymen!

Hymen!

Hymen!

Chapter 50...

BASES WERE LOADED. On one side of the chamber stood the Dark Alliance: Draknarkus, gun aimed at the disgruntled fairy queen; Michelle, eyes flicking from Draknarkus to Gambledolf; Derek, trying to reconcile differences with Perseus who hopped around nonchalantly, pretending he didn't know him; Rillit, who'd regained consciousness, but hadn't regained his feet. He whispered into a mobile phone he tried to conceal from the others.

On the other side of the chamber stood the surviving members of the Fellowship: the aforementioned disgruntled fairy; Mick the Knife, looking rather bored with proceedings; Plumporious, ever-vigilant of the threat of stray cobwebs hanging from the ceiling; and Gambledolf, his eyes switching from the dark wizard to his apprentice.

Mr. Grak, an unknown entity, had regained consciousness from his laughing fit and stood between the groups with his perpetual air of arrogance.

"Relinquish the Sword," said the dark wizard, gun aimed at the fairy queen's purported hymen.

Dan ignored her and swung the Sword slowly from side to side in a figure of eight. The Sword hummed through the air leaving a golden trace like a sparkler. Golden energy ran from the tip of the Sword, down the blade, into the hilt, and up his arm. The fairy queen grew in stature. His pocket crackled and sparkled too, his wand demanding freedom. It, too, had grown and stood out, impressively filling his trousers with at least five inches of metaphorical steel.

Michelle's eyebrows raised, but her libido didn't.

"Give me the Sword, damn it!" cried the frustrated dark wizard, a tremble creeping in to her gun hand.

Gambledolf clasped his hands together. "He's beginning to believe! It matters not, Draknarkus. Someone as evil as you could never use the Sword unless the wielder relinquished the power. No one can use it without his decree. He will become all-powerful. He is fulfilling his destiny!"

Draknarkus's eyes narrowed. "He may not care for himself, but there are others he cares for." With a sudden movement, smooth, and snake-like, the dark wizard twirled and tumbled, coming to her feet behind Michelle, who gave an extremely rare scream as the wizard's arm pulled tight into her neck. Blood rushed to Michelle's head and

Draknarkus drove the gun into her temple. Under normal circumstances Michelle would have fought, but there was more to this dark wizard's powers than met the eye.

"Now give me the Sword, fairy queen, or I'll blow her brains out. They won't be as pretty as the rest of her, I can assure you."

Sword swinging ceased. Dan steeled himself.

"You have the power, Danoclees," said Gambledolf, "You can harness magic. You can destroy life with a thought. You can bend nature with your will. You can defeat Draknarkus, but be careful, my apprentice, not to misdirect your power."

"Michelle...," said the fairy queen. Burning love still lingered in his heart.

"Don't worry about her!" cried Gambledolf. "She was being porked by that filthy goblin!"

The elf and the dwarf exchanged looks.

Mr. Grak grabbed at his crotch, which now occupied 25% of his lower half, and mouthed the words "*growspeck*," to the sword-wielding hero. But there was something else in the goblin's eyes, something Dan hadn't seen before. Mr. Grak's eyes flitted to Michelle and then back to Dan. Nerves? Was he nervous? He *did* have feelings for her! Which meant...he had...feelings?

"Do not grow angry, Danoclees!" said Gambledolf. "Rage clouds judgment. You won't control your power if you are angry."

"Then stop telling me about Michelle getting p...porked!" Dan felt the weight of the Sword, the magical weight. It embraced him. It was him.

"You can do it, Dan," said Gambledolf, "but you must concentrate all your will. You can't cock it up again."

"What?" said an incredulous apprentice.

"I'm getting bored of this," said Draknarkus, cocking the pistol. "Relinquish the Sword, you little shit."

"He's bloody useless, Gambledolf," said Mr. Grak, walking nearer the action and folding his arms. "You put it all on a plate for him, you made it easy, and he's still messing it up. How long have we worked at this? Setting it up so he occupied a jail cell with an elf of Darbenham, a dwarf of Dunhelm, and an arsehole centaur to sacrifice—and *still* he can't perform!"

"W...w...w....wh...wh...wha...wha...wha...wha...eh?" said Dan.

Draknarkus's eyes blazed. "Did you know about this, Michelle?" she said, pushing the gun harder into her temple, causing her victim to cry out. "Did you know your boyfriend was Gambledolf's puppet!"

"I had no idea!" she screamed.

Gambledolf raised placating hands. "Now, Dan, listen, everything has been done to regain the Sword."

"And he's going to give it to me!" cried Draknarkus.

"No!" cried Gambledolf. "Magic can find a way, Danoclees."

"Him!" cried Mr. Grak. "Magic? Did you see what he did to that polar bear? And you should see my *growspeck* now! He's all but ruined my sex life. I don't think there's a woman on the planet who can take the full length when it's in its ninth larval state of excitement." His sickly grin said the goblin didn't lose sleep over his predicament.

Dan, shook his head, trying to comprehend yet another betrayal. "Mr. G...Grak works for you!" he said to Gambledolf, hoping it wasn't true.

"We can discuss it later, Danoclees," said the wizard. "But first we need to use magic to get out of this predicament." He gestured to Draknakus with the tilt of his head. "She has a gun!"

Even though magic filled Dan and he was now the most powerful force in nature, the most powerful force within him was self-doubt. He'd not produced magic of any worth. He'd turned on a light once, maimed a polar bear, and increased the size of a goblin's *growspeck*, and that was it. *Finito.* And now someone's life was on the line, and not just anyone's life: Michelle's.

"Give me the Sword!" demanded Draknarkus. "I'm going to count to three, and if you don't relinquish it, I'm going to blow her head off, and then yours."

"You monster!" cried Dan. The Sword hummed.

"ONE," she snapped.

"Dan," cried Gambledolf. "If you give the Sword to me then I can use it. I can save us all. You must trust in me, Danoclees, if you do not trust in yourself."

"TWO," yelled Draknarkus.

"You have to trust me," said Gambledolf. "I know I've not been totally truthful, but everything has been about capturing the Sword and using it to save the world! Trust me, Dan!" He clasped his hands together and held his head high.

Dan had but a second left. The power was there, he could feel it, but putting someone with a provisional driving license in a F1 racing car did not guarantee the power would be directed in the right direction.

He'd been used from the very beginning, with all his "companions" in on the act. But what choice was he left?

Michelle could not die, even if the horrible goblin was porking her.

"THREE," yelled the black wizard.

"Take it!" he cried, before throwing the Sword through the air to Gambledolf. "I don't want it."

And then, several things happened at once.

The Sword sailed through the air, its golden glow disappearing as soon as it left Dan's hand. But the poor athletic ability of the fairy virgin meant it clattered onto the floor way before it reached its target. The wizard darted forward and picked up the Sword. Draknarkus's eyes widened and her hand took a firmer grip of the pistol.

But now Gambledolf had the Sword and the tide changed.

He cut a dignified and powerful stature, holding the ancient artefact in one hand, his great staff in the other, his eyes bright and challenging.

Draknarkus paused, her finger stroking the trigger, the gun still pressed to Michelle's head. A wizard of Anglor had the most powerful magical artefact on the planet under his control, and the physical world of guns and ammo was nothing but a fart in the wind.

Draknarkus stared at Gambledolf.

Gambledolf stared at Draknarkus.

"I have the power," he said, holding the Sword straight out in front of him.

She snarled, but shrugged, defeated, and slowly relinquished her grip on Michelle. She stepped backwards and Michelle turned to hit the dark wizard but stopped when the gun turned on her. "Don't even think about it," said Draknarkus.

"You know what must happen now," said Gambledolf.

"Aye, old one," Draknarkus answered. "I know exactly what must happen."

"LEG IT!" he yelled.

And before anyone could work out what the hell was going on, both wizards, along with the priceless Sword, bolted out of the front door as fast as their crooked legs could carry them.

Chapter 51...

FOR THE FIRST TIME, the Fellowship and the Alliance shared something in common: confusion.

Plumporious spoke first. "I don't think they're coming back."

"Oh, they're coming back, all right," said a red-faced Rillit, shakily getting to his feet. His clothes still smoked from the blast of magical energy he'd absorbed from the Sword. His hair hadn't reset and added a foot to the width of his head. But the heat of the magical blast had evaporated his cool exterior. "One thing that's certain is they're coming back." He shook his mobile phone at them.

"I thought you were my friends!" blubbed Dan, sobbing into his hands.

The elf and the dwarf ignored the fairy. "We should get after him," said Mick to his counterpart. "Bastard owes us money!"

Plumporious took a set of car keys out of his pocket and jangled them. "He isn't going anywhere."

Mick lit up a fag.

"I thought he was a wizard!" cried Dan.

"He couldn't even do a card trick," said Mick. "Useless old twat!"

"No one steals from my master. No one!" cried Rillit, stalking around the pantheon.

"Take your stick out of your arse for once," said Michelle.

"You should be as angry as I!" he cried, before consulting his phone again. "It doesn't matter. They won't get far. Even now, the master draws near."

"And why are you here?" asked Dan of Mr. Grak through a waterfall of tears.

"A fair question," said Mr. Grak, checking his Rolex. For once there were no japes, no putdowns. Something was very different about the goblin.

There was a commotion from beyond the pantheon, near the entrance to the ancient fairy dwelling. Rillit laughed manically. "I told you! See! I told you. No one steals from the master. No one!" He tried to cover his ears with his hair, but it was to no avail. His hair refused to obey.

The commotion grew and grew until Gambledolf, in all his

wizardry glory, came flying through the Blood Door and down the steps. He slid to a halt on the pantheon floor, his chin scraping on the flagstones, leaving blood in his beard.

"Tossers!" he cried, not quite as wizardly as he was an hour ago.

Draknarkus followed, although she was not treated as roughly. A squad of a dozen armed guards, consisting of men and orcs, marched through the great red doors behind them, spreading out to either side of the pantheon. Once they'd taken up position, the boss of bosses, Mr. Somersby, walked in, suited and booted, swinging the Sword like a dagger in his hands. He stood at the top of the steps so everyone could catch a look at his dignified figure.

"So *that* is the Chosen One?" said Mr. Somersby, pointing the Sword at a crying Dan. Mr. Somersby cast a disgusted look at Michelle. "*That* was your boyfriend?"

Michelle smiled sultrily and climbed the stairs to reach the boss. She draped her arms around him, pulled his head towards her, and kissed him hard on the mouth, her tongue driving down his throat.

Dan struggled to keep the contents of his stomach down. "What? Wha—? But? Wha—? That's...that's not...what? That's n...n...not right, surely?"

"They're very...erm...close," said Plumporious to Dan.

Dan looked to Mr. Grak, who'd turned his back on events. Eventually Dan found the disgusted words he was looking for. "She's your d...d...daughter!"

Mr. Somersby pulled away from the kiss and looked over to Dan. "What's the fairy talking about?"

"She's your d...d...daughter!" Dan squealed.

"No she's not, you fool," said Mr. Somersby.

Gambledolf struggled to his feet and he and Draknarkus cast nervous glances at the tough-looking guards holding very big guns.

"What exactly is going on here?" asked the boss, looking from Michelle to Dan to the two wizards.

"I haven't got a b...b...bloody clue!" cried the fairy.

Mr. Somersby pushed Michelle to one side and paced, as he often did of late, admiring the craftsmanship of the Sword. "Let's get back to business. There was a deal. At my expense, and there has been considerable expense." He pointed the Sword at Draknarkus. "I would fund an expedition to find the magical item I hold in my hands. In return, I'd be granted the ability to harness magic. I have come to collect what I'm owed."

Draknarkus approached the boss, guns trained on her. "Yes, Somersby, we can make all your dreams come—"

"So why did I find you running away with that old biddy—who I must say is considerably spritely for his age—with this sword? *My* sword?"

"I can explain everything," said Gambledolf, joining Draknarkus at the base of the steps.

"Go on then," said the boss.

"Ah," he said.

"Here's what I think," said the boss. "I believe you two are nothing more than a pair of con artists who've used me and my money to steal that sword that is of no more use than the stupid little shit down there, drowning in his own tears," said Mr. Somersby, indicating the red-eyed, snot-filled fairy.

"You hate me because of G...G...green Planet, don't you!" Dan cried.

"What the hell is Green Planet?" he said.

"Maybe it's best to keep quiet, Dan," said Michelle. "I think you're a little out of the loop."

"That may be, but one thing I'm certain, there is m...m...magic in that sword!" cried Dan. "Magic! I felt it c...course through my veins. I could have wielded it if I'd had but the c...courage."

"Then show me how," said Mr. Somersby offering the sword hilt to Dan.

No guns swung to the fairy as none of the guards saw him as a threat. Dan, with trepidation, got to his feet and joined Mr. Somersby at the top of the steps. He took the Sword with little ceremony and his heart sank.

There was no golden glow.

There was nothing.

Nothing at all.

It was dead.

The link between the Sword and the arcane was broken.

"It...it's not working," said Dan.

"Was it working earlier?" said Mr. Somersby, who had learned the art of patience since Derek the Debonair had come into his life. Derek was keeping a low profile at the moment, a wise, but not a difficult task for a halfling.

"Yes!" cried Dan. "I was linked to the cosmos when I wielded it!"

"Wielded!" said Mick, coughing on some laughter.

"So why doesn't it work?" asked the boss.

"He broke it!" cried Gambledolf, his finger judging the fairy heir.

"I broke it?" said Dan, incredulously.

"You relinquished the Sword and you relinquished all its power," said a former teacher who probably wouldn't be asked back for a second term.

"You're j...j...joking," said Dan, eyes fixed on the Sword.

"Nah," said Gambledolf.

"NOOOOOO!" screamed the fairy, with all the drama he could muster. "WHHHHHYYYYY!" he added, for a little more.

"I don't know," said the old trickster. "You did it!"

"You bloody told me to! So you could save Michelle from the woman you're in league with!" Dan shouted, rage trumping the stutter.

"Ah," said Gambledolf, seeing a flaw in his ruse.

"I could have saved the world," said Dan, pulling at his hair, "and you stopped it all! Why? WHY?"

Gambledolf blew out laboured breath and looked to his accomplice for support.

"Well, you might as well tell him," she said. "We're boned anyway."

"TELL ME WHY!" screamed Dan.

"Because that sword is made of an extremely rare metal and can be used in nuclear reactors," said Gambledolf, grudgingly. "And an old mate of mine has some contacts in North Korea who have offered us a bucket load of cash for it."

"So all this was for money!" cried Dan. "You turned your back on the planet for nothing more than cold hard cash?"

"Well, when you put such a negative spin on it...," said the old man.

"I could have harnessed magic if you hadn't made me relinquish the Sword!" said Dan, hysterical.

"Well, it was a possibility," said Gambledolf, "but chances were high you'd have cocked it up anyway, if it's any consolation."

Dan jumped up and down on the spot, stamping his feet as hard as he could despite his missing toes. "We could have saved the world, but you wanted to line your pockets. All this, using me, nearly killing me, crushing my dreams, endangering the environment—all just for cash!"

"Why else would he have done it?" said Mr. Somersby.

"I lost my toes!" screamed Dan.

"Only your little ones. And, in our defence," said Gambledolf, "we've worked really, really hard for this." He gave Draknarkus an acknowledging bow of the head. "We've been trying to get our hands on the Sword for many, many years."

"Years! You made out you were thousands of years old. How old are you?" asked Dan.

"Sixty-two."

"You lying...twa...twa...toerag!" Dan still couldn't bring himself to swear at someone, even if his head was screaming obscenities. "Is your name even Gambledolf?"

"Ken Fish," said Ken, offering a hand which wasn't taken. "Anyway, this caper took bloody ages to sort out. We had to research ancient fairy lore, which was really boring. The prophecies were genuine, and they all came true! Who'd have thought it!" he said, with a chuckle. "You really were the Chosen One! Once we knew the amulets lay in the hills of the Highland dwarves and the forest of the dark elves, we were ready to begin our adventure. We had to protect you, so Mr. Grak became your boss to stop you coming to physical harm, and Michelle became your girlfriend to protect your fairy hymen."

"I d...do not have a hymen!" Dan screamed.

"Protect your virginity," corrected Ken.

"You work for him!" spat Mr. Somersby in Michelle's face while pointing at Ken.

"For me, actually," said Draknarkus.

"How long has this been going on for!" the boss screamed. "You will all pay dearly for this! All of you are going to pay. You can't do this to me. I am a god!"

Draknarkus guffawed. "A god? Look around you." She raised her hands, indicating the statues. "These were the gods of the ages. They didn't need plastic surgery and a dick extension."

Mr. Somersby seethed, gnashing his teeth and readjusting a couple of million pounds worth of phalloplasty.

"Why string it out? Why?" cried Dan. "What was the point of p...pretending we were pursued by evil?"

Draknarkus answered, "To rinse the company credit cards."

"Harlot!" shouted the outraged Rillit.

"And why the hell is that halfling still alive!" said Mr. Somersby.

Derek took a break from stroking his bunny to wave. He was attempting to reconcile with Perseus with tickles, who, in turn, was attempting to hinder reconciliations with biting.

"I thought we'd need him as a sacrifice," said Draknarkus, "but the fairy pushed the centaur into death's door without a thought or care. It was a murder as cold as ever I've seen."

Dan took his foot off the outrage throttle and held up a finger, "That's n...not exactly true," he muttered.

"You were all responsible for the murder of that poor beast," said Michelle.

"Why on earth did you try to stop it," asked Draknarkus, suspiciously.

Michelle looked at Mr. Grak.

Mr. Grak looked at Michelle.

"And why is he here!" cried Dan.

Mr. Grak slowly reached into his pocket.

"FRRRREEEEEEZZZZEE!" yelled one of the armed guards, lifting his rifle.

"It's too late," said Mr. Grak, smiling, uncaring of the guns. "The Eagles are coming."

"What are you talking about?" said Mr. Somersby. "What are you holding?"

As commanded, Mr. Grak took his hand out of his pocket to reveal a small device, a light flashing on the front of it.

"What's that for?" asked Mr. Somersby.

Michelle's threw something on the floor. "That should answer you." Leather slapped stone and a wallet opened. Righteous silver gleamed, revealing a seven-point star with Her Majesty's crown sitting proud atop.

Every neck craned to see what had turned the boss of bosses so deathly pale.

"Is this some kind of SICK JOKE?" he screamed.

"Somersby," said Michelle. "I am arresting you for funding criminal terrorist activities, both domestic and international. You do not have to say anything—"

"KILL THEM!" screamed the boss to his private army. Somersby's eyes were as red as Dan's, but with murderous rage, not sniffles. "KILL THEM ALL!"

Chapter 52...

MR. SOMERSBY'S GUARDS HAD GUNS, but the Fellowship and the Alliance had the mighty fists and feet of Michelle, Mr. Grak's unfaltering electric razor, and Plumporious's berserker rage and cute skinny jeans. There was no longer any magic to be called upon in the battle ahead, which Dan thought the biggest crime of all, forgetting he'd contributed to a murder.

Bullets flew.

Michelle rolled to the side and bullets pinged off the flagstones where she'd stood a second before. She pulled out a handgun and returned fire.

Mr. Grak grabbed Rillit around the neck and used him as yet another elf shield, glad of the practise in the Dark Forest. Bullets thudded into the stuck up, quickly deceased butler, who'd become more supple once rigor mortis set in.

Mr. Somersby didn't blink at the death of a favoured employee; he was too busy pointing manically like a Bond villain, demanding the heads of his enemies.

Mr. Grak closed in on Mr. Somersby's guards, and when he was within reach, pushed the corpse of Rillit into them as a distraction and jumped over it and into the fray. In the tangle of bodies, guns were useless, but Mr. Grak's lightning fists, police-issue baton, and pepper spray were not.

Plumporious rubbed furiously at his jeans where a spot of blood had landed. "It's not coming out! It's not coming out," he squealed, and then his eyes glazed over and he cried, "ELPEEHS PU EKAW, DENEPPAH REVEN GNIDNAL NOOM EHT!"

He charged in behind Mr. Grak and dealt brutal haymakers when he was in range. The armour of the mercenaries might as well have been made of paper, so great was the power of The Black Rainbow.

Dan ducked and covered with the two false wizards, Derek the Debonair, and Perseus—who had either reconciled with the entertainer or was just taking a break from biting.

That left Mick the Knife. Mick hadn't looked for a place to hide, nor had he charged in behind the lifeless body of Rillit. No, Mick stood in the open and welcomed the gunfire. Dan watched, wide-eyed, wondering just how many other lies had been told to him as Mick ducked, weaved, and contorted, dodging the bullets with ease. He was a shadow. He was so lithe it was impossible that his tracksuit contained bones. It was as if Neo had become addicted to shoplifting and smack after leaving the Matrix. And then, as if bored of the dance, Mick drew knives out of his pockets and launched them with the fluidity of the world's greatest knifeman.

"But...but...," said Dan.

Six knives thrown, six guards dead. Out of throwing knives, he somersaulted this way and that, avoiding the bullets until he reached the guards. He pulled out a knife too brutal for a slaughterhouse, and Dan wondered how Mick fit such a large machete inside his jacket. He painted the walls with crimson with every flash and flick of his blade.

The echo of gunfire died with the last of Mr. Somersby's personal guard. The whole battle had lasted less than a minute.

And that left Mr. Somersby, aghast, holding the sword forged with the ideal of love, but had reaped nothing but death and destruction, like so many of allkind's creations. He turned to his former lover looking like a completely different person, shoulders slumped, eyes downcast. He'd never worn a humble expression in his life.

"Michelle, can we talk—" was all he said before she head-butted him. He collapsed into a heap on the floor, clutching his nose, staring at his blood, something he'd never seen before. And then he sobbed. The boss of bosses sobbed into the flagstones and Michelle got a little retribution.

"What...what's g...g...g...going on?" asked Dan to no one in particular.

The sound of inbound helicopters in the distance became ever louder.

"Eagle Squad is here," said Michelle to Mr. Grak.

Mr. Grak shook his head. "Late to the party, as usual." Then he said, "We're cops, Dan." This wasn't the Mr. Grak from yearly performance reviews. The goblin's hands shook and he took in great lungfuls of air, trying to regulate his breathing, adrenaline pumping, and not through rage. "I've been working undercover for years trying to bring down these two bastards." He nodded at Gambledolf and Draknarkus. "This was the big one for them. Michelle is an undercover agent. She's had bigger fish to catch. Her mark was that greedy bastard bleeding down there."

Michelle glared at her former target. "What I've gone through to bring him to justice...." She cleared her throat and spat a huge loogie that landed square on his forehead. The green slime oozed down to mix with the blood still gushing from Somersby's nose.

Mr. Grak put his arm around her and gave her an affectionate squeeze. "It's over now, my love. It's all over."

She kissed the goblin on the cheek. "I've worked for The Corporation for years," Michelle continued, "trying to find concrete evidence for the murders we knew occurred. I got wind of Somersby's magical desires years ago, so...." She ran a finger down Mr. Grak's chest. "We joined forces. And then we fell in love. In some ways it made it harder, but we became an incredible team. We soon crystallised a plan to bring them all down together."

Mr. Grak said, "Draknarkus, or rather Sharon Bush, and Ken Fish had operated separately but joined forces for this. Michelle infiltrated Sharon's group while I continued working for Ken."

"Magic was the key," Michelle said, "It was the only thing Somersby could not buy and the only thing giving us any semblance of an advantage."

"So I planned the heist with *Gambledolf*," said Mr. Grak, "and we made it work. Plumporious, Mick, and Steve were all promised pardons and cold hard cash—if they helped. I arranged it with the prison to let you all escape."

"Was that when you v...visited me?" asked Dan.

"Yes," said Mr. Grak.

"I wondered why the escape wasn't very magical," he said. "In fact, there was never anything very magical." He turned on Ken Fish, "C...can you even d...do any magic at all?"

"Pull my finger," he cried, eagerly.

Michelle went over to Derek. She made a sudden move towards him and he flinched, but she dropped to her knees and pulled him into a strong hug. His what-the-hell-is-going-on-here eyes bulged as she squeezed him tight. "I'm sorry for what I put you through," she said. "I thought that if I was mean to you, then it would save you from Draknarkus. I hoped she'd leave me alone with you so that I could pretend to kill you and let you escape."

"That's OK!" said Derek, patting her on the back. "No hard feelings!"

She let him go and kissed him on the cheek. "Not everything is about physical strength and monetary power," she said. "You were always a shining beacon, always upbeat and optimistic. You brought joy to those poor goblins in the town of Lashley when they were at the lowest. The world needs people like you, Derek the Debonair. Dan could have learned a lot from you."

Dan wanted to interject, but didn't.

"Oh, you!" Derek blushed and said, "And now I have my bunny back." The bunny bit him, but Derek danced a jig anyway.

Michelle rearranged her hair into a pony tail and stared up at the blood red door. "I'm just sorry I couldn't prevent Steve's death."

Mr. Grak took a knee next to the fallen centaur, legs pointing straight up to heaven, where he undoubtedly romped. Mr. Grak patted him on the side. "Good night, sweet prince," he whispered. "And flights of angels sing thee to thy rest."

Dan tried to find someone to exchange looks with—but failed.

Mr. Grak sighed. "You're right, Michelle. It's just a shame we couldn't have saved Steve. He didn't know the risks. I didn't get here fast enough."

"I had no idea the door would kill so fast," she said, voice cracking. "And I underestimated Draknarkus's strength."

Dan did his best not to blurt out that Steve was a wanker, as it didn't seem the right thing to do anymore, even though he had grounds.

Mr. Grak gave Steve one last pat before walking into the centre of the pantheon. "A murder charge will never stick, not when the weapon was magic."

"The biggest c...crime here today is the loss of all the magical p...potential," said Dan, looking at his former teacher, Ken Fish, with disgust.

"No, it isn't," said Mr. Grak, firmly. "The biggest crime is the murder I just mentioned, and that it will go unpunished."

"Ah."

"Count yourself lucky, son," said Mr. Grak.

"I was...I was trying to do g...g...good!"

"Good? Good?" cried Mr. Grak. He sat on a step, and wearily rubbed his face. Michelle took a place by his side. "I've been following you since the prison escape. Ken thought I was covering our tracks from the cops, but I was mostly putting right your wrongs, Smith. Do you realise the mess you made of that goblin town, Lashley?"

"That was Plumporious!" cried Dan.

The dwarf held up an apologetic hand and then said to Dan, "Thanks for the support, mate."

"He's a homicidal maniac," said Mr. Grak, matter-of-factly. "But you were meant to be the saviour of the world, powered by good."

Dan didn't like the direction this was going and did his best to protest. "But, the g...goblins were a b...bunch of hooligans, bullying the elderly and the local c...community!"

"They *were* the local community, you idiot!"

"They were horrible," said Dan.

"You ever wondered why they were horrible, huh?" lectured Mr. Grak. "You ever wondered why they are so different to you? You're a fairy heir to all-power, and you don't stop bloody whining. You're a cis-white male working for a FTSE 100 company in the capital of one of the richest countries on the planet. Do you know nothing of your privilege? What did those kids have, hey? Goblins are judged from the second they enter the world."

"Well...," said Dan. He preferred the other version of Mr. Grak. "Well...they were the ones that th...th...threatened—"

"Nothing. They had nothing. It's easy to judge someone who's had nothing from the start, no chance of an education, with no role models, where the most successful man on the street is the guy with a pocket full of smack to sell and a shotgun in the boot of his stolen car, and it appears that you have indeed been judge, jury, and part executioner."

Dan stared at the floor. He normally stared at the floor to avoid a shaving, but now he was starting at the floor because he felt like a right throbber.

"As for the elf community," continued Mr. Grak, "I did not want to beat that poor creature Jonquil, but I was left with no choice. They were likely to turn on us and I had to act, I had to scare them."

"Now they were a bunch of violent weirdoes if you ask me," said Dan. "Look how they treated M...Mick! Hang on...." Dan turned to the elf. "All that about not being able to fight was a load of rubbish."

"Total bollocks," said the elf, sucking on an ever-present fag. "I wanted out of that shithole society, but I let Jonquil give me a pasting so I could guilt-trip my dad, the old twat. I left home for good reason. But I didn't want him to lose the throne 'cos that would have upset me dear o' mum. The Grakster here was always meant to come to the rescue." Mick nodded at Mr. Grak and laughed. "I didn't expect Harry Shave-a-han to show up."

Mr. Grak and Mick the Knife shared a simultaneous double-point and wink.

"Why did you shave him?" asked Plumporious.

"A shaving avoids more violence," he said, righteously.

"The elves were still abhorrent!" cried Dan.

"Yes," said Mr. Grak, tiredly, rubbing his forehead. "But, they're cut off from the outside world. And that's why I had to stay behind. I've set up a new initiative to integrate the community with a couple of local villages. There's a mixed community close by, one willing to take the time to get to know its neighbours. There are some good people out there and it's just a case of finding them."

"So...erm...what now?" asked Dan, awkwardly.

"Justice, and hopefully a normal way of life for the both of us," said Michelle before grabbing Mr. Grak, embracing him, and kissing him good and long. Far too long for Dan.

"Can I...can I just interrupt for a second," he said, tapping Mr. Grak on the shoulder while trying not to cry over both of them. "C...c...can I just ask why you were so h...h...horrible to me?"

The couple faced him with lips covered in saliva. Both sets of eyes, one pair blue, one pair red, conveyed a similar message, hoping for a little privacy. But when they focused on Dan's cherubic yet dejected face, their apathy for the little fairy melted.

"I'm so sorry," they both said in unison, pulling him into a hug which he did not enjoy in the slightest.

"Eh?" said Dan, when they finally let him go. He gave them both double takes which made him a bit dizzy.

Michelle started to explain. "We had to keep your hymen intact—" she raised a finger to stop any of Dan's protests "—because if you were spoiled, nature would have known and the amulets wouldn't have sung to you."

Mr. Grak took over. "It may come as a surprise, but I didn't like bullying you, Smith. But I had to break your spirit in case you took hold of the Sword. With that in your hand you had the power to change the world. Power corrupts, and that sword is too much responsibility for one person, especially as bullied nerds turn into loose cannons when a bit of power comes their way. I couldn't let that happen. According to Ken, magic is wielded through will. I had to break yours, I'm afraid. I am sorry, but it was necessary to save the world."

"I'm not the b...b...bad guy!" said Dan.

"Tell that to the dead centaur," said Mr. Grak with a disgusted look one saves for salaried street fundraisers. "And the racism you expressed towards my goblin heritage was very hurtful."

"Hang on," said Dan, ignoring everything. "Are you saying when I held the Sword I really was all-p...p...powerful? I could have reversed g...global warming with a mere thought?"

"You could have, my boy," said Ken.

Dan collapsed on the floor and kicked and screamed and added an embarrassment element to the finale. "You fools! You fools!" he cried. "I c...c...could have saved the world!"

"Don't you worry, Smith," said Mr. Grak with a grin. "I worked plenty of overtime for Green Planet."

Chapter 53...

A FORTNIGHT LATER, Dan watched the events of the world unfold from the comfort of his living room. He no longer had a flat mate, so he could watch what he wanted on telly. It was best to take the positives wherever he could. He'd also bought a cat for company, now there was no chance of it being eaten. Mr. Grak hadn't been able to give him a decent explanation as to why, if he really was a good guy, he'd eaten Spartacus in the first place. The new cat, Bublé, hated Dan, and had clawed him until he stopped calling the cat Bublé and had started using his full title, Mr. Bublé.

The night previous, Mr. Grak had headlined the *Six o' Clock News* on BBC One, and now he was being interviewed on the Breakfast News by the nation's favourite morning presenter, Suzie McKelly, who was flirting terribly with him. He'd even stopped the interview once to tell her her manner was inappropriate. His name appeared on the bottom of the screen: *Mr. Grak QPM.* He'd been awarded The Queen's Police Medal for gallantry, as had Michelle, as soon as they'd returned to London to a hero's welcome. Even Derek was due The Queen's Commendation for Bravery.

"Mr. Grak, may I call you by your first name?" asked Suzie McKelly.

"No," he said, firmly.

She blinked and recoiled but a micron, and then carried on. "Mr. Grak, you and your partner Michelle have put behind bars one of the richest and most powerful men on the planet, Mr. Somersby. You have put an end to The Corporation, which has long been accused of environmental atrocities, as well as utilising child labour and having links to organised crime. It is quite incredible that you and your partner, just the two of you, have brought them to justice. And, I must say, you yourself are quite incredible," she gushed. "Whatever will you do next?"

The goblin took it all in his stride. He leant back on the sofa and tried to cross a sinewy leg, but failed on account of his *growspeck.* "I've been thinking long and hard, and although I'd like nothing more than to protect the British public on the streets, I must resign from my position."

A shocked hush came over the BBC studio.

"But—but why?" asked McKelly as the headline flashed on the

bottom of Dan's TV: *Mr. Grak Announces Resignation. Nation in Shock.*

Mr. Grak faced the camera. "I want to help the people of the world, not just the UK. When I worked undercover at Green Planet, babysitting and protecting Dan Smith's still-intact hymen, I'd a lot of time on my hands. Other than waste it, I decided to take a role in the company and make a difference, a real difference. I invested money in R&D, primarily renewable energy. I've funded the development of a solar cell for the third world. A cheap device. It won't produce much electricity, but it will change the infrastructure of the entire continent as it can be made for pennies from local, abundant materials and only a small amount of electricity is needed to help sanitise water and grow crops."

"So generous of you," said McKelly, breathlessly, playing with her silky black hair.

"That's not all. Green Planet's commitment is to reduce the greenhouse effect. We're developing new materials that will turn the water in the sea and the carbon dioxide in the air into fuel. We can reverse the greenhouse effect and power the world at the same time. I must see this work through to the end. Science must be embraced in order to save the planet!" His fist found his palm.

"This truly is an incredible story," said McKelly, fanning herself, the furnace burning inside her lady parts creating a greenhouse effect of its own. "Is there anything else you want to say?"

"Yes, there is." He turned to face the camera. "Michelle, I know we've had a tough time, with both of us working undercover, both in the most degrading and abhorrent of conditions, lowering ourselves every single day. The people we pretended to be were...were...." He shuddered and changed tact. "Now that's it's all over, and thank the heavens that it's over...will you be my wife?"

Michelle ran in from behind the cameras screaming, "Yes!"

"I didn't know you were here!" he cried, a tear forming in his eye—and on his nipple.

"I've just got back from an interview for BBC2," she said.

They embraced and kissed passionately before the camera that panned to Suzie McKelly, who also had a tear in her green eye. "Is this not the most remarkable piece of television you've ever witnessed?"

Dan got up and kicked the television screen. He tipped the set over and jumped on it. "You fucking bastard fucking g...g...g...goblin!"

Chapter 54...

WITH MR. GRAK AT THE HELM, the world had a bright future. The world could breathe easier, and not just because pollution in cities was tumbling under his directive. He would, undoubtedly, make a Utopia of this remarkable and unified world. Ken Fish (alias Gambledolf) and Sharon Bush (alias Draknarkus) were sent to prison for their crimes. They wouldn't be able to prey on the weak and vulnerable any longer. Mr. Somersby would likely never see the light of day again and still awaited sentencing. His assets had been stripped for the good of the world. Derek the Debonair went back to entertaining kids at their birthday parties, for he loved nothing more than bringing joy to the faces of the little ones.[26]

And then there was Dan.

There is nothing wrong with wanting to be a hero, but not everyone can step up and deliver. The rest must make the most of what they've got and be as good as they can possibly be. He was not proud to be the Last Queen of the Fairies, but that he was. Not that anyone knew. The media had got a whiff of the story but Dan did not have a face for television. A local newspaper reporter had stopped him in the street but had soon lost interest in his story and pushed Dan into a pile of dog poo.

A knock at the door disturbed him from his pit. He didn't get out of bed much lately. He hadn't shaved since his return to the Big Smoke, and his bum fluff was rampant. When he opened the door in dressing gown and slippers, Dan squinted at the daylight. Then he groaned in despair.

"What do you t...two want?"

"Hi, Dan," said Plumporious, posies in hand.

"You look rough as arseholes," said Mick the Knife.

"What do you c...care?" mumbled a very grumpy fairy, shielding his eyes from the sun.

"I don't," said Mick.

Plumporious gave Mick a frightful look and Dan went to shut the door but Plumporious placed a Gucci in the way and Dan knew better than to risk grazing the leather. "Dan, we've come to say we're sorry for what happened," said the dwarf.

---

[26] As well as landing himself a sneaky knee-trembler with divorcee mothers.

"Sorry?" said Dan, incredulously. "Sorry! Really?"

"Yes, sorry," said the dwarf.

Dan stormed back into his is flat, but left the door open. The two companions followed him into the stinking den. Plumporious did his best to avoid brushing against any surfaces.

"D...do you realise what happened to me?"

"Yeah, we were there, dickhead," said Mick.

Dan told them of his ordeal anyway. "I've lost my job, my girlfriend, and my purpose in life—and that b...bastard *goblin* stole all of them! And I've found out I'm the only one of my species left alive! I've b...been made a fool by an elderly c...conman and the only two people whom I thought I could call friends. You two were only with me because you were promised a p...pardon."

"And the cash!" added the Knife.

"Michael!" chastised Plumporious.

"You d...don't care about me at all," said Dan, grabbing a tub of ice cream out of the freezer and spooning too much into his mouth. "And you lied t...to me the whole time!" he said, in an explosion of dairy.

"That's not all entirely true, Dan," said Plumporious, stepping back to a safe perimeter.

"Which b...bit?" said Dan, mining to the depths of the tub.

Plumporious paused.

"He's got you there," Mick said to the dwarf.

"Look," said Plumporious, changing the subject. "We're here now, isn't that the main thing?"

"No."

Dan threw himself on the couch and the dwarf sat next to him.

"How about we make it up to you?"

"How can you p...possibly do that?"

"You've got to remember that we've suffered too, Dan." Plumporious put a hand on Dan's arm.

Dan pushed it away. "You've c...come out of this as free men!"

"So have you," said the dwarf.

"B...but I didn't do anything wrong!" he cried.

"You blew off that polar bear's leg!" said Plumporious.

"That's true. B...but I was really sorry about that," said Dan.

"And we're sorry too!" said Plumporious.

"I never wanted to hurt the b...bear," said Dan, blubbing again.

Suddenly, Mick looked rather sheepish. He took himself off to the window and looked out between a crack in the curtains and whistled a suspicious tune.

"Michael?" asked the dwarf.

Mick whistled a bit louder.

"Michael?" repeated the dwarf, drawing out the word.

The elf turned and leant against the windowsill. "Well...Dan didn't exactly blow the polar bear's foot off."

"Out with it, Michael!" demanded the dwarf.

"Well," he said. "Dan was actually doing what he intended. He gave the bear the power of speech with his will. Old Ken never saw that coming, I can tell you. Dan even granted the bear the ability to see into the Arctic too. Amazing really. I shit myself when I saw that flash of purple light."

"You...you were there!" cried Dan. "But...hang on...why d...did his leg explode then?"

"That wasn't exactly magic. That was sort of me and a high-powered rifle."

"Michael!" shouted Plumporious.

"You're both as b...bad as each other," cried Dan, jumping up and pointing at each of his former companions with his dripping spoon. "You're b...both selfish and you're both a p...pair of loony psychos."

"And what about you, Mr. High and Mighty?" asked Mick.

"What ab...about me?"

"You don't exactly shit rainbows, mate. Look what you did to that polar bear!"

"That was you!" shrieked Dan. "You just b...bloody told me!"

"Oh, yeah...," mumbled the elf, touching a finger to his chin.

"All I wanted to do was good, and I ended up b...b...being c...c...completely shafted."

"Stop it, the both of you," said the dwarf, placing his hands on his ears. "I can't stand fighting!"

"Yes, you can, you're a homicidal m...maniac!" said Dan.

"Oh, yeah...," mumbled the dwarf, touching a finger to his chin.

"C...cut the nonsense. Why are you b...both here? I can't imagine it's a social c...call?" said Dan.

"Dan, honestly, we've been feeling guilty," said Plumporious. "Why don't you come outside. We've come to take you for a drink."

"How c...can I trust you! By Uubla, you p...pretended that Gambledolf was healing you with magic!"

"You thought he was healing you too!" said Mick.

"That's true. B...but he did give me what, in hindsight, must have been p...painkillers. I did feel b...better after Steve spiked my drink that time and Gambledolf waved his wand around my head."

"That would have been psychosomatic," said the dwarf, knowingly. "Ken is a very good con artist. He hypnotised you with the help of your goblin flatmate and talked to you in your sleep, pretending he was appearing in front of you in the realms of Anglor."

"When he saved me in hospital, he made a g...goblin's *growspeck* tie itself into a knot," said Dan.

"They can do that," said Plumporious. "It's amazing what they can do with...," he trailed off.

"I wonder why I made Mr. Grak's bigger?"

"Definitely because of deep, masochistic, inter-racial, homosexual urges," said the Knife.

The dwarf shrugged. "It was kind of obvious, Dan."

Dan changed the subject. "I guess the appearing in p...puffs of smoke was just smoke b...bombs. But he did make the Blue-Eyed B...Boys disappear."

"They were in on it," said Mick.

"Should have known," said Dan. "Should have known. When he first ap...appeared in front of me in the street his clothes had repelled water. I thought it was magic, but I just watched an infomercial for water-repellent spray. Stupid bastard science," said Dan, grimly. "He never p...performed any magic. All the time I saw him d...doing stuff, there was no sense of the arcane. If there were, I would have known. It was all just smoke, mirrors, and hypnotism. I was the only one who ever d...did any real magic." He took his wand out of his pocket and it was incredibly short—and incredibly limp.

"Oh dear," said the dwarf, slapping a hand over his mouth.

"I've managed no magic since. It's d...deserted me."

And then a thought entered Dan's mind; a terrible, terrible thought that made him feel faint. He fell back on the sofa with a thud. "So that means he c...c...c...c...couldn't heal me...."

"Of course not," said Mick. "All magic is bollocks. Well, it is since you messed it all up."

Dan was too worried about another thought that had taken up residence at the front of his brain. "So when Steve injected me with that d...d...dirty needle...."

"Ah," said Plumporious.

"Ah," said Mick.

Dan raised his fists to the heavens. "THAT FUCKING BASTARD FUCKING CENTAUR!"

The Magic Continues...

Coming Soon

STEROIDS AND SORCERY

(Magical Modernity Book 2)

To be blamed for a crime one didn't commit is one thing, but to be blamed for a crime no one had committed is another.

Dan Smith could have been the most powerful wizard to have ever walked the Earth. He marched towards his destiny with righteousness in his small fairy heart—until the powers that be stopped him. They believed it dangerous to hand over infinite power to a nerd who'd been bullied and wedgied his entire life. The powers that be feared he'd become a malevolent dark force if he wielded the Lost Sword of the Fairy King, and Dan was tricked into severing his link to ancient fairy magic. And all this after discovering the "power that be" was porking his girlfriend.

Understandably, he was a little upset.

But there are other powers in this world beyond magic, and savage strength can be unlocked by reconstructing the atoms of life. Dan Smith, the last heir to the fairy kingdom, has discovered these powers. He has drunk deep from the wells of chemistry and has embraced the key to true power: anabolic steroids.

Dan Smith is massive, jacked, and tanned—and he is fucking angry.

About M. J. Jackman

M. J. Jackman writes horror, comedy, and fantasy, mostly at the same time. He wrote *The Sid Tillsley Chronicles* in his twenties and hopes to finish the *Magical Modernity* series before he hits forty in 2020. He's got two years (I've got two years ☹).

When he isn't writing, he's an exponent of the science. He studied chemistry at the University of York and obtained a PhD in nanoscience from the University of Manchester. He's currently working on nanomedicines. Hailing from Great Yarmouth, he now lives in Cambridge where he prepares for his mid-life crisis (I've got two years ☹).

Visit M. J.'s website at http://mjjackman.com/.
Stop by his Amazon Author page: https://www.amazon.co.uk/Mark-Jackman/e/B0034PZJW2/

Sign up now!

Don't miss out!
Get M. J.'s (occasional) Newsletter
http://eepurl.com/dnnz9P

Get More of M.J. Jackman!

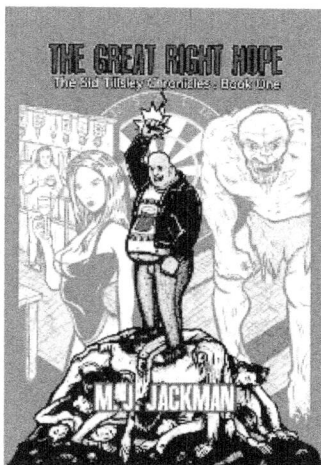

THE GREAT RIGHT HOPE
The Sid Tillsley Chronicles - Book One
M. J. JACKMAN

A FISTFUL OF RUBBERS
The Sid Tillsley Chronicles: Book Two
M. J. JACKMAN

ACRACKNOPHOBIA
The Sid Tillsley Chronicles: Book Three
M. J. JACKMAN

Get any/all of the *Sid Tillsley Chronicles* at Amazon!
UK: https://www.amazon.co.uk/Mark-Jackman/e/B0034PZJW2/
US: https://www.amazon.com/Mark-Jackman/e/B0034PZJW2/

Printed in Great Britain
by Amazon